J.A. JANCE

PROOF OF LIFE

A J. P. BEAUMONT NOVEL

WILLIAM MORROW
An Imprint of HarperCollinsPublishers

"Still Dead." Copyright © 2017 by J. A. Jance.

PROOF OF LIFE. Copyright © 2017 by J. A. Jance. All rights reserved. Printed in the United States of America. No part of this book may be used or reproduced in any manner whatsoever without written permission except in the case of brief quotations embodied in critical articles and reviews. For information, address HarperCollins Publishers, 195 Broadway, New York, NY 10007.

First William Morrow premium printing: April 2018
First William Morrow trade international printing: September 2017
First William Morrow hardcover printing: September 2017

Print Edition ISBN: 978-0-06-265755-8
Digital Edition ISBN: 978-0-06-265756-5

Cover design by Richard L. Aquan
Cover photograph © urbanglimpses/Getty Images

William Morrow and HarperCollins are registered trademarks of HarperCollins Publishers in the United States of America and other countries.

18 19 20 21 22   QGM   10 9 8 7 6 5 4 3 2 1

By J. A. Jance

J. P. Beaumont Mysteries

UNTIL PROVEN GUILTY • INJUSTICE FOR ALL
TRIAL BY FURY • TAKING THE FIFTH
IMPROBABLE CAUSE • A MORE PERFECT UNION
DISMISSED WITH PREJUDICE • MINOR IN POSSESSION
PAYMENT IN KIND • WITHOUT DUE PROCESS
FAILURE TO APPEAR • LYING IN WAIT
NAME WITHHELD • BREACH OF DUTY
BIRDS OF PREY • PARTNER IN CRIME
LONG TIME GONE • JUSTICE DENIED
BETRAYAL OF TRUST • RING IN THE DEAD (NOVELLA)
SECOND WATCH • STAND DOWN (NOVELLA)
PROOF OF LIFE • STILL DEAD (NOVELLA)

Joanna Brady Mysteries

DESERT HEAT • TOMBSTONE COURAGE
SHOOT/DON'T SHOOT • DEAD TO RIGHTS
SKELETON CANYON • RATTLESNAKE CROSSING
OUTLAW MOUNTAIN • DEVIL'S CLAW
PARADISE LOST • PARTNER IN CRIME
EXIT WOUNDS • DEAD WRONG
DAMAGE CONTROL • FIRE AND ICE
JUDGMENT CALL • THE OLD BLUE LINE (NOVELLA)
REMAINS OF INNOCENCE
RANDOM ACTS: A JOANNA BRADY
AND ALI REYNOLDS NOVELLA
DOWNFALL

Walker Family Novels

HOUR OF THE HUNTER • KISS OF THE BEES
DAY OF THE DEAD • QUEEN OF THE NIGHT
DANCE OF THE BONES: A J.P. BEAUMONT
AND BRANDON WALKER NOVEL

Ali Reynolds Novels

EDGE OF EVIL • WEB OF EVIL • HAND OF EVIL
CRUEL INTENT • TRIAL BY FIRE • FATAL ERROR
LEFT FOR DEAD • DEADLY STAKES • MOVING TARGET
A LAST GOODBYE (NOVELLA) • COLD BETRAYAL
NO HONOR AMONG THIEVES: AN ALI REYNOLDS
AND JOANNA BRADY NOVELLA
CLAWBACK • MAN OVERBOARD

Poetry

AFTER THE FIRE

*For Howard G. Malley, whose ongoing battle
with muscular dystrophy constitutes a daily and
courageous Proof of Life.*

PROOF
OF LIFE

PROLOGUE

THE DOOR SLAMMED shut and Chrissy Purcell's eyes popped open. She groped under the covers until she found the comforting softness of her frayed teddy bear, Oscar, and then lay there, staring up at the ceiling, waiting to see what would happen next. Maybe, if she was lucky, he would go to sleep. That's when the window-rattling snoring would start, but she could sleep through that. They all could.

The bedroom door was shut, but it wasn't dark in the room. The lights from the parking lot made the ceiling above her glow in a strange, orangish light. Chrissy was grateful for that light. Sometimes, when she did something wrong, Daddy would lock her in the closet, where the only light was from that tiny crack that showed at the bottom of the door. She would lie there with her heart pounding and gasping for breath until Mommy would finally come and let her out.

Mommy knew Chrissy was afraid of the dark. That was why, when they set up the bunk bed, Chrissy had been given the top bunk.

"You're three years older than Lonny," Mommy had said. "Since he still falls out of bed sometimes, he should be in the lower bed. Besides," she had added, "the lower bunk is a lot darker than the upper one."

The part about their ages was true, of course. Chrissy had just turned seven. Lonny was only four—a baby almost. But so was the part about the lower bunk being darker. Once or twice, when the scary sounds from the other room got to be too much, Chrissy had scrambled down the ladder and tried snuggling in with Lonny, but that hadn't worked. It was too dark—like being in a cave. She needed the brightness of the ceiling overhead.

And so Chrissy lay there and waited, sometimes holding her breath, sometimes not. Grandma Louise, Mommy's mother, said that when you were scared like that, it was a good idea to pray. The problem was, whenever Chrissy prayed, she always asked for God to take Daddy away and not let him come home. Obviously her prayer hadn't been answered, at least not tonight.

Time passed, and she had almost drifted off again, when the expected quarrel finally started. At first it sounded like the distant rumbling of a thunderstorm blowing in off the ocean. Soon after that came the sound of raised voices.

"You stupid . . ." Chrissy wasn't sure what that last word was or what it meant, but she knew it was one of her father's mean words. Whenever he called her mother that, it usually made Mommy cry. Only tonight that didn't happen. Instead of crying, her mother argued back. Chrissy knew that was a mistake and she understood what would happen next. Not right away, but eventually, she'd hear the unmistakable sound of flesh on flesh. In the morning there would be a new bruise somewhere on her mother's body—on her upper arm maybe or else on her back. The bruises usually ended up in spots that didn't show once Mommy put her clothes on.

Waiting for it to happen was worse than listening to it happen. Finally, unable to stand it any longer, Chrissy climbed out of bed and clambered down the ladder, dragging both Oscar and her blanket with her. Instead of crawling into the lower bunk with Lonny, she made her way to the foot of the bed and to the spot where Rambo lay curled up on her own bed.

Rambo was a tall, scrawny dog, coal black, and with fringes of long, soft hair on the ends of her ears and on her shoulders. When Grandma Louise had first brought her to live with them, the dog had been a lot smaller—little more than a long-legged puppy. Naturally, that had caused another big fight, with Daddy insisting that he didn't want a dog and wouldn't have one, but that time Mommy hadn't backed down. Rambo had stayed, but only on the condition that Daddy give her a new name.

When Grandma Louise showed up with the dog, she had brought along a dog bed. Back then, the bed had been too big for the dog. Now it was too small. As she lay stretched out flat, Rambo's nose rested on the floor on one side of the cushion and her long tail trailed off the opposite side. When Chrissy approached the bed, Rambo raised her head and thumped the floor with her tail.

Pulling the blanket down over both of them and still clutching Oscar, Chrissy snuggled up next to the dog, with her back pressed tight against Rambo's very warm tummy. Once Chrissy was settled, Rambo gave a contented sigh. With the dog's warm breath humming steadily in Chrissy's ear, the angry voices from the other room receded into the background, and after a time they both slept.

CHAPTER 1

WHEN THE PHONE rang and my son's name appeared in the caller ID window, it was as though someone had thrown a lifeline to a drowning man. "Hey, Pops, it's Scotty," he told me unnecessarily. "How're you doing?"

Most of the time when people ask a question like that it's rhetorical only—no one expects a real answer, and my reply was a long way from real.

"Great," I said with as much heartiness as I could muster. "Couldn't be better."

Which could not have been further from the truth. I was anything but great. I was at home alone at Mel's and my recently remodeled cliffside home on Bayside Road in what real estate professionals like to refer to as Bellingham's "historic Edgemoor neighborhood." The view outside our floor-to-ceiling west-facing windows was gray—an unrelenting gray sea beneath a gray sky, glimpsed through a gray fog of drizzle. Despite the splashes of color our talented decorator, Jim Hunt, had installed here and there as furnishings and wall hangings, the mood inside the house was unremittingly gray as well. Mel Soames, my lovely wife, was hard at work at her relatively new job as chief of police in Bellingham, Washington, while I was stuck at home alone, trying to come to terms with the realities of retirement.

I had done some occasional work for TLC, The Last Chance, a volunteer cold case unit that my friend and attorney, Ralph Ames, had hooked me up with. That included a case I'd been able to help resolve that had come up just prior to Thanksgiving. The reality of TLC work is that it often involves plowing through old police reports searching for something someone else has missed. The problem with plowing through police reports is that it's too much like... well... plowing through old police reports.

Besides, what alternatives did I have? Golf has never been my thing, and there are only so many crossword puzzles you can do in the course of a week before you're ready to blow your brains out. As our neighbor up the street, Johannes Bodner, a guy who spent his formative years in the South African Defense Force, likes to say, I was not a happy chappie. The words "clinically depressed" hadn't yet surfaced in my consciousness, but they were lurking around the edges.

"How are things for you?" I asked.

"So-so," Scott replied, which was probably a far more honest answer than mine had been. If you're in search of actual information, listening in on father-son conversations probably isn't the right place to go looking.

"Any chance you'll be coming into Seattle tomorrow?"

The truth of the matter is, I was free as a bird—no schedule to speak of; no mandatory meetings; no due dates on case reports. And I have to admit, the idea of having a chance to spend some one-on-one time with my son when there wasn't a houseful of holiday company gladdened my heart. Driving eighty-some miles one way to do it? No problem, but I didn't want to sound too eager. When it comes to father-son relations, being too eager is also bad news.

"Hadn't planned on it," I said cagily. "Why? What's up?"

"I'm having my wisdom teeth pulled," Scott answered. "Because of the anesthetic, I'm required to have someone there to drive me home afterwards. The trouble is, when I made the appointment I forgot that Cherisse is in Vegas for the big consumer electronics convention this weekend. Still, it's not that big a deal. If it's not good for you, I can always run up the flag to Uber."

The problem for me is that it really was that big a deal. I wasn't there on the day when Scotty Beaumont, age six, bit into a Taco Bell burrito, lost his first tooth, and swallowed same. My first wife, Karen, was in charge of parental duties at the time because, when the initial lunchtime crisis happened, I was in Seattle conveniently at work as a Seattle homicide cop. I wasn't home later on when the second part of the lost tooth incident occurred, either—when Karen sat Scott down at the kitchen table and helped him pen a note to the Tooth Fairy, explaining how, although the tooth itself had gone AWOL, he hoped money would appear under his pillow all the same. (It did, once again as a result of Karen's due diligence.) By that time of day—night, really—I was done with actual work, but I had stopped off for a few stiff ones on the way home, with the ready excuse that I needed to have some "decompression time" between being a cop and being a husband and father.

This is a scenario that will be all too familiar to far too many—including all those guys I've met during the intervening years as a result of my long-term involvement with Alcoholics Anonymous. It's usually among the collection of regrets that are a common denominator in one AA drunkalogue after another. That's what happens when people finally decide to sober up and begin discovering what they missed out on while they were drunk out of their gourds, sometimes for years on end.

Occasionally, though, life reaches out and gives you a second chance, and this was one of them—a missed Tooth Fairy do-over, if ever there was one!

"What time's the appointment?" I asked. "And where? Just let me know what time you want to be picked up."

Because the appointment was set for 9 A.M., and because I didn't want to be driving into Seattle from Bellingham at the peak of rush-hour traffic, I decided to go down that evening—early afternoon, really—because I didn't want to be driving in afternoon rush-hour traffic, either. That's one of the advantages of Mel's and my keeping the condo at Belltown Terrace in downtown Seattle—it makes it easy for us to come and go whenever it suits us.

It turns out police chiefs need decompression time every bit as much if not more than homicide cops do, so I usually drive into Bellingham proper at midday each day so Mel and I can have lunch together, as long as she doesn't have to go hobnobbing with some visiting dignitary or other.

Our favorite spot is a greasy spoon diner on Dupont called Jack and Jill's. Jack died years ago. Jill, somewhere north of seventy, is a wiry, white-haired dynamo who is at the restaurant every day, running the show and keeping an eagle eye on things. The restaurant is two blocks from Mel's office and comes with a side door that allows her to slip inside and duck into our permanently reserved back-corner booth without garnering a lot of attention.

Some second or third wives might have objected to my driving eighty miles each way in order to take a forty-something son to a dental procedure, but not Mel. She's been a huge asset in helping me reestablish better relationships with all my offspring—Scott and Cherisse along with my daughter, Kelly, and her husband, Jeremy, who live down in Ashland, Oregon, with their own two kids. Taking my poor parenting history into account, let's just say I've had some serious overcoming to do, and Mel has guided and facilitated that process as much as possible.

"What time are you heading out?" she asked, tucking into her Cobb salad.

Salads aren't exactly my thing. I've always been more of a burger or bowl of chili kind of guy. "Right after lunch," I told her. "I want to get a haircut this afternoon and then go to a meeting tonight."

I may have changed residences, but I haven't changed barbers, and my AA meetings of choice still mostly take place in Seattle's Denny Regrade neighborhood, or as it's currently referred to, Belltown.

"You've probably forgotten that Saturday afternoon is when we have our Fifth Avenue tickets," Mel mentioned.

The Fifth Avenue is a longtime theater in downtown Seattle that specializes in musical productions. Mel has had season tickets for as long as she's lived and worked in Seattle. She used to go with a friend. Now she goes with me. She was right, of course. I had completely forgotten about our theater date, but I managed to spare myself some embarrassment by not asking which show.

"Since you'll already be in town," she continued, "how about if I come down after work tomorrow? We can grab a late dinner at El Gaucho and then see *Man of La Mancha* the next day."

Whew. At least I now knew which play we were seeing, and I took the idea of Mel giving herself a weekend off as a very good sign. "Sounds good to me," I said. "Like an actual date."

"Right," she said. "Let's just hope nothing happens to screw it up. I have a meeting with Mayor-Elect Appleton this afternoon. Keep your fingers crossed."

When Mel had signed on for the Bellingham chief of police gig, she had walked into a political hornet's nest where she'd been forced to go head-to-head with the then mayor, a woman named Adelina Kirkpatrick. From the moment I met Mayor Kirkpatrick, I'd had a bad feeling about her—a gut instinct that unfortunately had turned out to be dead-on right. Mel had uncovered some serious corruption issues in Mayor Kirkpatrick's administration, which had resulted in the now former mayor's surprise election-day ouster by a dark-horse, write-in candidate named Lawrence Appleton. The new mayor's swearing-in ceremony was scheduled for two weeks from now. That meant that Mel was currently walking a tightrope between her incoming boss and her outgoing boss. Not fun.

"One-on-one?" I asked.

"Yup," she said, "a cozy little meeting for just the two of us."

Mel had met the man previously, but this would be their first comprehensive meeting. Given what had gone on before, I didn't fault Mel for being concerned about it.

"You'll do fine," I assured her with more confidence than I actually felt. "He'll be totally blown away."

"Thanks," she said. "I needed that."

By the time lunch was over, my bad attitude had been adjusted for the better. As I headed south on I-5, it was raining pitchforks and hammer handles, but I even found a way to be grateful for that. The mountain passes were a mess, but down in the lowlands it was rain rather than snow, and a warm rain at that —a Pineapple Express, as the talking weather-heads like to call it. Unfortunately, according to the weather reports, the rainstorm was likely to be followed by an arctic blast—a sudden dry spell that would drop temperatures to frigid and turn wet road surfaces to glass. No doubt that was just the kind of foul-up Mel was worried about. From my point of view and considering our plans for the weekend, continuing rain for as long as possible was just what the doctor ordered.

I pulled into the parking garage at Belltown Terrace, parked on P-4, and then stopped off in the lobby on my way upstairs to empty the nonforwarded junk mail from our mailbox. Bob, the doorman, greeted me like a long-lost pal.

"Hey, Mr. Beaumont," he said. "Great to see you. How's retirement treating you these days?"

"Terrific," I said, passing off the lie with what I hoped appeared to be a sincere smile. "Couldn't be better."

"Have you heard about Marge?"

Margie Herndon was a registered nurse—a cranky one at that—who happened to be a longtime friend of Bob's wife, Helen. That connection was enough to explain why I had ended up with her as my home-health nurse in the aftermath of my bilateral knee replacement surgery. She had turned out to be your basic Nurse Ratched–style rehab Nazi. Naturally she and Mel had gotten along like gangbusters. To be fair, the fact that my no-longer-new-but-still-fake knees work as well as they do can be attributed, in large measure, to Marge Herndon's ability to crack the whip. We had gotten through rehab together, but it hadn't exactly been a match made in heaven.

"What about her?"

"Helen tells me that she and Harry I. Ball are planning to tie the knot."

Back before my unexpected and unwelcome retirement, Harry Ignatius Ball used to be my boss. That was when I still worked for the attorney general's Special Homicide Investigation Team, S.H.I.T. (Unfortunate acronym. Sorry about that, but the name is not my fault.) Slightly more than a year earlier, Ross Connors, the attorney general, and Harry had been involved in a spectacular Christmastime traffic accident near Seattle Center. Ross Connors had been declared dead at the scene.

By the time someone used the jaws of life to extricate

Harry from the smashed limo in which he'd been riding, the man was barely clinging to life. He survived. For months he had been a wheelchair-bound double amputee, only recently being fitted with prosthetics. Shortly after the incident, when he had required nursing care in order to be released from the hospital, I had suggested that Marge Herndon might fill the bill. At the time I had expected interactions between the two of them to be your basic oil-and-water combo. For a serious romance to have blossomed between the two of them? Nobody saw that one coming, most especially me.

Stunned by this unanticipated development, I believe my jaw literally dropped. "Are you kidding?"

"Nope," Bob replied with a grin. "Obviously someone out there in the world of matchmaking is trying to see to it that chain smokers hook up with other chain smokers. Makes life easier for everyone else. Helen says they're planning on getting married in Vegas on Valentine's Day. Your smoke-drenched invitation is probably already in the mail."

"I can hardly wait," I said, heading onto the elevator. "That'll be one to remember."

"Your fault," Bob said as the door started to slide shut.

I pushed it back open. "Nope," I told him, "not mine, yours."

I rode on upstairs and let myself into the penthouse unit. I had inherited a fortune from my second wife, with the money landing during what had been a serious downturn in terms of Seattle's real estate. I had bought the condo at Ralph Ames's suggestion because it was totally a buyer's market back then, and the developer needed to unload it. Now it's worth far more than I paid for it.

One of the things I like about living in a high-rise is that you can go away for days or weeks or even months at a time, but when you come home, it's always there waiting for you—just the way you left it. Nobody has broken out one of the windows or strung your trees full of toilet paper.

Without turning on any of the interior lights, I walked over to the windows and stared outside. The Space Needle was lit up, still lined with red and green lights and topped by the traditional tree. Brightly lit trees in Seattle Center sparkled through the downpour, as did the decorated radio towers on the flanks of Queen Anne Hill. As far as Seattle was concerned, Christmas wasn't over, but seeing all the celebratory decorations reminded me of everything that had been lost the previous Christmas. On the drive down, I had about talked myself out of going to a meeting that night. Why not just stay at home, holed up from the cold and wet? But now, thinking about Ross Connors losing his life and Harry losing his legs made me do an about-face.

Besides, I could hardly cite inconvenience as an excuse for not going. When I first landed in AA, my meetings of choice had taken place a few blocks up the street at a lowbrow dive on Second Avenue called the Rendezvous. Back then, a lot of the attendees were beaten-up old construction workers and ex-fishermen. (Sorry, I refuse to use the more politically correct version, *fishers*. I believe "fishers" are actually weasel-like mammals, but I digress.)

One of the regulars at the Rendezvous had been a

grizzled old retired halibut fisherman named Lars Jens-sen, who first became my AA sponsor and eventually my step-grandfather as well, when he married my widowed grandmother, Beverly Piedmont. Although both of those wonderful folks are gone now, their short-but-sweet happily ever after was almost as unanticipated as the newly announced romantic entanglement between Marge Herndon and Harry I. Ball. Go figure.

Now, with the Regrade's ongoing gentrification, the local AA meeting is held much closer to home—directly across Clay Street from the entrance to Belltown Terrace's parking garage—in a building that was once a union hall which has now been transformed into a church. The distance I have to travel up and down in the elevator is farther than I have to walk to get from one building to the other.

As for the meeting itself? That has changed, too. For one thing, attendees are younger. As Amazon takes over more and more pieces of South Lake Union, the electricians and carpenters have been replaced by IT guys and gals, and yes, these days more women have been added to the AA mix. Even so, when I showed up that night, there were still a few old-timers around who recognized me on sight. One by one they came up to greet me, shake hands, and remind me to "keep coming back."

I'm not one of those superobservant AA guys. I'm not someone who goes to a meeting every day (Did that. Ninety meetings in ninety days. Got the T-shirt.) or even every week. Despite the objections of straight-arrow AA guys, I drink the occasional nonalcoholic O'Doul's, and I go to meetings when I need to go to meetings—as in when I'm down in the dumps. This was one of those times.

Roger, the guy who stood up and spoke at the meeting that night, looked like a kid. He was probably midthirties, which means, compared to me, he really was a kid. He'd been picked up for DUI on Christmas Eve. When he'd called his wife to come bail him out, she had told him to go to hell. When he'd finally gotten cut loose and made it home on Christmas morning, his wife had packed up the two kids and gone home to her mother. I looked at the nodding heads around the room as we all remembered our own holiday screwups, which had routinely devastated our kids and broken our spouses' hearts.

Fortunately for Roger, someone had dragged him to an ER to go through withdrawal under medical supervision. The idea that DTs can actually kill you isn't something widely recognized outside the world of Alcoholics Anonymous. Now, having been properly medicated, Roger was through the worst of it—including the shakes, chills, and hallucinations—but this was his first regular meeting. I gave him high marks for having balls enough to stand up, say his piece, and remind the rest of us why we were there.

When the meeting was over, I walked back across Clay, rode upstairs in the elevator, went to bed, and slept like a baby for the first time in weeks.

The next morning, at what seemed like the crack of dawn, I headed for Ballard, the neighborhood north of Seattle where Scott and Cherisse live. Ballard is also where I grew up. Back then, it was primarily a Scandinavian enclave. I was raised in an apartment situated over a bakery where I lived with my mother who was a World War II–vintage single mom.

My mother, left to raise a child on her own and with little formal education, had supported us by working out of our home as a seamstress. Women in town would bring her photos of dresses gleaned from catalogs and magazines, and she would make knockoff copies. She was obviously very talented, something I regret to say I failed to recognize as a kid. Going to school in a shirt she'd made on her Singer sewing machine was always something of an embarrassment when all the other boys were wearing clothes from JCPenney or Sears. I should have told her I was sorry about that before she died, but of course I never did.

These days, Seattle cops, even cops in the Tactical Electronics Unit, are strongly encouraged to live inside the city limits. Because Cherisse's IT job comes with flexible hours and the ability to telecommute on occasion, it wasn't necessary for Scott and Cherisse to live close to her job and out in the burbs on the east side of Lake Washington. Originally they had made an offer on a house in a suburb called Burien, south of Seattle proper. When that deal fell through, they ended up buying a place in Ballard, a sweet little 1930s bungalow on NW 57th Street just a few blocks from the now long-demolished apartment building where my mother and I had once lived.

I never met my father. He died before I was born and before my parents married as well. A few years ago I met up with some long-lost relatives, including my father's aging sister, Hannah Mencken Greenwald. She generously saw to it that both of my kids—Scott and Kelly—came into sizable inheritances that grew out of a collection of family-owned oil wells in eastern Texas. My last name, bestowed on me by my unmarried mother, came as a result of where my father was from—Beaumont, Texas—rather than his family name.

Hannah's bequest meant that Scott had been able to quit a well-paying engineering job in Silicon Valley, one for which he had trained extensively but ended up hating, and left him free to sign up for his dream job—at Seattle PD. When I learned my son was intent on following my footsteps and going into law enforcement, you could have knocked me over with a feather. His work in the TEU is a whole different can of worms from working Patrol or Homicide, but a cop is still a cop.

Armed with their inheritance, Scott and Cherisse had been able to pay cash for their new house and completely update it before move-in day. (A long family history of my never exactly completed DIY remodeling projects may have had something to do with that.) They had also been able to retire their mutual collection of student loans, so not only were they living mortgage-free, they were almost completely debt-free as well. I could have helped them on both of those scores. My second wife, Anne Corley, left me with a bundle, but they seemed to view help from me as coming with some kind of strings attached, while the money from a great-aunt they had never met could be accepted and used without similar complications.

I pulled up in front of their house at seven thirty on the dot. Then, with Scott belted into the passenger seat, I made my way through gridlocked traffic going back into the city. His appointment was with a dentist in downtown Seattle on Olive in a building unimaginatively named the Medical Dental Building. I slid into the coffee shop on the third floor, whipped out my iPad, and spent the next two hours or so reading the news and, yes, doing that day's crossword puzzle. At the ripe old age of seventy-two, I find that even the Friday puzzles no longer faze me. Practice makes perfect.

At ten thirty-five, Scott sent me a text saying that he was done and ready to go home. We went downstairs, where the attendants extricated my Mercedes from its individual elevator-accessed parking spot and sent us back up the narrow driveway and out onto Sixth Avenue.

Full confession here. I love watching *America's Funniest Videos*. I worked as a cop all my adult life. Out on the street, people who do stupid stuff often end up dead. The people pulling stupid stunts on *AFV* may end up bruised and battered on occasion, but they aren't dead, and I find that refreshing.

So I've seen the videos—several of them prize winning—of drugged-up folks yammering away while being driven home from dental procedures—usually the extraction of wisdom teeth. Maybe it's a sudden lack of wisdom that makes them blab their heads off. Although I didn't have a camera running, that was certainly the case here. Scott was high as a kite and running off at the mouth.

"Am I too old?" he mumbled.

"Too old for what?" I asked. "Too old to have your wisdom teeth pulled?"

"Too old to have kids. Cherisse always said she didn't wanna have kids, and now all of a sudden I think she does."

Because of the meds, he had trouble getting his

tongue around the necessary *s*'s. Listening to him try to talk around that severe lisp made it hard to keep from laughing, but I managed.

"Look," I said. "From where I'm sitting, age forty-four looks like a long way from the end of the line. You're just a couple of years older than that Ross guy who hit a home run for the Cubs in the final game of last year's World Series. I was twenty-eight when you were born. Your sister was eighteen when she had Kayla, so we're all over the map here. If you and Cherisse want to have kids, go ahead and have 'em."

"I don't know," he said. "My gut's telling me that it's just too late." At that point he burst into tears.

There's no sense trying to reason with people who are a) drunk or b) high, so I didn't. Instead I drove Scott home, handing out a huge helping of well-worn platitudes along the way. I walked him into the house and settled him in a recliner in the family room. (Scott is his father's son, after all. Of course he has a recliner.) After making sure his iPad, the TV remote, and a pitcher of water were all within easy reach, I let myself back out of the house and drove back to Belltown Terrace.

"So what do you think's going on with him?" Mel asked.

It was Friday evening, and we were having our late dinner in our favorite quiet corner of El Gaucho, seated in a raised booth that nonetheless gave us a front row view of the frenetic action happening in the kitchen.

"I don't know. Midlife crisis maybe? I didn't bother asking him, not when he was clearly under the influence. That's a conversation we'll need to have some other time when he isn't."

Mel sighed. "Could be it has nothing to do with how

old he is and there's something else going on with the marriage."

Mel's pretty much on the beam when it comes to relationships, and I had a feeling she might be right. "Could be," I agreed.

"How about my own guy's postmidlife crisis?" she asked, breezily changing the subject and pointing the conversation in my direction. I'm gradually adjusting to Mel's sudden shifts in conversation and learning to negotiate same, but that one still caught me flat-footed.

"I'm bored," I admitted finally, after a pause. "I miss the action. I miss doing something useful."

What was it my mother used to say? "Ask and you shall receive." In this case it was a matter of from my lips to God's ears. I was about to be thrown back into the action, all right—in spades.

CHAPTER 2

PART OF THE general malaise that had been affecting me was only to be expected. Mel and I had just come through a frenetic round of holiday activities, an overly booked endurance race that had started with a driving trip from Bellingham to Ashland for Thanksgiving with my daughter and her family and hadn't let up until well after New Year's Day, when the last college bowl game finally came to an end.

This time around, with Mel fully preoccupied with her new job, the complex holiday preparations, which she had previously handled effortlessly and without so much as turning a hair, had all fallen on my inexperienced shoulders. That had included sending out the Christmas cards and seeing to the holiday decorating at both places—the new house in Bellingham as well as the condo in Seattle. It had all gotten done eventually but not, I'm sorry to admit, without a bit of serious grousing on my part.

Fortunately, when it came to organizing and installing decorations, I'd had professional help from our interior designer, Jim Hunt, who saw to it that all our halls were decked to the max, at both places.

Mel is big on family, and the decorations in Seattle were mostly part of our family holiday celebration. As for the ones in Bellingham? Those were mostly business—Mel's business.

I think that I may have mentioned before that when Mel landed her new job as chief of police, she walked into a political maelstrom. She immediately launched what she likes to call a "charm offensive," which entailed the two of us hosting several preholiday parties—one for Mel's top brass, another for her rank and file, and a third for her civilian employees.

Yes, I spent years being a cop, but somehow it never occurred to me that the job of chief would turn out to be quite such a social undertaking, but then perhaps I hadn't ever envisioned someone like Mel Soames tackling that role.

The preferred management style of Bellingham's previous mayor, Adelina Kirkpatrick, had been to create as many adversarial situations as possible. While her underlings went after each other tooth and nail, the mayor had been free to do whatever she damned well pleased. Mel's idea, revolutionary as it might seem, was to get people to work together, and those preholiday gatherings had been part of Mel's determined effort to put some of the department's previous bad blood in the rearview mirror and come up with strategies for dealing with the incoming administration. My role in the festivities had been that of corporate/political spouse, which is to say, I arranged for the caterer. When it came to the events themselves? I made sure I was on hand, properly bibbed-and-tuckered, and prepared to make a certain amount of inoffensive small talk. It was also my job to oversee the cleanup of several spilled beverages. In other words, you can mark me as present but not essential.

Now, though, at the end of the first week in January, the last of the decorations in both places had been taken down, packed up, and put away. I was dealing with a curious combination of relief and letdown. Given the weather at the moment, I was probably also suffering from something locals like to refer to as SAD—seasonal affective disorder.

"So how'd it go with Mayor-Elect Appleton?" I asked, as our favorite waiter at El Gaucho cleared away dinner plates to make way for dessert. We'd already decided on the bananas Foster.

"Okay, I think," Mel said. "He seems like a pretty squared-away guy."

"He's a politician," I warned.

"A beginning politician," Mel said. "This is his first elected office."

"They all have to start somewhere," I said.

"Ross Connors started out as King County attorney," Mel countered.

She had me there. Ross, our much-lamented late boss, had indeed started his political career by running for elected office as the King County prosecutor. He had gone on to spend several decades as Washington State's attorney general, where his bipartisan support had meant he had served with governors on both sides of the aisle. That's where Mel and I had both encountered Ross and each other—when we'd signed on to work with his statewide Special Homicide Investigation Team.

"Okay," I said, conceding defeat. "You've got me there. And I hope you're right—that Lawrence Appleton turns out to be the same kind of straight shooter Ross Connors was."

"Larry," Mel corrected. "He told me to call him Larry not Lawrence."

"That's a start then, I suppose."

"Well, well," someone said, stopping next to our table. "I spotted you earlier as you came in. What are you doing in town? I heard you'd moved up north."

Fully expecting the arrival of the bananas Foster dessert cart, I was dismayed to find myself looking into the face of one of my least favorite people on the planet—Maxwell Cole, a former columnist for a now Internet-only newspaper, the *Seattle Post-Intelligencer*. Suffice it to say, Max and I have a long history together, and not in a good way.

It had been years since I'd seen the man, and at first I almost didn't recognize him. For one thing, he was much smaller than I remembered—thin, almost. Where he had once boasted a full head of hair, his head was now shaved bald, and his signature handlebar mustache was nowhere in evidence. Standing there in the aisle, he leaned heavily on one of those three-pronged, self-standing canes. Parked behind him was a rolling portable oxygen container. My first impression was that the intervening years had been far harder on Max than they had been on me, but I said nothing to that effect. We were out in public. There was no point in being rude.

"Long time no see, Max," I said, rising to my feet and holding out my hand. "How's it going?"

"Not bad," Max said. He swayed slightly as he spoke,

as though he might have had a bit too much to drink. Then, nodding briefly in Mel's direction, he added, "I presume this is the little woman?"

His looks may have changed, but clearly he hadn't improved in the brains department. Talk about getting off on the wrong foot! Take it from me, calling Mel Soames "little anything" is not recommended.

"Please," I said. "Allow me to introduce my wife, Melissa Soames—Chief of Police Melissa Soames. Mel, this is Maxwell Cole."

She offered him her hand along with a frosty look that was one step short of lethal. "Glad to meet you," she said.

"From Bellingham, I believe?" Max asked, wading in where angels fear to tread.

"That's correct," she told him. "I'm chief of police in Bellingham."

"Is that where the two of you are living now?" he asked.

I sat back down. "We have a place there," I answered, "but we kept the condo here as well."

"The one just up the street?" Max jerked his head in the direction of Belltown Terrace.

I wasn't much liking this Spanish Inquisition style of questioning, but short of making a scene, I had to go along to get along. "That's right," I said. "How about you?"

"I'm back in my folks' old place up on Queen Anne," he said. "I rented it out for a time while I was down in California, but I hung on to it just in case I might want to come back. Someday I suppose someone will make me an offer that's too good to refuse. Once they do, I'll be out of there and living it up in Palm Springs or somewhere warm. What about you? What are you up to these days? I guess that cold case gig with Ross Connors came to a screeching halt."

Considering the terrible wreck that had happened just blocks from here, the one in which Ross Connors had lost his life and Harry I. Ball both his legs, it was a shockingly poor choice of words. Whether or not it was deliberate on Max's part, I couldn't tell, but I spotted the grimace of distaste that flashed across Mel's face and knew that Max had just managed to dig himself an even deeper hole.

"Keeping busy," I said noncommittally.

What I really wanted was for him to shut up and walk away. He didn't.

"I've been doing some blogging of late," Max offered, although I hadn't asked. "Just to keep my hand in, as it were. I've come up with an idea that might actually be worthy of turning into a book. Maybe we could sit down and chew the fat about it one of these days."

"Sure," I said, not really meaning it. "Any time. Just give me a call."

Our waiter showed up, pushing his dessert cart, but he was forced to park it on the far side of the Maxwell Cole roadblock. This being El Gaucho, the waiter was too polite to say anything. Instead, he stood there silently with his arms crossed waiting for Max to get the message and take his leave.

"Glad to," Max said, "but I'll need a number."

Reluctantly, I hauled out my wallet and handed over the only business card I had in my possession at the time—one that happened to be from TLC—The Last Chance.

Max held the card up to his eyes and peered at it,

frowning. He was groping for a pair of reading glasses when the helpful waiter whipped out one of the tiny flashlights the restaurant provides to make menu reading easier for people of a certain age.

"Who's The Last Chance?" Max asked, reading from the now-illuminated text.

"It's a volunteer cold case squad, one I work with on occasion," I explained. "A friend of mine hooked me up with them a few months ago."

"Oh," Max said, nodding. "I see." He pocketed the card. "Weren't you working on that cold case from Seattle PD, the one where that lady cop got blown away?"

That was a topic I most assuredly did not want to discuss with Maxwell Cole.

"The 'lady cop' in question happened to have a name—Detective Delilah Ainsworth."

Something in my voice must have warned Max away. He took a backward step. "I believe that was a very old case," he said. "Did you get much pushback?"

"Not so much," I said, struggling to keep my voice even. I didn't dare glance in Mel's direction. I knew she understood how much Detective Ainsworth's senseless death still haunted me.

For the first time Max seemed to notice the presence of our very patient waiter.

"Okay then," he said, giving us a half wave as he finally moved away from our table. "See you around."

He headed out, leaning heavily on his cane as he dodged between tables and dragging his oxygen cart behind him. Mel waited until the waiter had performed his flaming-bananas magic and the dessert plates had been placed in front of us before she said anything more.

"So that was Maxwell Cole!"

By the time Mel and I had met up, the digital age had overtaken the *Seattle Post-Intelligencer* and Maxwell Cole had gone south looking for greener journalistic pastures. Since he was now back from what had obviously been a brief sojourn in California, those hoped-for greener pastures must not have materialized. That also meant, however, that beyond the bare bones of the narrative—long-term loathing and disrespect on both sides—Mel wasn't exactly completely up to speed on Max's and my mutual history.

She knew, for example, that Max and I had been fraternity brothers back in the day at the University of Washington. She also was aware that I had scored my first wife, Karen, by stealing her out from under Max's nose. I'm pretty sure I neglected to tell her about my punching the guy's lights out once—not one of my finest hours. As we dug into our bananas Foster, I saw no need to go into any of those gory details right that minute. We were out on the town, having fun, and enjoying the moment. Given all that, it seemed silly to dig up that ancient history, so I didn't.

"That's the guy all right," I agreed, "the very one."

During dessert, the waiter reappeared twice—first to proffer a box of selected teas to the lady and second to present a box of cigar choices from El Gaucho's famed humidor. The cigars were offered even though the health police have seen to it that the restaurant's beloved cigar lounge no longer existed. Mel accepted the tea; I passed on both counts, although I have to admit the idea of settling in to smoke a handmade cigar was more than a little tempting.

I glanced at Mel, who was shaking her head as she stirred Splenda into her Earl Grey.

"What?" I asked.

"Didn't you see the cigar in his pocket? You'd think someone who's on oxygen might have gotten the memo that smoking cigars is a bad idea."

Now that she mentioned it, I remembered that there had been a cigar tucked discreetly in Max's vest pocket. "You'd think," I agreed with a nod.

It was a tiny, sharp shard of conversation in an evening's worth of pleasant and relaxing talk, but one I would have reason to remember in the coming days—and definitely not in a good way.

CHAPTER 3

WE WENT TO the play on Saturday afternoon. Dulcinea was a knockout, and Sancho Panza was great. Don Quixote, however, was only so-so. I guess it's true, you really can't win 'em all. I had expected the play to be followed by a quiet evening all to ourselves, dining on the previous night's leftovers, but that was not to be. The city of Bellingham had other ideas.

The report of an officer-involved shooting in Bellingham meant that Mel had to head back up I-5 immediately after the show ended. A call to Scott told me that he was doing fine and needed no further hand-holding. With that in mind, I packed up the leftovers and headed north as well.

The torrential downpours continued. I drove through several squalls where the windshield wipers couldn't keep up with the rain, to say nothing of the spray kicked up by jerks in sports cars, SUVs, and eighteen-wheelers who didn't have brains enough to slow down even a little bit. The talking heads on the radio reported that the Cascades continued to be hammered with snow.

With both Stevens and Snoqualmie Passes currently closed, I was glad to be traveling north rather than east or west. Along I-5, the highway's proximity to the ocean meant there wasn't any snow or ice to deal with, just water—but the radio reporter's daunting list of nearby rivers at or approaching flood stage made me glad our house in Fairhaven was up on a bluff rather than down in a valley.

Just so you know, Fairhaven was founded in the 1880s, but in the early 1900s the village was incorporated into the city of Bellingham. One of the reasons we had bought a house there was that although it was officially "in" the city, it was also "out" of it. Considering Mel's highly visible position as chief of police, we needed at least a modicum of privacy.

Halfway there, I called Mel to see how things were going. "My officer is fine and out on administrative leave," she told me. "The guy he shot is not. He's not room temperature at the moment, but he's hospitalized in critical condition."

"What happened?" I asked.

"A DV," she said.

DV is cop speak for domestic violence. "The woman who called 911 reported that her husband had a gun. Naturally my officers showed up with weapons drawn. What the wife failed to mention and maybe didn't even know was that the gun in question was a BB gun, which the bad guy promptly fired. We found at least one of the BBs. It had bounced off my guy's vest and ended up in his shirt pocket."

A civilian hearing that might think, *Wait a minute here. A cop uses his service weapon to shoot the shit out of some poor guy armed with nothing but a BB gun? How unfair is that and how do you spell police brutality?* The problem is, that civilian is probably thinking about one of those Daisy BB guns from back in the old days, like the one the poor kid's mother worries may cause him to shoot his eye out in *A Christmas Story.*

I'm definitely not a civilian. "What kind of BB gun?" I asked.

"A Beretta Px4 Storm Pellet-BB Pistol," Mel answered.

I happen to have a nodding acquaintance with those. They're made by Umarex. If you have a computer handy, you might want to google them just for the hell of it. Once you do, I double-dare you to come face to-face with one of those in the heat of battle and decide it's a BB gun instead of the real thing. Cops in those kinds of situations are scared to death and jacked up on adrenaline. Confronted with armed assailants with guns in their hands and fingers on triggers, they tend to shoot first and ask questions later. And although pellets fired from one of those aren't likely to kill you, without that officer's vest in place, the BB that hit Mel's guy in the chest would have smarted some.

I knew that. Mel knew that. But there are plenty of people out there—the second-guessers of the world— the Monday morning quarterbacks who have never once put their own lives on the line—who want to turn every police shooting into a media crap storm. Reporters were probably already descending on Bellingham en masse. I knew full well that, along with the officer who had pulled the trigger, Mel would be their next-best target.

"Where are you?" I asked.

"Still at the scene," she said. "As far as the investigation is concerned, we can't afford to leave any stones unturned. There'll be a press conference later tonight, and I'll need to stop by the hospital before that."

"In other words, I shouldn't wait up?"

"That would be my guess."

"Okay," I said. "Stay safe and stay warm."

"Too late for the warm part," she said. "I'm already soaked to the skin."

I drove on home, where I divided the leftovers scrupulously in half and then ate my share. I watched the boob tube for a while, but I was in bed and fast asleep long before Mel got home.

When I crept out of bed the next morning, she was sawing logs, and I left her to it. I fired up the coffee machine and then turned on the news. It was Sunday morning, so the third-string newsies on the local channels hadn't yet built up a good head of steam as far as the officer-involved shooting was concerned. The would-be shooter was still hospitalized with his condition listed as critical. As for the officer? He was still on administrative leave. There was nothing new to report other than the fact that neither the shooting victim nor the officer was African-American or Hispanic. Hopefully that meant the race card wouldn't be played in this case, but the report failed to mention that the hospitalized "victim" had been in the process of beating the crap out of his wife when he had been rudely interrupted by the arrival of the cops.

I checked the TV guide to see when the Seahawks' game was due to start. I'm not a huge NFL fan, but when your local team ends up in the playoffs, you're more or less duty bound to pay attention, especially when Seattle is pitted against Green Bay with the Packers already in the playoffs as well. Then, while the TV droned in the background, I took my iPad over to my new and surprisingly comfortable easy chair by the front windows, where I settled in to "read the papers." Be advised that I use the term *papers* very loosely, because the electronic news media I follow these days and the sites where I do my crossword puzzles have nothing to do with paper and ink.

The talking heads were blabbing away in the half hour leading up to kickoff when I saw a headline on the *Seattle Times* site that caught my attention: ONE DEAD IN QUEEN ANNE HOUSE FIRE. Local news is local news, and Queen Anne Hill is the next neighborhood over from the Denny Regrade. Since proximity is everything, I read the whole article.

> *Overnight the Seattle Fire Department responded to an early morning two alarm blaze on Queen Anne's Bigelow Avenue where at least one victim is known to have perished. The fire was spotted at 2:30 AM by a passerby who immediately called 911. By the time units arrived on the scene, the upper story of the house was fully engulfed.*
>
> *Fire department personnel are still on the scene, checking for hot spots. The victim, presumed to be the owner, was transported to Harborview Hospital, where he was pronounced dead on arrival. His identification is being withheld, pending notification of next of kin.*

That was it. It's the kind of article I've read countless times over the years—a snippet of news that's long on drama and short on details. I had no inkling at the time that it would have anything at all to do with me, nor did I guess that the unnamed victim would turn out to be someone I knew personally.

Mel, wearing a robe and with her hair still damp from the shower, emerged from the bedroom about then, in search of coffee. As far as Mel Soames is concerned, her taking a shower before drinking coffee could mean only one thing:

"You're going in to the office?" I asked.

"What do you think? How bad is the media playing it?"

"Relatively even-handed so far," I told her.

"That'll change if the victim croaks out."

"I thought he was okay."

"Still critical," Mel answered. "I checked on him just a couple of minutes ago. He took a turn for the worse overnight due to some kind of complications. He's currently back in the ICU. So yes, I'll be going to the office. I'll probably be there most of the day."

"Breakfast first?" I asked.

My asking the question should not be confused with an offer on my part to actually cook. I'm useless when it comes to kitchens, and Mel isn't much better. Our favorite Sunday morning breakfast treat turns out to be huevos rancheros at Pepe's, a family-run Mexican food joint in downtown Fairhaven. It's only a little over half a mile away from our house, and lots of Sundays we walk it. (Thank God for my new knees.) But this cold January morning, with torrential rain still pounding down, was not the kind of day to go for a midmorning stroll.

"The usual?" Mel asked.

"Works for me," I said, "although if you're going into

work, you should probably pass on your customary mimosa."

In the end, we took separate vehicles and were both soaking wet by the time we walked from our cars to the restaurant. Because of the nature of Mel's job, she's on everybody's radar in town, so we didn't talk shop during breakfast. I sent her on her mimosa-free way as soon as we finished eating our late-morning meal, while I returned home to watch the remainder of the game—a 17–14 nail-biting victory that the Hawks pulled off by scoring a Hail Mary 48-yard field goal with thirty seconds left on the clock.

I confess, I felt a bit silly, sitting there all by myself, yelling my head off, but it was that kind of game. When it was over, I made another cup of java and returned to my iPad, intent on working the crosswords. That's when I noticed the updated headline: LONGTIME SE-ATTLE REPORTER DIES IN FIRE.

Longtime Post-Intelligencer *crime reporter and columnist, 72-year-old Maxwell Oscar Cole, perished overnight in a fire at his home in the Queen Anne neigh-borhood.*

Firefighting units were summoned to the blaze at 2:30 AM by a passerby who dialed 911 after seeing flames inside the two-story home on Bigelow Avenue. By the time units arrived on the scene, the upper level of the home was fully engulfed.

Firefighters were able to effect a rescue, although Mr. Cole was unresponsive at the scene. He was trans-ported to Harborview Hospital, where he was pronounced dead on arrival. The investigation is continuing.

For many years, Mr. Cole was considered to be one of

the city's leading crime reporters. Once the PI *switched* over to being a virtual publication, Mr. Cole left the Seattle area to work in newsrooms first in San Francisco and later on in Los Angeles. In recent years, he's maintained a blog dealing with reminiscences of his years as a local crime writer. He was said to be at work on a book at the time of his death.

Funeral arrangements are pending.

CHAPTER 4

WHEN I WAS in my twenties, I was immortal and didn't bother reading the obituaries. Yes, my mother had died of cancer, but she was old—in her midforties. Then, in my thirties and after I became a homicide cop, I started paying more attention because people I knew did die. Bad guys died. Fellow officers died. Some were taken out by car crashes or struck down by physical ailments, but some, who found the pain of living more than they could bear, went out of their own volition and on their own timetable.

By my forties, whether I knew the deceased or not, I began paying attention to the ages of the people who had died. It always felt better somehow—or at least less threatening—if the dead person in question happened to be "really old," which is to say at least a couple of decades older than I was. Now that situation has changed dramatically. People a lot younger than I am routinely show up among those death notices along with plenty of people my age.

Maxwell Cole was one of the latter—a contemporary. Because we had been in the same fraternity back in college, I happened to know that his birthday preceded mine by a mere three months. His birthday in the frat house at the end of August our freshman year was the excuse for the first drunken party I experienced after enrolling in the University of Washington—or the U Dub, as that institution of higher learning is known to locals.

Even with all the bad blood between us, Max's death hit far closer to home than I would have expected, especially since Mel and I had seen him on Friday night, only two nights before his death. With Mel gone for the day, I had plenty of time to think—and if you've been a homicide cop for as long as I have, extended periods of solitary thought have the potential to be hazardous.

I've investigated fatality fires. To say they're gruesome is a huge understatement. Once you've been exposed to the distinctive smell of burnt human flesh, it's something that never goes away. There's always the faint hope that the victim was overcome by smoke long before the flames reached him. Sometime in the course of that long afternoon, I had a heart-to-heart chat with my Higher Power hoping that had been the case here—that Max had died as a result of smoke inhalation rather than from something much more horrific.

Had I wanted to, I could have found out about what was really going on by checking with some of my long-time contacts at either Seattle PD or at the medical examiner's office. I could have done so, but I didn't. At the time it was none of my business. During the course of the day, as the story was updated, I contented myself with reading the updates, and toward the end of the day, a familiar name jumped out at me.

A close family friend, Erin Kelsey Howard, serving as family spokeswoman, said that funeral arrangements are pending with the Poindexter Funeral Home and will be announced once the medical examiner's office releases the body. In the meantime, in lieu of flowers, it is suggested that donations be made to the local chapter of the Right to Try.

My initial impression was that "Try" was a misprint of some kind—a mistaken rendition of the Right to Die, but then I googled the term and discovered that Right to Try is a national organization devoted to passing laws that allow terminally ill patients to avail themselves of groundbreaking drugs that have not yet been completely vetted by the Byzantine obstacles put in place by the FDA.

Here's the deal. Imagine you're someone who has just been given a terminal prognosis by your friendly neighborhood oncologist. In the course of giving yourself a graduate-level education in whatever version of the Big C is currently threatening your existence, you have just discovered that there is an experimental drug that is thought to improve life expectancy of patients dealing with that malady.

In hopes of helping yourself and, as a consequence, helping others as well, you sign up to participate in a trial. Because the drug has not yet been deemed safe, if you're actually allowed into the program, you have a fifty-fifty chance of receiving a) the drug you want or b) a placebo. If you do sign on, that means you're agreeing to a situation where you may get the real medication—the one you want—which *might* kill you, or the placebo, which for sure will do nothing to help you. Good luck with that. Any resemblance to a rousing game of Russian roulette is purely coincidental.

I thought about a thin, bald Maxwell Cole—a mere shadow of his former self—standing in El Gaucho, minus his mustache, leaning on his cane and dragging an oxygen canister behind him. Had he been a cancer patient perhaps? Maybe. And then I remembered that cigar—no doubt of the Cuban, hand-rolled variety. Cigar versus cancer? If you're already terminal and you want to smoke a cigar, why the hell not?

The first thing I did, right then and there, was locate the Right to Try's website, where I made a sizable donation in memory of Maxwell Cole.

About that time, the clouds parted and the sun came out. After days of unrelenting rain, that burst of sunlight was especially welcome. Before the sudden clearing had time to turn frigid, I decided that after days of being cooped up in the house, I needed a walk.

Ever since our move to Bellingham, or rather, our half-move to Bellingham, Mel and I had been discussing the possibility of getting a dog, partially under the most likely mistaken impression that having a dog would make me walk more. Mel's take on the matter was that I should make some effort to walk without using a dog for cover.

So I threw on a jacket and went outside. As I started off through the winding up-and-down streets of Edgemoor, despite having salved my conscience with a monetary donation, my mind was still stuck on what had happened to Maxwell Cole and on the fact that, for the second time in my life, I felt sorry for him. And that realization took me back to the first time I felt sorry for him, some twenty years or so earlier, and to the familiar name that had leaped out at me from the online article—Erin Kelsey Howard.

It had been about this same time of year and in the aftermath of a record-breaking snowstorm that I, along with my least favorite partner of all time, Detective Paul Kramer, was summoned to a double homicide in the old Seattle Public Schools District office up on Queen Anne Hill. One of the victims, Marcia Kelsey, was thought to be Erin's mother. Unfortunately, our subsequent investigation revealed that everything Erin thought she knew about her past and her presumed family had been a complete fabrication.

When I first met her, Erin was a college sophomore—an Oregon Duck. Her real father and Marcia's first husband, a nut job by the name of Chris McLaughlin, was a sometime drug dealer with delusions of polygamous grandeur. He had enticed Marcia to marry him and run away to a commune in Canada despite the inconvenient fact that he was already married to someone else. I'm sure at one time I knew the name of the first wife, but as I walked around Edgemoor that cold but sunny Sunday afternoon, I couldn't for the life of me remember it.

Once at the commune, things went haywire in a hurry. Chris and his first wife already had one child and were expecting a second when eighteen-year-old Marcia turned up on the scene. She came from a staunch Mormon household. At the time of the elopement, she may or may not have known about the existence of that other wife. That early on, she also may or may not have known that she was prone to lesbian leanings. I've often wondered if her running off with Chris was an attempt to squelch those very tendencies.

Sometime after she arrived, the commune experiment went south. For one thing, the other women involved—including Chris's first wife—all seemed capable of getting pregnant at the drop of a hat. Marcia, desperate to have children of her own, could not. I learned later that she was what's known in the West as a "downwinder."

During the fifties, as a young child visiting her grandparents in Utah for summer vacation, the family farm was directly in the path of fallout from a particularly dirty nuclear bomb set off on the Nevada test site. As a result of that exposure, both grandparents subsequently died of cancer. As for Marcia? She might have developed cancer eventually, but she was murdered long before that happened. Still, from what her husband told me at the time of her death, she always attributed her inability to have children to that one fateful fallout encounter.

Once the commune experiment blew up, Marcia returned to Seattle to live with her parents, go back to school, and try to put the whole Canadian experience behind her. Meanwhile, things weren't going so well for Chris. With money in short supply, he tried his hand at drug smuggling, sometimes using his infant daughter's blankets and diapers as cover for his illicit goods. Whether it was done with or without the consent of the baby's mother, that moderately successful scheme continued for a time, until the day Chris ended up dead, stabbed to death in the course of a drunken brawl in one of his favorite south-of-the-border hangouts—a bar in Puerto Peñasco, aka Rocky Point—in Mexico.

At the time of Chris's death, the bartender on duty happened to be an American expat, a Vietnam

War army deserter named John Madsen. A day after McLaughlin died, the local woman he had hired to look after his daughter, Sasha, while he went drinking, turned up at the bar with the baby in hand, along with a collection of Chris's goods. Worried that she might be accused of kidnapping the Anglo child, the woman was eager to have someone else take charge of Sasha, and that's exactly what John Madsen did.

Hidden in the bottom of a diaper bag, he discovered a cache of several sets of fake IDs, ones Chris had had created for both himself and for Sasha in order to facilitate their being able to move back and forth across the border at will. John Madsen's physical resemblance to McLaughlin was close enough that in cursory examinations, the photos worked. Madsen saw that collection of fake IDs as nothing short of a godsend—as a way of ending his long exile from the States. Choosing one set of IDs—those for someone named Pete Kelsey and his daughter, Erin—John Madsen packed up Sasha and headed north.

Among Chris's effects, Madsen had found Marcia's name and address. Thinking she might be able to point him in the direction of Sasha's real mother, that's where Pete and Erin headed—to Seattle. When he reached out to Marcia, she did indeed know where to find Sasha's biological mother. Unfortunately, Marcia also knew that the commune she had left behind was no place for a child to grow to adulthood. The fact that Chris had used his own child as an unwitting accomplice in his drug trafficking pretty much sealed the deal.

In the end, Pete Kelsey and his "daughter" stayed on in Seattle. Considering his identity irregularities, finding a regular job was out of the question, so he established himself as a star in the local home remodeling industry. In order to legitimatize their relationship, Marcia pulled a fast one on one of her long-term acquaintances, Maxwell Cole, and duped him into believing that he was the one who first introduced Marcia to Pete.

Their resulting marriage came with a number of benefits for Pete and Marcia. He acquired newfound standing in the community while an otherwise childless Marcia had a child to raise. In addition, Pete and Marcia's stable but nontraditional relationship provided cover for Marcia's longtime relationship with a female lover. And what did Erin get from all this? A supposedly stable family that, upon examination, turned out to be nothing but a pack of lies.

The whole scheme had collapsed when one of Chris McLaughlin's other children, Erin's half sister, Jennifer, came to Seattle intent on taking revenge on Pete Kelsey—the man her mother had held solely responsible for her father's death. Jennifer had murdered Marcia, attempted to frame Pete for the crime, and burned the family home to the ground. Her final act, one that very nearly succeeded, had been an attempt to drag Erin to her death in a suicidal plunge off the Magnolia Bridge.

I had been caught up in that terrible life-and-death tug of war, with me grasping Erin by the wrist and pulling in one direction while Jennifer attempted to drag her in the other. When it was over, Jennifer had fallen to her death, and Erin was still alive—broken but alive.

All these years later, during my increasingly chilly walk through Edgemoor that suddenly icy Sunday afternoon, I could still hear the dull pops as Erin's shoulders dislocated, along with the howls of agony that followed.

It was after that awful confrontation that I'd finally had to tell Maxwell Cole the ugly truth—that for the better part of twenty years he'd been played for a fool by Pete and Marcia Kelsey, the two people he had assumed were his best friends in all the world. Much as I disliked the man, I couldn't help but feel sorry for him when he finally learned the truth.

Police involvement in the aftermath of Marcia's death meant that Pete Kelsey's decades-long charade came to an end. Unmasked as a Vietnam-era army deserter named John Madsen, he had been taken into custody. Charged with desertion, he was eventually released from federal custody with a general discharge from the U.S. Army. He emerged from the process a seemingly broken man. His wife had been murdered and his house destroyed. The resulting notoriety had cost him not only his business, but also the love of the girl he had raised and loved as if she were his own. Erin was his no longer.

From what I had learned today, the only piece of Erin's previous life that had evidently remained intact was her friendship with Maxwell Cole. Sadly, now that, too, had come to an end. Since the online article had referred to Erin as Maxwell Cole's "family spokesman," their close relationship had endured despite everything that had gone before. The connection between them, forged in the fire of mutual betrayal, was a bond even death itself couldn't sever.

Wheels crunched on the roadway as a car pulled up beside me. The honk of a horn and a flash of headlights startled me out of my reverie. I had no idea how long I had been walking, but I was chilled to the bone, and the sun was definitely going down.

"What the hell are you doing out here?" Mel demanded as she buzzed down the passenger window of her shiny new Ford Interceptor. "Come on. Get in. You'll catch your death."

For as long as I've known her, Mel Soames has always been one sweet talker. How the hell could any guy in his right mind resist an invitation like that? I got in, and away we went.

CHAPTER 5

"How are things?" I asked.

"You might want to take a look in the backseat," Mel said.

I turned around to check. There was a lumpy black blob huddled in the corner of the backseat, directly behind where I was sitting. It might have been a blanket or a coat, but then we passed under a streetlight and the glow from that lit up an unblinking pair of black eyes. What I thought was a blanket turned out to be a dog—a very large dog.

"What the hell?" I demanded.

"The name is Rambo," Mel said with a sigh, "and it's a long story."

One of the things I've learned in life is that you have to watch out what you ask for or even what you think about because Someone is out there listening— Someone with a very dry sense of humor.

"Are we taking him to the pound maybe?" I asked hopefully.

"Rambo's a girl actually," Mel answered. "And she's not going to the pound. She's coming home with us."

Okay, so if you can have transgender bathrooms in this day and age, maybe having a transgender-named dog isn't completely out of the question, either.

Mel eased down the steep hill that is our driveway, pulled into our two-car garage, and popped the trunk latch. "Rambo's stuff is in the back. If you'll get that, I'll take her inside."

Once out of the car, Mel opened the back door and picked up a leash, which she attached to the dog's collar, one of those very fierce-looking pinch collars designed to keep troublesome dogs under control.

"Come on, girl," Mel urged. "Let's go." Obligingly Rambo unwound her incredibly long legs, stood up, and gave herself a full-body shake. She was nothing short of immense. A fringe of smooth, six-inch-long hair dangled from the ends of both her ears, and a cape of similarly long hair covered her massive shoulders.

"What the hell kind of dog is that?" I demanded.

"Mostly an Irish wolfhound," Mel told me, "possibly mixed with something else."

Once out of the car and on the ground, Rambo was tall enough that the top of her head was even with the top of Mel's hip. I believe I may have mentioned before that Mel isn't anybody's idea of a "little lady." Not only was Rambo tall, but she probably weighed in at a hundred pounds or so. She was a big dog—a very big dog— who accompanied Mel into the house without making any objections, so I did my part, too. I went to the back of the car to collect Rambo's "stuff."

It consisted of a large but very worn gray dog bed; a grocery bag full of several battered chew toys; a pair of equally worn tennis balls; two large metal dog dishes; and a forty-pound bag of dry dog food that was more than half-empty. It took two trips to drag everything into the house. I put the dog bed down in one corner of the kitchen, next to the trash drawer. When I came back into the house with the other load, Rambo was already curled up on her bed. With only her eyes moving, she watched me warily while resting her nose on her outstretched front paws. Her coat was black and so were her eyes. I found the steady gaze from those unblinking eyes to be unnerving, to say the least.

I filled one of the two dishes with water and the other with a measuring cup full of food and put them down on the floor next to her. She didn't budge. "There you go, Rambo," I said. "Make yourself at home."

Because Mel had gone to work that morning expecting to have interactions with the press, she had worn her dress uniform. When she reappeared in the kitchen a couple of minutes later, she had already changed into the fleecy lavender tracksuit I had given her for Christmas.

Mel gave me a glancing kiss as she crossed the room, then knelt down in front of the dog and patted the animal's head. "There you go, Rambo," she crooned softly. "How's it going?"

Rambo responded with a weak thump from her long, lanky tail.

"So tell me," I said, "what's the deal with the dog, and how's the guy in the hospital?"

"The guy in the hospital is named Purcell—Kenneth Purcell," Mel told me. "Things have settled down with him for now, and it looks like he's going to make it."

"That's got to be a huge relief."

Mel nodded. "A shooting incident is bad enough, but a fatality shooting would be a whole lot worse."

"Purcell," I repeated. "Sounds Anglo."

"That's right," Mel answered. "He's not even Hispanic, and neither is my cop, which might help dial back some of the deadly-force outrage and rhetoric."

"Good luck with that," I said.

"Turns out that long before Saturday, Purcell had multiple arrests for domestic violence—three of which occurred in the last six months. Each time, even with a no-contact order in place, his wife took him back the minute he got out of the slammer. This time, though, I think the presence of the weapon—BB gun or not—got her attention. After a full day of urging on our part, she finally agreed to get help. One of my victims' advocates spent the day finding a shelter that would take the wife and the two kids, but…"

"But not the dog," I finished.

"Right," Mel agreed. "Not the dog, and that left the kids—Chrissy and Lonny—absolutely heartbroken. Rambo evidently came to them as a pound puppy, and they didn't want her having to go back there. Since it was the only way to get the wife and kids taken care of, I offered to look after Rambo until they have a chance to get settled somewhere else."

"That could take months," I objected.

"Exactly," Mel said with a nod. "But still, it's only temporary, and we do have a fenced yard. Besides, wasn't the plan all along that that once we got settled in here, we'd look into getting a dog?"

That had been somebody's plan, just not necessarily mine. I glanced at Rambo, who continued to study me with unwavering concentration. There's a big difference between discussing a hypothetical dog and looking at a creature who seemed fully capable, if she once set her mind to it, of eating me for lunch. Compared to Rambo, Snooks—my first wife's ankle-biting dachshund—was a lightweight.

"I don't think she likes me," I said.

"If you had met Kenneth Purcell, you wouldn't blame her," Mel said fiercely. "The guy's a piece of work who has terrorized his family for months on end, and he's probably done the same thing to the poor dog."

So there it was—a done deal. For good or ill, either temporarily or maybe forever, Mel and I were now responsible for a dog—this dog. Another lesson I've learned over time is that once you're beaten, give in gracefully and get on with it.

"Okay then," I said. "What's for dinner?"

The remodel on our newly acquired house had included the installation of a gourmet kitchen. The ironic thing about that is that neither Mel nor I qualifies as a gourmet cook. Our very high-end, six-burner gas range boasts two ovens along with both a stovetop griddle and grill. The last two items—the grill and the griddle—are the ones that get the most use. That night, with Rambo watching our every move, we heated up a can of tomato soup and made a stack of grilled cheese sandwiches.

Our kitchen is part of a great room that looks out over the water of Bellingham Bay. On the far side of the kitchen island is a dining room table and beyond that the living room. I prefer eating at the table so we can enjoy the view. By then it was fully dark outside, so the view wasn't exactly an issue. Nonetheless, Mel and I took our usual places. We had barely tucked into our own food when we heard an unaccustomed crunching noise coming from the far side of the island.

"Good," Mel said. "At least she's eating."

A few minutes later, Rambo made her grand entrance. Leaving the kitchen behind, she sniffed her way around the dining area and living room before stopping in front of the outside door. Then, with her nose practically touching the doorknob, she glanced back in our direction.

"I think she needs to go out," Mel offered.

This was uncharted territory for me. "What should I do?" I asked. "Put the leash on her to take her out?"

Like water-view houses everywhere, the back door of our house is the one we use for most of our comings and goings. The front entrance, located at the near end of the living room, opens onto a porch and into a grassy yard, which runs steeply downhill and ends in a cliff-side fence overlooking the water. There was no doubt in my mind that in this weather, the wet grass would be very slick. I didn't relish the idea of going out in the dark and cold and being dragged down that slippery slope by a dog the size of a small Shetland pony.

"How about if we trust the fence," Mel suggested. "Let's let her out and see what happens."

I got up from the table, walked over to the door, and switched on the yard lights. When I reached for the door handle, however, Rambo cringed away from me as though I was about to hit her. It broke my heart—damn Kenneth Purcell!

"It's okay, girl," I said, opening the door and then stepping aside to give her room. "Off you go."

She bounded outside and I walked over to the window. Using the yard lights, I was able to observe her progress. She sniffed around some, exploring again, but soon got down to business. When she finished, she came right back to the porch. Despite the cold, I had left the door ajar so she could come in when she was ready. Once she did so, Rambo went straight back to the kitchen and curled up on her bed without stopping off for any unnecessary interaction with us.

"He must have hit her a lot," Mel observed, when I resumed my place.

"That's what I think, too," I said. "But the good news is, she's clearly housebroken, and she knows enough to ask to go out when she needs to."

"We'll need a doggy door," Mel said.

"I thought having her here was a temporary arrangement."

"A temporary doggy door, then," Mel replied. "But we still need one."

Rambo stayed in the kitchen while Mel and I hung out in the living room, where we ended our evening in front of the gas log fire, Mel with a glass of her favorite Cab in hand and me with a single bottle of O'Doul's. In the course of the evening, I recounted everything I had learned about Maxwell Cole's death as well as the whole convoluted story surrounding the Marcia Kelsey homicide. It took time for me to recall the name Alvin Chambers. He was a security guard at the school district offices at the time of Marcia's murder. As far as we were able to ascertain, he was an innocent bystander, a piece of collateral damage who was mowed down in the course of Jennifer McLaughlin's murderous pursuit of vengeance.

"What a sad story for all concerned," Mel said when I finished. "Whatever happened to John Madsen?"

"No idea," I told her. "For all I know, maybe he went back to wherever it was he came from—somewhere in the Midwest, I think."

"And Erin?"

"You've got me there, too. People don't always stay in touch, you know. When something like that is over, the best thing for some folks is to leave it as far in the past as possible."

"What about Maxwell Cole?" she asked. "Are you planning on going to the funeral?"

"I don't think so," I answered. "He was a jerk. We weren't the best of friends while he was alive. Now that he's dead, showing up at the funeral would make me feel like a complete hypocrite."

"He must not have seemed like a jerk as far as Marcia and Pete Kelsey were concerned," Mel observed mildly.

She didn't say anything more than that. She put the idea out there and left it hanging in the air, leaving me free to draw my own conclusions.

When it was time to go to bed, I took Mel's empty glass and my empty bottle back to the kitchen. When I got there, Rambo was still lying on her bed. The food dish was empty; the water dish half-empty. I refilled it on the spot. As I did so, she looked at me and I at her. She was a stranger in our midst. I had no idea if we even spoke the same language.

"Do you need to go out?" I asked.

Obligingly, Rambo rose to her feet, shook, and then walked to the door. Obviously "out" was a word that worked for both of us. I stood shivering in the open doorway, watching while the dog made her rounds. Tomorrow I'd need to go out and revisit those locations, cleaning up behind her. When she finished and came back inside, I set about walking around the house, turning off lights. With that nightly ritual completed, I undressed in my walk-in closet and stopped off in the bathroom long enough to brush my teeth.

When I came into the bedroom, Mel was already in bed with the lamp on her side of the bed turned off. (I'm more than a little envious of that sometimes. She's someone who is able to fall asleep as soon as her head hits the pillow. I'm more of a tossing/turning kind of guy.) Mel was asleep on her side of the bed while Rambo was stretched out full length on mine.

I lifted the covers on my side of the bed and made as if to get in. At that point, the dog raised her head and bared her teeth. She didn't say a word; she didn't have to. Irish wolfhounds have very long canines, and sometimes not having an argument is the best way to win it.

Without another word, I shut off my bedside lamp and then retreated to the guest room. Obviously something had to give, but tomorrow would be plenty of time to deal with that. Right now, as far as J. P. Beaumont's sleeping arrangements were concerned, the guest room would have to do.

CHAPTER 6

"HOW'D YOU SLEEP?" Mel asked the next morning when I stumbled into the kitchen in search of coffee. We have a Dux bed in our master bedroom. The mattress situation in the guest room is a lot less posh than that, and my back was killing me.

"I'm surprised you didn't inquire about where I slept," I grumbled, without really answering the question as she passed me my coffee mug. "That would have been more to the point."

"If Rambo was in your spot, why didn't you just make her get off the bed?"

"Because she growled at me," I answered, "and showed me her very sharp teeth."

"Did you do that, Rambo?" Mel asked the dog. "Really?"

The miscreant in question was already in the kitchen and snugly curled up on her own bed at the moment. Reading Mel's tone of voice as entirely nonthreatening, she thumped her yardlong tail briefly, all the while keeping her black eyes focused on yours truly.

"Obviously she hates me," I said.

"Hating you and being scared of you aren't the same thing," Mel corrected, "but we can't have her booting you out of the bedroom. If need be, we'll put her in the bathroom when it's time for us to go to bed tonight."

"Good idea," I said. It may not have been a final solution, but it was a step in the right direction. "What's on your agenda today?"

"Officer-involved shooting day three," Mel answered. "I'm sure it's going to be an absolute blast."

She left for work shortly thereafter, leaving Rambo and me alone in the house, maintaining an uneasy truce and tolerating each other rather than getting along. I took my coffee and iPad and retreated to the living room to read the online papers. Rambo stayed in the kitchen. When the need arose, she would venture into the living room, but only as far as the front door, where she would stand staring pointedly at me until I got the message. When her water dish hit empty, I filled it. Ditto for her food dish.

I briefly considered gathering up the leash and taking her for a walk, but I got over that in a hurry. After days of rain, the clouds cleared, the temperatures dropped, and we got hammered by an arctic blast that turned everything remotely damp into ice. Walking on ice is not recommended for people with even one fake knee, let alone two.

Halfway through the day, I decided to make myself useful. I put on a Crock-Pot of Senate Bean Soup. (The recipe is so easy even I can follow it.) Then I bestirred myself from the house. Grateful to have all-wheel drive, I motored over to Home Depot, where I studied the doggy door situation. Not wanting to saw a hole in our very expensive front door, I opted for one that would work with the patio slider at the far end of the family room. I bought the one labeled "large." If they'd had a size called "immense," I would have come home with that, but large was as good as Home Depot got. I had to use bungie cords to tie the box in the open trunk long enough to get it home.

I also stopped by Target, where I bought the largest leather dog collar I could find. I wouldn't have wanted to wear a pinch collar, and I didn't see why Rambo should, either. She apparently agreed. When I finally managed to remove that sprocketed mess, she rewarded me with a semi-wave of her tail and a vigorous shake of her very floppy, hair-fringed ears.

The supposedly easy installation instructions for the doggy door turned out to be not so easy at all. Standing half in and half out of the house on a wooden deck, I damned near froze my butt off getting the damned thing properly placed. Not only that, the weather stripping provided in the carton was pretty much useless. I fixed the draft problem with what's known as the Man's Home Companion—several layers of carefully applied duct tape. Once done, it was not a thing of beauty, but, as Mel and I had both agreed earlier, it was only temporary.

Worried about icy road conditions and tempted by knowing Senate Bean Soup was on the menu for dinner, Mel arrived home at a surprisingly early hour—6 P.M. I think she was also concerned about whether or not open warfare had broken out between Rambo and me during her absence.

Predictably, Rambo welcomed Mel home with tail-wagging enthusiasm. "How'd it go?" Mel asked.

"We survived," I told her, "but you need to come see this. Your DIY guy rides again."

I led Mel into the family room, where she allowed herself to be suitably impressed by the doggy door. Rambo? Not so much. She sniffed at it, but that was all. When Mel went out onto the deck and tried to coax the dog to join her by way of the clear plastic flap, Rambo was having none of it. You can't really say that she turned on her heel, since dogs don't actually have heels, but she did an immediate about-face and returned to her spot in the kitchen. Later, while Mel and I were in the dining room savoring our soup and Rambo needed to go out, guess what happened? She went straight to the front door—the nondoggy one—and then glanced at me over her shoulder with a look that said, "Well, are you going to open this or not?"

"So much for that," I said. "I hope we have better luck with the sleeping arrangements."

As we often do, Mel and I talked shop over dinner—supper, as my mother would have called it. We didn't talk so much as Mel vented and I listened. She and I were partners long before we were lovers, and the idea of your partner having your back never goes away. In this case, she didn't need answers from me so much as she needed to unload.

I don't envy Mel's job, but I understand it. Being the top cop in a small city is complicated. Not only do you have to navigate the variable ups and downs of police work, but you have to do so under a microscope of public scrutiny and with a whole lot of small-town politics thrown in on the side. Toss in the current climate, where the news media yells police brutality first and asks questions later, and you've made an already difficult situation virtually impossible.

In the course of her rant, I learned that although Kenneth Purcell remained hospitalized in serious condition, his doctors were planning to release him on Tuesday or Wednesday. Once that happened, he would be placed under arrest on a variety of charges and transported to the Whatcom County Jail. How long he'd be in the lockup after that would be up to a judge.

"How about the wife and kids?" I asked.

"They're in a YWCA shelter down in Redmond, one where they've moved into a fully furnished apartment complete with pots and pans, dishes and linens," Mel told me. "Serena Holland, my victims' advocate, thought that, considering the violence involved, putting that much distance between Kenneth and the rest of the family was our best recourse. Which reminds me," she added, pushing away from the table and pulling out her phone, "I need to take a picture of Rambo so Serena can send it along to Nancy and the kids. Chrissy needs to know the dog's okay."

"To prove you didn't go back on your word and send Rambo to the pound?"

"Exactly."

"Are they still hoping to get her back?"

"I guess."

"But is that a good idea?" I wondered.

"What do you mean?"

"How old are the kids?"

"Four and seven, something like that."

"Look," I said. "Pardon my saying so, but Rambo is one big mother of a dog. When she growled at me, she made a true believer of me in a hurry. What happens if one of those little kids gets on her wrong side? What happens then? With those fangs of hers, she could tear someone limb from limb in a matter of minutes."

Mel left the table, shaking her head. I noted the flash as she took the photo. Shortly after she returned to the table, I heard the swoosh as she forwarded the picture off to someone else.

"You really think Rambo's that dangerous?" she asked.

"I do."

"Crap," Mel said. "What if you're right?"

I didn't want to be right, but the fact that I might be scared the hell out of me. I was glad when Mel changed the subject, although the new topic wasn't much of an improvement.

"Any word on the Maxwell Cole situation?" she asked.

I've learned enough about women over the years to understand that in this case, Mel's use of the word "situation" was actually code for "funeral." She was still of the opinion that I ought to go, while I remained convinced that the final arrangements for my longtime frenemy were none of my business.

"As far as I can see online, the ME has yet to release the autopsy results," I told her. "Not only that, the fire itself is still under investigation."

Mel nodded. We both knew enough about fire investigations—especially fatality fire investigations—to understand that those take time.

At that point, by mutual agreement, we got up, cleared away dinner, did the dishes, and again repaired to the family room, where we turned on the fireplace and watched an evening's worth of mindless entertainment on television just like any other normal married couple. When it was time to turn off the boob tube and go to bed that night, Mel suggested that she turn off the lights while I hit the sack first.

Once I was safely in bed—fully occupying my side— she came into the bedroom, dragging Rambo's dog bed behind her. Mel placed it on the floor in front of her bedside table. As soon as Mel went into the bathroom to undress and make her ablutions, Rambo ignored the bed on the floor and hopped up on the bed beside me. She circled once and then, with a contented sigh, settled down on the bed with her head neatly positioned on Mel's pillow.

Afraid Mel might hear me, I was careful not to allow the slightest hint of a chuckle to escape my lips. Instead, I feigned sleep and waited to see what would happen.

I heard the toilet flush and the bathroom light switch off. I squinted my eyes open wide enough to see Mel standing beside the bed, looking down at the dog.

"Off, Rambo," she ordered, pointing at the bed. And do you know what happened? Rambo got off! Just like that, leaving me to spend the night wondering, *Why the hell didn't I think of that?*

CHAPTER 7

I WON'T SAY I slept like a baby, but I slept well enough that by the time I woke up, Mel was already up, showered, and dressed.

"Rambo's already been out," she told me as she handed me my morning cup of java. The dog bed had been moved back to the kitchen, and Mel's handover of coffee was done under the dog's watchful eyes.

"And not through the doggy door, either, I'm willing to bet."

"Rome wasn't built in a day," Mel retorted. "Rambo grew up living in an apartment complex. Renters aren't allowed to install doggy doors. I'm sure yesterday was the first time Rambo ever saw one. She's a good girl. Give her a break."

Mel went off to work shortly thereafter, leaving it up to me to maintain what was clearly an uneasy truce between me and our new addition. Part of the rhythm of bringing a new dog into your home is learning to keep track of the pees and craps. Since Rambo was a large dog, potential problems with those were not insubstantial. After meeting Mel for lunch, I stopped off at Home Depot on the way home and invested in a proper pooper-scooper along with an outdoor trash container and a box of large garbage bags. I went back to Target and dragged home another large dog bed. I didn't see any logical reason for us to have to keep hauling that one bed back and forth between the bedroom and the kitchen.

I know I'm coming from a whole different era in terms of the fundamentals of relations between the sexes, but in my book, yard work is still something menfolk are supposed to do. Once I got home, I went out to the front yard and started doing exactly that. I was in the midst of walking a sizable scoop of dog leavings over to the trash can when my cell phone rang with Scott's name in the caller ID. I took the time to empty the scooper before answering the phone.

"Hey, Scotty," I said. "What's up? Are you back at work?"

When I had spoken to him last, he'd been considering taking Monday off, and with all the Rambo hullabaloo, I hadn't taken the time to check in on him.

"Yeah," he said. "I'm back at work today, and I just had a strange call."

"What kind of strange call?"

"Someone called into the homicide department looking for you, and whoever took the call was smart enough to put it through to me."

Considering how long I'd been away from Seattle PD Homicide, whoever was looking for me obviously wasn't someone I knew well.

"She said her name was Erin Howard," Scott continued, "but that you would probably remember her as Erin Kelsey. She asked me for your phone number. I suggested that she give me hers instead. Do you want me to give it to you?"

"I'm out in the yard scraping up doggy doo-doo at the moment," I told him. "How about if you text me the number?"

"Doggy doo-doo?" Scott repeated. "Does that mean you and Mel have a dog?"

"Long story," I said. "And it's more like a temporary dog rather than a permanent one."

"Does this dog have a name?"

"Rambo."

"If you've already named him, that means you own him," Scott told me. "I've gotta go. I'll send the number."

He was gone without giving me a chance to explain that Rambo was really a girl. As I slipped the phone back into my pocket, I heard the ding of an arriving text. I picked up the scooper and headed back toward another pile of poop, one I had spotted on my way to the trash can. When I was halfway there Rambo silently appeared beside me. I turned back toward the front of the house and checked to make sure the door was closed. It was. That meant she had deigned to use the doggy door for the first time.

"Good dog!" I exclaimed enthusiastically. "What a good out!"

Rambo rewarded me with a dignified wag of her tail. It may not have been a gesture of complete accord between us, but it was a mutual acknowledgment that you can teach old dogs new tricks, human ones included.

With my scooping job done, we headed back inside.

Rambo was happy to be let in through the front door as opposed to using the plastic flap, but I considered the whole transaction a huge step in the right direction.

Inside, I washed my hands, made a new cup of coffee, and then pulled out my phone to dial up Erin Howard. She answered on the second ring.

"J. P. Beaumont here, Erin," I said when she came on the line. "My son mentioned that you had called. I heard about what happened to Maxwell Cole, and I know the two of you were very close. I'm sorry for your loss."

The strangled sound that greeted my words of condolence was, no doubt, a half-stifled sob. "Thank you," Erin murmured. "I wasn't sure you'd even remember me."

The truth was, I had spent a good deal of my Sunday afternoon hike thinking about little else—of her and that whole long ago tragedy. "Of course I remember you," I said. "How's your dad these days and what's he doing now?"

"If you're referring to my father, Chris McLaughlin," Erin said stiffly, "he's been dead for more than forty-five years. If, on the other hand, you mean Pete Kelsey, the guy who pretended to be my father, I have no idea."

Whoa! That gave me a pretty clear view of the lay of the land. As far as Erin was concerned, nothing that had happened all those years earlier was either forgotten or forgiven.

"Are you planning on coming to Uncle Max's funeral?" Erin asked.

That took me aback. John Madsen, aka Pete Kelsey, the man who had rescued her from an uncertain fate as an abandoned baby in Mexico—the guy who had brought Erin home and cared for her for years as his own—had been summarily kicked downstairs, while Max had somehow been elevated to honorary uncle status. That didn't seem right, at least not to me. As far as the funeral was concerned and despite Mel's urging, I wasn't planning to go, but I didn't want to come right out and admit that.

"I didn't know it had been scheduled," I hedged.

"The ME's office released the remains to the Poindexter Funeral Home a little while ago," Erin said. "The memorial service will be tomorrow morning at eleven in their chapel in Interbay. I'd like you to be there."

Given the circumstances, it was an unexpected request, but not one I could reject out of hand. "Of course," I agreed at once. "I'll be happy to show up." That was an outright lie. In actual fact, I didn't expect to be happy about it at all, but I knew Mel would be.

"Has there been any word on the cause of the fire?"

The pause before Erin answered was long enough to make me think we'd been disconnected. I actually checked the screen on my phone to see if the call had failed.

"Everyone keeps trying to tell me it was an accident," Erin said at last. "They say he was smoking in bed, the bedding caught fire, and his oxygen equipment made the fire more intense. I don't believe a word of it," she added, "not one word. That's why I need to talk to you."

For the life of me, I couldn't see how the one thing would automatically lead to the other, but I wasn't prepared to argue the point.

"No problem, then," I said. "Whenever you'd like to talk, just say the word."

"Uncle Max was a well-known figure in town back in the day, but I don't know how many people will actually show up for his funeral," Erin continued, "probably not that many. How about if we get together to talk after that?"

"Sure," I said. "Would you like to do lunch?"

"Yes, please," she said, sounding as though I had just lifted the weight of the world off her shoulders. "I'd like it to be just the two of us."

I finished my coffee and my last online crossword puzzle toward the middle of the afternoon. Rambo was in the kitchen on her bed when I took my coffee mug to the sink. Her food dish was empty and so was the water dish. As I filled the food dish, I made a mental note to see about finding a larger water dish. Leaving Rambo to crunch her kibble, I went into the bedroom and looked through the clothing in my walk-in closet. (The fact that our proposed master bedroom had included two matching walk-in closets had been a big selling point as far as Mel was concerned when it came to designing the house. In actual practice, my closet is only half-filled with my clothing, with the remainder being encroached upon by Mel's.)

I searched through my collection of clothing bags until I located a pinstripe suit that looked suitably funereal and also still fit—something for which I was immensely grateful. I also located a suitable tie and a fresh-from-the-cleaners white shirt and put them on the bar next to the suit.

Having done my best to prepare for the unwelcome duty of attending Max's services the next day, I went back to the living room, turned on the gas log, and prepared to enjoy the sunset over Bellingham Bay, which gave every evidence of being magnificent. (As far as I'm concerned, being able to watch sunsets in the late afternoons and evenings is one of the unheralded side benefits of being retired.)

I had settled into my easy chair and was totally relaxed when the dog appeared at my feet. Her arrival was accompanied by an unfamiliar thump, thump, thump on the hardwood floor. Looking around the hassock to see what had made the racket, I spotted one of Rambo's worn tennis balls go rolling back toward the dining room table. The dog chased after it, brought it back, and dropped it for the second time on the far side of the footstool. While the second thump, thump, thump sounded, Rambo gave me a quizzical look with those fathomless black eyes of hers as if to say, "Don't you get it?"

The night before she had nosed the doorknob to tell me it was time to go out. Tonight she was telling me it was time to play ball. I took the hint. I put on a jacket, grabbed the ball, and escorted her outside. Flinging the ball as hard as I could throw, I could bounce it off the fence at the far end of the yard. Running low to the ground, Rambo raced after it, catching it each time on the first bounce. Once she had the ball in her mouth, she galloped straight back to me and dropped the slobber-covered mess at my feet, and then stood waiting impatiently for me to throw it again.

Which I did. I have no idea what the sunset looked like that evening, because I never saw it. I was out in the yard having way too much fun playing ball with a dog who wasn't supposed to be my dog but, as Scott had pointed out, probably already was.

CHAPTER 8

THE NEXT MORNING, once I was properly attired and ready to head south to Seattle, I was faced with the dilemma every owner of a newly acquired dog must face sooner or later, which is to say—what happens when I have to leave the house? I understand that crating dogs is sometimes recommended, but we didn't have a crate. Besides, I was going to a funeral almost a hundred miles away and had no idea how long I'd be gone. Would Rambo use the doggy door if she needed to go out and relieve herself? In terms of size alone, if she ended up doing her duty in the house, it was bound to be a big problem. As househusband of the moment, I had a pretty clear understanding of whose problem that would be.

Rambo was lying on her bed in the kitchen, regarding my every move as I picked up the car keys and put them in my pocket. "You be a good girl now," I admonished. "I'll be back in a little while."

Did she understand what I was saying? I don't know. Maybe the words "good girl" registered. Her head didn't move. Her eyes didn't move, but her tail gave a tiny, halfhearted thump.

I got into the car, turned on the heated seat, and headed for I-5. Driving time has always been my best thinking time. These days I often find myself resenting the way cell phones have intruded on those formerly peaceful drives. On that Wednesday morning, however, the phone in my pocket remained blessedly silent, leaving me free to contemplate the strange dream I'd had the night before about my grandfather. It occurred to me that the dream had been sparked by Erin Kelsey's sudden reemergence in my life. (No matter what she calls herself these days, that's how I'll always think of her.)

But back to my grandfather. By the time my mother was eighteen, she was an unwed mother with an infant son. With World War II still in full swing, she had fallen hard for a young sailor named Hank Mencken, who hailed from Beaumont, Texas. My mother was pregnant with me and they were engaged to be married when Hank died in a motorcycle accident on his way back to base.

When my mother refused to give me up, her father, Jonas Piedmont, had disowned his daughter on the spot. In taking care of me, my mother had no help from her side of the family. As for my paternal grandparents? When my mother appealed to them for help, Hank's parents, too, turned their backs on her.

The whole time I was growing up and long after I achieved adulthood, I remained estranged from my maternal grandparents, had never even met them and most likely never would have—had it not been for the murder of Marcia Kelsey.

In the course of that investigation, I had been searching the phone book for the telephone number of a witness whose last name started with a *P*. Driving into Seattle that morning, I couldn't remember the witness's name at all—Pierson, maybe? At any rate, at the very top of the page where I eventually found the witness's name and number, I saw something surprisingly familiar—my own names and also my grandfather's— Jonas Piedmont. I suspect now that my mother named me after her father in hopes of one day sparking some kind of reconciliation between them, but that never happened.

However, on that long-ago day, there was my name and his, printed in bold black and white—staring back at me from the page of a phone book. (This was back in the nineties, when phone books still existed and people actually used them.) Not only was his name there, but so was an address on Dayton Avenue along with a listed phone number. In the ensuing weeks, I tried working up enough nerve to pick up the phone and make the call, but I never did. Instead I drove by the house several times before finally stopping the car one day, getting out, and walking up onto the front porch of what turned out to be little more than a humble clapboard cottage.

There had been a dog on the porch that day, an aging platinum-colored golden retriever named Mandy. She seemed happy enough to see me, but I still remember how my heart pounded in my chest as I stood outside that closed front door, trying to summon the courage to knock. When I finally did, a tiny, bent-over old woman answered the door and let the dog inside.

I'm not sure what kind of welcome I had expected, but as soon as my grandmother, Beverly, peered up into my face, she recognized who I had to be, greeted me by name, and welcomed me with open arms. She led me into the house and introduced me to the long-estranged grandfather I had never met. I'm sure that once upon a time Jonas Piedmont must have been a powerful figure of a man, but by the time I met him, he had been felled by a series of paralyzing strokes, leaving him only a frail echo of that. While I stood there dumbstruck and watching, Mandy had walked over to the side of his wheelchair, ducked under his hand, and then stood there patiently with his useless fingers resting on top of her head.

My grandfather and his dog—Jonas Piedmont and Mandy—were the two unsettling characters who had marched through my dreamscape the night before. In the dream, I was the same age I am now, but both the dog and my grandfather had been young and healthy. My grandfather and I were walking somewhere together (around Greenlake maybe?) while the joyous dog raced back and forth ahead of us.

None of that ever happened in real life—not once. By the time I met my grandfather, his walking days were long over, but maybe that's what dreams are for— to fill in the blanks and allow us to glimpse things that would otherwise remain forever invisible.

Over the next few months after that initial meeting, my grandfather and I had that long-delayed reconciliation, the one my mother had always prayed for. When he passed away sometime later, my grandmother held on to his ashes until Mandy finally died, too, allowing my grandfather's ashes and those of his beloved canine companion to be scattered together.

And just like that, a name came back to me out of

the blue—the Academy of Canine Behavior. After my grandfather's death and before Mandy's passing, that was the place where my grandmother had boarded the dog on the rare occasions when she traveled. Beverly had raved about the place—said the spacious grounds had reminded her of some books she'd read as a girl, ones that featured generations of collies. She'd also mentioned that whenever she sent Mandy to board at the academy, they always did a certain amount of training.

About the time I pulled into the parking lot at the Poindexter Funeral Home and Chapel, I made a note to myself, as a newly appointed dog owner, to look up the academy online and see if it was still in business. Having a place in mind for us to board Rambo should the need arise seemed like a good idea.

When it came to estimating the anticipated attendance at Maxwell Cole's funeral, both Erin Howard and I couldn't have been more wrong. The place was packed, wall to wall. I ended up among the standing-room-only crowd stuck at the back of the room. A small wooden table on the dais was flanked by a metal tripod containing a single spray of flowers. (Obviously people had taken that "in lieu of flowers" admonition seriously.) On the polished surface of the table stood two items: a bronze funeral urn along with an easel-backed color photo of a much younger Max—a robust man with a full head of hair and a perfectly groomed handlebar mustache.

The reason cops routinely show up at homicide victims' funerals is that the vast majority of the victims are killed by someone they know. That reality makes it reasonable to assume that the killer or killers are likely to be in attendance right along with everyone else. And so, with the situational awareness skills honed from a lifetime spent as a cop, I kept my eyes peeled for anything or anyone out of the ordinary.

Since I was in the SRO crowd at the back of the room, I couldn't help but notice the single attendee who came in after the doors had been closed, just as the service began. The newcomer was a scruffy-looking guy. His mane of shoulder-length gray hair was pulled back in a ponytail, and he sported a long, unkempt beard. He seemed vaguely familiar somehow, but I couldn't for the life of me place him. He did nothing out of line, however, nor did he appear to be in any way threatening. He listened attentively to everything that was said, occasionally nodding in agreement. Eventually, since he looked like a contemporary, I wrote him off as maybe having been one of Max's coworkers during his time at the *P-I*.

Max would have found the number of attendees gratifying. He had been Seattle's best-known crime reporter for decades on end, and he had most definitely not been forgotten. During Max's writing career, cops of all kind, but most especially homicide cops, had been the targets of his many published diatribes. As far as I could tell, I was the only current or former member of the thin blue line in attendance. As for everybody else? Point of view is everything.

Many of the people who crowded into the funeral home that day turned out to be family members of long-ago crime victims. Several of them stepped forward to speak, standing in front of the assembled group of mourners and heaping praise on the deceased. They told how much it had meant to them and to their families that Max had seen fit to air their side of some long-ago atrocity. Because that's what murders are, after all—atrocities. For the family members who are left behind, memories of those events may diminish over time, but they never go away.

The last person to stand up and speak on Max's behalf was Erin Kelsey Howard herself. When someone passes out of view for years at a time, it's easy to freeze-frame them as they were when you saw them last. It's what happens when months pass between visits with my grandkids. It seems like they're always so much bigger than I expect them to be and so much older. The same was true for Erin Howard.

The last time I had seen her, she'd been a cute coed in her early twenties—a smart young thing with what should have been a bright future ahead of her. The middle-aged, overweight, black-clad woman who made her way to the microphone was in her late forties, but she looked far older than that—older and careworn. Her shoulders slumped. The corners of her mouth seemed permanently turned down. If there had ever been a smile on her face, there was no hint of it now, and I had the sense that it wasn't just Max's death that had robbed Erin Howard of all joy.

She approached the lectern warily and then stood for a moment, leaning on it, as if fearing she might topple over. Then, taking a deep calming breath, she finally began.

"Maxwell Cole was a part of my life from my earliest memories," she said, reading aloud from a piece of paper that trembled visibly in her hand as she held it. Obviously Erin Howard was not a person accustomed to public speaking.

"Although I always called him Uncle Max, he was not my uncle nor was he any kind of blood relation. The people I thought to be my parents appointed him to be my godfather. When I discovered that everything else they ever did or told me turned out to be nothing but lies, Maxwell Cole was the one thing in my life that remained good and loyal and true. He was always there for me when I needed him—always. I miss you, Uncle Max. I will always miss you."

Weeping openly now, Erin fled the stage. Once she was seated, the funeral director in charge of the service offered a brief benediction. When that ended, he approached Erin in her place in the front row, helped her rise, and then led her to the back of the room, where, as mourner in chief, she was expected to preside over the grip-and-greet honors as people exited the room. Two people hurried out the door before Erin arrived at her appointed place. One was the scruffy-looking man who had arrived after the service was under way. The other was a tall woman, dressed in flamboyant funeral finery, who had sat silently in the back row throughout the service.

As Erin attended to her duties, I took a seat on one of the chairs near the back of the room and waited. I watched while several funeral home employees went around the room gathering up abandoned programs and stacking chairs, leaving behind only two chairs— the one I was sitting on and the one next to it. By the time the cleanup concluded, the only remaining evidence that a funeral had recently taken place in that now eerily empty room were three items—the spray of flowers, the urn, and the photo—still standing forlornly at the front of the room.

That was the third time in my life that I felt sorry for Maxwell Cole. To give Mel her due, I was also grateful that I had taken her suggestion and come to offer my respects. I could tell from what Max's eulogists had said that he and I had been opposite sides of the homicide coin. While I had been trying to solve crimes, he had been trying to help families somehow make sense of what had happened.

When the last of the attendees left, Erin came over to where I was sitting and sank down on the chair next to mine. "Thanks for coming," she murmured.

"You're welcome," I said. "It was the least I could do."

"You didn't have to."

"You asked me," I reminded her. "And you look as though you could use some sustenance about now. Have you thought about where you'd like to go for lunch?"

As soon as she nodded, tears mixed with mascara began to slide down her cheeks. She mopped at them with the fistful of soggy tissues.

"Chinook's at Fishermen's Terminal," she said. "It was one of Uncle Max's favorite places. Mine, too. We used to go there a lot."

The funeral director materialized behind us, discreetly clearing his throat. "Do you wish to take the flowers and the urn with you now, Ms. Howard, or would you rather come back and collect them later? There's no rush, of course, none at all."

For some reason, funeral directors always speak in hushed tones that remind me of the announcers who used to hold forth during bowling tournaments back in the early days of television, when Saturday bowling was standard network fare. This guy, whose name tag identified him as Ralph Poindexter, was no exception.

"I'll take the photo and urn now," Erin said, "but I've got no place for the flowers. I guess I'll just leave them."

"Of course," Mr. Poindexter said. "As you wish."

He collected both the photo and the urn from the table and brought them back to us. He handed the picture to Erin and then held out the urn to me.

I was surprised by the weight of it, because Maxwell Cole's cremains turned out to be far heavier than I expected. Whoever said, "He's not heavy, he's my brother," lied. Technically, Max was my fraternity brother. As Erin and I made our way out of the funeral home, the irony of the situation wasn't lost on me.

Fifty years after Maxwell Cole's and my initial interactions as freshmen at the University of Washington, J. P. Beaumont, who was never Max's friend, became his sole pallbearer. Unbidden, several almost simultaneous visions from the past came flooding back—pranks from those long-ago carefree college days; the holiday formal where I'd snatched Karen away from him; and the regrettable time much later when I'd actually bloodied the man's nose.

I remembered all those things and something else besides. Max was gone; I was still standing. As Erin and I stepped out into the cold winter sunshine, I was grateful about that—very grateful. We walked together across the parking lot, where I loaded the urn onto the passenger seat floorboard of her aging Honda, using Erin's very large purse to wedge the urn against the seat in a way that I hoped would keep it from falling over. A pile of spilled funeral ashes would be a nightmare to clean up.

Erin and I drove to the restaurant in separate vehicles. Geographically, Seattle's Interbay area is, as you might surmise, between two bays—Shilshole Bay to the West and Salmon Bay to the East, with Fishermen's Terminal at the halfway point of the latter.

Salmon Bay used to be a saltwater inlet fed by a creek, with tides that rose and fell along with the tides of Puget Sound. Now it's connected to Lake Union by way of the Fremont Cut, which follows the old creek bed. The completion of the Chittenden Locks turned Salmon Bay into a freshwater lake that empties into Puget Sound through the locks complex.

Fishermen's Terminal, as the name implies, offers moorage and a host of other services for fishing vessels—work boats rather than pleasure craft. It's also the home of the Seattle Fishermen's Memorial, which features a thirty-foot-tall column topped by Ronald Perry's magnificent statue of a spear-wielding fisherman. At the base of the statue, engraved in bronze, are the names of all members of the local fishing fleet—halibut, crab, and salmon fishermen—who have been lost at sea. In case you don't consider those to be dangerous occupations, please be advised that new names are added to the memorial each and every year.

In terms of both time and distance, Fishermen's Terminal was practically next door to Poindexter's Funeral Home, and Chinook's, one of two restaurants located there, is on many people's must-do list when hosting visitors from out of town.

WE ARRIVED AT the restaurant a little after two. It was late enough that the lunch crowd had thinned. We were shown to a table by the window, where the delivery of our menus was immediately followed by a basket full of piping-hot focaccia bread that was both irresistible and delicious. I ordered my favorite—clam strips with extra tartar sauce. Erin chose the planked salmon.

"Okay," I said, once the waiter walked away with our order. "As well as you knew Max, I'm sure you're aware that he and I were never the best of friends. I came here today because you asked me to, but I can't for the life of me understand why you wanted me to show up."

"I didn't want you here," Erin said quietly. "Max did."

I wasn't sure I had heard her correctly. "You're saying Max wanted me to attend his funeral?"

"Yes," she answered.

"Was he worried that something might happen to him?"

Erin nodded. "He wanted something else, too."

"What's that?"

"He wanted you to find out who is responsible."

"Wait, wait, wait," I said. "I read an article online that claimed that the fire that killed him has been ruled accidental."

"That may be the official ruling, but it can't be right," Erin declared hotly. "There's no way that fire was an accident. Somebody set it. Uncle Max was murdered, and he wanted you to figure out who did it."

"It's your belief that he knew in advance that he was being targeted?"

Erin nodded. "It is. He told me so himself."

"When?"

"In a text he sent me on Saturday afternoon."

"This past Saturday?"

"Yes."

"Did you mention the text to the cops?"

"No, because I didn't think Uncle Max would approve. He wanted you to look into it, not them."

"Regardless of what he may or may not have wanted, you can't withhold information in a possible homicide investigation."

In response, Erin pulled out her phone, turned it on, scrolled through her messages until she found the one she wanted, and then handed the phone to me.

I'm onto something big. Unfortunately, the people involved may be onto me as well. If anything happens to me, whatever you do don't go to the cops. People at Seattle PD will just cover it up.

No doubt you remember JP Beaumont, the guy who solved Marcia's homicide and who kept Jennifer from being able to drag you to your death. I never liked Beaumont much, but he's a straight shooter, and he's been away from Seattle PD long enough that if anyone can get to the bottom of things, he's the one to do it.

I know he's still around, because I saw him and his new wife last night at El Gaucho. If someone comes after me, I think he can be trusted to go after them. And if things go completely south, be sure he turns up at the funeral. He'll be smart enough to notice if something is off.

That set me back. Clearly Max had been worried, and he had indeed wanted me in attendance at his funeral. Still mulling what I'd read, I handed the phone back to Erin, and she slipped it into her jacket.

"He sent that to me on Saturday afternoon, and the very next day he was dead," she said.

"The report calling the fire accidental made some mention about his smoking in bed," I suggested. "That's plausible enough, isn't it? I remember seeing him with a cigar on Friday night as he was leaving the restaurant."

"Uncle Max adored his cigars," Erin agreed, "but he never smoked in bed or even inside the house, at least not to my knowledge. Once he started using oxygen, he only smoked out on the covered porch."

"Did you tell the cops any of that?"

Erin shook her head. "As far as I can tell, once they decided the fire was an accident, that was the end of it."

"What if Max committed suicide and wanted to make it look like his death was accidental?"

Erin's dismissal of that idea was as vehement as it was instantaneous. "No way!" she objected. "Who would be dumb enough to commit suicide by setting his own bed on fire?"

"But he had been ill, hadn't he?" I asked.

Erin nodded.

"Cancer?" I asked.

She nodded again. "Third-stage lung cancer when it was first diagnosed. His doctors said he was in remission, but his lungs had been so badly compromised that he still needed oxygen."

"And cigars apparently."

"Yes," she agreed sadly, "and cigars. I also thought he drank too much but what are you gonna do?"

I could see her point. Telling someone walking around with a cancer diagnosis that he needed to stop smoking and sober up was a bit like locking the barn door when the horse was already miles away.

"But he wasn't in imminent danger of dying?"

Erin shrugged. "The cancer would probably have come back eventually, but for right now he wasn't at death's door."

"So what about that whole Right to Try thing? What's the deal there?"

"Uncle Max got involved in that because of a friend of his down in Tucson, Arizona. Jean Egan was retired Air Force. I'm not sure how they met initially, but they were pen pals for years. She died a year ago, less than two years after she was diagnosed with ALS."

Somehow, knowing that I'd been suckered into making a contribution to Right to Try made me feel better about the whole thing—as though Maxwell Cole had somehow managed to pull the wool over my eyes and have the last laugh after all.

"So will you help me?" Erin asked.

"Yes," I answered with some reluctance. "I'll do what I can."

CHAPTER 9

OUR FOOD CAME then. I dove into my clam strips as though I were starving while Erin barely picked at her salmon.

"How did you learn about the fire?" I asked.

"A uniformed cop from Renton came to see me the next morning. Uncle Max was already gone by then— DOA at the hospital—but they found my name listed as next of kin on his driver's license. He didn't have anybody else. I was it."

Erin's eyes brimmed with tears once more. I didn't blame her. I've been on both sides of those kinds of notifications. They're hellish, plain and simple. But the fact that Seattle PD had passed the job off to Renton PD meant they were treating Max's death as a very low priority. Rather than dwell on that, I attempted to steer the conversation away from the next-of-kin notification.

"Max said he was onto something big. Do you have any idea what?"

"Not really, just that he had stumbled on something

from before...you know, from back around the time when everything happened."

The way Erin grimaced when she said the word "everything" told me what she really meant. That would be back when Marcia Kelsey was murdered and when the world as Erin knew it fell apart.

"But he didn't say what?"

She shook her head. "No."

"Or who all might be involved?"

"Not that, either."

"Is it possible all of this might have something to do with Marcia's murder?"

"Maybe," she said. "I don't know."

"To your knowledge, did Max have any enemies?"

"You mean other than you?" she asked, giving me the faintest hint of a smile.

"Yes," I said, "other than me."

She shook her head.

"Is there anyone who would benefit financially from his death?"

"That would be me," she said. "Uncle Max had his will redrawn a few years ago. I just happen to have a copy. The original is at the lawyer's office."

She reached into her capacious purse—no longer doing urn control duty—and pulled out a thick business-size envelope. Dusting clam strip crumbs off my fingers, I opened the envelope and pulled out a document that turned out to be a photocopy of Max's last will and testament. I scanned through it and saw that other than a few relatively small charitable bequests, everything else went to Erin Kelsey McLaughlin Howard. In the event of her death, Max's secondary beneficiary was listed as Christopher Cassidy.

"You took your grandfather's name?" I asked.

"For legal stuff," she said, "and why wouldn't I? Everything about Pete and Marcia Kelsey was a lie. At least Christopher McLaughlin was real."

"And who's Christopher Cassidy?" I asked.

"My son," Erin said. "He's eighteen and a freshman at WSU. He's a good kid, going to school on a full-ride academic scholarship."

No doubt the boy's name, too, had come by way of his birth grandfather, Mr. Lowlife Chris McLaughlin. If Erin's son was an honors student, however, he most likely wasn't your basic chip off the old block.

"Sounds like you lucked out as far as kids are concerned," I observed.

That comment was greeted by Erin's first genuine smile of the day. "Yes," she agreed. "I certainly did."

I folded the document, put it back in the envelope, and returned it to her. "You realize what this means?"

She frowned. "What?"

"Since both you and your son stand to benefit financially from Max's death, and if this does turn into a homicide investigation, it's possible you'll both be under suspicion. That leads me to ask a pertinent question. Where exactly were you and Christopher on Saturday night?"

"Chris was in Pullman," Erin answered. "I was at work."

"Doing what?"

"I'm a bartender," she said. "I work at Jake's Place, a bar in downtown Bellevue. I got off at midnight and was home in Renton by half past twelve, which is much earlier than when the fire must have been called in to 911. I went home and stayed there the rest of the night. I don't live in the best of neighborhoods. My apartment complex has had more than its share of car prowls. In case you're interested, there are security cameras all over the parking lot outside my building. You're welcome to check for yourself. You're bound to see me coming and going."

"That's probably not necessary," I told her, "but all the same, if you could give me the name and number of the property manager, it would probably be a good idea."

Frowning in concentration, she consulted her phone and read off the requested information. If Erin did end up needing an alibi at a later date, it couldn't hurt to have one that came complete with a time and date stamp. That in turn meant I'd need to track down the security footage before it had a chance to disappear for good.

"Christopher didn't come home for the funeral?" I asked.

"No," she answered. "He wanted to, but I wouldn't let him. For one thing, the weather in the pass has been a mess. He was on his way back to Pullman after Christmas vacation when that first storm came through. The trip took more than eight hours, and he barely made it. I told him I didn't want him to risk life and limb coming back over the mountains for the funeral."

"Does Christopher have a phone?"

Erin gave me a quizzical look. "Are you kidding? He's a college student. Of course he has a phone."

"Could I have his number?"

"Why?"

"Because if you need an alibi, so does he," I said. "It'll

be far easier to nail one down now than it will be weeks or months from now, if and when someone from Seattle PD's Homicide Unit finally gets around to asking questions."

Reluctantly, Erin recited another phone number, which I typed into my phone.

"Yours?" I asked.

In answer she reeled off several numbers—home, work, and cell. I took those down as well.

"Is there a Mr. Howard?" I asked.

Erin looked uncomfortable. "As far as I know," she said. "I suppose if he had corked off, someone would have let me know. I haven't seen the man since our divorce was final six years ago." She paused and then shrugged. "Married three times, divorced three times. I guess you could say I have trust issues."

Given her history, that was hardly surprising.

"But I don't understand why you need all this information," she added.

"Because you've asked me to look into this matter," I explained. "That means, since I'll be working for you, presumably I'll need to contact you from time to time."

"So you really will do it, then?" she asked.

"With some conditions," I said.

"What kind of conditions?"

"As Max mentioned in his text, I'm no longer a cop. However, if my investigation turns up information that points in the direction of homicide, I will go to the cops. Understood?"

Erin nodded. "All right," she agreed, "but there is one other thing that worries me."

"What's that?"

"How much is all this going to cost?"

"You mean how much is my involvement going to cost?"

She nodded again. "I don't have much money right now. I suppose, with the will situation, when all is said and done, there'll be some money, but I don't know how much or how long it will take for me to receive anything from an inheritance. If you'd be willing to wait until that all comes through for me to pay you . . ." Her voice drifted off.

All you had to do was look at Erin Howard to know she was leading a hardscrabble life. Scholarship student or not, she had a kid in college, and that's bound to cost money. Her less-than-fashionable clothing, the unbecoming cut of her hair, the fact that she was driving a car that was probably the same age as her son—all of those things pointed in the same direction. She was getting by financially, but just barely.

When I first met Erin all those years ago, she had been a pert college sophomore with ambitions of going on to law school after graduation. The murder of Marcia Kelsey had evidently derailed all those plans. Now she was a middle-aged bartender and a single mother, surviving on minimum wage and tips, which couldn't be easy. For someone living in such straitened circumstances, any bequest like the one from Max would be a huge windfall, but I doubted she had any clear concept of what that would amount to, just in terms of property values, if nothing else.

If Queen Anne Hill is considered to be one of Seattle's most desirable areas, Bigelow is one of the neighborhood's most desirable streets. Yes, Max's house may have been severely damaged in a fire, but these days a lot of prospective buyers go looking for properties with the express intention of tearing down existing dwellings in order to build anew.

In the case of Max's house, extensive fire damage might make a teardown unavoidable, but with or without a house, the lot itself comes with a killer view of downtown Seattle, and it would be worth a bundle all on its own. In addition, there was bound to be a hefty settlement from Max's homeowner's insurance. That amount, combined with whatever sums were realized from the sale of the house, would leave Erin sitting pretty, most likely with enough funds to pay cash for a modest place of her own somewhere else.

She was still grieving the loss of Max, her trusted friend and godfather, so now wasn't the time to mention that there might be a silver lining in all this, but I was pretty sure that, due to Maxwell Cole's generosity, Erin, after years of living a hard life in the low-rent district, was about to be better off financially than she'd ever dreamed possible.

Right now, though, I decided it was time to take her current concern about paying for my services off the table. "I'm not a licensed private investigator," I told her. "That means, you can't hire me at any price."

Disappointment washed over her face. "But I thought you said ..." She shook her head, took a deep breath, and grabbed for her purse. "Sorry for wasting your time. I'll be going then."

"Wait," I said, motioning her back into her chair. "Don't rush off. That doesn't mean that I won't do the work, but it does mean I won't charge you for it."

She sank back down on her chair. "You won't? Really?"

"Really," I answered. "I believe you qualify for what I like to call the friends-and-family discount—you and Max both."

Erin's eyes brimmed with tears again—tears of gratitude this time rather than grief. "Thank you," she murmured.

At that point she seemed to regain her appetite and did more than pick at her salmon. When the meal was over and the server had cleared our plates, we settled in to do a more in-depth interview.

As far as I could see, Max had no other close relations. Erin was his sole survivor. If I was going to gain any traction in finding out the truth about his death, it was important to understand who his friends were—if any; what he'd been doing both while he was in California and since his return to Washington; and, since he had evidently believed himself to be in danger as late as Saturday afternoon, what kinds of current projects he'd had in the works.

Now that our rules of engagement had changed, Erin was more forthcoming. She said that Max had recently told her that his literary agent had found a publisher who was interested in buying the book he was working on.

"What kind of book?" I asked.

"Some kind of overview of his career that would include stories about some of the investigations he'd covered through the years as well as follow-ups with some of the people involved."

"Journalistic cold cases, in other words," I offered.

Erin nodded. "I suppose."

"How far along in the process, would you say?"

She shrugged. "I'm not sure. I know he'd signed a contract. He may have even received an advance."

"Do you know the name of the publisher?"

"Sorry, no idea, but he did have an agent."

"A literary agent?"

"Yes."

"Had you seen any of what he'd written?"

"Nope," Erin said. "Uncle Max promised that I'd get first dibs when it was finished, but he was afraid that letting someone else read the manuscript before he was done writing it would be bad luck."

"And this 'big thing' he'd found, it's something he discovered in the process of writing the book?"

"I guess," Erin said.

For me, in the process of embarking on an investigation into Max's death, talking to someone who had read all or part of the manuscript would be a huge first step.

"Do you happen to know his agent's name or how I could reach him?" As I asked the question, I envisioned a shady-looking guy holed up in a dinky office somewhere in a less-than-desirable neighborhood in New York City.

"Sure," Erin said. "His name is Tommy Raines, although it's probably really Thomas. Tommy is what Max always called him. They've been friends for a long time—since high school. I'm not certain, but I think he lives in Madison Park somewhere."

If Thomas Raines had been at Queen Anne High School with Maxwell Cole, he had most likely also been attending at the same time as Erin's adoptive mother, Marcia Riggs Kelsey. Years later, after Queen

Anne High was shuttered, the building was sold to a developer who turned the old classrooms into condos. In a supreme irony, at the time Marcia was murdered, her long-term girlfriend was living in one of those converted units.

Pete and Marcia themselves had seemed entirely at ease with the idea that a third person was part of their somewhat unorthodox relationship, but I was relatively certain that that was one of the parental lies that still haunted this troubled woman who had once thought of herself as their daughter. That being the case and out of fear of bringing our now-civil exchange to a screeching halt, I made no mention of any of that to Erin.

Instead, I dutifully thumbed the name Thomas Raines into the note page on my cell phone. In the old days, when it came time to locate someone, I generally carried a phone book in the car along with the latest edition of the local *Thomas Brothers Street Guide*. Now I have my cell phone and a GPS. If this Raines character was doing business somewhere in the greater Seattle area, I was pretty sure I'd be able to find him.

"No problem," I said. "I'll be able to track him down."

I was about to ask something else when Erin glanced at her watch and then jumped to her feet. "Crap!" she exclaimed. "Sorry, I've gotta go. I'm supposed to be at work in a little over an hour. If I don't leave right now, I'll be late."

It hurt me to think that her job situation was so sketchy that she couldn't even take the full day off for her godfather's funeral. "Sure," I said, waving her away. "Go."

She left the restaurant at a half run. Driving distance from Fishermen's Terminal to Jake's in downtown

Bellevue is around sixteen miles, give or take. But it was after three now, which meant rush hour was already under way.

I recently read an article that said that in terms of traffic congestion, the Seattle/Tacoma area is home to 5 of the top 21 knottiest traffic jam spots in the country. Last year Seattle tied for the dubious honor of being fourth worst in terms of overall traffic congestion. When it comes to evening rush hour, however, the traffic needle dials all the way up to number two, directly behind San Francisco. We're the kind of place where something as relatively minor as a semi spilling a load of frozen crab onto a stretch of single roadway can turn the whole region's hour-long evening commute into a six-hour ordeal.

As I watched Erin race out of the restaurant, I wished both of us luck in dealing with traffic, and luck was definitely needed. There's no direct way to get from Fishermen's Terminal back to I-5. Rather than zigzag up and over Phinney Ridge, I headed back toward downtown, planning to enter the freeway from Mercer. That proved to be a strategic error of massive proportions.

On I-5 the Mercer interchange is the nearest one to Seattle Center. For generations it has been referred to as "the Mercer Mess." Despite years of unending detours around supposed traffic improvement projects, it still merits the name—that day especially.

I was on Mercer itself, inching along toward the freeway entrance in gridlocked traffic, when a fire engine and an aid car blasted their way past and onto the northbound lanes. Not good. At that point I turned on the radio for a traffic update—something I should probably have done before leaving Chinook's. There

was a multicar injury wreck northbound on the Mont-
lake Bridge. Alternate routes were suggested.

Thank you so very much. Giving up northbound
I-5 altogether, I went south and got stuck in another
mess crossing the I-90 bridge. Two hours after leaving
the restaurant, I'd made barely fifteen miles of progress
and was inching northward at two miles per hour on
I-405. Just past the turnoff to Woodinville, I was in
the right-hand lane when I realized I was approaching the intersection I had used several times on those
occasions when, as a favor to my grandmother, I had
either dropped Mandy off at or picked her up from the
Academy of Canine Behavior. Curious after all these
years to learn if the place was still in business, I posed
the question to the lady whose voice lives in my GPS.

"Directions to Academy of Canine Behavior," I
told her.

The mechanical AI response came through the
speaker only a few seconds later. "In one half mile, exit
to the right on 195th," she said. "Then keep right."

I didn't have to worry about changing lanes in a hurry.
Traversing the half mile from there to the exit took another twenty minutes. By the time I turned off, it was
twenty past five. By then I didn't give a damn if the academy was open or closed. What I needed more than anything was to get off the freeway and out from behind the
vehicle directly in front of me, a looming motor home
that belched diesel exhaust and was plastered with tro-
phy state emblems from all over the country. No doubt
it belonged to a retired couple who wanted everyone to
know that they'd been everywhere there was to go. That
was perfectly fine with me, as long as they took their obnoxious bragging rights somewhere I wasn't.

CHAPTER 10

As a cop—make that as a former cop—I pride myself in having pretty much a total recall when it comes to places I've visited in the past. If you're on patrol and some kind of emergency arises, knowing how to get into some obscure neighborhood or out of same in the most efficient manner possible can mean the difference between life and death.

The neighborhood just off the freeway qualified as an obscure one, all right, but as far as remembering it, I could just as well have landed on the planet Dalvar. Nothing was familiar. The last time I had been in this neck of the woods, I had a pretty clear recollection that it was mostly rural in nature—forested terrain, in fact. Now was made up of full-fledged industrial parks complete with low-rise office buildings, a hotel, stoplights, and, of course, the obligatory Starbucks.

As for the academy? It's located at the crown of a nearby hill. In my memory the road leading there had been lined by mostly empty fields. Now recently constructed housing—apartment complexes and single occupancy houses—lined both sides of the street. The gated entrance to the academy complex was as I remembered it, but the grounds themselves, not so much. Just inside the gate, I encountered yet another traffic jam. Most of the cars waiting in line seemed headed in the direction of what a banner on the side of the building proclaimed to be DOGGY DAYCARE. Really? I have kids and grandkids. I know about day care for children, but for dogs? I guess if something doesn't seem to apply to you and yours, you just let those items flow past without their registering.

I dodged the day care melee and drove around to the main building. The parking area there was jammed as well with people and dogs coming and going—either being picked up or dropped off for training and/or boarding. Inside the lobby area, some of the dogs along with their owners were being given lessons on how they should conduct themselves in public.

"Are you picking up or dropping off?" a young woman inquired as I approached the front desk.

"Neither," I said. "My grandmother used to bring her dog here a long time ago. Now my wife and I have sort of inherited a dog, and I'd like to talk to someone about it."

"Name?" she asked.

"My name? Beaumont—J. P. Beaumont."

"Dog's name?"

"Rambo."

Without a pause, she picked up a phone. "Colleen," she said, "would you please come to the front desk? A Mr. Beaumont is here to discuss Rambo."

Soon a small woman with brown eyes and short curly hair emerged from a back room. The name tag on her plaid flannel shirt identified her as Colleen McDaniel. She glanced around the waiting area and then settled on me. I guess the fact that I was there accompanied by no visible dog made me something of an anomaly.

"You're here about Rambo?" she asked.

It was clear to me that at the academy, the dog's identity took precedence. "Yes," I said, nodding, then held out my hand. "That would be me."

The academy boasted no such thing as a private office. Colleen invited me into a side room where a large long-eared mutt named Mitzi was practicing something called "wait on the rug." Watching a dog perform "wait on the rug" is about as interesting as watching paint dry, but the trainer was explaining to the dog's entranced family how mastering this command would make the arrival of newcomers at their home far less traumatic for everyone involved.

"Tell me about Rambo," Colleen commanded. "What kind of dog is he?"

"She," I corrected. "And she's big. We believe she's all or part Irish wolfhound."

Without mentioning any names, I launched off into the whole long story, including the part where Rambo had bared her teeth at me and effectively kept me from climbing into my own bed.

Colleen listened, nodding now and again as I spoke. "Wolfies are very protective," she said finally. "That's what they were bred to do originally—to protect their families from whatever. Since Rambo comes from a background with a history of domestic violence, when you were trying to get into bed, she may have read your actions as somehow threatening to your wife and she was protecting her."

I have to confess, that thought had never occurred to me. As far as I could tell, Rambo wanted my side of the bed. Period.

"Considering her environment and the possibility that she has probably witnessed her share of family violence," Colleen continued, "there's a good chance she's insecure. In my experience, insecure dogs can be dangerous dogs."

I had always thought that vicious dogs were just that—vicious. It never crossed my mind that the dogs might actually be scared out of their wits.

"So by taking in this dog—temporarily or not—you're saying it's really a rescue, correct?" Colleen asked.

"I suppose," I said. "If we hadn't taken her home with us, she would have had to go back to the pound. But still, she's a big dog—a huge dog. We have young grandkids, and the family she came from and may go back to has small kids."

"And you're worried about that—about how she'll interact with children?"

"Yes."

Without another word, Colleen stood up and walked back to the desk, where she collected a clipboard and a pen. She spent several moments, writing something on a piece of paper. Only when she finished did she look back at me.

"One of the things we do here at the academy is evaluate rescues," she told me. "Your concerns about large dogs and especially insecure large dogs as posing a danger to small children are not at all misplaced. Some so-called rescue dogs have been so severely damaged in their previous homes that they simply shut down and can never be safely integrated into new ones.

"Here at the academy we make it our mission to facilitate successful and safe rescue situations. In order to do so, we take in newly rescued dogs and keep them here at the academy for a week at no charge to the adopting family. That allows us to evaluate the dogs' personalities and assess their ability to successfully integrate into a new family dynamic. Given Rambo's troubled background, I think that kind of assessment would make sense for your peace of mind going forward, regardless of whether Rambo stays with you on strictly a temporary basis or if the situation morphs into something more long term.

"The fact that she knows to ask to go out would indicate that she's had some training, but oftentimes animals from those kinds of situations have not been properly vaccinated. And even if she has been, you won't be able to access those records."

With that, Colleen handed me the piece of paper on which she'd been writing, explaining the contents as she did so. "The three items listed at the bottom of the sheet are the three vaccinations Rambo would need to have had—rabies, distemper, and Bordetella— in case you decide that you're interested in dropping her off here for an evaluation. The last one, Bordetella, prevents what we call kennel cough, and dogs can't come here for anything including boarding and training without up-to-date vaccination records. Do you have a family vet?"

"No," I answered. "I've never had a dog before."

"Check with PetsMart then," she suggested. "They generally have a vet on hand, and they'll also have a chip reader."

"A what?"

"A microchip reader," she answered. "When a dog is being adopted, some agencies install a chip in the dog's shoulder prior to its being placed. That way, if the dog is lost, it's possible to locate the owner even if the dog isn't wearing tags. A chip can also lead you back to the vet who originally inserted it. If Rambo has one, with any luck, the vet in question will have access to the vaccination records. If you decide this is something you want to do, once you ascertain that Rambo's shots are current, call here, so I can schedule a time for you to stop by and drop her off."

"Thank you," I said. "Will do. But what's this at the top of the page?" Without my reading glasses, I had to squint to make out the two words she had written there—Beth Gelert. Even after reading them, however, they made no sense whatsoever.

"It's the name of a poem," she explained. "It's also your homework assignment. Go home, look it up on the Internet, and read it. It'll teach you everything you need to know about the wonders of having an Irish wolfhound in your life."

"Thank you," I said, pocketing the paper along with Colleen's business card. "I'll do that."

"What's your wife's name again?" Colleen asked.

"Mel," I answered. "Melissa really, but everyone calls her Mel."

"Just for the record," Colleen added, "I suspect that Rambo is lucky to have you and Mel in hers."

I may not have had the dog with me at the time, but I walked out of the Academy of Canine Behavior feeling as though I'd just been given an excellent report card.

It was ten to seven when I got back on the freeway

headed northbound. Traffic was moving fairly well—at least compared to what it had been doing earlier. However, even though I had to drive eighty miles between Bothell and home, I still arrived well before Mel did. Have I mentioned that the job of being chief of police is not a nine-to-five endeavor?

Once back home I was greatly relieved to discover that all was well. Rambo had indeed deigned to use the doggy door. There were no messes of any kind inside the house. Considering Rambo's relative size, you could say that was a huge relief. Her water dish was empty. I filled it. Her food dish was empty, and I filled that as well. It was far too late for sunset watching or playing ball, either, so I turned on the fireplace. With iPad in hand, I settled down in my chair to do my homework. It turns out that Beth in Beth Gelert is a misspelling of Bedde of Gelert, which doesn't mean "bed" at all. In this case it means grave, and the poem Colleen McDaniel had assigned for me to read ended up telling a very sad story.

It seems a prince of Wales—I'm not sure which one —loved to go hunting with his hounds. One day, when it was time for the hunt, his favorite dog, a wolfhound named Gelert, was nowhere to be found, so the prince went hunting without him. When he came home that evening, the dog came to greet his master, completely covered with blood. With his heart filled with dread, the prince went inside searching for his baby. The crib, also covered with blood, was empty. Assuming the dog had killed his child, the enraged father stabbed the dog, who, as he was dying, gave out a piteous howl. The sound was answered by the cry of a baby.

The father soon found the child, safe and sound, hiding in another room. Nearby lay the body of the wolf Gelert had slain while bravely protecting his charge.

Talk about a miscarriage of justice! Bedde of Gelert indeed! And wouldn't you know? I was still sitting there mopping my eyes when Mel showed up. "You look upset," she said. "What's going on?"

"Nothing," I said. "I was just reading a poem about an Irish wolfhound."

Mel gave me a look of utter disbelief—as though I really were from the planet Dalvar. "Sure you were," she said. "And I'm a monkey's uncle. So why don't you come into the kitchen and tell me about it while I fix something for us to eat. With you out of town, I missed lunch today. I'm starved."

Because she gets home so late most nights, we tend to eat our main meal at lunchtime. More often than not, our evening repast consists of gourmet peanut butter and jelly sandwiches prepared in our gourmet kitchen, where I was surprised to discover that Rambo loves peanut butter.

Over the course of making and eating the meal, Mel and I compared notes. It was while I was telling her about Max's funeral and about Erin Kelsey being totally estranged from the man who had rescued her as an abandoned child in Mexico that I saw the similarity between what had happened to Pete Kelsey and what happened to that damned dog. That wasn't fair, either.

"So what are you going to do about all this?" Mel asked.

"Tracking down Max's literary agent is probably the first step," I answered. "If the cops are wrong and the man really was murdered, the who and why may be found in something he uncovered in the course of working on the book. I'll also want to check with some of my sources and see if I can get details on the fire investigation."

"Scott?" Mel asked.

"No, definitely not Scott," I replied. "If this ends up going sideways, I don't want to have him hauled up on charges of providing unauthorized information to someone outside the department."

"Makes sense," she agreed.

"And since Erin said this may have something to do with Marcia Kelsey's homicide, I should probably track down Pete, her widower, as well."

After dinner—I have a hard time calling PBJ sandwiches dinner, but there you are—we wandered back into the living room and sat down in our matching chairs by the fire, where Mel brought me up to date on the Ken Purcell situation. He'd been released from the hospital and was now in police custody, being cared for in the infirmary at the county lockup.

"He's scheduled to go before the judge tomorrow morning," she said. "The prosecutor says that because it wasn't a deadly weapon—BB guns are considered to be about the same danger level as a stun gun—the best we can hope for on the shooting is assault in the third degree."

"What about the domestic violence charge?"

"That remains to be seen," Mel said. "Serena is working on that. It depends on whether Nancy Purcell is willing to press charges and testify. So far she says she will, but you know how that goes."

Unfortunately I did. All too often, victims in domestic violence cases end up caving when it comes time to lock up their abusers. I didn't know either one of the people involved personally, but I figured the odds were good that Nancy Purcell would pull the same stunt when it came time to put her asshole hubby in jail. What that meant was that Kenneth Purcell would be back on the streets in no time.

"So he'll be able to post bail?" I asked.

Mel nodded. "Most likely," she said, "and probably sooner than later, which isn't good news for my department or for Nancy and her kids, either, especially if he ends up arming himself with something other than a BB gun."

"So maybe it's not such a crazy idea for Nancy and her kids to have an oversized dog on the premises after all?"

"Maybe not," Mel agreed with a smile, "but that reminds me. I promised Serena this afternoon that I'd send her another photo."

When Mel and I had turned off the lights in the kitchen and gone into the living room to sit by the fire, Rambo had eventually followed us there. When she had entered the room, she had stopped by the sofa—black leather, by the way—where she paused for a moment, looking first at me and then at Mel. Then, without any further hesitation, she had hiked her long body up onto the seat and stretched out full length—using up a surprising amount of acreage on that six-foot-long couch. Obviously she was accustomed to being on furniture, and neither Mel nor I had bothered to tell her otherwise. Now she was apparently sound asleep.

"Hey, Rambo," Mel said, aiming the camera on her cell phone in the dog's direction. "Look here."

Obligingly, Rambo opened her eyes and raised her

head just in time for the flash to go off. When Mel examined the resulting photo a few moments later, she burst out laughing. "That's not going to cut it," she said, handing me the phone. "Take a look."

I did. Against the black background of the couch, the dog's body was completely invisible. All that showed were a pair of eerily glowing eyes—two fiery orbs that seemed to float, like smoldering embers, in midair.

"She looks more like a devil than a dog," I observed, passing the phone back to Mel. "You should probably take one of her on the new bed in the kitchen. It's blue and gray—better contrast."

"No," Mel said. "I think I'll send this one anyway. That way Nancy and the kids will be able to see for themselves that we're not mistreating her."

Was that good for the dog? Probably. Good for the furniture? Probably not. But there you are—live and learn.

CHAPTER 11

THAT NIGHT MEL, Rambo, and I all managed to crawl into our respective beds without incident. Seeming to understand this new arrangement, Rambo settled down without complaint or objection on her old ratty bed next to Mel's side of ours. As per usual, Mel went straight to sleep.

Maybe she could sleep like a baby, all the while ignoring the possibility that Ken Purcell might post bail and come looking for trouble, but I could not. In my opinion and regardless of the caliber of weapon they use, people who go around shooting at cops need keepers and shouldn't be allowed out on their own.

After I'd tossed and turned, wrestling with that one for a while—to no avail, I might add—I turned my attention back to the Maxwell Cole situation. It was like approaching an investigation the way we did it back in the old days, long before DNA and the microscopic examination of trace evidence became the be-alls and end-alls of modern police work. Back then we started with the crime, a theory of what had happened, and worked from there, investing a lot of time, energy, and shoe leather along the way.

In this case, since Erin's theory that Max had somehow been murdered was completely at variance with the official findings, I would be doing my investigation with no legal backing or assistance. Clearly, my obvious first step was to talk to Max's literary agent. Finding him wouldn't be that big a problem, but before I spoke to him, I needed to know something about him. On that score, I had a powerful ally available to me, one I was reasonably sure I could bring into play, namely the only forensic economist I know, a guy named Todd Hatcher.

Todd actually hails from the same neck of the woods where my friend Sheriff Joanna Brady hangs out— Cochise County in southeastern Arizona. The son of a waitress and a failed and consequently convicted bank robber, Todd saw his life forever impacted when his father was released from prison and into the care of his mother only after he had come down with early onset Alzheimer's. The financial, emotional, and physical impact of caring for the impaired ex-con had proved to be too much for Todd's mother, and she had survived her husband's death by only a matter of months.

Todd spent his summers as a cowboy in southern Arizona while working his way through college, earning both a B.A. and a master's in economics. By the time his mother died, he was at the University of Washington, working on his doctorate. His thesis, a study of the long-term fiscal impact of an aging prison population, hadn't won him a lot of accolades among the faculty at the U Dub, but it had brought him to the attention of the then state attorney general and my old boss, Ross Connors.

Mel and I had been working for Special Homicide at the time, and that's where we first met Todd Hatcher. He's a geek, all right, but an unlikely-looking one—a long, lanky, bowlegged guy who prefers to dress in jeans, boots, and cowboy shirts and who looks, for all the world, as though he just stepped off a horse. He and his wife, Julie, and their new baby, Sabrina, live on a small farm down near Olympia where they're raising quarter horses on the side.

Even with Ross Connors out of the picture, however, Todd continues to do yeoman's labor for any number of governmental agencies at state, county, and local municipal levels. He likes to say that when he gets tired of shoveling all the bureaucratic horseshit, he goes out to the barn and shovels the real kind to help get his mojo back.

Since the family lives out in the boonies, I'm not at all sure how Todd manages to maintain a to-die-for Internet connection, but he does. And, because of the kinds of work he does, he has unlimited access to information about pretty much anything and everything.

My last waking thought before I drifted off to sleep that night was that I'd check with Todd in the morning. I was relatively sure he could help me look up Maxwell Cole's literary agent, Thomas Raines. I was also hoping he'd be able to give me some context on the man. That way, even before I started asking questions, I'd have some idea if what the literary agent told me was worth listening to or if I should take his answers with a grain of salt. I also hoped that, in addition to giving me background on the literary agent, Todd would be able to point me in the direction of John Madsen, formerly known as Pete Kelsey.

As I've mentioned, Mel is your basic early to bed, early to rise kind of woman, and the next morning was no exception. She was up, showered, and dressed before I finished sawing logs. I stumbled into the kitchen as she was gathering up her purse and car keys and getting ready to leave. She paused long enough to give me a dual-purpose kiss that covered both hello and good-bye.

"I already fed Rambo," she warned. "Don't let her trick you into believing she hasn't eaten."

"Are we having lunch?" I asked.

"Nope," Mel told me, "not today. Ken Purcell's arraignment is scheduled for late this morning. I want to put in an appearance at that. Then, at noon I'm scheduled to be the dog and pony show at a lunchtime Rotary meeting."

I didn't envy her either of those chores. "Have a good one then," I mumbled, making for the coffee machine and pressing the button. While the coffee dribbled into my mug, I glanced down at the dog. Rambo may have been lying on her bed, but she was watchfully keeping me in her field of vision.

"How are you this morning?" I asked.

Since there was no one else within hearing distance, Rambo seemed to understand that I was addressing her. She thumped her tail accordingly, forcing me to come to the inarguable conclusion that I had fallen so far down the rabbit hole that I was actually talking to a dog.

"You're losing it for sure," I chastised myself aloud, which I admit wasn't a big improvement over talking to the dog. Rambo may not have understood a word I was saying, but she thumped her tail at that comment, too.

Unplugging my phone and iPad from their chargers,

I took them and my cup of coffee into the living room, where my first call of the day was to Todd Hatcher.

"Hey," he said. "Long time no hear. How are things up in Bellingham?"

"So-so," I told him.

"Right," he said. "I heard about the OIS. Those are always tough." (OIS is cop shorthand for officer-involved shooting.) "How's Mel doing on that score?"

"All right, I guess. The bad guy's arraignment is today."

"How's the officer?" Todd asked.

"Still on administrative leave. The jerk shot him with a BB gun that looked for all the world like the real thing. I have no doubt that the incident will end up being declared a righteous shooting."

"Good," Todd said. "Glad to hear it. Now, to what do I owe the honor?"

"I'm calling to ask a favor," I said. "I need some background information on a guy named Thomas Raines. I believe he's a literary agent operating somewhere in the Seattle area."

"A literary agent?" Todd shot back. "Are you about to turn your hand to writing—like maybe you want to be the next Lieutenant Joe Kenda?"

I knew about the TV series; in fact I had even watched a few episodes of *Homicide Hunter*. Although Kenda and I operated in different parts of the country, our mutual years in homicide more or less paralleled each other's, and I sort of liked the guy's plainspoken, matter-of-fact way of dealing with life-and-death matters.

"Hardly," I answered. "I'm investigating the death of an old acquaintance of mine, a guy named Maxwell

Cole. Supposedly he was writing a book, and I'm told Raines was his agent. Max died last week in a house fire that has been officially ruled as accidental, but some of Max's nearest and dearest think he may have been murdered."

"And something in this manuscript may have had something to do with it?" Todd asked.

"Exactly," I said. "I've been led to believe that what happened may have something to do with a homicide I investigated years ago. The victim's name was Marcia Kelsey. I'd like to see if you can locate her widower— a Vietnam War–era army deserter whose real name is John Madsen. I'm short on details at the moment. I think he hailed from somewhere in the Midwest— North or South Dakota maybe."

"Okay," Todd said. "I'll be glad to look into all of this, but it won't be until later on today. I'm fighting a dead-line at the moment."

"Whenever you get around to it will be fine," I told him. "Say hi to Julie for me."

"Will do," he said and signed off.

I read the online papers for a while. When it was time for my second cup of coffee, I returned to the kitchen to find that Rambo hadn't moved. And that's when I made up my mind. While I was waiting to see what Todd came up with, why not take a crack at find-ing out about Rambo's situation as far as microchip and vaccination records were concerned?

I located the phone number for the Bellingham PetsMart and learned that they did indeed have a vet on the premises. Taking my coffee with me, I returned to the master bedroom long enough to shower, shave, and dress.

Once back in the kitchen, I gathered up my keys and wallet. Then, collecting the leash, I looked down at the dog and asked, "Do you want to go?"

That's when I discovered the word "go" happened to be one Rambo understood completely. She bounded off her bed and headed straight to the door, and not just any door, either, but to the correct one—the one that led out back to the garage and to where the car was parked rather than to the front yard.

I fastened the leash to her brand-new leather collar and away we went. On Sunday evening, when she'd been riding in the back of Mel's car, the dog had been through a trying day and had huddled miserably in a corner of the backseat. Obviously, today she was feeling better—more secure maybe? This time Rambo stood in the backseat of my S 550—taking up most of it, by the way—with her chin resting on my left-hand shoulder while I drove. I couldn't help but be touched by the gesture—in more ways than one. By the time we arrived at our destination, I discovered a trail of dog slobber had left indelible tracks on the shoulder of my sport jacket.

When we got to the parking lot, I wasn't sure what to do—leave the dog in the car or take her inside? Looking around the parking lot, I noticed that other people, accompanied by dogs on leashes and seemingly without a care in the world, were walking in and out of the store. It wasn't long before I decided to do the same. I'll admit, I was more than a little worried about how Rambo would react not only to unfamiliar surroundings but also to the presence of strange dogs. Much to my surprise, she seemed totally at ease.

When I asked a clerk up front about checking for a

microchip, she immediately directed us to the veterinarian's office located at the back of the store. On the way there, some fuzzy but fierce little leashed dog came charging out of a side aisle, barking its little head off. Much to Rambo's credit, she shied out of the way but kept right on walking.

When we reached the vet's reception area, Rambo was tall enough that she could stand flat-footed with her chin resting on the counter. Giving the dog a wary look, the clerk seated there asked, "May I help you?"

"I'm fostering this dog," I explained. "I need to see if she has a microchip and to figure out whether or not her shots are up to date."

"Of course," she said. "No problem. We check for chips all the time. Right this way. What's your dog's name?"

"Rambo."

"What kind of dog is he?" she asked, bringing out a wand that looked like something the TSA might use at an airport check-in.

"Irish wolfhound we think," I answered. "And it's a she not a he."

"Rambo's a girl?" she asked. "Are you kidding?"

"Look," I said. "we're just adopting the dog; we didn't get to name her."

"Okay then," she said, passing the wand over Rambo's shoulder, "here we go, and yes, she does have a chip." The woman studied the wand for a moment or two, and then scribbled some information onto a piece of paper, which she handed over to me. On it were two sets of numbers. The first one was long enough to resemble the serial number on a refrigerator. The second was a phone number.

"What do I do with these?"

"The first number is the one on Rambo's chip," she told me. "The other number is the chip provider's toll-free number. If you call there, someone should be able to tell you what you need to know."

I was in the process of dialing the number when a woman approached the counter with two little dogs who immediately and vocally decided that Rambo was their sworn enemy. What the hell is it about little dogs? At any rate, I decided that the phone call would be best made from the privacy of my car. Back to the parking lot we went, and I placed the call from there.

Although the clerk had said the people at the chip company would help me, it turns out that wasn't exactly true. As the agent at the call center carefully explained to me, it was her job to take the chip number and then call the pet's owners to let them know the missing animal's current location. I tried to explain to her, quite reasonably, I thought, that Rambo wasn't actually missing. I was the dog's new caregiver—"new human" were the words the call center agent used—and I was merely attempting to locate Rambo's shot records.

Mel is an expert at bucking bureaucracies—at going over, through, or around them. Me? Not so much. I didn't try explaining that any call to the telephone number the chip people had on record would most likely go unanswered due to the fact that a) Kenneth Purcell was in jail and b) the rest of the family was in hiding. In any event, the call center person was utterly obdurate. She didn't come right out and say, "You'll find *sympathy* in the dictionary between *shit* and *syphilis*," but it was very close.

I upped my volume and asked to speak to her supervisor, and to her supervisor, and to the supervisor beyond that. Eventually I was advised that although they were unable to give me any additional information about Rambo's owners (which I already had, by the way), they could at least give me the name of the vet who had installed the microchip. Hallelujah!

Within minutes I was on the phone to the practice of someone named Dr. Dennis White. The woman there listened quietly while I told her that Rambo was temporarily in my wife's and my care and that I needed her shot records. Moments later I was both surprised and relieved to be told that Rambo's shots were completely up to date. That meant I didn't have to take the poor dog back inside PetsMart and have her shot full of unnecessary holes. Not only that, but Rambo had a valid license in Bellingham, although the tag itself wasn't currently in my possession.

"If you're going to board her or take her on a plane and someone needs her info," Dr. White's clerk advised me, "just have whoever it is call here. I'll be glad to fax them whatever information they need."

"Thank you," I said. "Thank you so much."

I was about to hang up. "One other thing," Dr. White's assistant added.

"What's that?"

"Are Nancy and the kids okay?" she asked.

Clearly the clerk knew more about the Purcells' family situation than I would have expected.

"They're fine," I said.

"Thank goodness," she breathed. "And whoever you are, thank you for looking after Rambo. She's a very good dog."

CHAPTER 12

RAMBO AND I were on our way home from what I regarded as an altogether successful trip to PetsMart when the phone rang. It was Todd.

"I thought you were on a deadline," I told him. "I didn't expect to hear back from you this soon."

"I don't have all of your info, but I do have some," Todd said. "I have a couple of student interns working for me these days, and I put one of them on the case. From the information she just handed me, I can tell you that Thomas Raines is seventy-six years old, a Seattle native who attended Franklin High School. In the eighties he was an outspoken gay activist, raising money for AIDS research on the one hand and for comprehensive care for patients diagnosed with AIDS on the other. From what I can gather, back then the care in question amounted to little more than hospice kinds of services due to the fact that regular hospitals weren't eager to admit patients suffering from AIDS."

Remembering back to the bad old days, I knew all of

that to be true. In the beginning, being given an AIDS diagnosis had been an automatic death sentence.

Look, I came of age in the fifties. I know how gay people were treated back then—the insults, the name-calling, the bullying. Much as I'd like to pretend otherwise, I'm sure I was guilty of those kinds of baiting on occasion. Kids who didn't quite fit in were in for it. As for the ones who were suspected of being gay? They had more to deal with than just the torment dished out at school or on the playground. I'm sure plenty of scorn and denial was served up by their families at home, right along with the evening meal.

I remember a long-ago homicide case where a woman, the mother of a recently deceased AIDS victim, had insisted to her son's grieving partner that if her son had somehow developed AIDS, he must have gotten it from a toilet seat! That was the beginning of my own personal wake-up call.

As for Thomas Raines? "If the guy was 'out' in public back then," I told Todd, "we're talking about a gay guy with balls."

Todd laughed. "I have to agree with you there. He was a lot more 'out' back then than he is these days. He started his literary agency about fifteen years ago. The authors he represents are mostly mainstream fiction—mysteries and sci-fi both. He also represents a couple of true crime writers, and several of those seem to be doing very well. Raines and his longtime partner, a retired real estate developer, live in a penthouse condo out in Madison Park. That's where you come in."

"I beg your pardon?"

"Have you ever heard of six degrees of separation?"

"Sure," I replied. "It's the idea that every person is somehow linked to every other person through a network of intersecting lines."

"Close enough," Todd agreed. "In this instance, you and Thomas Raines share the same interior designer. There was a big spread about Raines and his partner's condo in a national architectural magazine. I recognized the designer's name because Julie and I met Jim Hunt when we came to the open house for Harry I. Ball's condo remodel, remember?"

It turns out I remembered very well. I had roped Jim, my personal decorator, into spearheading the project to make Harry's place more accessible to someone who was a double amputee. It had been a complex undertaking, and we had all been there—Jim, Mel, and me along with all the other people from S.H.I.T.—to welcome Harry home from the hospital upon his release from rehab. Come to think of it, Margie had been absolutely aglow that day when she drove him home and wheeled him into the house. I should have known at the time that something was up.

As for Thomas Raines and Jim Hunt? They were about the same age—mid-seventies. The AIDS scourge in Seattle in the eighties had greatly reduced the numbers of surviving gay men in that demographic. Based on that, it was hardly surprising that the two of them would know one another.

"Anyway," Todd continued, "I'm e-mailing you a report of sorts. It includes contact information, addresses, etc. Remember it was done by an intern, so don't expect it to be professional grade, highly organized, or grammatically correct, but I think it'll give you what you need."

"Thanks, Todd," I told him. "I owe you big-time. The next time you and Julie are in town, dinner's on me."

I hung up the phone and immediately dialed Jim Hunt's number. He is not your basic morning person, but it was early afternoon now, and I was pretty sure he'd be up taking nourishment.

"What gives, Beau?" he asked when he answered the phone. I still haven't quite adjusted to this new world order in which everyone on earth knows who's calling on the phone long before they even say hello.

"I'm looking for some help," I told him.

"You've bought another house," he said at once.

That made me laugh. "No," I said, "not that. An acquaintance of mine died in a house fire on Queen Anne Hill last weekend, and I've been asked to look into the situation."

"Maxwell Cole?" Jim asked.

That stopped me cold. "You knew him?" I asked.

"I knew of him," Jim corrected. "I remember reading some of his stuff back in the day, but it was big news over the weekend. Not that many fatality house fires on Queen Anne Hill recently. I put two and two together and came up with four."

"I'm really calling about someone else right now," I said. "Thomas Raines."

"What about him?"

"My understanding is that Max was working on a book—had most likely even sold a book—and that Thomas Raines was his literary agent. What can you tell me about the guy?"

"When it comes to furniture, he has way better taste than you do," Jim said, "although that's not really saying much."

"No, it's not," I agreed, "but I need to talk to this Raines character and see if he has any idea about what was going on in Max's life in the months and weeks before his death."

"As in did someone have it in for him?"

"Exactly, so I'm planning on giving Mr. Raines a call, but before I phone him up, introduce myself, and start asking questions, I was wondering if there was anything up front that I needed to know about the man."

"Tommy's true blue, all wool, and a yard wide," Jim said. "He's also a man of his word."

I could hardly have expected a higher recommendation than that, but I was about to get one.

"Would you like me to give him a call and tell him what's up?" Jim asked. "I think he and his partner, Sid, are planning to head down to their place in Palm Springs in the next little while. If you want to talk to him, you should do it sooner rather than later."

"A personal introduction from you would be a huge help," I said.

"Okay," Jim replied. "Let me see what I can do."

Once back home, I pulled into the garage and immediately led Rambo around to the front of the house, where I let her off leash to relieve herself. By the time I unlocked the front door to let myself inside, she had already dashed in through the doggy door and was lapping water in the kitchen. Note to self: Rambo is one fast learner!

The lunch pickings at home were exceedingly slim. I settled on a package of Top Ramen and was in the process of heating same when my phone rang with CALLER UNKNOWN showing in the window. I expected it to be some kind of robocall with an automated survey of some kind or letting me know that I'd just won an all-expenses-paid two-day cruise to the Bahamas.

"Mr. Beaumont?" said a male voice.

"Yes."

"Thomas Raines here. I just got off the phone with our mutual friend, Jim Hunt. I understand from him that you're looking into Max's death and need to speak to me about it. Do you really think his death wasn't accidental?"

"That's what I'm trying to find out."

"Dying the way he did is utterly horrifying, and if someone is responsible, I'll be happy to do everything in my power to help."

"I was wondering if there would be a time when the two of us could sit down to talk?" I asked.

"That's the whole problem," Thomas continued. "My partner and I are flying out of town early tomorrow, and we won't be back for the better part of a month. If you want to get together before then, it'll have to be this evening sometime."

"Sure," I said, "no problem. What time?"

"Say seven?"

"Sure," I said. "I can do that. Where?"

"We live out in Madison Park," Raines said. "Let me give you the address."

I wrote it down, but I was just being polite. I was pretty sure the address was in the material Todd Hatcher had just sent me.

"Okay then," I told him. "See you at seven."

Only after setting the appointment did I really think about it. If the meeting with Raines lasted until eight thirty or so, that would leave me with a late-night two-hour drive back home in the pitch dark on possibly icy roads. I immediately sent Mel a text:

Going to town to interview Max's literary agent. Meeting is at seven. Going to stay overnight at the condo.

Her response was immediate, so obviously she'd finished the latest round in her charm offensive, her visit with Rotary:

What about Rambo?

I was used to coming and going as I damned well pleased. What about Rambo indeed? I looked down at the dog, who was curled up on her bed once more and regarding me with no small interest.

I'll have to get back to you on that. What about Purcell?

Showed up with his public defender. Pleaded not guilty. Bail is set at $500,000. That seems to be a little out of his price range.

Good. The longer he's under lock and key the better.

But the really good news here is that Serena got Nancy to swear out a no-contact order. If he does manage to track her down and show up on her doorstep, he's back in the slammer no questions asked.

Good for Serena. Best you can do then. Later. Gotta run.

Finished texting, I dug through my wallet until I found Colleen McDaniel's business card. When I asked to speak to her, she wasn't in, of course. "I expect her back shortly," I was told. "May I say what this is about?"

"My name's Beaumont," I replied. "I spoke to her yesterday about my new dog—a rescue named Rambo. Colleen told me I could bring the dog in for a possible evaluation as soon as I could verify that her shots were up to date, which I have done."

"Colleen personally handles all rescue evaluations," the receptionist told me. "I'll have her get back to you on that."

Right, I thought without saying anything aloud, *sometime in the next century if I'm really lucky.*

I turned my hand to one of my newly assumed duties—filling the dog dishes, food and water both. Then I went outside to do the other one—doggy latrine duty. As I wielded my pooper-scooper, I did so with a respectful hat tip in Todd Hatcher's direction. It occurred to me in the process that shoveling Irish wolfhound crap was probably less problematic than shoveling horse poop.

Surprisingly, not more than ten minutes after my leaving a message for her, Colleen McDaniel did indeed call me back. I let her in on everything I'd learned in the course of the morning—that Rambo's shots were current and that her vaccination records were available on demand from Dr. Dennis White's veterinary practice in Bellingham.

"Given all that," I finished, "would it be possible for me to bring her in this afternoon to drop her off for that adoption suitability evaluation? I've been called back down to Seattle this evening, and it would be easy for me to drop her off on my way."

"Let me check to see if there's room," Colleen said. She turned away from the phone for a moment, and I could hear her speaking to people in the background. "Okay," she said when she returned to the line. "What time?"

I checked my watch. "Four," I answered, "or maybe a little before."

Shortly after two, Rambo and I were back in the car and headed south on I-5. Once again, Rambo positioned herself in the backseat, standing on all fours with her chin resting on my shoulder. I'd noticed the slobber stains on the jacket I'd been wearing earlier, so I had abandoned that one in favor of a clean one. I may be slow at times, but at least I had been smart enough to bring along a towel, which I placed on my shoulder as a drool deflector.

Three different times during the drive south, cars in the passing lane drove slightly past my front bumper and then inexplicably came close to losing control, swerving back and forth before finally straightening up. For the life of me, I couldn't understand the sudden outbreak of bad driving. No one was speeding excessively, and weather certainly wasn't a factor. There had been a bit of afternoon clearing, so although the road surface may still have been slightly damp, it wasn't icy and there weren't pools of water on the roadway that might have caused hydroplaning.

It wasn't until the fourth time it happened, when I noticed passengers in the backseat, pointing in my direction and laughing their heads off, that I finally realized what was going on. Rambo is so large that, with her chin positioned on my shoulder, her head probably totally obscured mine. As far as the occupants of passing cars were concerned, it must have looked for all the world as though a dog were driving the car. With my side and rearview mirrors in play, she wasn't really blocking my view of surrounding traffic, but I was happy not to have a discussion about that with a uniformed member of the Washington State Patrol.

Rambo and I arrived at the Academy at what I now realized was the beginning of afternoon rush hour for doggy day care pickup. I drove up to the office and then stopped. It took me a moment. I felt more than slightly guilty about dropping Rambo off among a new group of strangers. After all, she was just now getting used to Mel and me. Nevertheless, there was nothing for it. With a heartfelt sigh, I got out of the car, opened the back door, picked up Rambo's leash, and led her toward the door.

I may have been suffering some trepidation about all this, but Rambo seemed perfectly fine. She stepped through the front door with her ears up and her lanky tail plumed out behind her. With several other sets of people and dogs coming and going, I more than half-expected to get into some kind of tugging match with mine, but that didn't happen. Rambo looked every bit as mellow in these new surroundings as all the other dogs did. Amazing!

"J. P. Beaumont and Rambo," I said, in answer to the desk clerk's query. "We're here to see Colleen."

While I stood by the front desk, waiting, I occupied the time by glancing through one of the color brochures displayed there. I was astonished to see how much a six-week session of obedience training cost. The eye-popping total came out to more than twice what I paid for a year's worth of college tuition back when I was attending the U Dub!

I was still mulling over that when Colleen entered through the front door just behind me. "Mr. Beaumont?" she began.

I turned toward her voice. Rather than stepping forward to greet me, Colleen stopped short with her attention focused solely on the dog. "Oh my goodness!" she exclaimed. "Lucy, is that you?"

At the sound of her voice, Rambo lunged forward so unexpectedly, she yanked the leash from my hand. Before I could react in any way, Rambo was on her hind legs with her front legs resting on Colleen's shoulders, licking the woman's face.

"Off!" Colleen ordered, talking and laughing at the same time. "Off!"

Instantly Rambo dropped to all fours.

"Sit!" Colleen said.

Rambo sat, but as soon as she did so, Colleen knelt beside her, cradling the dog's huge head in her hands and crooning at her. "Lucy, you sweet, sweet thing, you! How good to see you again."

I stood there utterly agog. "You know this dog?"

"Not by the name of Rambo," Colleen said. "Her name was Lucy when I first met her. She's one of the smartest dogs we've ever trained."

CHAPTER 13

THE GOOD NEWS was that Lucy Rambo—it made perfect sense to me that her first name would be Lucy and her last name Rambo—was a *cum laude* graduate of the Academy of Canine Behavior. As such she needed no "suitability evaluation" and, as a consequence, there was no reason for her to stay overnight.

I, on the other hand, was completely in the dark. "I was under the impression that this dog came from a pound," I objected. "And I just now saw how much you charge for training. How could the Purcells afford to spend that much money on a pound puppy?"

"Maybe we should discuss this in private," Colleen said. She turned to the girl behind the desk. "We're going over to the house for a few minutes. If anybody needs me, I'll be back shortly."

Colleen reached down and picked up Rambo's leash. "Okay, Lucy," she said. "Right here."

While we'd been conversing, Rambo had been sitting patiently on the floor between Colleen and me. Now, coming to attention, she stood up and stationed herself at Colleen's left knee. "Let's go," Colleen added.

They started toward the door with the leash dangling loosely in Colleen's hand. At the door, Colleen looked down at the dog. "Wait," she said. The dog stopped and waited long enough for Colleen to go out first before allowing the dog to follow. "People go out before dogs," she explained for my benefit. "It's a matter of respect. The problem is, Lucy already knows the rules and you don't. We're going to have to give you a crash course."

Colleen led the way across a broad driveway and into a low-slung brick house that served as the McDaniels' residence. We entered a comfortably lived-in living room filled with well-worn furnishings and heated by a glowing fire in a wood-burning fireplace. The pleasant aromas in the air told me that somewhere inside the house someone was cooking dinner. There were two other dogs in residence at the moment, small, noisy ones, stationed behind a dog gate in a doorway that evidently led to the kitchen. The two dogs barked their objections to Lucy's arrival, but Colleen ignored them.

"Go ahead and have a seat," Colleen told me. Then, dropping Rambo's leash, she addressed the dog. "Lucy, go get on the rug."

Rambo stopped short and looked around before finally locating a likely looking rug lying on the floor in front of the fireplace. She went straight there, circled twice, lay down, and curled up.

" 'Go get on the rug' and 'Wait on the rug' are two of our most useful commands," Colleen explained. "They're especially useful if you have a swarm of guests coming into the house. It's a way of taking the dog out of play long enough for visitors to come inside and settle down. 'Get on the rug' is different from 'Wait on the rug.' The first one means go there. The second one means the dog is supposed to stay put until you release her by telling her it's 'Okay.'"

"I'm going to need a list," I told her. "Rambo maybe knows all this stuff, but I'm way behind."

"Don't worry," Colleen told me. "I'll give you a study guide." She turned to the dog. "Okay, Lucy. Come."

Obligingly, Lucy rose to her feet and walked straight to where Colleen was sitting. "Sit," Colleen commanded. The dog did so. "Good sit," Colleen told her. "Now lie down." Again, Rambo complied instantly. "Good lie down." Colleen glanced at me before explaining, "It's always a good idea to reinforce the idea that the dog has just done what you wanted them to do."

With that Colleen rose to her feet. "Lucy," she said, "stay." Colleen left the room and was gone for the better part of two minutes. When she returned, the dog hadn't moved so much as an inch. "Good stay, Lucy," she said, patting the dog's head and ruffling her ears. "Very good stay."

"That's impressive," I said.

"I told you she was one of my top students."

"But you still haven't explained how all this happened. As I said earlier, I was under the impression that this dog was rescued from the pound."

"Not exactly a pound but close," Colleen said. "She actually came from a wolfhound rescue outfit in Montana. Nancy Purcell's mother, Louise Crocker, and I went to school together, both elementary school and high school. We're still the best of friends. She was adamantly opposed to Nancy marrying Kenneth, but you see how far that got her. She thought the first time Ken beat the crap out of Nancy that she'd up and leave him."

"But that didn't happen," I interjected.

"Correct," Colleen agreed. "She took him right back, and not just the first or second time, either. That's when Louise came up with the idea of maybe adding a dog into the mix."

"For protection, you mean—for Nancy and the kids?"

"That's right. And that's why I went looking for a wolfhound in particular. They're known to be gentle giants, but only up to a point. Go too far and whammo! They'll come after you tooth and nail. I taught Lucy a command that most of my dogs never learn. I'm going to spell it for you. G-E-T H-I-M! If you use that one with Lucy here, she'll tear whoever you're pointing at limb from limb. And the only way you'll get her to back off is to tell her to L-E-A-V-E I-T!"

If that was true, I couldn't help wondering why Nancy hadn't turned the dog loose on Ken when he'd come after her with that BB gun. Maybe nobody had given her the applicable commands.

"So I found Lucy, brought her here, and trained her," Colleen continued. "Once the training was over, Louise gave the dog to Nancy and the kids for Christmas, claiming she'd been rescued from the pound. According to Louise, Ken was pissed about it, but the kids loved the dog so much that he was overruled for a change."

"I'll bet he was the one who decided to call her Rambo," I suggested.

"I wouldn't be surprised. So where are Nancy and

the kids? The girl's name is Chrissy, I think. I'm not sure about the little boy."

"They're in a YWCA shelter in Redmond. No dogs allowed. But what about Nancy's mother? No one mentioned her being involved. Maybe she'd like to have Ram... Lucy with her."

"Unfortunately, Louise has her own set of health issues," Colleen answered. "She lives in an assisted living facility over in Shoreline, and she can't have pets, either."

"Okay then," I conceded. "I guess Mel and I are in for the duration."

"Good," Colleen said. "I'll give you a copy of our command cheat sheet. You and Lucy will be just fine." Her phone rang. "Okay," she said after listening for a moment. "I'll be right there."

She looked over at me. "Stand up and tell Lucy 'Come.'"

I did so, and it worked—perfectly. Lucy came to me without a moment's hesitation.

"Now pick up the leash and tell her, 'Right here.' She should position herself at your left knee. When you start to move, she should stay at your side, but at the door, be sure to tell her 'Wait.' She's supposed to wait long enough for you to go first through any given opening."

It was a lot to remember, but I managed. Lucy had no difficulty with any of it.

"Go ahead and get her loaded, while I go find a command sheet," Colleen told me. "And she might want to get busy before you drive off."

"Get busy?" I repeated. "Is that another one of those commands?"

Colleen grinned. "You bet," she said. "Having dogs go on command before you put them in a car comes in very handy at times. Oh, and if you need one, we have poop bags just inside."

I tried out the "Get busy, Lucy" command then and there. (By the way, if the name Rambo came from Kenneth Purcell, I had already decided that I was calling the dog Lucy from then on.) "Get busy" worked like a charm first time out. Lucy immediately did exactly what needed to be done. Fortunately that particular pit stop didn't require the use of a poop bag.

About the time I drove out through the academy's front gate, with Lucy's chin once more resting comfortably on my shoulder, I realized I was screwed. Rather than dropping the dog off, she was with me and headed into Seattle to a high-rise condo where she had a) no bed; b) no food; c) no dishes; and d) most important, no yard! At the next stoplight, I consulted the GPS and was directed to the nearest PetsMart, a couple of miles away in Woodinville.

This time I went inside without the dog in tow. I collected everything I thought I might need, including what appeared to be a lifetime supply of poop bags. When it was my turn to check out, the clerk wanted to know if I wanted to sign up for their savings club. All I had to do was provide my name and phone number. Having purchased two dog beds in as many days along with forty pounds of kibble, I figured what the hell. I signed up.

Southbound traffic on 405 was a zoo, but no surprises there. This is Seattle, after all. When isn't it?

I drove into the garage at Belltown Terrace and collected the shopping cart that hangs out in the P-4 elevator lobby to facilitate dragging groceries upstairs. I loaded my purchases and then went to get Lucy. I worried about how she'd react to walking along with someone pushing a grocery cart. It turns out that wasn't a problem. She was fine with that. What I should have worried about was her riding in an elevator. (That was not fine!) Having a hundred pounds of dog suddenly cowering against my leg almost knocked me over.

We stopped off in the lobby long enough to collect the mail. "Good evening, Mr. Beaumont," Bob, the doorman, said. "What have we here?" he added, eyeing Lucy, "a new addition to the family?"

"It's only temporary," I said, although the assorted collection of dog-centric items in the grocery cart probably gave the lie to that. "Her name's Lucy."

"She's one handsome animal," Bob observed. "You do know where the nearest dog walking area is, don't you?"

That's one of the things I like about Bob—he's in the business of solving problems, sometimes long before the building's residents even know there *is* a problem.

"I have no idea," I told him, and that was the God's truth.

"Just go out through the garage entrance. It's right across the street. There's some grass, streetlights, poop bags, and even a proper disposal canister."

"Thanks for the tip," I said. "Under the circumstances, that's vitally important information."

Back in the elevator, we rode up to the penthouse. This time Lucy wasn't quite as spooked. I let her into the unit, unloaded the cart, and then left the dog there to explore while I rode back down to P-4. By then I could see I was running low on time. Back upstairs, I dished up food and then waited impatiently while Lucy thoughtfully worked her way through her kibble, one piece at a time.

When it was time to leave for my appointment with Thomas Raines, I had a choice to make—take Lucy along or leave her home? In the end, I took her with me. Madison Park is a pretty nice part of town, but if I had to park on the street, I figured that having a hundred-pound canine security guard in the backseat would prove to be an effective deterrent to any prospective car thieves.

CHAPTER 14

THE ADDRESS TODD Hatcher had given me for Thomas Raines led to Madison Park Gardens, a low-rise condominium development near Prospect and Harvard, which—surprisingly enough—did have several spaces of designated visitor parking. The Gardens consisted of six separate four-story buildings built around a common courtyard. Each building held four luxury units—one per floor—with a coded elevator stop leading directly to each non-ground-floor unit.

My directions said Building A. At the entrance and despite all the dog-related delays, I punched the button labeled Raines/Cutler at the stroke of 7 P.M. "I'll let you in," a disembodied voice told me. "Once inside the elevator, you won't be able to operate it without a keycard, but don't worry. Once you're in the elevator, we'll be able to summon it from here."

Having a remotely controlled elevator was a step up from Belltown Terrace's security system, but our building has a round-the-clock doorman and this one did not. Given all that, the elevator arrangement made sense.

I entered the building and pressed the elevator call button. When it came, I stepped inside and waited. As soon as the doors glided shut, the elevator seemed to rise of its own volition. When the doors opened again, rather than finding myself in a building corridor of some kind, I discovered I was already inside an apartment. The tall, distinguished man waiting there to greet me was a few years older than I am. He was strikingly good-looking and exceptionally fit.

"Mr. Beaumont?" he asked.

"Yes," I said, "but please call me Beau."

We shook hands. "And I'm Thomas Raines," he replied. "Everybody calls me Tommy. Come on in."

He ushered me out of the entryway decorated with only two items—a massive, gold-framed mirror hanging over a delicately fashioned inlaid wood table that announced its unequivocal status as a legitimate French antique even to an interior decorating dummy like me.

I stopped in the middle of an eye-popping great room and took stock. The place was a marvel. The entire east-facing wall consisted of floor-to-ceiling windows in which Bellevue's glittering nighttime cityscape gleamed in the distance. That could only mean that the pitch-dark area in the foreground had to be a totally unobstructed view of Lake Washington.

Raines motioned me into a chintz-covered easy chair that was as comfortable as it was stylish. "I'm having scotch," he said. "Care for a cocktail?"

"No, thanks," I told him. "Went off the sauce a few years ago."

Raines didn't lose a beat. "Club soda and lime then?"

"Sure," I answered. "That would be great."

While he busied himself at the bar, I glanced around the room, noticing the touches of what Jim Hunt refers to as "glitz and glam" that are his signature style, while at the same time taking his clients' individual tastes and preferences into account.

"How long have you known Jim Hunt?" Raines asked, handing me an icy rocks glass along with a coaster. The table next to my chair, also blatantly antique and costly, had a totally unblemished surface, and I didn't want to be responsible for leaving behind a water ring.

"Long time," I said. "Since the eighties, anyway. He did my first bachelor pad condo right after my divorce, and my second one, too, a few years later when I came into some money. Recently he helped my relatively new wife and me rehab a place up in Bellingham."

A knowing grin suffused Thomas Raines's face. "Wait a minute. Are you the guy who had to be black-mailed into unloading his recliner?"

"My reputation precedes me," I conceded, "and you're right. I'm the one. Jim's a great guy to work with as long as you do things his way."

Raines laughed aloud at that. "Isn't that the truth! Now, what can I do for you? I believe you said on the phone that this has something to do with your belief that Max's death wasn't accidental."

"Not my belief necessarily…" I began, but Raines held up his hand to stop me.

"Here's the thing, Beau. Having read some of Max's manuscript—not all of it, by any means—I couldn't help but recognize your name. From what he wrote about you, it's clear the two of you were never pals, so how is it you're the one here asking questions rather than a homicide detective from Seattle PD?"

"I used to work homicide at Seattle PD," I told him, "but as I said on the phone, their official investigation into the incident seems to have concluded that the house fire that killed Max was accidental in nature. Erin Howard, who is, to the best of my knowledge, Max's sole heir, disagrees with that finding. She's the one who contacted me about the situation."

"Ah, yes," Raines said. "That would be Erin Howard née Kelsey?"

I was taken aback by the idea that not only did Raines know about Erin Howard but he also knew she was formerly known as Erin Kelsey. "You know that how?" I asked.

"Because that's what Max's book *Tangled Web* is all about," Raines answered, "or, rather, that's what he told me it was going to be about. I sold the book based on the premise that it would be a retrospective of the cases Max had covered during his years as a crime reporter here in town. Once he started working on the book in earnest, however, the Kelsey case quickly got moved to the front of the queue, in part because of the personal betrayals involved. I don't think Max ever fully recovered from those, and I can't say that I blame him. In the last few weeks he indicated that something else had been added to the mix. He was excited about it, but he didn't divulge what that was—at least not to me. But are you saying Erin Howard is the one who asked you to investigate?"

"Not exactly," I hedged.

"What does that mean?"

"I said she contacted me, but the person who asked me to look into the situation was Max himself."

"Max did that?" Raines echoed. "Are you sure?"

"Yes, he sent Erin a text on Saturday saying that if anything happened to him, she should ask me to handle the investigation because he was afraid Seattle PD would cover up their findings, and he didn't think I would."

"So he thought he was in some kind of danger?" Raines asked.

"He didn't just *think* he was in danger," I corrected. "If what Erin believes is true, he *was* in danger. As I said, he sent the text about involving me to Erin on Saturday afternoon and died early Sunday morning. I'm wondering if what happened to him could have had something to do with whatever he was working on. I was hoping I might be able to get a look at the manuscript itself."

"Unfortunately, I can't help you there," Raines told me. "I sold *Tangled Web* for what's considered to be a reasonably good advance these days. The sale was based on the first three chapters of the book along with a detailed proposal. You're prominently featured in those first three chapters, by the way. But after that, once Max got into the material, he told me he was focusing far more on the Marcia Kelsey case than he had initially intended. As for anything he might have uncovered recently? I don't have a clue about that. His deadline was fast approaching, however, so I'm assuming there's quite a bit more to the manuscript now than what I've seen."

Raines paused for a moment. "What about Erin?" he asked. "Did Max show any of the material to her?"

"She claims not. He told her he'd give her first dibs

on reading it, but not until after he was completely finished."

We fell silent after that. Raines's glass was empty. He held it up to the light, rattling what remained of his ice cubes. "Care for another?" he asked.

"No, thanks. I'm good. But back to the manuscript. Did Max work on a computer?"

"I'm sure of it."

I sent myself a brief reminder to try to check with Seattle PD to see if any electronic devices had been recovered from the remains of Max's residence. In this instance having access to either his phone or laptop records could prove to be vital. An address book would put me in touch with his contacts. His word-processing program would let me see his progress on the unfinished manuscript and maybe even allow me to read it for myself. In addition, being able to view Max's phone records and calendar would bring me up to date on everything going on in his life in the days leading up to his death.

"Would it be possible for me to read the part of the book he had already given you?"

"No can do," Raines said at once. "As far as I'm concerned, that material is part of Max's estate. If, as you say, Erin Howard is Max's heir, she should be able to authorize my showing it to you, but I'm not sure how long it will take to clear all those legal hurdles. In the meantime, as I told you, my partner and I are heading out for Palm Springs tomorrow morning."

Had I still been an official cop investigating an official homicide, it would have been a simple matter to get a warrant and demand that he hand over the material. As far as I know, literary agents don't get the same kinds of client privilege protections that attorneys and doctors get. In this instance, however, I didn't have a leg to stand on.

"All right then," I said. "I don't like it, but I suppose that makes sense."

"Anything else?"

"Max was a client of yours, but I notice you weren't at his funeral."

"You're right. I wasn't," Raines answered. "I had a scheduling conflict—a long-standing conference call appointment with another of my authors, his editor, and a Hollywood producer. It can take months to get a whole bunch of people like that on the same page, to say nothing of on the same call at the same time. Besides," he added, "since Max was already dead, I doubt he was offended by my absence."

"An agent/client relationship, then," I suggested, "but not close friends."

"Yes, not that close."

"All right," I said, rising to my feet. "I guess I'll be going." I started toward the elevator and then, turned back to Raines and delivered my very best imitation of that great old-time television sleuth Columbo. "By the way, where were you on Saturday night?"

Surprisingly enough, although Raines clearly understood the implication behind my question, he didn't object or even hesitate before he answered. "Sid and I went to a dinner party right here in the Gardens. There were three other couples involved. Before it was all over, I'm afraid things got a little wild. If you check with your sources, I believe you'll discover that Sid and I were the subject of a noise complaint late that night, sometime between one and two. I believe there's also video footage of all comings and goings in the buildings here. You'll need to check with the association office in order to access them. I can tell you right now that Sid was in no condition to be driving back and forth to Queen Anne that night, and neither was I."

Having a couple of tipsy seventy-something gay guys hauled up on wild partying charges was a story that was too good to make up. It was also way too easy to check.

"All right then," I told him. "Asked and answered, so I'll be on my way."

Raines followed me as far as the elevator door. "On the off chance that Max's death wasn't an accident, that doesn't necessarily mean it's connected to the book, you know. There could be some other simple explanation."

"Like what?" I asked.

"It could be a hate crime."

"A hate crime?" I echoed.

"There are people like Sid and me and Jim Hunt who have been out of the closet for so long that we don't bother giving that aspect of our lives another moment's thought. But there are plenty of people out there who have never come out. It so happens Maxwell Cole was one of those. In awkward situations where no one is quite sure about if you is or if you ain't, there's a lot of room for serious misunderstandings."

I was utterly gobsmacked. "Wait a minute. Are you serious? You're saying Max was gay?"

"Sure," Raines answered. "Didn't you know that?"

Believe me when I tell you. I hadn't had a clue!

CHAPTER 15

I MULLED THAT unexpected bit of information all the way home and all the way through Lucy's and my dog walking exercise. It was a source of some humiliation to discover that the dog walking area recommended by Bob, the doorman, was a piece of lawn outside the church where I regularly attend AA meetings. He was right. There was a post with a supply of poop bags as well as a poop bag disposal container. How many times had I walked right past all that without paying any attention? Plenty.

That's one of the reasons eyewitness testimony is so unreliable. People notice what's important to them and forget the rest.

By the time Lucy and I got back upstairs, it was nearly nine. My noontime Top Ramen had long since evaporated. When I showed Lucy her new bed, she was happy to settle down on it. I took that as a sign that I was free to go.

I went back down in the elevator, out through the garage door, and hiked the few chilly blocks from Belltown Terrace to El Gaucho. It was cold enough to need a coat, but proximity to Puget Sound meant at least it wasn't freezing.

Back when Karen and I were first married and didn't have two nickels to rub together, the idea of going to El Gaucho for a meal would have been a splurge far beyond our means. Now it's more or less Mel's and my neighborhood joint, in the same way the Doghouse used to be, except the food is better and the atmosphere isn't nearly as dicey.

Roger, the maître d', greeted me by name and led me to a table in the bar where I ordered crab cakes along with a Caesar salad and let it go at that. I was about to order an O'Doul's, but realizing what time of night it was, I ordered coffee instead. For the kind of under-the-radar investigation I was launching, I needed to check in with some of my law enforcement contacts at times when they had the least amount of adult supervision. For tonight, at least, I'd be pulling a night shift.

A few minutes later, when the maître d' passed by my table again, I flagged him down. "It's such a shame about Maxwell Cole," I observed.

"Who?" Roger looked genuinely puzzled.

"Maxwell Cole," I repeated. "He's the guy who died in that house fire up on Queen Anne Hill last Sunday morning. He was here for dinner just last Friday."

"That's not a name I recognize, I'm afraid," Roger said with a frown. "You're sure he was here?"

Roger walked away but reappeared a few minutes later carrying the leather-bound volume that they usually keep at the front desk to track reservations. "About what time would Mr. Cole have been here?" Roger asked.

"Mel and I were about to have dessert as he was leaving, and we got here about seven thirty or so. He must have come sometime earlier than that."

Roger scanned the page. "Nope," he said at last. "No sign of anyone named Cole, so the reservation must have been under someone else's name."

When he walked away, I sat there sipping my coffee and wishing I knew exactly what the missing name was. There was a good chance that whoever Max had dined with on Friday night had been among the last people to see him alive.

I was partway through my Caesar salad when Mel called. "I just got home from a city council meeting," she complained. "Why didn't someone tell me that being a chief of police is way more about politics than it is about doing police work?"

In the run-up to Mel's accepting the position, I had a reasonably clear memory of a conversation in which I had attempted to make that precise point. Fortunately I was smart enough not to mention it right then. Sometimes silence is golden.

"So where are you?" she asked.

"El Gaucho," I said. "The cupboard was bare at the condo."

"It's pretty bare here, too," she said. "PBJ two nights in a row is not my idea of how to live."

My waiter delivered the crab cakes. I let them cool off without mentioning their arrival to Mel since she adores that particular dish.

"Did you get Rambo dropped off all right?"

"Not exactly," I said. "And it turns out her name is Lucy. Since Ken Purcell is most likely the guy who changed it to Rambo, we're changing it back."

"How would you know anything about how Rambo got her name, and what do you mean 'not exactly'?"

So while my crab cakes went from hot to cold, I told Mel the whole story.

"You're saying the dog is completely trained?"

"Completely," I said. "You should see what all she can do! Colleen McDaniel gave me a cheat sheet of commands for easy reference. But tell me one thing. When your officers responded to that domestic violence call, where was Lucy?"

"Locked in the bathroom, apparently, and tearing the place apart," Mel replied. "She was so ferocious that everybody at the scene was scared to death of her. Nancy was the only one who could get her to settle down."

Huddled in the backseat of Mel's Interceptor, Lucy hadn't looked particularly fierce. In fact she had looked downright harmless. That missing bit about the bathroom was one of those telling details my wife might have considered mentioning to me in passing, but she hadn't. It wasn't a lie, exactly—more like a sin of omission. Sort of like not mentioning the crab cakes.

Let's just call it tit for tat.

"All right," Mel said. "I'm off to bed. Talk to you in the morning."

"Sleep tight," I told her.

I finished my salad, mowed through my dead cold crab cakes—no fault of the chef's—swilled down two more cups of coffee, paid my bill, and headed out. As I was leaving, the lobby area was relatively deserted. Roger was there, but no customers.

"Would you mind doing me a favor?" I asked.

"Sure thing," he said. "What do you need?"

"Would you mind letting me take a photo of your reservation page from last Friday night? I've been asked to look into Mr. Cole's death, and it would be a big help to be able to contact some of the last people who saw him alive."

Roger hesitated, but only for a moment. Mel and I were regulars after all, and what I was asking must have seemed reasonable enough. He thumbed back to the proper page and then turned the book in my direction. I took several pictures, just to be on the safe side, and made for the door as the next group of exiting diners filed out toward the lobby.

Back in the condo I found Lucy stretched out on her new bed with no evidence that she had moved a muscle in my absence.

Phone in hand, I headed for the family room. I checked out the photos I'd just taken and found them to be wanting—which is to say, fuzzily out of focus and impossible to read.

Knowing Todd Hatcher's knack for computerized wizardry, I dialed his number.

"What's up?" he wanted to know.

"Can I put you on retainer?" I asked.

"For what?"

"Maxwell Cole had dinner with someone at El Gaucho two nights before he died, and it would be helpful to know who that person was. I took a photo of the restaurant's reservation register, but it's not exactly legible. I'm hoping you'll be able to enhance it for me."

"No problem," Todd said, "and no payment, either."

"Thanks," I told him.

After sending the e-mail, I put in a call to Dr. Rosemary Mellon at the King County medical examiner's office. Mel and I first encountered Dr. Mellon—or Dr. Roz, as she prefers to be called—when she was a relative newcomer to the ME's office. We were investigating the deaths of a Seattle homicide detective named Delilah Ainsworth and that of a former partner of mine, a long-retired and exceedingly crooked cop named Rory (Mac) McPherson.

When I'd had my knee replacement surgery, a bad case of opiate-induced hallucinations had brought me face-to-face with a very old cold case. The grisly murder of teenager Monica Wellington was the first homicide I ever worked as a full-fledged detective, and it had never been solved. In hopes of gaining permission to reexamine the case, I had gone looking for help in my old stomping grounds at Seattle PD. Detective Ainsworth was the one who had gotten the call.

In the course of the investigation, when both she and Mac were found dead, the initial assumption had been one of murder/suicide. Cops on the scene theorized that, after shooting Delilah, Mac had committed suicide by locking himself in his garage along with an idling motor vehicle. Dr. Roz, a relative stranger to me at the time, was the one who had set the record straight by determining that the two deaths were actually the result of a double homicide. In addition, Dr. Mellon had tracked down some critical and long-neglected DNA evidence that had put us on the trail of Monica's killer once and for all.

When Dr. Roz first arrived at the ME's office in Seattle, she was regarded as something of a maverick. Several years later her designation as maverick still held sway, possibly even more so than in the beginning. As far as she's concerned, her role as a medical examiner was more of a sacred calling than it was a job. She's someone who, as the saying goes, faithfully spoke for the dead, and she was utterly passionate about doing so. She moved to Seattle from Chicago because, as she told me once, "Chicago has too much snow and too many homicides." She prefered to work the night shift because "that's where the action is." And because she had zero interest in so-called career advancements, she wasn't afraid to color outside the lines.

"Why if it isn't my old friend J.P.," she said, obviously lifting my information from caller ID. "Long time no see. Now that S.H.I.T. is shut down, what are you up to these days?"

"This and that," I said disingenuously.

Dr. Roz laughed aloud. "Liar, liar, pants on fire!" she declared. "You wouldn't be calling me at work at ten o'clock at night if you didn't have a damned good reason to do so."

"You've got me there," I admitted.

"So?" she prodded.

"Before I say another word, be advised," I warned her. "It's a case where I've got zero official standing."

"Which one?"

"I've been asked to look into the death of Maxwell Cole."

"Oh, well," she said. "That's a hot mess."

Dr. Roz's penchant for unrepentant gallows humor might possibly be another reason she was remoted, as opposed to demoted, from Chicago to Seattle. I get a kick out of her off-the-wall humor, but in my experience, higher-ups—the people hanging on to the brass ring for dear life—find it very easy to take offense at the slightest little thing.

"Yes," I agreed, "but does it happen be a hot mess you can discuss?"

"On the record or off?" she asked.

"Off," I said, "as in just between old friends."

"All right then," Roz said, "here goes. I'm calling it as an accidental death. It shouldn't come as a big surprise to anyone that knocking off a few stiff ones and then taking a sleeping aid before crawling into bed to smoke a cigar is a pretty bad idea, especially if there happens to be an oxygen tank in use at the same time."

During my years in Homicide I learned that fires are often set in hopes of covering up evidence connected to some other crime, one that directly preceded the arson. Most crooks aren't nearly as smart as they think they are. A lot of them are school dropouts who, as a result, are sadly lacking in terms of basic scientific knowledge. They have no idea, for example, that the human body consists of approximately 60 percent water. That means that trying to use arson in order to disappear incriminating evidence in a homicide case is generally a bad idea. Absent a crematorium designed especially for that purpose, human bodies are deucedly difficult to transform from flesh and blood into ash.

"Wait, the guy was burned to a crisp, but you were able to do a tox screen?" I asked.

"He wasn't burned to a crisp," Roz said. "He made it out of the bedroom, but that was it. By the time the firefighters reached him, he had some second- and third-degree burns, but smoke inhalation is what really got him, probably sooner than later."

"Thank God for small blessings," I said.

"You can say that again," Roz agreed. "The victim was unresponsive at the scene, but he wasn't dead. The tox screen results still aren't back, but his blood alcohol level was off the charts. The EMTs said they found the remains of a partially smoked cigar in the room. In other words, the man was blitzed out of his gourd and smoking in bed. What more do you want?"

"So you're saying his death was accidental then—with no wiggle room?"

"Not as far as I'm concerned."

"Do you happen to have the name of the lead homicide investigator on the case?"

"There is no lead homicide investigator," Roz replied, "only the duty sergeant from ABS."

ABS stands for Arson Bomb Squad. In terms of Seattle PD's callout order, when there's a fire that may result in injury or death, Dispatch summons the on-duty sergeant from ABS. He's the one who makes the final determination about whether or not to call in homicide detectives.

"And the sergeant in question would be?"

"Al Thorne," Roz answered at once. "Sergeant Albert Thorne. Do you want his numbers?"

Getting Thorne's numbers from someone else would mean my having to go through channels, a course of action I definitely didn't want to tackle.

"Absolutely," I told her.

Al Thorne's name happened to be one I recognized. I suppose everyone who signs up to become a cop does so with illusions of somehow saving the world. Inside that group, however, there are two distinct subgroups. The first consists of the ambitious ones who are determined to go to the head of the class no matter what. Those are the guys who end up being the stars—what I like to call the FBOAs—Future Brass of America. With their eyes focused on the prize, they mostly keep their noses clean. They spend hours writing impeccable reports in which all the *i*'s are properly dotted and the *t*'s are properly crossed and that consistently show them in the best possible light. Those are the guys and gals, for that matter, who will make a big show of following all the rules exactly, especially the most insane ones, and you can damned well bet that they will be one hundred percent politically correct at all times—at least in public.

On the opposite side of the coin are the worker bees—the ones who want to be left alone to do their jobs so they can go home safely at the end of their shifts. They have zero interest in climbing the rungs of departmental ladders. Their reports are probably less than perfect, but they perform their jobs dutifully and with workmanlike attention to detail. If they do happen to bend a rule or two now and then? Too bad. And because they have no delusions of grandeur about rising to the top of any given heap, they don't give a crap about being politically correct, either.

A notable exception to those two generalizations would be my wife, Mel Soames, who happens to be an interesting amalgam of both—full-tilt brass and worker bee.

Sergeant Al Thorne, a known entity, was an old hand and definitely a member of the worker bee category. He's several years younger than I was, but he had long been to Seattle PD's Arson Bomb Squad what I was to Homicide. Once he got where he wanted to be, he stayed put. Just knowing that he was involved in Max's case buoyed my spirits. He was a lot more likely to talk to me than some young hotshot homicide cop who's still trying to learn up from down and who would have immediately dismissed me as a pathetic has-been.

"Anything else?" Rosemary Mellon asked once she finished giving me the phone numbers.

"Not right now, Dr. Roz," I told her. "Thanks for the help."

I hung up. At that very moment, Lucy appeared in the doorway of the family room and stood staring at me. I am trainable. I got the message from those impenetrable black eyes. I also got the leash. We rode down in the elevator, went out through the locking gates on P-1, and walked kitty-corner across the street.

Out there in the dark and the cold, I was a bit startled to find that Lucy and I were not alone. Another man, bundled against the cold, was walking what looked to me like a pit bull. To my surprise, neither dog took much interest in the other.

"Fine-looking animal you've got there," the man said, nodding in Lucy's direction. "What's his name?"

"Thanks," I said, "her name's Lucy."

"Surprised to have company out here," he continued. "Billy Bob and me usually have this park all to ourselves this time of night."

"We're a little new at this," I said. "You live around here?"

"You could say that," he replied with a mirthless chuckle. "We're in the neighborhood."

Lucy did what needed doing, after which I busied myself doing my part. By the time we were done, Billy Bob and his owner seemed to have vanished into midair. Only as we headed back into Belltown Terrace did I notice him unloading tarps and blankets from a parked grocery cart and setting up camp inside a small sheltered alcove outside one of the building's emergency exits.

When I first moved to Belltown Terrace, the Regrade was relatively free of crazed bicycle riders, homeless people, and drug dealers. In those days the most challenging enforcement areas in the downtown Seattle area had been down around Pioneer Square and at Third and Pike. Now those issues are everywhere.

I guess that's what the city fathers really meant when they told us we should "share the wealth."

CHAPTER 16

IN THE OLD days, I would have come back inside, picked up the phone, and dialed Al Thorne's number on the spot. Since he'd been working the third watch on Sunday morning, there was a good chance he was either on the job or not sleeping anyway. In this case, however, I decided it was time for me to hit the hay.

I moved Lucy's new bed from the living room, where I had placed it originally, to the bedroom. When I got into my bed, she seemed content enough to climb into hers. I awakened the next morning, fighting to breathe, and it wasn't because I was having a heart attack. The huge black dog was looming over me, breathing in whenever I breathed out and leaving me gasping for air.

The clock said 7:30. Wishing profoundly that the condo had a doggy door, I crawled out of bed, threw on some clothes. Before Lucy and I made our trek downstairs, I stuffed a Ziploc bag filled with some of Lucy's kibble in my pocket, just in case Billy Bob and his human companion were still camped out across the street.

By the time we got there, however, they had already packed up and gone elsewhere. Lucy and I were back inside and riding the elevator when my phone rang. Expecting a morning wake-up call from Mel, I was surprised to see my daughter-in-law's name in the caller ID window.

"Morning, Cherisse," I said. "How are things?"

"I'm taking the day off," she announced. "I was wondering if I could come up and see you."

That's the weird things about cell phones. In the old days, when Ma Bell was the only game in town, if I placed a call to my mother, say, I was pretty sure that when she answered, she'd be standing by the black rotary dial phone mounted on the wall next to the kitchen table. The moment she said hello, I could picture the scene exactly. When Cherisse asked if she could come visit, she most likely thought she'd have to drive up to Bellingham. She had no way of knowing I had answered the phone from the elevator of our downtown Seattle condo.

"No problem," I said. "As it happens, I'm here in town at the moment. When would you like to get together and where? Would you like me to stop by the house?"

"No," she said quickly—a little too quickly. "Don't come here. I'd rather meet somewhere else."

A little warning bell sounded in my head. Something was amiss. "Name the time and place," I said. "I'll be there."

"Julia's in Wallingford?" she asked tentatively. "In about an hour?"

"Cherisse," I said, "is something wrong? Are you okay? Is Scott?"

"He's fine," she said, again a little too quickly. "I just need to talk to you."

I've learned over time that when women tell me something is "fine," it ain't necessarily so.

I dished up Lucy's food and water and then showered and dressed while she was eating. When I was ready to leave, I was up in the air about what I should do with the dog. Should I take Lucy along or leave her at home? Without knowing how long I'd be gone, there wasn't much choice.

"Do you want to go?" I asked, picking up the leash.

The dog's answer was a definitive yes. With her dancing at the door, it was all I could do to fasten the leash. We drove without incident to Wallingford, where I was amazed to find on-street parking. As I got out of the car, Lucy seemed poised to leap after me.

"Wait in the car," I told her. It wasn't exactly "Wait on the rug," but close enough. Then, switching my phone to silent, I went inside.

When I arrived, Cherisse was already seated at a table with a menu laid out in front of her. Ordinarily, Cherisse is a beautiful young woman—a brunette with flashing brown eyes. Today that beauty was lacking. She looked wan—her skin color was sallow. There were dark circles under her eyes, and she looked as though she hadn't slept in days.

"Hey, Cherisse," I said cheerily, slipping onto the chair directly across from her. "How are things?"

For an answer she simply burst into tears.

Like most men my age—no, like most men of *any* age, I don't do well with weeping women. I'm always at a loss about what I should say or do, so in this case,

I said nothing. I simply let her cry. Other people in the room noticed. From the stink-eyed looks leveled in my direction, customers and waitstaff alike held me entirely responsible for whatever was wrong. As far as they were concerned, Cherisse's meltdown was all my fault.

Finally she managed to get a grip. "Sorry," she mumbled, using an already soggy tissue to blow her nose and wipe her eyes.

I reached across the table and covered her hand with mine. "Is there anything I can do to help?"

"I wish you were my dad," she said.

Oh boy! At that point, so did I, but that wasn't possible, because Cherisse's father, Pierre Madrigal, had succumbed to a recurrence of prostate cancer years earlier, soon after Scott and Cherisse's fairy-tale wedding on a beach on Oahu.

The two kids had met as undergraduates while earning degrees in electrical engineering down in California. At the time, Cherisse, a native of France, had been in this country on a student visa. Their wedding, several years later, had pulled her out of the immigration limbo world of H-1B visas by giving her access first to a green card and eventually U.S. citizenship.

As far as I could tell, Cherisse and Scott were getting along fine. Other than Scott's tearful fit the other day, I had seen no signs of trouble anywhere along the way, but what do parents ever know about their kids' relationships? What does anyone ever know about what goes on behind closed doors in someone else's life? Maybe what I had viewed as a happily-ever-after story was in fact one of those complicated sham green-card marriages. Sitting across the table from her, I worried that perhaps, since Cherisse now had her U.S. citizenship in hand, she was about to throw poor Scotty under the bus.

"I'm sorry about your father," I said at last, breaking a long silence during which my phone had vibrated twice inside my pocket, signaling two different calls. "I'm sure you miss him terribly."

I think Mel would have been incredibly proud of me for making such an adroit deflection.

"I do," Cherisse said. "Most people can talk to their mothers about things like this, but not me. I was always closer to my dad."

I felt a stab of envy. I doubted my own daughter, Kelly, would ever say she was closer to me than she was to her mother—never in a million years.

"Things like what?" I asked.

"Like having kids," she said.

Suddenly I was transported back to the previous Friday, when Scotty had been out of his head on post-op anesthetic and blabbing to me about his being too old to have kids. And now here was Cherisse broaching the same subject? With me? Her father-in-law? Unfortunately I already knew way more about this than I should have. I played dumb.

Our waitress came over with her ticket pad at the ready. We both ordered coffee and said we weren't ready to order food.

"What about having kids?" I asked once the waitress left.

Cherisse searched through her purse, took out a single piece of paper, and pushed it across the table to me.

It resembled a very blurry photograph, but it wasn't exactly an appropriate time to go searching for my reading glasses.

"What's this?" I asked.

"It's from an ultrasound," Cherisse said, "proof of life. I'm pregnant."

That wasn't at all the news I had been dreading, but there it was. I knew that Scott and Cherisse hadn't planned on having kids ever, but despite all that, they were about to. Surprise, surprise. That happens. All the time. If you don't believe it, just ask my daughter . . . or my mother.

"We discussed the topic while we were still dating," Cherisse went on. "We always said we weren't going to have kids. And we've been using protection, but . . ."

"It didn't work."

She nodded miserably. "When I tried to tell Scott—when I tried to bring it up—he had such a bad reaction, I just couldn't tell him. I couldn't, and now I don't know what to do. If he's completely opposed to having kids, maybe I should just go ahead, get it over with, and have an abortion."

Now I was totally and completely out of my depth! Where the hell was Mel when I needed her? If Cherisse was pregnant with Scott's child, that baby was my grandchild. Mine! The last thing I wanted was to miss the chance to meet and cherish that unknown little one. And yet . . . I had no right to tell Scott and Cherisse how to live their lives. Except she had asked for my advice, right? And in a way, so had Scott.

I knew I was walking an emotional tightrope here. I couldn't risk saying something that would betray the unwitting confidences Scott had shared with me. I also couldn't leave poor Cherisse sitting there trapped in such abject misery. Another deflection was in order.

"You love Scott, right?"

She nodded.

"And he loves you?"

"Yes."

"You have to talk to him about this, then," I said. "You have to. I don't think it's so much that he doesn't want to have a baby—this baby or any other. I think he's afraid he won't measure up and be a good enough father."

"You think that's all it is?"

"I know that's all it is. He's over forty, he's recently embarked on an entirely new career, and he's a Beaumont."

"What's that supposed to mean?"

"That Scott has a terminal case of thinking he's not good enough. It's one of those unfortunate family traits that are passed on from generation to generation."

I had noticed our server keeping a wary eye on our table. Now that Cherisse seemed to have recovered her composure, the waitress returned to take our two orders—mine for ham and eggs and Cherisse's for nothing but dry toast.

"Queasy?" I asked as the waitress walked away.

Cherisse nodded. "Very," she said.

During that brief order-taking interlude, I searched my soul for the right thing to say. Still coming up empty, I dragged out my reading glasses and then picked up the black-and-white photo that still lay on the table. After peering at it for some time, I eventually made out the ghostly image of a baby.

"If your father were here, what would he want you to

do about this?" I asked, with my eyes still on the ultra-sound image.

"Keep him."

Him? So this baby wasn't just an it—he was my grandson!

"What about you? What do you want to do?"

"The same—keep him."

And that's when the answer came to me—like a bolt out of the blue—in the form of a mostly unwanted dog, one who was even now sitting outside in the car, waiting for me.

"I'm guessing you know that Mel and I have been talking about getting a dog—sort of a maybe, maybe-not situation?"

Cherisse nodded.

"It turns out now we have one."

She looked surprised—more like astonished. "Really?"

I nodded. "Her name's Lucy, and take my word for it—she's an ugly-looking beast. When I first met her late on Sunday afternoon, I was more than a little wary, but do you know what's happened? In just a matter of days, that damned dog has grown on me—and I have a doggy door, forty-plus pounds of kibble, four dog dishes, and three dog beds to prove it."

Cherisse gave me a faint smile. "So?"

"There's a huge difference between wanting or not wanting a hypothetical dog and meeting a real one. I think the same thing will hold true here."

I handed the paper back to Cherisse. "All you have to do is show Scott this," I continued. "Once he sees this little person, he's going to want him, too."

"You think so?"

"Yes, I do," I told her. "I believe it with all my heart."

The truth is, I'm every bit as much of a Beaumont as my son is. What I was hoping, of course, with my out-of-sight fingers crossed under the table, was that this little riff of *Father Knows Best* would be good enough to do the trick.

CHAPTER 17

As Cherisse and I left Julia's after breakfast, we stopped by the car long enough for me to officially introduce Lucy to my daughter-in-law. On the way back to Belltown Terrace, with Lucy's head once again resting on my shoulder, I attempted to explain to the dog how grateful I was that she had helped me out of a tight spot with Cherisse and Scott. Did she get the message? Maybe. Her lanky tail thumped against the back of the front passenger seat a couple of times.

I waited until Lucy and I were back upstairs at the condo before answering any missed calls. One of the buzzes on my phone had been from Mel. She had left a message saying she was jammed up with meetings all day and wondering when I'd be home. Would Rambo (Mel had yet to make the name transition over to Lucy) and I be coming up to Bellingham for the weekend, or should she plan on joining us in Seattle? Gratified to know that Mel actually missed me, and hoping to spend at least part of the weekend working on the Maxwell Cole situation, I sent her a text suggesting that she come south once she finished up at work, adding that, for today only, she was in charge of dinner arrangements.

This constituted a clear win/win for me. That way I wouldn't be making some kind of dinner reservation for which Mel might or might not arrive on time. And presumably, if she picked up some kind of takeout along the way, she and her relatively hot food would arrive simultaneously.

The other buzz announced an e-mail from Todd with a subject line that said, "With regard to your earlier question." The message included a downloadable PDF and a single telephone number—one with a 360 prefix, which meant it was somewhere in Washington State but outside the Seattle area. Once I downloaded and opened the PDF, I saw a photocopy of what was apparently a Washington State driver's license. I had to enlarge the image several times before I was able to read it.

Once I did, it stopped me cold. The name on the license was that of John David Madsen, with an address in Chehalis, Washington. But what really got my attention was the familiar face of the man in the photo, because I had just seen him—hurriedly ducking out through the back door after Max's funeral. In the photo the beard was much shorter than he wore it now and so was the hair, but this was definitely the same guy. No wonder that he had seemed familiar but unplaceable, and no wonder he had been in such a hurry to leave. The man I had once known as Pete Kelsey had wanted to escape the funeral without having to encounter his estranged foster daughter.

Todd had thoughtfully tracked down Madsen's phone

number for me and sent it along. I dialed the number at once but got no answer. When the prompt asked me if I wanted to leave a message, I didn't. I thought it was best that when I finally did get around to speaking to John Madsen, it would be a surprise.

Temporarily stymied on that score, I dialed another number—this time the one Dr. Roz had given me as Albert Thorne's home number.

"Hey, Beau," Al said once I identified myself. Obviously Al was someone who still used his landline phone; otherwise he would have known who was calling without my having to tell him. "How's it hanging?" he asked. "And how the hell did you get this number?"

Answering the second question took a fair amount of explanation and lots of detail. "So let me get this straight," Al said at last when I finally finished my long spiel. "Maxwell Cole sent this Erin person an e-mail saying that he was worried someone might knock him off and telling her that he wanted you to investigate whatever might happen. In the process, he also asked her to invite you to his funeral?"

"That's about the size of it."

"If he was that worried someone was after him, why the hell didn't he call the cops his own damned self?"

"Believe me," I said, "I've asked myself that same question and come up with no reasonable answers."

"Regardless," Al said, "I'm telling you right here and now that the fire that killed Maxwell Cole wasn't arson."

"You know that because…?" I prompted.

"No multiple ignition spots, for one thing," Al told me. "No sign of any accelerants, either, other than the spilled bottle of scotch that got knocked onto the floor beside his bed. I'm sure that flamed up like nobody's business. I've seen this scenario way too often, Beau. You drink yourself into oblivion and then go nighty-night with a smoke of some kind in your hand, what do you expect? But given all that, you still think this wasn't an accident?"

"I'd like to be sure."

Al sighed. "Anybody ever mention that you're a complete pain in the ass?"

I couldn't help but laugh aloud at that. "Plenty of people; plenty of times. You're certainly not the first."

Al laughed, too. "Now tell me again, when's the last time you saw our mutual dead guy?"

"Last Friday night late as he was leaving a restaurant here in the Regrade—El Gaucho. He told me he was working on something—an old case maybe—and he was concerned about the possibility of some kind of pushback. On Saturday he sent Erin that text I told you about, urging her to contact me if anything happened to him. In other words, between Friday evening and Saturday afternoon, things must have changed for the worse, or he would have spoken to me about it directly the night before, right?"

"Makes sense, I suppose," Al agreed. "So what exactly are you looking for?"

"What I need more than anything is to locate one or more of Max's electronic devices—a computer, a cell phone, or an iPad. Once we find them, Erin can go through the legal hoops to give me access to his files. So that's my question: did someone from Homicide collect any of Max's equipment as evidence and cart it out of the house on Sunday morning?"

"Not on my watch," Al assured me. "In dealing with a fire involving possible injuries or fatalities, it's ABS's

job to make the call as to whether or not Homicide
is brought in on the case. Based on what I saw at the
scene, I opted to leave Homicide out of the loop. Didn't
think they were needed. And I certainly never autho-
rized that anything at all be removed from the house.
Once the fire was out, it was Seattle FD's job to board
up the place and install crime scene tape."

"In other words, unless there was interference from
looters of some kind after the firefighters left, whatever
was in the house at the time of the fire should still be
there?" I asked.

"Should be."

A long silence followed. I worked my way through
college as a Fuller Brush man. I suppose Fuller Brush
boy would be closer to the mark, but my manager back
in that long-gone era of door-to-door sales taught me
that if you're in some kind of negotiation and the other
person goes completely quiet on you, it usually means
your opposition is busy considering his or her options.
In that case, the first person to open his trap is bound
to lose.

"Tell me about this Erin person again—your
client…" Al began.

"Erin Howard is a friend rather than a client," I corrected.

"Whatever," Al said impatiently. "Whoever she is,
she's of the opinion that somebody came into Maxwell
Cole's house, somehow doped him up with a combination of sleep meds and booze, lit up his cigar, and then
walked out of the house and left him to die? A scenario
like that doesn't seem very realistic to me."

I had to admit, the whole thing seemed far-fetched

to me as well. "You're saying there were no signs of any kind of struggle?"

Al laughed. "Come on, J.P. You know the drill. By the time the fire department finishes putting out a fire, you'd better believe there are going to be signs of a struggle—all kinds of signs. But you're asking if there were any troubling signs of a struggle that preceded the fire, in this case, I'd have to say no. I saw no indication of forced entry or of any kind of confrontation between the victim and someone else. By the way, you ever hear of an attorney by the name of Delia Rojas?"

"Can't say that I have."

"It turns out she's Maxwell Cole's attorney—at least that's who she claims to be. She left a message for me late last night, and I called her back this morning. She's attempting to initiate the homeowner's insurance claim, and time is of the essence. In situations like this, water damage from fighting the fire can be far worse than that caused by the fire itself. In order to get the cleanup ball rolling, a claims adjustor needs to have access to the dwelling. Since the residence is currently red-flagged, no one is allowed inside until a building inspector from the city of Seattle deems the structure safe. It so happens, I've got an appointment to meet up with the inspector at three o'clock this afternoon."

"What are you telling me?"

"I'm saying we could go through channels and ask the attorney if she'd be willing to allow you to go inside or…"

"Or what?"

"Or maybe you'd like to do a ride-along."

As far as my investigation was concerned, getting a

firsthand look at the crime scene would be invaluable. "You bet," I said at once. "I'll be there with bells on. Should I meet you there?"

"No, sir," Al said. "When I said, 'ride along,' that's exactly what I meant. You tell me where you are, and I'll come pick you up. That way, when you arrive on the scene in an official vehicle with your very own hard hat, the building inspector won't be any the wiser. Unless you get hurt, of course. In which case my ass is grass."

"Fair enough," I said.

"There's one more condition," Al added. "Nothing gets touched and nothing leaves the scene. If you find one of Mr. Cole's so-called devices, it stays right where it is until we get official permission from either Ms. Rojas or that Erin person saying you're allowed to touch it. Got it?"

"Understood," I told him.

I gave him my address and got off the phone feeling like I'd won a lotto jackpot. Al Thorne had just given my "unofficial" investigation a big step up. As far as I was concerned, it didn't get much better than that.

To his credit, Al was good to his word. When he showed up outside Belltown Terrace at ten to three in one of the old, clunky metallic blue departmental sedans, I was already down in the lobby waiting. He had to move a pair of hard hats out of the way in order to clear a spot on the passenger seat so I could have a place to sit. He gave my clothing—a pair of slacks, a white shirt, and a sport jacket—a once-over and followed with a disapproving shake of his head.

"You're not exactly dressed for the occasion," he warned.

When we stopped in front of Max's house on Bigelow and stepped out of the car, I noticed that he was wearing a full-body khaki jumpsuit embroidered with the monogram ABS just above the Seattle PD emblem. Knowing whatever clothing he was wearing underneath was fully protected, I felt a little envious. Still, if he had brought along an extra jumpsuit for me to wear, we both would have been walking dangerously close to the line of my impersonating a police officer—a crime, by the way. Later when Al introduced me to the building inspector as his "colleague, J. P. Beaumont," we were both pretty close to that slippery slope.

The building inspector, however, couldn't have cared less who either of us was. Accepting our presence as the real deal, he demanded no badges or identification of any sort. Armed with his own hard hat, jumpsuit, and clipboard, he marched purposefully up to the house and used a battery-powered screwdriver to remove the sheet of plywood someone had screwed into the frame to cover the front door. I noticed that all the windows had been similarly shuttered.

"Here," Al said, handing me a miniature Maglite. "We're both going to need one of these."

We stepped through the door and into an evil-smelling murky darkness. Saturated wall-to-wall carpet bubbled and squished underfoot. The place recked of smoke and mold and mildew. Firefighters had managed to confine the fire to the upper floor of the house, but the water used to fight the flames had run downstream, soaking everything on the lower floor into a sodden mess.

While the building inspector did his thing, Al and I took a look around, including making a brief foray into the burned-out upstairs bedroom. A charred booze bottle lay on the floor next to a mound of naked bedsprings. I recognized the melted remains of Max's three-pronged cane, lying among what appeared to be the ruins of an overturned bedside table. Nearby something shiny caught the beam from Al's flashlight and glittered in the darkness.

Al bent over to examine the item more closely. "Rolex," he pronounced, but he left the watch where it was. Nearby lay a tangle of bare wires, all of them devoid of their respective casings. Those were readily identifiable as several different charger cables, but there was no sign of any accompanying devices.

I flashed my light around the charred ceiling and eventually found what I was looking for. "Isn't that a smoke detector?" I asked.

Al went over to where I was pointing and stared up at it. "Yup," he said. "That's what it is all right. Looks like the battery's been removed, most likely by the dead guy himself. You'd be surprised how often that happens. People get sick and tired of listening to that annoying new-battery warning, so they disable the damned things, which, if you ask me, is pretty damned stupid."

"Do you mind taking a look in the bathroom?"

"Why?"

"Just curious," I said.

The bathroom was severely smoke damaged but otherwise mostly intact. "What?" Al asked.

"Can you open the medicine chest?"

Shaking his head in annoyance, Al complied, prying the medicine cabinet door open with the point of a pencil. "What now?" he asked.

I shone my light across the contents: toothbrush, toothpaste, shaving equipment, cologne, nail clippers, and several varieties of over-the-counter cold medicine. The cabinet also included a hair brush and a jar of mustache wax, neither of which, sadly enough, Max had needed to use in the recent past. The top shelf contained a lineup of prescription bottles, but an examination of those didn't yield what I was looking for—a brand-name sleep aid. I realized that didn't mean one hadn't existed. A plastic prescription bottle might well have melted into charred invisibility in the debris of that burned-out bedside table.

At that point we heard the building inspector coming up the stairs. Al used the pencil to close the medicine cabinet and off we went, back down to the main floor. I had been inside Max's house only once before, and that had been years earlier, in the course of the Marcia Kelsey homicide investigation. Max and I had sat in this very living room for our heart-to-heart talk, and I remembered that there had been a den of some kind just off the living room. If Max had been using either a laptop or a desktop to work on his manuscript, it seemed likely that was where we'd find it.

Once inside the murky room, we discovered it to be more of a library than it was a den. The shelves sagged under the heavy weight of bulging, water-saturated books. There was a desk of sorts—an old-fashioned library table. Both ends of it were covered with loose papers that had welded themselves into sodden masses of mush. In the middle of the table, however, was a four-foot-wide clear spot. And on the floor on the far side of the table lay one of those multiple-outlet extension cords. Situated next to that was a perfectly recognizable cable modem along with an older model daisy-wheel printer.

"The modem's here and so's the printer," I told Al, "so where the hell is his computer?"

"Here you go again," Al grumbled, "back to the same old song and dance. But let me ask you this. If a crook went to the trouble of setting the place on fire, why would any bad guy in his right mind take off with a computer that, depending on its age, wouldn't be worth more than two hundred bucks on the open market and leave behind a perfectly good Rolex?"

I didn't have a ready answer for that one, but once a homicide cop, always a homicide cop. Instead I posed a question of my own. "Do you happen to have an evidence bag on you?"

With an annoyed sigh, Al extracted a clear bag from his hip pocket. "What exactly would you like me to bag and tag?"

"That extension cord," I said, pointing. "Max lived here alone, so his prints should be on that cord. If he had a cleaning service of some kind, his housekeeper's prints might be there as well. But if someone else, some third party, was in the house that night and if they'd already started the fire upstairs, they would have been totally focused on getting the hell out of Dodge. Supposing they came down here in search of Max's computer. Even if the guy had worn gloves the rest of the time, he might have thought he was in the clear enough to risk stripping them off down here. After all, he fully expected that oxygen tank would blow sky-high any minute and that the house would burn to the ground."

Al gave me a dubious smirk. "You really think we're going to find a killer's prints on this extension cord? You want to bet money on that?"

"Sure," I said. "How about ten bucks? Just take the

damned thing down to the crime lab and have somebody check it out."

"Okay," Al conceded, "ten bucks it is."

By the time the building inspector reappeared in our midst on the ground floor, the extension cord—evidence bag and all—had disappeared into one of the capacious pockets on Al's ABS jumpsuit.

"We're done here," the building inspector told us. "I'll notify you once I finish filing my report so you can green-light the insurance folks. The sooner they get this nasty mess of wet carpet dragged out of here, the better."

CHAPTER 18

WHEN AL AND I headed back down Queen Anne for Belltown Terrace, I was surprised to see that it was almost five. We had spent the better part of two hours poking around in the murky ruins of Maxwell Cole's home. I didn't remember touching anything other than the sodden carpet, but my clothing—my very pores—reeked of smoke and mold.

Lucy came to the door to greet me. I was sure she was overdue for a walk, but after giving me a cursory sniff, she sneezed and then stalked back to her bed in the kitchen. Obviously my unpleasant mixture of odors offended her as much as it did me. I went straight into my bathroom, where I stripped off my clothes and stepped into the shower. When I finished, I noticed that although I was now smoke-free, the bathroom sure as hell wasn't. As soon as I was dressed, I retrieved my smoke-drenched clothing and shoes and banished them to the lanai just off the bedroom in hopes of airing them out.

Emerging from the bedroom, I discovered that a

plastic bag of takeout food had magically appeared on the kitchen counter. That meant Mel was already home, and you could color me surprised about that. Even in Bellingham she seldom arrived home before six. The fact that she had made the eighty-mile drive to our Seattle condo prior to five thirty told me she had left work far earlier than usual.

Curious about what was for dinner, I sorted through the three food containers inside the bag. The two larger ones, labeled with a Magic Marker, contained beef stew and Caesar salad, respectively. No doubt the smaller one contained dressing for the salad.

Leaving the food where it was, I decided to take the dog out for her somewhat delayed walk. Since she wasn't in her usual spot in the kitchen, I went looking for her. "Hey, Lucy," I called. "Do you want to go get busy?"

When there was no response, I headed for Mel's room in search of both wife and dog. It hadn't taken long after the wedding for Mel and me to discover that the condo's bathroom and closet—which had worked just fine during my bachelor existence—were totally inadequate for the two of us together. We overcame the woeful lack of closet and counter space by converting the guest suite into Mel's private domain, giving her not only a separate sitting room/dressing room combo but also her own private bathroom and closet, which counted for a lot in her book.

I found Mel's purse and briefcase in her room. Her uniform had been draped over the back of the love seat. Her high heels and pantyhose had been abandoned nearby, but Mel was nowhere in sight and neither was Lucy. Doubling back to the kitchen, I noticed for the first time that Lucy's leash, which I had left hanging on the doorknob, was no longer there, either. That's when I pulled out my phone and dialed Mel's number.

"Where are you?" I asked.

"I took Rambo for a run," she panted into the phone. "We're down in Myrtle Edwards Park."

"Okay," I said. "Call me when you're on your way home. I'll have dinner on the table."

I puttered around the kitchen—setting the table, loading the stew into a microwavable bowl, and tossing the dressing into the salad before dividing it into separate bowls. But while I was performing all those mindless tasks, I was worrying, because I had the distinct impression something was wrong. Chief Melissa Soames wasn't one to take off work early on a Friday afternoon. To my knowledge, this was the first time it had happened. As for going on a run in the middle of a wintry late afternoon squall? That wasn't a good sign, either.

Mel and Lucy turned up forty-five minutes later, both of them soaking wet. One look at Mel's face told me I had been right to be worried. Something was definitely amiss. While she went to shower and change, I toweled off the dog and fed her. By the time Mel emerged from the shower, wearing a robe, I had dinner on the table.

"So what gives?" I asked, handing her a glass of Cabernet.

"It's that obvious?"

"Pretty much."

"Somebody posted Ken Purcell's bail," she answered bleakly. "Just like that, he's back on the streets. I let Nancy know, and we also informed the people at the shelter, so they'll know to keep an eye out for him, but still . . ."

Mel has been a cop for a long time. By now she should be accustomed to the whole law enforcement catch-and-release game, but this case was different somehow, and she was taking it personally.

"Who coughed up the bail?"

"Some relative or other," she said. "I don't even know, and it doesn't matter. The point is, he's out, and for right now I don't want to discuss it. Let's talk about something else. What have you and Rambo been up to?"

With the conversational ball squarely in my court, I had plenty to tell her. I told the stories more or less in chronological order, starting with what I'd learned from Colleen McDaniel at the academy about Lucy Rambo's history.

"It's a shame the poor dog was locked in that damned bathroom when all hell broke out," Mel observed. "It would have served Purcell right if she'd taken a hunk out of his hide. But I'll bet you're right. He's probably the one who stuck her with that name, so from now on, it's Lucy all the way."

Mel listened quietly through my recitation of the surprising information I'd gleaned from Thomas Raines about Maxwell Cole's sexual orientation and gave me high marks for the way I'd handled the complexities surrounding the impending arrival of Scott and Cherisse's unexpectedly expected baby.

"I'll give Cherisse a call tomorrow and see if there's anything I can do."

"Would you?"

"Of course."

I told her about how Todd Hatcher had managed to come up with a location for Erin's estranged foster father and gave her a blow-by-blow description of Al Thorne's and my exploration of Max's burned-out house earlier that afternoon. By the time I finally ran out of steam and subject matter, Mel seemed more relaxed. When she got up to clear the table and pour herself a second glass of wine, an alert on my phone announced an arriving e-mail, which turned out to be from Todd:

You probably shouldn't go looking for a career in photography. You suck. The enhancement isn't much better than what you sent. What follows is a typed version of what I believe was on the page, including names and phone numbers along with the time of the dinner reservation. Be aware, some of the numbers may be off by a digit or two. Hopes this helps.

T.

Below the body of the text was a list of forty or so names—sometimes first and last names and sometimes a first name followed by an initial only—but all of them were followed by a phone number.

"What's that?" Mel asked, peering over my shoulder.

"It's the list of people who had dinner reservations at El Gaucho last Friday night," I told her. "Since Maxwell Cole's name isn't on the list, I have to assume that he either didn't have a reservation or else he was there as someone else's guest."

"Who would most likely be one of the last people to see him alive," Mel concluded. "You're going to call all of them?"

"That's the plan."

"Don't let me stand in your way, then," she said. "I may have left the office early, but I brought home a mess of paperwork because it's impossible to get any of it done with the phone ringing off the hook every ten seconds."

While she retrieved her briefcase and spread papers out across the dining room table, I took my phone and retreated into the family room, far enough away, I hoped, that my phone conversations wouldn't disturb her.

I was about to dial the first number from the reservation list when I noticed the last number on my recent calls list was the one with the 360 area code that had gone unanswered. John Madsen hadn't been home earlier in the day, but maybe he was now. I hit redial.

After the third ring and just when I expected the call to switch over to voice mail, he answered.

"Hello."

"John Madsen?"

"Yeah, who's this?"

"A voice out of the past," I told him, "and probably not a very welcome one at that. It's Beaumont, J.P."

"Detective Beaumont?"

"I haven't been Detective Beaumont in quite some time, but yes, that's me. I tried calling earlier today, but you weren't home. I didn't want to leave a message."

"I was at work."

That surprised me. Since John was several years older than I was, I thought he would have been retired by now, but then who was I to talk?

After a small pause and as though he had somehow read my mind, Madsen continued. "It's not work, really," he explained. "I volunteer one day a week at the

Veterans Museum here in Chehalis. Since you know all about me, that probably strikes you as odd—that someone with my history and who was an army deserter back in the day would volunteer at the museum. But you'd be surprised. I'm not the only one who got screwed up by that war. When I went there the first time, I wasn't at all sure what I would find or even why I felt compelled to go."

John Madsen fell silent again.

"What did you find?" I prompted.

He cleared his throat before he answered. "Forgiveness," he said quietly, "a whole lot of forgiveness from the very people I would never have thought would be able to forgive me. And now, when other guys like me show up—which they do occasionally—I try to do unto them as was done unto me."

That took my breath away. I wouldn't have expected that result, either—that a suffering army deserter would find comfort in the company of veterans who had served with honor, but then again, maybe forgiveness is part of what serving with honor is all about.

"But no forgiveness from your daughter," I suggested quietly.

I heard John's sharp intake of breath. "No," he agreed, "not from Erin."

"She's the reason I'm calling," I said.

"Really? She wanted you to call me?"

The naked hope in his voice was heartbreaking.

"No," I said. "I'm sure she has no idea that I'd be reaching out to you. She's asked me to look into the circumstances surrounding Maxwell Cole's death. I was at the funeral. I saw you there."

"I only went because I hoped Erin would be there,"

he said. "I wanted to see her and know firsthand that she's all right."

"She's struggling," I said. "Max's death has hit her hard."

"It hit me hard, too," John said quietly. "I know that what Marcia and I did to Max was terrible, but it turns out our faith in him wasn't misplaced. He's been there for Erin all this time when we couldn't be."

"Are you aware that Erin is Max's only heir?" I asked.

He seemed dumbstruck by that. "You mean like in his will?"

"From the document I saw, he left her everything. I'm guessing that when the dust settles, she and her son will both be in pretty good shape financially."

"I'm relieved to hear it," John said. "He never told me he was considering doing such a thing, but I'm aware of Erin's financial struggles. I tried reaching out to her several years ago, after her most recent divorce, but she refused to have anything to do with me. Still, if she didn't ask you to contact me, why are you calling? You don't think I had something to do with Max's death—"

"No," I said, cutting him off, "nothing of the kind. It has come to my attention that Max was working on a book—something that might hark back to around the time when Marcia was killed. Do you have any knowledge of that?"

"I did know about the book," John said. "Max told me about it."

Now I was the one taken aback. "Max told you?"

"We've been in contact for a number of years now," John continued. "From time to time he would keep me in the loop about what was going on with Erin and her son. As for the book? He said something to the effect that what he was writing might bring up some of that bad old stuff, and he wanted me to have some advance warning."

"Did he go into specifics about what kind of bad old stuff?"

"Not really," Madsen said. "He hinted around that it maybe had something to do with a crooked cop, but that was about it. No other details. Why do you ask?"

A crooked cop? That one gave me pause. As far as I knew, the only cops involved in the Marcia Kelsey homicide had been Paul Kramer and me. I sure as hell wasn't crooked. And Kramer has always been a brown-nosing jerk, but nothing I'd seen about him said he was dirty!

"Because," I answered finally, "some of that bad old stuff may be the reason Maxwell Cole is dead."

CHAPTER 19

Once off the phone with John Madsen, I didn't immediately try dialing any of the other numbers. Instead, I sat there puzzling over the crooked-cop comment. Truth be told, Seattle PD has had its share of crooked cops—my first partner in Homicide, Rory "Mac" McPherson, being a prime case in point. His malfeasance hadn't come to light until decades after the fact, and that revelation had been accompanied by especially dire consequences for any number of people.

What if this was the same thing? Max had made no secret of the fact that he was writing a book that would most likely deal with some aspects of the Marcia Kelsey homicide. If a crooked cop had been lurking in the shadows back then, he might still be there, hiding in plain sight and worried about being thrust into the light of day.

Still, besides Kramer and me, what other cops had been involved in the case? That one left me stumped. The two who immediately came to mind were our sergeant in Homicide at the time, Watty Watkins, along with the guy running the unit, Captain Lawrence Powell. As far as I knew, both of those guys—now long retired—were as honest as the day is long.

Of course, once Erin's sister, Jennifer Lafflyn, had fallen to her death off the Magnolia Bridge, that incident had sparked another whole line of investigation. Since I had been directly involved in the confrontation, Kramer and I had both been excluded from that aspect of the investigation. Was Jennifer's death where the crooked-cop angle came from? Much as I didn't want to, I resigned myself to the distinct possibility of having to hold my nose and reach out to Paul Kramer to see if he could shed any light on the subject.

Right then, what would have helped the most would have been having access to the murder books on either one of those two cases—Marcia Kelsey's and Jennifer Lafflyn's. Had Ross Connors still been alive, he would have waved his magic wand and access would have been a done deal. But then again, so could someone else—another former partner of mine, Seattle PD's current assistant chief of police, Ron Peters.

We hadn't been partners for very long when, in the course of a high-speed chase, the van in which Ron had been riding had plunged off an unfinished off-ramp on I-90. The accident had left Ron a paraplegic. He had spent months in recovery, first in the hospital and later in rehab. It was no accident that one of his many nurses was now his wife, Amy. Come to think of it, maybe what was going on between Harry I. Ball and Margie Herndon wasn't all that surprising, either.

But back to Amy Peters. Not only is she Ron's wife, but she's also the mother of my namesake, Jared Beaumont Peters.

When I dialed their home number, Amy answered the phone. "Hang on," she said. "Let me go find him. He and Jared are having a father-and-son chat."

That sounded ominous, but Jared's a little kid. How bad could it be?

"Hey, Beau," Ron said when Amy handed him the phone. "How's it going?"

"Things are fine with me. What about on your end?"

Ron sighed. "We're being hassled by Jared's fifth grade teacher. Jared wants to conduct a ballistics test for his science project. The teacher is objecting on the grounds that she won't allow guns to be mentioned in her classroom."

I wanted to whack my forehead with the phone. Jared's father is a cop. Guns are the tools of his trade just as they are of mine. If a carpenter's son wanted to do a science project related to hammers, for instance, would that cause a hue and cry? About that time, the other part of Ron's stunning statement pierced my consciousness.

"Wait," I said. "Jared's already in the fifth grade? Are you kidding me?"

"Time flies," Ron said with a chuckle. "Now what's up?"

"You've heard about Maxwell Cole, I presume?"

"Yup," Ron said. "No love lost there as far as I'm concerned."

When Ron first came back to work, he had landed a job in the Public Information Office, or as that department is currently known, Media Relations. I suspected he hadn't enjoyed dealing with Maxwell Cole any more than I had.

"He was working on a book, which evidently has

something to do with a homicide Kramer and I worked years ago," I said. "The murder of Marcia Kelsey."

"Wait, you mean the school district murders?" Ron asked.

I always focus on Marcia's death, because she had been Jennifer Lafflyn's main target, but another person had been found dead at that same crime scene. Alvin Chambers, a lowly school district security guard who'd had the misfortune of being in the wrong place at the wrong time. His death was always considered to be something of an afterthought.

"Yes," I said, "exactly. Marcia's foster daughter, Erin, has been close friends with Maxwell Cole all her life. She's of the opinion that his death wasn't accidental at all, and she's asked me to look into it."

"Beau," Ron cautioned, "if you're asking me to give you information on a current case ..."

"I'm not," I said quickly. "Obviously current investigations are off-limits."

My fondest hope, of course, was that Al Thorne from the Arson Bomb Squad wouldn't spill the beans as far as where we'd been earlier in the day. I doubted he would, if for no reason other than self-preservation. After all, Al was still on the job and, as a consequence, could still be fired. Because I'm approximately older than dirt, I'm already fired.

"I'm just trying to get a better idea of the direction Max's book was taking," I explained. "Having a chance to sit down and look through those murder books would be a huge help."

I shut up then and gave Ron a chance to think it over. "I don't see why that would be an issue," he said at last. "When would you like to do it?"

Slipping in and out of the Evidence Unit on a weekend day would be less obvious than visiting during the week, when my turning up might attract unwanted attention. "Tomorrow maybe?" I asked tentatively. "Early afternoon, maybe, say one or so?"

"Sure," Ron agreed. "I'll call down to the EU and let them know you're coming."

"Thanks, Ron," I told him. "I really appreciate it."

I set a reminder for the evidence room appointment on my phone and then turned my attention to the names on the reservation list Todd had sent me. It was easy to discount the guests whose expected arrivals came later than Mel's and mine. Since we'd been ready for dessert as Max was leaving, I focused in on parties that were listed as having started an hour or so before we did.

Before placing the first call, I came up with a lame-brain cover story that had the advantage of being partially true. I tried it out for the first time on someone named Loretta Mason, who was listed as a four-top at 6:00 P.M.

"I ran into an old fraternity buddy of mine at El Gaucho last week," I told her. "Unfortunately, I've misplaced Max's phone number. I was wondering if maybe you could put me in touch."

Obviously if the person knew Max's last name or was aware that he had croaked out in the meantime, the story wouldn't fly. Loretta, however, fell for it hook, line, and sinker. "I'm so sorry," she said. "I can't help you. I don't know anyone named Max."

Despite Todd's warning to the contrary, the phone numbers all worked. I expected people to hang up on me or demand to know how I had acquired their number, but they didn't. They were all unfailingly polite and sorry about being unable to help. It wasn't until call number ten or eleven, one placed to someone named Amelia R at 6:45, that I finally hit pay dirt.

The phone was answered with what sounded like a series of letters—"DQC" maybe? When I asked for Amelia, the phone was banged down on a counter. While I waited I wondered if the "DQ" in question stood for Dairy Queen perhaps, but the music playing in the background along with occasional bursts of laughter made me think that couldn't be right.

Eventually a husky-voiced individual came on the line. "Amelia," she said.

I launched off into my scripted story, but I never made it past the word "unfortunately" because Amelia stopped me cold. She not only knew who Max was, she knew who I was, too.

"You're the guy who used to be the detective," she said. "Max pointed you out to me when you first came into the restaurant the other night. It's about time someone got in touch with me. I thought I would have heard from Seattle PD long before this."

"Because?" I hinted.

"Because Max put on a good front—at least he tried to, but I could tell he was scared to death and with good reason, as it turns out. What is it they say? 'You're not being paranoid if someone really is out to get you.'"

"You don't think the fire that killed him was an accident?"

"No," Amelia said at once. "Do you?"

I started to say I was warming to the idea, but I stifled myself just in time. Indulging in gallows humor outside the walls of law enforcement establishments is not recommended.

"That's a distinct possibility," I hedged. "But if you thought there was more to his death than its being just an accident, you could have contacted Seattle PD on your own."

She laughed aloud at that one. "Sure," she said, "someone like me calls the cops to argue that what they're calling an accident is actually a homicide? Don't be silly. A story like that is never going to get any traction."

"That's not true," I said. "Private citizens call in to report crimes all the time."

"Drag queens don't," she said pointedly. "Now, Friday nights are busy around here, and I've got a business to run, so how about you get off the dime and tell me the reason for your call."

A drag queen? Had I stumbled into another aspect of Maxwell Cole's secret life? Leaving that to be sorted later, I launched off into my explanation.

"As you said to begin with, I was a detective, but I'm not any longer. However, a woman named Erin Howard contacted me. She's apparently of the same opinion you are—that Max's death wasn't an accident—and she wanted me to look into it."

"Ah, Erin," Amelia said, "my new partner."

"Excuse me?"

"Never mind," she responded. "We'd probably be better off discussing all this in person rather than over the phone."

"I'd be glad to drop by if that would be convenient," I offered.

"Drop by here?" Amelia asked. "Exactly how straight are you, Mr. Beaumont?"

"Pretty," I admitted.

"You do know what the initials 'DQC' stand for, don't you?"

"Not the foggiest."

"It's Drag Queen Central," she said. "We specialize in drag queen stand-up comedy. Things can get pretty raunchy around here later on in the evening, but if you think you're tough enough, feel free to stop by."

"Where are you exactly?"

"Up in Wallingford," she said. "Right on the main drag in a storefront that used to house a movie theater."

I glanced at my watch. It was only eight o'clock. "Okay," I said. "See you soon."

I got up and headed for the dining room, where Mel was still poring over her paperwork.

"Care to take a field trip?" I asked.

"Where to?"

"To see a friend of Maxwell Cole's," I answered. "Her name's Amelia Rourke, and she runs a drag queen comedy joint up in Wallingford."

Mel gave me a raised-eyebrow look. "Drag queen, really?"

I nodded.

"Best offer I've had all day," she said, pushing back her chair. "Are we taking Lucy or leaving her here?"

"She's with us," I said. "Let's go."

CHAPTER 20

AMELIA ROURKE (MAN or a woman? I wasn't sure) had mentioned that DQC was located in what had once been a movie theater. Mel and I approached the place on foot, having had to park several blocks away. When we arrived, the establishment was awash in splashes of vivid neon signage, and it looked for all the world as though it still was a movie theater, albeit one from a much earlier era.

Under a sheltering overhang, a crowd of smokers—most of them outlandishly overdressed in ball gowns and tuxedos—milled around outside an old-fashioned ticketing booth, laughing and talking. Standing in line with Mel, I tried not to stare. Some of the folks were women dressed up in men's clothing, and vice versa. Surprisingly enough, some of those faux females were actually drop-dead gorgeous. Let's just say it was all very unsettling.

The young woman in the ticket booth, however, was clearly that—a young woman. A sign in the window said that the Friday night cover charge was fifty bucks.

I was about to hand over the money when she glanced first at Mel and then back at me.

"Mr. Beaumont?" she asked.

"Yes."

"Your cover is covered," she said. "Tell Jack I said so. Tell him to take you to see Auntie Em."

"Who's Jack?"

It turned out Jack was the bouncer—and a serious-looking one at that. I was sure that there was plenty of muscle hiding under his S-E-C-U-R-I-T-Y emblazoned windbreaker.

When we approached him, he gave a slight bow, opened the door, and gestured us inside. My first impression was that I had left Seattle far behind and wandered into some upscale casino in Vegas. The DQC was what Jim Hunt refers to as "all glitz and glam," with an interior as lavishly overdone as some of the waiting customers we had seen outside. The back wall of the lobby, where popcorn and sodas had once held sway, was now a respectable bar, complete with a highly polished counter and a row of padded barstools. It came complete with what I recognized as a commendable collection of top-shelf booze.

"Right this way," Jack said, holding aside a red velvet curtain. "You'll find Miss Amelia's table over there in the far corner of the room, all the way in the back."

I stopped for a moment, taking it all in and remembering all those Busby Berkeley musicals that used to be on TV back in the fifties. Any surface that wasn't covered with lush velvet curtains was covered with mirrors. The immense chandelier in the middle of the room would have been totally at home in any bus-and-truck show's traveling production of the *Phantom of the Opera*.

Yes, Jim Hunt definitely would have given the place an enthusiastic two thumbs up.

Long ago I'm sure a silver screen hung on the far wall of the slope-floored room. That was no longer the case. In its place was a small stage area backed by a layer of lavish red velvet curtains. The stage itself was empty except for two items—a microphone stand and a tall armed stool—both of them at the ready and awaiting the arrival of the evening's first performer. In the background, behind the din of pleasant laughter and partying chitchat, Johnny Mathis's recorded voice crooned *"Misty"* over what I deemed to be a respectable sound system.

I had no doubt that the place had once been filled with row upon row of auditorium-style seating. Those had now been replaced by risers holding small cocktail tables and upholstered banquet chairs. Most of the tables were already occupied, with scantily clad cocktail waitresses darting back and forth among them. Were they or weren't they? Who knows and probably best not to ask. Let's just say that none of this glitzy operation looked like the butt-sprung, down-at-the-heels version of Wallingford I had expected.

As for the blonde holding court in the far corner of the room? I recognized Amelia Rourke at once as the person who had left Maxwell Cole's funeral immediately after the service ended, following hard on John Madsen's heels. From a distance she looked like one of those glamorous movie stars from the forties. Up close and personal I realized Amelia was definitely one of the drag queens in question. She stood to greet me, offering a bejeweled hand along with a surprisingly firm handshake.

"Mr. Beaumont, I presume?"

I nodded. "Yes," I said, "and this is my wife, Mel Soames."

Amelia gave Mel an appraising once-over. "Are you an investigator, too?"

Mel responded with one of her most dazzling smiles. "Don't pay any attention to me," she said. "I'm just here as backup."

Amelia actually hooted with laughter at that. "Welcome then, both of you," she said. "Have a seat. The first set starts at ten. Once that happens, having an actual conversation won't be possible. Would either of you care for something to drink? I gave up drinking years ago, so I'm having Earl Grey, but you're welcome to whatever."

So Amelia Rourke, a man dressed in women's clothing who also had sobriety issues, was running an upscale bar? How much stranger could it get?

"Earl Grey works for me," Mel told her while I took a pass.

Once Amelia had given Mel's order to a passing waitress, she turned back to me. "Now," she said, "how can I help?"

"On the phone earlier, you mentioned something to the effect that Erin Howard is now your new partner. What's that all about?"

"When I came up with the idea for Drag Queen Central, one of the first stumbling blocks—a major one at that—was landing a liquor license. Max and I had been friends for years. Decades even. He knew people who knew people, and he put me in touch with someone who was able to help me obtain what I needed. It turned out to be a frightfully costly undertaking. When I came up short in terms of funding, there weren't any banks back then who were willing to step up, so Max did. He advanced me the shortfall in exchange for a ten percent ownership of the business—a silent partnership, mind you. That agreement remains in effect to this day, and he's been receiving a ten percent share in the profits for as long as there have been profits."

Mel's tea was delivered. As she stirred in sweetener and lemon, I glanced around the crowded room, realizing as I did so that profitability clearly wasn't one of DQC's problems.

"In fact, that was one of the things Max and I were discussing at dinner at El Gaucho last week," Amelia continued. "My buying out his interest in the business. We even established a price point—one hundred and forty thousand dollars. He told me that night that he'd meet with his attorney the following week—this week—and have her draw up the paperwork."

"That would be Delia Rojas?" I asked.

"Yes," Amelia answered, "I believe that's her name. His hope was to have the deal finalized within a matter of days."

"Paying out that much money all at once wouldn't have been an issue for you?" Mel inquired.

Amelia smiled as she answered. "DQC is a going concern, Ms. Soames, and these days banks are far more understanding than they used to be when it comes to financing alternative kinds of establishments. Since the sale never went through, however, I'm now stuck with a silent partner who doesn't know the first thing about me or my business. If she's straight, there's a good chance that she won't approve of either one. That's the whole reason Max wanted us to do the buyout sooner rather than later—so I wouldn't end up being encumbered with a business partner I didn't know and also because, truth be told, if something bad did happen to him, he'd be able to keep a lid on that as far as Erin is concerned."

"You mean as in not letting her know he was gay?" I asked.

Amelia favored me with a searching look. "That aspect of Max's life has always been a closely guarded secret," she said. "In fact, I'm surprised to hear you know about it."

I suspect she was hoping that I'd shoot off my mouth and reveal my sources. I didn't, however, and eventually Amelia continued.

"Max saw himself as a writer first and foremost. He kept his sexual orientation quiet because he didn't want to be pegged as a gay writer. It probably doesn't matter as much nowadays as it did when he first went to work for the *P-I*, but if word had gotten out back then, it likely would have impacted everything he wrote. I have a feeling that under those circumstances, some of the people who showed up at his funeral out of gratitude for his stories might not have been there."

"Erin's going to have to know the truth at some point," Mel said.

"Yes, she is," Amelia replied, "and with any luck I won't be the one to tell her."

I had a sinking feeling that I'd be the one left doing the dirty work, which would add yet one more stunning betrayal to Erin's already overwhelming collection of same.

"Let's go back to last Friday night for a moment," I suggested. "That was the sole purpose of your getting together with Max that night—to discuss the buyout?"

"As I said, he and I were friends—pals, even. We've known one another for years, and we tried to go out for an elegant dinner every so often—once a month or so. Over the course of the evening, we talked about a lot of things, but I could tell he was upset and uneasy about something. It wasn't until he caught sight of you across the dining room that he finally got around to telling me about the book he was working on."

"About *Tangled Web*?"

"I hadn't known about it before then. He said that in the course of researching it, he had stumbled onto something he hadn't expected to find, something that might, as he put it, end up having serious repercussions in the here and now."

"Serious as in his being afraid someone might come after him?"

Amelia nodded. "That was my impression. I told him if that was the case, he needed to go to the cops. He said that was the whole problem—that the bad guy was someone who used to work for Seattle PD and probably still carried a lot of weight around there. After a while, though, he got this sort of thoughtful look on his face and said that you'd been away from the department long enough that maybe you could help."

"I wish I could have," I said. "He stopped by our table on his way out of the restaurant and hinted that there was something he wanted to discuss, but we never had a chance to go into it. Did he give you any more details—anything at all?"

Amelia thought about that for a moment. "He did say something odd. That if he'd had any idea where it was going to lead, he never would have talked to that drunk."

"Did he say which drunk?"

"No."

One of the waitresses hurried over and whispered something in Amelia's ear. "Sorry," she said. "There seems to be a problem out front. I'm going to need to go take care of it. If there's anything else..."

"That's all for the time being," I said. "You've been most helpful."

"You really don't think his death was an accident?"

The accident part was seeming less likely all the time, but I couldn't come right out and say that.

"We're working on it," I told her.

"I hope you get the bastard who did it and string him up by his toes," Amelia said fervently, wiping away a tear before it managed to ruin her mascara. "Max spent months doing hand-to-hand combat with lung cancer and fought his way back from the edge. He deserved better than this. He deserved to have more time."

With that, Amelia Rourke rose to her feet, plucked a small beaded purse off the table, and then sashayed toward the entrance on what looked to me like dangerously high heels.

"Look at those Jimmy Choos!" Mel exclaimed in admiration. "I'd kill to have a pair like that. I wonder where she got them."

Not wanting to stay for the show, we followed Amelia out to the lobby, where bar customers clustered around the window, watching whatever was happening outside. "What's going on?" I asked the bartender.

"Some young punks are out there causing trouble," he explained. "You should probably wait a little while before you leave. I've already called the cops."

Mel didn't say the words "We are cops" aloud. She

didn't have to, because she was already out the door with me two steps behind her. Jack, the bouncer, was fully engaged. He had one hooded kid in an armlock, holding his face pressed against the back of the ticket booth while two more hoodie-wearing thugs whaled away at his back. No weapons were visible, but plenty of fists were flying. It turned out, however, that Mel's and my assistance was totally unneeded. We arrived on the scene just as Amelia grabbed one of the hoods, pulled that guy out of the melee, and then decked him with a powerful left hook.

The kid's eyes rolled back in his head, and he crumpled to the worn terrazzo floor. Worried Amelia might come after him too, the other kid immediately backed off. That's all they were—three kids hopped up on something and out looking for trouble.

"Let him go, Jack," Amelia ordered. "The cops will be here in a couple of minutes. If these guys know what's good for them, they'll grab their friend, Mr. Sack of Potatoes there, and make themselves scarce."

Which they did, by the way, in a hell of a hurry!

"You all right, Jack?" Amelia asked.

"Yes, ma'am," he said. "Thanks for the help."

"You'll tell the cops that they got away?"

"Yes, ma'am. Will do."

"All right then," Amelia said, snapping her purse shut. "It's almost showtime. I'd best get back inside." She nodded in our direction on her way past. "Sorry about that," she said. "Occasionally things do get a little too exciting around here."

"That left hook was something," I told Mel as we made our way back to the car. "I've never seen anything like it."

"The brass knuckles helped," Mel said.

"What brass knuckles?"

"The ones Amelia put back in her purse after she KO'd the kid."

Brass knuckles? Really? Talk about being put in my place! I had noticed Amelia snapping the purse shut, but I had missed the brass knuckle bit completely. Maybe my much-vaunted situational awareness isn't all it's cracked up to be after all.

CHAPTER 21

SATURDAY MORNING FELT like we were starting to get the hang of things as far as having a dog in the family was concerned. Mel took Lucy for a walk and another run in Myrtle Edwards Park while I drank coffee and did crossword puzzles. After she showered, we left Lucy at home and walked over to the Five Points to have a late breakfast at the counter.

"So who's the powerhouse cop Max was so scared of?" Mel asked, while we waited for our order.

I had spent much of the night, with Mel slumbering peacefully beside me, pondering that very question.

"Beats me," I told her. "I know there were a few bad apples back then. There always are, but the problem is, none of them were connected to the Marcia Kelsey investigation."

"Are you going to ask Kramer?"

Mel had had the distinct misfortune of interacting with Detective Kramer several years earlier, and she didn't like him any more than I did.

"Not if I can help it," I told her.

Back home after breakfast, Mel resumed her paper-work challenges while I settled down with my phone to do some work of my own.

On the off chance that the investigation into Max's death did end up turning into a homicide case, it was time for me to work on establishing alibis for both Erin and her son. I started with the management for her apartment complex. The young man I spoke to was surprisingly accommodating when I asked him for copies of the building's overnight security footage for the previous Saturday night and Sunday morning.

"Do you just want the parking lot footage for her building, or the interior footage as well?" he wanted to know. His cordial response was jaw-dropping. I had expected him to tell me to a) take a hike, b) talk to the company's lawyer, or c) show up with a search warrant.

"Both, please. If you don't mind."

"No problem," he said agreeably. "Just tell me where to send it. It's usually boring as hell around here on Saturday mornings. At least this gives me something useful to do."

Once I gave him my information, I dialed the number Erin Howard had given me for her son's cell phone.

"You're the guy who's helping my mom, right?" Christopher Cassidy asked once I finished introducing myself.

"That's correct."

"Thank you for that. Uncle Max's death has been really hard on her. I offered to come home and help out—you know, just be there for her—but with all the snow in the pass, she wouldn't hear of it."

"It turns out maybe you can help, even without com-ing home," I told him.

"I can, really? How?"

"It turns out that your mother is Max's primary heir. As such, she, and ultimately you, stand to reap substantial financial benefits from his death. As long as everyone accepts the premise that Max's death was accidental, there's no problem. However, if this eventually turns into a homicide investigation..."

"We'll both be suspects," Christopher concluded.

"Exactly."

"My mother would never do something like that!" he declared vehemently. "Uncle Max was like a father to her. Mom would never hurt him, and neither would I!"

"I'm sure that's all true, but we'll need a way to prove it."

"How do we do that?"

"I'm in the process of obtaining security footage that should confirm that it would have been physically impossible for your mother to have been involved in what happened. Now I need to do the same for you."

"What do you mean?"

"Where were you on the night Max died?"

"Here in Pullman."

"Can you prove it?"

"I work in the CUB in the food court," he said, "at the Subway. I didn't get off work that night until after we finished cleaning up, a little after ten."

I don't speak fluent Wazoo, but I suspected that the CUB was some kind of student union building on the WSU campus. As for the driving distance from Pullman to Seattle? It is, as one of my AA friends likes to call it, "a fur piece." In good weather, it's a five-hour drive for a hot-shoe young driver. Under winter weather driving conditions the trip through Snoqualmie Pass there is usually accumulated snow and ice on the roadway. There's also the increased possibility of both weather-related accidents and intermittent Department of Transportation traffic closures due to avalanche control. Taking our recent flurry of inclement weather into consideration, that five-hour drive now probably averaged more like eight to ten. No way Christopher Cassidy could have gotten off work at 10 P.M. and ended up in Seattle in time to set fire to Maxwell Cole's house.

"Do you happen to have a time sheet showing exactly when you clocked in and out?"

"Yes, sir."

"And a manager who will verify you were there?"

"Yes."

"Good," I said. "That's all I needed to know."

"What about my mom?" Christopher asked. "Doesn't she need an alibi, too?"

"She does, but as I said, I'm reasonably sure she has one, and I'm in the process of verifying it."

Christopher heaved a relieved sigh. "Good. I'm glad she has someone to help her with all this." He paused for a moment before asking a question that surprised me. "Did you really save my mom's life once?"

My own pause before answering matched the one that had preceded the question. "Yes," I said finally, "I did."

"What was that all about? She mentioned something about a crazy girl who was trying to kill her. Is that true? And if so, who was she, and why was she after my mom? Could it maybe have something to do with her family? I mean, Mom never talks about any of her relatives. I don't even know if there are any. Do I have grandparents out there somewhere or maybe some cousins?"

There was a whole lot I could have told him about those crippling family dynamics, but I didn't want to. "It's not my place," I said. "You'll need to ask your mom."

An incoming-call alert came in. "I've got another call, Christopher," I told him. "But if you think of it, have your manager text me a copy of your time cards from last week."

"Okay," he said. "Will do."

I switched over to the other call. "Hey, Beau," Al Thorne said. "How's it hanging?" Even if I hadn't recognized the voice, his customary greeting was unmistakable.

"Good," I said. "How about you?"

"Well, sir," he said, "it looks like I owe you that sawbuck after all."

"What do you mean?"

"We got a hit on the prints off that extension cord just like you said we would."

"Great," I told him. "Who is it?"

"His name's Duc Nguyen, a lowlife gangbanger, a full-fledged member of the Local Asian Boys from down in Columbia City."

"Are you going to go talk to him?" I asked.

"Can't," Al said. "Nguyen just happens to be dead as a doornail. Turned up as a victim of a hit-and-run down in Pioneer Square just a few hours after Maxwell Cole corked it. Estimated time of death for this guy is approximately five A.M."

"If it happened the same day Max died," I suggested, "that probably means it's not an accidental hit-and-run, either."

"Probably not," Al agreed.

"Can you send me a mug shot?"

"Sure thing," Al said, "but I don't know how much good that's going to do you. Since there's already an ongoing vehicular homicide investigation, the prints I found are bound to start connecting the dots back to the Cole situation. That's why I'm calling—to give you a heads-up. I told the crime lab that when I went to the Cole residence with the building inspector, I noticed that some of the electronics seemed to be among the missing and was concerned that looters might have been in and out of the house after we sealed it up. That's the excuse I used for asking them to run the prints.

"The prints tell us that one way or the other, Nguyen was in Cole's house, and now he's dead, too," Al continued. "That means the cause of that fire is starting to look more and more suspicious."

"Suspicious enough for you to stop labeling the incident as accidental?" I asked.

"Yup," Al answered. "That's it exactly. My next call will be to Homicide to advise them of the change in status and put them on the case."

"No doubt my name is bound to come up in the course of one or the other of those investigations."

"Or in both," Al added. "At least that's how I see it. I'd take it as a huge favor if, when you talk to the detectives, you somehow fail to mention that you were with me at the crime scene yesterday afternoon."

"As in withhold evidence?"

"Maybe just a tiny bit of evidence."

"All right then," I said with a chuckle. "What they don't know won't hurt them."

"As long as you didn't touch anything."

That was both a statement and a question. "Believe me," I assured him, "I kept my hands to myself the whole time."

"Good-o, then, Beau," Al said, sounding relieved. "Best for all concerned if nobody talks out of turn."

He hung up. I couldn't help but be grateful that Al was in ABS rather than Homicide. If I'd had to work with him for any length of time, I probably would have been clichéd to death years ago.

Moments later, my phone dinged with an arriving text that included both a rap sheet and mug shot for Duc Nguyen, age twenty-three. He was a surly-looking kid who, despite his tender age, already had prior arrests for armed robbery, assault, and . . . wait for it . . . attempted arson. In the first two instances, he'd been given a suspended sentence. In the arson case—a fire at a local smoke shop—he'd done six months in the King County Jail.

The smoke shop was an establishment in the Rainier Valley that was, as the media likes to say, "known to law enforcement." In the Seattle Metro area, Rainier Valley is considered to be the Wild West. It's a location where an assortment of gangs—Asian, black, Samoan, and Hispanic—constantly duke it out, vying for supremacy.

But what was the connection? Rainier Valley gangbangers seldom venture far outside their designated territories. In that regard, the distance between the hood and Queen Anne Hill was almost infinite. Given Nguyen's history of arson and the fact that his prints had been found at the crime scene, it was certainly conceivable that he was behind the fire at Maxwell Cole's home. So had this been arson for hire then? If that was the case, was it possible that whoever had ordered the hit on Max had taken out Nguyen as well? The likelihood that Max's death had been an accident was growing more remote by the minute.

It was getting on toward time for me to head down to Seattle PD. With Mel still preoccupied with paperwork, I took Lucy downstairs for another walk. While she was getting busy, I was free to think about my two linked homicides, because, regardless of my lack of jurisdictional authority, that's how they seemed to be now—mine.

I had just picked up a steaming pile of dog poop and tied the bag shut when my phone rang with Scott's name in the caller ID. I managed to drop the bag into the designated container before I answered.

"Dad?"

"Hey, Scott," I said. "How are you feeling? What's up?"

"Are you sitting down?"

I didn't feel like filling him in on the gory details. "No, I'm actually out for a walk," I said.

"You're not going to believe this, never in a hundred years."

He sounded beyond excited. I had a feeling I knew exactly where this was going, but I played dumb. "What?"

"Cherisse and I are going to have a baby!"

I looked down gratefully at Lucy, who had unwittingly helped me navigate some potentially rocky generational shoals. Cherisse had taken my advice and spilled the beans to Scott. Just from his tone of voice, I could tell it had worked. Whatever objections he'd had to becoming a father had disappeared in a puff of smoke.

"That's wonderful news, Scotty!" I told him. "Congratulations to you both."

"Cherisse has been under the weather some lately," Scott continued, "enough so that I've been worried about her, but now it turns out to be nothing but..."

"Morning sickness?" I supplied.

"Exactly," he said. "Morning sickness. So, the reason I'm calling—if you and Mel are in town this weekend, we wondered if maybe the two of you would like to come over for dinner on Sunday evening so we can celebrate. I have the day off, and I'll be doing the cooking."

"I'll have to talk it over with Mel once I get back upstairs," I told him, "but I'm pretty sure you can count on our being there."

Feeling lighter than air, I rushed back to the condo to report the conversation to Mel, who immediately put our Sunday dinner date into the calendar.

"Scott thought Cherisse was 'under the weather,'" she repeated, "and he never once made the connection between that and the possibility of morning sickness?"

"Evidently not," I answered.

Mel shook her head. "How can men be so dim sometimes?"

"Give us a break," I told her. "Isn't that part of our natural charm?"

CHAPTER 22

BACK IN THE old days at Seattle PD, the evidence room was downstairs in the basement of the Public Safety Building. When they built the new police headquarters on Fifth Avenue, the sky-high, square inch value for downtown Seattle real estate made the cost of keeping mountains of evidence there prohibitive. As a consequence, the Evidence Unit was moved to Sodo, an industrial area south of the city center.

Originally the name Sodo was shorthand for "south of the dome," the dome in question being the Kingdome. Then, of course, some local brainiac busy spending other people's money decided to knock that venue down and build two stadiums—not for the price of one—and both in the same general area. Nowadays some people claim Sodo means "south of downtown," but I'm not one of them.

Currently, Sodo's biggest claim to fame is the "homeless encampment," a lawless stretch of derelict RVs, buses, and other assorted vehicles that are allowed to park on city streets with complete impunity. The residents of same have a tendency to rape and murder one another with wild abandon and with few, if any, consequences.

Fortunately, the building housing the Evidence Unit, which looked like one of those commercial self-storage outfits, was located a fair distance south of the actual encampment. Since it's also just up the street from the Washington State Patrol Crime Lab, there's usually a considerable police presence in the area. I parked in a designated visitor spot in the lot out front and walked into the building with some confidence that the car would remain undisturbed until I came out again.

I soon discovered that Ron Peters was good to his word. The clerk at the front desk was expecting me and passed along a visitor pass with no hassle. I was ushered into an area my guide referred to as "the vault." Signage was everywhere. NO FOOD OR DRINK ALLOWED! NO ELECTRONIC DEVICES IN EVIDENCE CUBICLES! I did as instructed and deposited my phone and iPad in the locker next to the door before being allowed into the cubicle itself.

The room contained no furnishings other than a single table and chair. In many ways it bore a very real resemblance to a law enforcement interview room, including the presence of an overhead camera eye designed to make sure no one perusing the contents of the evidence boxes did anything untoward. An old-fashioned yellow legal pad and a pen had been left on the table for my handwritten-note-taking convenience.

Since I was allowed to examine only one box of material at a time, I started with the container labeled with Marcia Kelsey's name. When I removed the top from the banker's box, I discovered a sign-out sheet attached to the lid. The log called for the first and last names of the person requesting access as well as dates and times. It came as no surprise that the name just above mine on the list turned out to be that of Maxwell Cole, and it wasn't a one-time thing, either. He had come here to study the contents of the box on four separate occasions, all of them within the last two months. Clearly I wasn't the only one with old-time connections. I doubted that Ron Peters had allowed Max into the evidence room, but someone had.

For me, opening that evidence box was like stepping into a time machine. The murder book was front and center, but I set that aside to sort through a collection of physical evidence that consisted mostly of the blood-stained clothing—the heavy woolen skirt and the maroon turtleneck—Marcia had been wearing the night she was gunned down in the old school district offices on Lower Queen Anne Hill.

I remembered standing and peering into the janitor's closet that was the crime scene for that long-ago homicide and looking down at the tangle of limbs that had once been two living, breathing people. Our initial theory of the case was that Marcia and Alvin Chambers had been involved in some kind of romantic relationship and that Marcia had shot Alvin Chambers before taking her own life. We had dug the spent bullet from the .38 special out of the brain-spattered Sheetrock behind Marcia's shattered head. A twelve-by-twelve square of sheetrock containing the bullet hole had been cut out of the wall. That hunk of sheetrock was there in the evidence box along with the misshapen slug that had taken Marcia Kelsey's life. That deadly chunk of lead, no doubt still containing traces of blood, was properly sealed away in a labeled evidence bag.

Back when all this happened, DNA analysis of evidence was not yet a blip on the radar of forensic science. These days crime scene techs might well have been able to find traces of Jennifer Lafflyn's DNA on the bodies of both her victims, but that was not the case when the school district homicides occurred. In addition, since that little sexy number had been employed in the building and had every right to be there, both Kramer and I had discounted the importance of her having been the one who discovered the bodies. Our bad—and a mistake that had very nearly cost Erin Kelsey her life.

Marcia's case hadn't remained unsolved long enough to go cold. The investigation into her death hadn't occupied detectives for months or years. In fact, it had been resolved in only a matter of days with the perpetrator dead of her own volition after that fatal plunge off the bridge deck. The relatively quick resolution meant there was far less material in the box than there would have been otherwise.

Crime scene photos were present, of course, along with Doc Baker's autopsy results. In addition, there was an assortment of reports, some handwritten and some typed, with most of them signed by Paul Kramer, who had hogged the report-writing duties on that case in order to make himself look good and make me look bad. When I came across reports written in my own handwriting, the first thing I noticed was that my penmanship back then was a lot neater and more readable than it is now.

As I paged through the murder book, bits and pieces

of the investigation came back to me. We had learned that the murder weapon had belonged to the second victim, Alvin Chambers. I had been surprised that a school district security guard would have been packing a loaded weapon, but it turned out the school district had been under siege due to a number of unpopular school closures along with some sticky labor union negotiations in which both Marcia Kelsey and her lover, Andrea Stovall, had been directly involved.

As a result of all the public turmoil, the district office had been targeted by a number of bomb threats. While striving to downplay the seriousness of the threats, school officials had gone to the extraordinary length of hiring armed security guards rather than unarmed ones. Unfortunately for Alvin Chambers, although he had been carrying a loaded weapon at the time, he had lacked the kind of combat training that might have enabled him to maintain control of his weapon rather than allowing his assailant to turn it against him.

As soon as I saw Charlotte Chambers's name in the murder book, I remembered the next-of-kin notification, when she had absolutely discounted the possibility that her husband might have been involved in an adulterous affair with another woman—an assertion that had eventually proved to be true—and the Pete Kelsey notification, in which everything he told us about his and Marcia's "perfect" marriage had wound up being a total fabrication. In the course of the investigation, Kramer and I had stumbled on the fact that Maxwell Cole was close friends with both our murder victim and her widower.

I skimmed along through the pages of the murder book, picking out a word here and there, but mostly relying on memory to fill in the details. Then I hit on something odd—a single page where the corner had been turned down. The page in question turned out to be one of my handwritten reports dealing with a kid named Todd Farraday.

That obnoxious little dork had been the son of Seattle's then mayor, Natalie Farraday. I may have forgotten about him in the meantime, but just seeing his name brought everything about him back to me in a flash. Todd had been a smart but troubled kid, living in the shadow of a political powerhouse of a mother. He'd made the school district bomb threats in hopes of earning points with the other kids so he could be considered one of the regular guys. Instead, when Todd's mother had pulled strings and gotten him off, the whole game had blown up in his face. I doubted that the shenanigan had improved his status with the other kids. In fact, on that score he'd probably ended up worse off than he'd been before. And although he may have come away with a clean record as far as criminal charges were concerned, I suspected that his hard-nosed mother would most likely have exacted her own pound of flesh.

When Ron Peters and I had called on Todd at his mother's home up on Kinnear, it had been on the very off chance that the bomb threats might somehow be related to the Marcia Kelsey homicide investigation. Ironically enough, although Todd and the bomb had nothing directly to do with our case, he had nonetheless pointed us in the direction of a friend of his, Jason Ragsdale, who, although not directly involved in the bomb threats, had turned out to be the very eyewitness we needed.

The day before the homicides, Seattle had been hit

by a terrific snowstorm. With traffic pretty much shut down city-wide, Jason had snuck out of the house for some late-night unauthorized urban skiing on the snow-covered slopes of Queen Anne Hill. Speeding past the school district office, he had not only seen the assailant with her weapon in hand, but also later heard gunshots. His first instinct had been to dismiss the sound of the shots as a car backfiring. Later, though, when he became aware of the homicides, he had been afraid to come forward, for fear of landing in hot water with his parents. His eyewitness account of having seen an armed young female at the scene initially led us to wonder if perhaps Erin had been responsible for her mother's death. Only later did we discover the Jennifer Lafflyn connection.

If, as I suspected, Max was the person who had turned down the corner of that particular page, which of the two names written there—Todd's or Jason's—had snagged his attention? I jotted both of them onto my yellow pad for future reference and then continued to leaf through the book, scanning as I went.

One piece at a time, the fiction that had been Pete and Marcia Kelsey's lives fell apart. I read through the parts where we had learned Pete Kelsey's real identity as an army deserter named John Madsen. Finally I read about the arson fire that had obliterated the Kelsey home. A late-night meet-up with me down at the old Dog House Restaurant on Seventh was the only reason Erin hadn't been home alone when the fire was set. The fact that Erin hadn't died in the fire was what had fueled that final life-and-death struggle on the Magnolia Bridge.

When I finished with Marcia's evidence box, I called for the clerk and sent that one back in exchange for one labeled with Alvin Chambers's name. Once again, Maxwell Cole's name was listed on the log sheet, but it appeared only once. In other words, Max hadn't been as interested in the material devoted to Alvin as he had in that relating to Marcia, and understandably so. Pete, Marcia, and Erin had been Jennifer's primary targets. In the evidence room, as in the homicide itself, poor Alvin had been little more than second banana.

Taking my cue from Max, I made a far more cursory examination of the second box than I had of the first one. I set aside the bloodstained security guard uniform and focused my attention on the murder book. Some of the reports I found there were virtual copies of the ones I had previously read in Marcia's. Reading between the lines, I recognized the gradual downward arc of Alvin's life. He had once been a minister of some kind, but the presence of a troubled wife, one suffering from a combination of both physical and mental issues, had eventually forced him to leave the church. He'd ended up taking the security guard position as a way of making ends meet.

As for his wife? It was during an interview with Charlotte Chambers where we had finally started to learn the truth about the *ménage à trois* reality of Pete Kelsey's life and about Marcia's long-term relationship with her lover, Andrea Stovall. Now, knowing what I did about Maxwell Cole's own secret life, I couldn't help but wonder how he must have felt back then when the lies surrounding his friends' existence had been stripped away and dragged out into the harsh light of day.

Two hours into the process, I left the cubicle for a pit stop and a detour in the corridor long enough to check for messages on my phone. There were two new e-mail notifications, along with a voice mail from Erin. I listened to that one before checking the others.

"A Seattle PD homicide detective was here up until just a few minutes ago asking questions about Uncle Max," Erin's recorded voice told me. "His name is Blaylock—Detective Kevin Blaylock. He's investigating the hit-and-run death of someone named Duc Nguyen. He asked me if I knew of any connections between Max and this Nguyen person. I told him I'd never heard of the guy. I gave him your name and number. I hope you don't mind.

"Before he left, though, Blaylock gave me some good news. He told me that Uncle Max's death is now considered suspicious rather than accidental. Thank you, Mr. Beaumont. I don't know how you made that happen, but you did."

I appreciated being given the credit for the change of status on Max's case, but that really should have gone to Al Thorne. As for the vehicular homicide situation? Cases like that are investigated, of course, but resolving one of those doesn't come with the same kind of public awareness or as much departmental oversight and focus as one sees in the more high-profile ones.

Shootings and stabbings automatically garner media attention for both the victims and the detectives conducting the investigations. Vehicular homicides are usually handed off to someone near the bottom of the homicide unit's pecking order—either a beardless newbie youth or some gimpy old guy on his way out. Either way, those cases have a high probability of being shelved as opposed to solved.

It occurred to me that if I passed along the fingerprint evidence connecting Duc Nguyen to the death of Maxwell Cole, it might improve the odds for both of those cases to have a successful outcome.

I thought about that for a moment or two as I started checking my e-mails. The first one came from the management team at Erin's apartment complex. As promised, the "bored" Saturday morning guy had delivered, and the message contained several video files. Three were labeled parking lot. Two others were marked "Building J. Interior" and "Building J." Combing through security footage is about as much fun as watching paint dry, so I marked that one as unread and went on to the next message. That one came from Christopher Cassidy and contained what appeared to be time cards. I marked that one as unread, too, and then called Erin back.

"Beaumont here," I said when she answered. "If Max's death has been booted into the suspicious column, it sounds like good news all around. Does that mean I'm fired?"

"Do you want to be?"

The truth is, I didn't. I was feeling engaged and focused in a way I hadn't felt for months on end. And with the fingerprint stuff still in abeyance, I knew I was holding an important piece of the puzzle.

"I'd still like to know exactly what Max was investigating," I told her. "I've spent the last couple of hours going through the old evidence boxes, and it's clear Max was doing the same thing."

"He went through the evidence boxes, too?"

"Yes."

"But why? What was he looking for? Something to do with Pete and Marcia, maybe?" Erin asked. "Maybe they were involved in something else besides just pretending to be my parents."

I had heard the profound regret in John Madsen's voice when he spoke of his long estrangement from Erin. I knew that his love for Erin as well as his parenting of her had been anything but empty pretense. That had been true back then, at the time of Marcia's death, and his anonymous presence at Max's funeral showed that it still was. However, I couldn't very well go into any of that with Erin, at least not right now. Nor was this the time to discuss some of the more colorful details my investigation into Maxwell Cole's existence had so far revealed about his own hidden life. Those kinds of disclosures—including Erin's unsuspecting involvement with Amelia Rourke and the DQC—would have to be done in a face-to-face encounter.

"If you don't mind, I'd like to keep digging," I added after a pause. "Whatever Max found has to have more to do with the present than it does with the past, but what exactly did you say to Detective Blaylock?"

"Like I said, he asked me if Max and the other dead guy, Nguyen, were friends or acquaintances. I told him I had no idea. I've certainly never heard the name before, and I couldn't imagine why Max would be involved with a young gangbanger from the Rainier Valley."

"Is there anyplace special where Max actually did hang out?" It was a question I should have thought to ask much earlier, and I kicked myself now for not having done so.

Erin thought for a moment before she answered. "Sneaky Pete's, I suppose," she said. "That was probably his favorite. It's right at the bottom of the Counter Balance and only a few blocks from his house. He liked to go there in the evenings, grab something to eat, gab for a little, and have a drink or two before heading home."

I remembered how that worked from back in my own boozing days. If you're going to drink and drive, you're always better off having to navigate a couple of blocks than a couple of miles.

"I heard you talked to Christopher," Erin said, abruptly changing the subject.

"Yes," I told her. "He sent me his time cards from last week. And I have the security footage from your apartment complex as well."

"Does that mean we'll both have provable alibis?"

"Yes," I told her, without adding the words "assuming they check out."

"That's a relief, but I'm going to have to go. There's a big private party at work tonight, and I offered to come in a couple of hours early to get ready."

"Take care," I told her. "I'll be in touch."

CHAPTER 23

I WENT IN search of a cup of coffee and was directed to a break room where the pay-to-play coffee machine yielded a cup of something that bore zero resemblance to real coffee. Knowing I wouldn't be allowed to take the vile stuff into the cubicle with me, I took a chair in the break room and fired up my iPad.

My study of Christopher's time cards and the films from Erin's apartment complex soon led me to believe that both of their alibis would indeed stand up to investigative scrutiny. Then I went browsing on the Internet. As a member of S.H.I.T., I had become accustomed to and incredibly spoiled by having access to the extensive data available through LexisNexis as well as any number of other official and unofficial sources whenever I needed information. Now I was reduced to the thin gruel of what was routinely available online, which, to tell the truth, wasn't much.

Remembering that page with the turned-down corner in the murder book, I googled the star witness in the Marcia Kelsey case and came up with any number of hits on Jason Ragsdale. What popped up on my screen were mostly connections to various legal proceedings. Reading between the lines, I came to the conclusion that Jason had grown up, attended law school, and come out the other end as a prominent divorce attorney in the Seattle-Tacoma area.

When I typed Todd Farraday's name into the search engine, I expected a variation on that same theme for Mayor Farraday's much-coddled son. What I ended up with instead was a brief obituary.

Todd Michael Farraday, age 43, went to his reward on Wednesday, January 4, after a long illness. He was laid to rest during a private ceremony at the family plot in Holy Name Family Cemetery in West Seattle. He was preceded in death by his parents, William M. Farraday and his mother, former Seattle mayor, Natalie Farraday Harden. He is survived by his loving stepfather, Lawrence Harden.

In lieu of flowers donations may be directed to The Refuge, P.O. Box 728, Seattle, 98143.

I read the article through once and then again because, in those few words, everything I had thought I knew about the case suddenly shifted into clearer focus. What is it they say? When it comes to politics, the cover-up is always worse than the crime itself. Nixon and Watergate? There you are. Todd had been the mayor's son while he was busy making his school district bomb threats, and the whole thing had been kept dead quiet. Even now, however, I remembered the name of the guy who had warned Ron Peters and me away from looking into the issue. Larry Harden had been only a captain at the time, but eventually he had gone on to become chief of police.

During his brief tenure as head of the department—less than six months—Harden's relationship with the rank and file had been anything but cordial. He was routinely referred to as either Chief Hard-nose Harden or Chief Hard-on Harden, depending on how pissed the speaker was at the time the name-calling occurred and whether or not it happened in mixed company. Forces had been lining up to expel him, when Harden had beaten everyone to the punch by resigning abruptly in order to run for some elective public office or other. After that he had fallen completely off my radar.

Considering the fact that I was newly sober at the time, it wasn't surprising that I had neglected to notice that sometime after his departure, the former police chief and the former mayor had tied the knot. But now that I knew how things had turned out, I suspected that their lovey-dovey relationship predated both his promotion and their wedding by a number of years. In hindsight it was easy to understand how such a totally inept turkey had ended up being appointed chief.

That's when the last pieces of the puzzle slipped into place. Wasn't that exactly what Amelia Rourke had told me? That Max had been concerned about pushback from some big fish at Seattle PD, someone from back in the day who might still have enough pull inside the department to carry out a whole new cover-up?

Lawrence Harden certainly qualified as far as being a big fish was concerned, and he also understood the subtle ins and outs of finagling a cover-up. From where I was sitting in the Evidence Unit's break room, it seemed likely that he would have been in favor of making sure the bomb threat accusations against his future stepson went nowhere. That had taken a good deal of political pull back then, but did Harden still have the same kind of juice at his disposal all these years later? It seemed likely to me that Lawrence Harden was the can of worms Maxwell Cole had inadvertently kicked over, and that he was also the reason Max was dead.

I ran through the time line in my head. Mel and I had run into Max at El Gaucho on the evening of Friday the 13th. (I'm a superstitious guy. I remember things like that.) Todd had died a few days earlier. It was possible that at the time Max had been chatting with Mel and me, he had yet to hear the news of Todd's death. If Max had learned about it sometime during the day on Saturday, that might account for his sudden uptick of concern about his own safety, resulting in his asking Erin to contact me in case something untoward happened to him.

I went back to the obituary and read through it again, parsing all the words and making notes along the way. Todd had succumbed at what I thought to be a very young age from what was termed "a long illness," a euphemism that could be used to conceal a multitude of sins, including long-term drug or alcohol abuse. So what exactly was Todd's cause of death? Thinking the notice's "in lieu of" suggestion might provide a clue, I clicked on the word "Refuge" and was taken straight to a link for the Refuge Shelter, located on Aurora Boulevard North, a self-described "wet house" for hopeless alcoholics who also happen to be homeless.

Long illness indeed! In most homeless shelters, sobriety is mandatory rather than optional and the *sine qua non* for being granted admission. If you go seeking shelter from, say, the Salvation Army, for example, there's no point in showing up drunk or high. In recent years, however, a number of do-gooders out there—ones who generally regard themselves as the smartest people in the room—have begun to push back on that way of thinking. Maintaining that mandatory sobriety raises the bar for admission far too high; they have branched off into creating shelters where homeless drunks can check in and keep right on drinking. Seattle boasts two wet house facilities. The first one, located on Eastlake, has been operational for years. The Refuge seemed to be the new kid on the block.

As a former drunk, allow me to say, straight out, that I think the whole idea of "wet houses" is nuts. Giving drunks places to stay while they proceed to drink themselves to death seems counterproductive. The world is a funny place, however, and it takes all kinds. That's when something else Amelia Rourke had said to me came to mind. Max had mentioned that he wished he'd never talked to "that drunk," without mentioning anyone by name. Was Todd Farraday the drunk in question? Right that minute, I was prepared to bet money on it.

I've seen search-and-rescue bloodhounds on the job occasionally, and once one of those animals catches a scent, the dog is on it. Homicide investigators operate the same way. I was up and out of that break room so fast it would have made your head spin. Telling the clerk I was done for the day and that he could have his evidence box back, I made for the parking lot, dialing Todd Hatcher on the way.

"Do you happen to have that intern handy?" I asked when he answered.

"It's Saturday," he reminded me. "Student interns don't work on weekends. Why? What do you need?"

"Everything there is to know on three people—Todd Farraday, recently deceased; his mother, Natalie Farraday Harden; and Natalie's second husband and Todd's stepfather, a guy by the name of Larry Harden. Harden may be listed as either Larry or Lawrence. I'm not sure which."

"And how soon do you need this information?"

"ASAP, of course," I told him.

"Right," Hatcher said. "I get it, immediately if not sooner, but just for the record, I ought to charge more if I'm having to investigate someone named Todd."

"You're charging now?" I asked.

"No," he said with a laugh, "just kidding."

I got in the car and typed the name "Refuge" into my GPS. The shelter's physical presence turned out to be in the 3900 block of Aurora Avenue North, otherwise known as State Route 99.

For years Highway 99 provided a usable secondary controlled-access route running north and south through downtown Seattle. Much of that was via first a raised highway known as the Alaskan Way Viaduct and then the Battery Street Tunnel, which leads back to surface streets. The Washington Department of Transportation is currently revising that route and is in the process of constructing a tunnel to carry Highway 99's traffic.

Naturally the project has been beset by huge delays and mounting cost overruns. A couple of years ago the drilling machine they're using, affectionately dubbed "Big Bertha," got tangled up in some unexpected construction debris and was out of service for months on end. The ongoing traffic delays have made using the viaduct an iffy proposition, but my GPS said Highway 99 through the Battery Street tunnel was my best option. Since this was a Saturday and construction workers were most likely not working, I crossed my fingers and took her advice.

That stretch of Highway 99 on the far side of the Aurora Bridge has long been a haven for dodgy flophouse-style motels rife with prostitution, drug use, and, yes, homelessness. I suppose part of the rationale for locating a wet house shelter in that neighborhood was that their most likely clientele would feel more at home in that part of the city than they would anywhere else.

Once I arrived, it was apparent that someone had bought up two of the former motels, given them an extensive upgrade, and deemed them fit for their current higher purpose. I parked in a visitors' slot. After pressing a button to be buzzed inside, I walked into a well-furnished lobby area that, despite the polished floor and upscale furnishings, still reeked of the same antiseptic scents that you find in low-end rehab facilities, which, come to think of it, this one was. Rather than being for the old and the frail, this was for unrepentant drunks, several of whom were seated here and there around the lobby. They eyed me suspiciously as I entered and continued to monitor my every word and gesture with rapt attention. No doubt they had me pegged as some kind of cop, and they were wondering who among them was about to have a world of hurt visited on his or her head.

The muscle-bound young man seated behind the front desk reminded me of the bouncer at DQC. "May I help you?" he asked. His name tag identified him as Mr. Bannerman.

"I'd like to speak to someone about one of your former clients," I said, "a man by the name of Todd Farraday."

"Our residents all have HIPAA protections," the gatekeeper told me.

I thought he was probably blowing smoke just to get rid of me since the Refuge didn't seem to have all the trappings of a health-care facility. Refusing to take the hint, I pointed toward the visitor sign-in sheet.

"I'm actually investigating one of Mr. Farraday's visitors," I told him, "a man named Maxwell Cole. Since Mr. Cole wasn't a resident here, I'm pretty sure he didn't have HIPAA protection."

Mr. Bannerman crossed his arms. "We regard our residents' visitor information as confidential as well, although I suppose, if you had a warrant, I could let you check the guest register."

We both knew I didn't have a warrant, not on me, and since I hadn't shown any kind of ID, he knew good and well that I wasn't a cop. But since the other people in the room were still paying attention, I let things play out a little longer.

"Mr. Cole was murdered just under a week ago," I continued, "a few days after Mr. Farraday passed away. It's possible the two deaths were somehow related, at least that's my current theory."

Mr. Bannerman didn't budge. "Due to their alcohol consumption, our residents often have issues," he said. "On occasion, those issues lead to unfortunate results and even untimely deaths. I can assure you, however, that Mr. Farraday's death was neither unexpected nor avoidable, may he rest in peace."

The last, I'm sure, was for the benefit of those listening in on the conversation. I had the distinct impression that Bannerman wasn't nearly as sympathetic about Todd Farraday's untimely demise as he wanted the other residents to believe. Bannerman had a job to do, and he was doing it, but he was there for his paycheck and not because he had the milk of human kindness running in his veins.

Two newly arrived visitors approached the desk, and Mr. Bannerman was quick to turn his attention on them. I waited while he called one of the other residents to let him know he had a pair of visitors waiting in the lobby. From that conversation I was able to ascertain that visitations usually took place in the lobby area rather than in the individual units themselves. Under the circumstances, that seemed reasonable enough. The last thing the Refuge needed would be drunken private parties attended by people who weren't residents of the facility.

Finished with the newcomers, Bannerman turned back to me, shaking his head in annoyance when he realized that his pointed attempt at brushing me off hadn't worked.

"As I said before," he told me, "if you want access to the visitors' log, you'll need to come back with a warrant."

Cops aren't allowed to offer bribes. Had I been carrying a badge, I could never have done this. I knew going in that Bannerman would never take me up on it. However, for the benefit of the audience in the lobby, I reached for my wallet. "What about if I brought along my friend Franklin?" I asked. "Would that work?"

Bannerman's meaty muscles flexed under his shirtsleeves. "I don't take bribes," he snarled at me. "Either bring me a warrant or it's no deal. Now get the hell out of here, and don't let the door hit you in the butt on the way."

I retreated as far as my car. Rather than starting it up, however, I pulled out my iPad and spent a few minutes completing that morning's unfinished crossword puzzle, all the while waiting to see if I had managed to set the hook. Sure enough, a few minutes later, there was a sharp rap on the window next to my head. A grizzled old guy, leaning heavily on a walker, stood just outside the car. As soon as I buzzed down the window, the unwelcome stink of secondhand vodka flowed into my Mercedes. People who claim vodka doesn't smell don't know what the hell they're talking about. It's unmistakable.

"Is that hundred bucks still on offer?" he wanted to know.

"Depends on what you're prepared to give me," I told him.

"Todd was good friends with a guy by the name of Patrick Donahue. I'm pretty sure he's up in his room right now. I could go tell him you need to talk to him."

I immediately pulled out my wallet and handed over the hundred. "You can tell Mr. Donahue from me that I have one of these for him, too, in case he's interested. Let him know that I'm here to talk to him about Todd's connection to a friend of mine, Maxwell Cole."

"The guy who's dead?"

Obviously Mr. Walker Guy had been paying very close attention to the conversation between me and Mr. Bannerman.

"That's right," I said, "Cole is the one who's dead."

The guy stuffed the hundred into his shirt pocket and then shuffled back indoors as fast as he could go, reminding me for all the world of Arte Johnson, that doddering old character who used to be on *Laugh-In*—the one who could never quite manage to wrap his arms around that elusive sweet little beauty, Goldie Hawn.

Now that my first bribe had borne fruit, I settled in to see if the second one would do so as well. The next tap on the window was on the passenger side. I opened the window. "Patrick?" I asked.

A tall, painfully thin guy leaned down and peered inside. "That's me," he said.

"Do you have a couple of minutes to talk?" I asked.

"That depends," he said. "Show me the money."

Like his predecessor, he pocketed the bill first thing. Once the cash was stowed, he reached for the door handle. "We can't talk here," he said. "No telling who might be watching. We should probably go for a ride."

"All right," I told him. "Get in."

He did, and off we went. As we pulled onto Aurora, I noticed that Patrick kept a close eye on everything around us. Considering the wary focus he aimed at the rearview mirror on the passenger side of the car, I didn't think he was just checking for oncoming traffic.

CHAPTER 24

I STARTED TO ask, "What's your poison?" but thought better of it. The yellowish cast to Patrick's skin and the distended belly on an otherwise skeletal frame was something I had seen before, mostly at AA meetings. Those two symptoms taken together generally mean liver disease—late-stage liver disease.

"Where to?" I asked.

Instead of heading off to the nearest bar as I had more or less expected, Patrick directed me to a hip little coffee shop in Greenlake. "It's a little out of my price range most of the time," he said wistfully. "My daughter won't have anything to do with me these days, but my granddaughter brings me here occasionally as a special treat."

I couldn't help but feel a moment of gratitude that despite my own similar history of drinking, I still had my health, and my kids and grandkids were all a part of my life.

Once inside the coffee shop, while I stood in line to order the drinks—a mocha for him and a plain Jane coffee for me—Patrick managed to score two leather chairs in the front window of the place.

"He was murdered, you know," Patrick muttered as I set the cups down on the scarred coffee table between his chair and mine.

That, of course, was precisely the premise on which Erin and I and even Al Thorne had been operating, but Patrick's air of dead certainty surprised me.

"You know that how?" I asked.

"Because he'd stopped drinking," Patrick declared. "We both had."

That statement left me confused. Based on what I'd seen that Friday evening at El Gaucho, I was pretty sure Maxwell Cole had still been on the sauce at the time of his death.

"I quit three months ago," Patrick continued. "Todd would have gotten his thirty-day chip at the next meeting, but he died first. They claim his blood alcohol level was 0.36. Someone got him to fall off the wagon in a big way. I'm not saying they bodily poured the booze down his throat, but once he started drinking, he didn't stop until it was too late, and he was a goner."

Mrs. Reeder, the hoyden who was my senior English teacher at Ballard High School, was fierce when it comes to the grammatical sin of faulty pronoun reference. "Hells bells, people," she would say, "a pronoun must refer to the noun that immediately precedes it!" The missing noun in Patrick's statement had led me to the wrong conclusion.

"Wait, you're talking about Todd Farraday being murdered? I thought you meant Maxwell Cole."

Patrick shrugged. "They're both dead, aren't they?

And that's the last thing Todd ever said to me—that he was going downtown someplace to have dinner with an ex-*P-I* reporter named Maxwell Cole. Todd said Cole wanted to interview him—something concerning Todd's mother and maybe something else about that earthquake that happened a few years back."

"Which one?" I asked. "The Nisqually Quake, maybe?"

"Beats me," Patrick said. "That's all he said—that earthquake. He didn't come right out and name it."

"Did Todd happen to mention where he and Max were meeting?"

"A joint on Queen Anne, I think."

"Sneaky Pete's maybe?"

Patrick frowned and then nodded. "That's probably the place," he said.

"And then what happened?"

"That Cole guy arranged for a cab to come pick Todd up. He left here late in the afternoon."

"What day?"

"It was a Wednesday."

"Wednesday, January fourth?" I asked.

Patrick nodded. "Sounds about right. Todd left and never came back. Early the next morning he turned up on the front porch of his mother's old place on Queen Anne. The house belongs to his stepfather now. Todd wasn't just dead drunk; he was actually dead. Acute alcohol poisoning is what I heard. His stepfather's wife found him there first thing in the morning when she went out to get the newspaper. Once I heard what happened, I figured Maxwell Cole must have plied Todd with booze in order to get him to talk. A few days ago, when I found out Cole was dead, too, I didn't know what to think. This afternoon, when I heard you had come around asking questions about both of them, I was afraid I might be next."

"But you still came out to talk to me?" I asked.

Patrick shrugged. "It's a long time until my next check. I wanted that hundred bucks. Besides," he added, "compared to what's coming down the pike to get me, I figured going out fast might not be such a bad idea. So what's the deal here? If you're not a cop, what's your connection to all this?"

"I used to be a cop," I explained, "but I'm not anymore. Someone asked me to look into what happened to Maxwell Cole. In the course of going through some old case files, I stumbled across Todd's name. When I tried to look him up, I found his obituary instead. It said he died after a long illness."

"Alcoholism is an illness," Patrick said. "Just ask anyone in AA. Besides, family members are usually the ones who write up those death notices. They get to say whatever they want, and I wouldn't be surprised if there was a lot of sugarcoating in those. After all, just because someone takes himself out by swilling down too much booze doesn't mean mom and pop want to come right out and say so in front of God and everybody."

Patrick wasn't wrong there. I knew for a fact that some families, especially the more prominent ones, are able to airbrush away any number of inconvenient or unsavory details in publicly disseminated obituaries. Todd may not have been Larry Harden's blood relation, but the connection would have been close enough that having it widely known that his stepson had died of booze might have besmirched Hard-on Harden's public image. I guessed that he would have had a hand in directing how Todd's death notice was written, and that kind of misdirection would have been far easier to do since no one had shown any interest in mounting an official investigation into Todd's death.

"So Todd went out to meet with Maxwell Cole and then, after tying one on with him, he went to visit his stepfather?"

"I doubt he went to the house under his own steam," Patrick said. "I figured once Todd was bombed out of his gourd, Cole must have dropped him off there."

I was trying to make sense of Patrick's story, and I couldn't see why Max would have done that. But then, at that point, maybe Max thought Todd was already too drunk to send him back to the Refuge.

"You don't think Todd would have gone to his stepfather's place of his own accord?" I asked. "Why not?"

"Because Todd hated Larry Harden's guts, that's why, and ditto for the guy's new wife."

"So Harden has remarried?"

"I guess," Patrick answered. "According to Todd, if it hadn't been for Harden, his mom wouldn't have thrown him out of the house and out of his job, and just maybe she wouldn't have disowned him, either. To be fair, she didn't disown him completely. When she died, she left him a small trust fund. Todd was also supposed to receive part of the proceeds if and when his stepfather sold the house. Rent at the Refuge is based on ability to pay. Most of the residents, me included, live there on the state's dime. Todd had enough money that he was actually paying his own freight."

"If that's how Todd felt about his stepfather, I can't see any reason for him to go to their house, drunk or sober."

"Me, either," Patrick muttered. "When you figure that out, let me know."

"After you heard about Todd, did you speak to anyone at the Refuge about what had happened?" I asked. "For instance, did you mention to anyone that you thought Maxwell Cole might have been the one responsible for getting him so drunk?"

Patrick laughed outright at the question. "Let's see," he said bitterly. "I seem to remember trying to talk to the head counselor about it. Guess what? He told me to get lost. He said Todd was a drunk who had fallen off the wagon, gone on a binge, and wound up dying in the process. Big deal. Drunks die all the time. Good riddance and who cares? One less boozer to worry about, and now the Refuge has an open bed, right?"

"No cops came around asking any questions?"

"Cop or no cop, as far as questions are concerned, you're the first."

I had no doubt that a quick call to Dr. Roz would provide me with whatever official information existed concerning Todd Farraday's death, but it was pretty clear no one had regarded it as suspicious.

I paused for a moment and looked through my notes. "So you and Todd were friends?"

"Neighbors more than friends," Patrick answered. "People who turn up at the Refuge usually have issues that don't work out well when it comes to being friend material."

"But, given the circumstances, you were close?"

"I suppose."

"Was there anyone else, either a resident or someone on the outside who was friends with Todd?"

"The only person I can think of would be Jason."

My ears pricked up. Was this another name from the murder book? "Jason Ragsdale by any chance?" I asked.

"Maybe," Patrick answered. "Don't think I ever heard his last name, although Todd said they'd been friends since they were kids. Jason would drop by every once in a while, always dressed in a fancy suit and tie and driving a BMW. I got the feeling that Jason was the guy who helped Todd get off the streets and into the Refuge."

Here was someone else from the distant past whom I'd need to track down.

Patrick looked at his watch. "If there's nothing more, I should be getting back home. It's time for my pills."

We left the coffee shop. It was quiet in the car as I drove Patrick back home, and I could tell our long conversation had taken a toll on him. "Todd was lucky to have you as a neighbor," I assured him, as I pulled into the parking lot. "I'm sorry for your loss."

"Thanks," he said. "Nobody ever said that to me before, and I appreciate it. Losing Todd hurt a lot more than I expected, but would you mind doing me a favor?"

"What's that?"

"If you do find out what really happened to him, would you let me know?"

"Glad to," I told him. "You can count on it."

Once Patrick was out of the car, I checked my phone. A call had come in while we'd been talking. The number wasn't one I recognized, and I had let the call go to voice mail. When I checked the message, it was short and to the point. "Detective Kevin Blaylock here, with Seattle PD Homicide. I'm investigating the death of Duc Nguyen. Could you please give me a call."

I returned the call, but when the voice mail prompt

came up, I didn't bother leaving a message. The things I wanted to discuss with Kevin Blaylock were too complex to leave on an answering machine. My next call was to Todd Hatcher.

"What now?" he asked, sounding very much as though he was tired of hearing from me.

"I need some phone numbers."

"You do realize that it's still Saturday, and my interns still aren't on duty, right?"

"Sorry," I said.

"Okay," he said with a sigh. "Shoot."

I asked for numbers on both Jason Ragsdale and Todd Farraday.

"Don't hold your breath," he advised. "I'm putting together a file of material for you, but I don't know how long it's going to take."

Once we hung up, I dialed Mel's number. It was getting on toward evening. The sun had come out briefly. I had a feeling Mel and Lucy would once again heed the call of Myrtle Edwards Park, and I wasn't wrong.

"Where are you?" Mel panted into the phone. "And what's for dinner?"

I had now heard mention of Sneaky Pete's from two entirely separate sources. It seemed reasonable to stop by and pay the joint a call, and picking up some takeout would provide as good a cover story as any.

"Don't worry," I told her. "I'll bring something home. We won't starve."

Sneaky Pete's is right at the bottom of what's known as the Counter Balance. Back in the old streetcar days, counterweights were used to haul the trolleys up the steep hillside. On the way back down, they provided braking. Sneaky Pete's, located on the site of a former church, did, as advertised, have customer parking available at no charge. I availed myself of same and went inside.

Based on the name alone, I expected the place to be something of a dive, but it wasn't. There was a gas log fireplace burning at the far end of the room. The room was pleasantly lit, and the leather armchairs at the cocktail tables looked reasonably comfortable. Knowing this was close to the time when Max would have come in for one of his dinnertime visits, I made straight for the bar and for the curious cop's best friend—the bartender.

"What'll you have?" the portly man behind the counter asked.

"Club soda with lime and a takeout menu," I told him.

"Coming right up."

The drink and the menu came together. "You new around here?" the bartender asked.

"Not new," I told him. "My wife and I live part-time down in the Regrade. This is my first time here, though A friend of mine used to be a regular."

"What friend?" he asked.

"Maxwell Cole."

The bartender's jaw tightened slightly before he changed the subject. "Did you figure out what you wanted?"

I ordered two to-go orders of fish and chips with coleslaw and then settled in with my drink.

"Shame about poor old Max," the barkeep said the next time he came back down the bar. "Usually stopped by in the evenings to grab a bite to eat, and then he liked to sit here at the bar, working on his laptop. He was a good tipper, but I suspect he was a bit on the lonely side."

I pulled out my phone and scrolled through until I found the mug shot Al Thorne had sent me. "Ever see this guy before?"

Rather than checking out the phone, the bartender gave me a wary look. "You a cop?" he asked.

"Like I said, Max was a friend of mine, and you're right, what happened to him was a crying shame. The cops seem to believe his death was an accident, but I'm beginning to wonder about that. I suspect there's a good chance the guy in this photo could have been involved in what happened."

The bartender pulled out his own phone. He removed a tiny pair of reading glasses from a leather case on the back of the phone and then perched the cheaters onto his nose. He studied the mug shot and then passed the phone back.

"I've seen him before all right," he said, "but he sure as hell didn't look like this."

"What do you mean?"

The bartender pointed at the photo. "See there," he asked, "that little teardrop tattoo? I recognized that right off."

Now it was my turn to track down my reading glasses. Once I did, a closer examination of the mug shot revealed the presence of the tattoo.

"So how was he different?" I asked.

"He wasn't wearing a jail jumpsuit, for one thing," the bartender said. "He was all gussied up in a suit and tie, enough so that at first I thought he might be one of those foreign engineer types working for Google or

Microsoft. Except this guy spoke with an American accent. This guy was here the same night Max was."

"The last time he was here?"

The bartender nodded. "Max had been here for a while. He left and then came right back in, complaining he had a flat tire and would need to wait for Triple A to show up and fix it. To my surprise, Tattoo Guy here hopped off his barstool and offered to go outside and change the tire for him."

"Wait," I said. "He offered to change Max's flat?"

"Yup," the bartender said, handing me back the phone. "I thought it was damned decent of him to do that for a complete stranger."

"So they weren't friends or acquaintances?"

"Not as far as I know."

"Did the two of them leave together?"

The bartender nodded. "The Good Samaritan left his drink on the bar. When he didn't come back to finish it, I figured Max must have given him a ride home. The next thing I knew, Max was dead, but since everything I heard said it was an accident, I didn't give much thought to the tire-changing thing. Is it possible Tattoo Guy had something to do with what happened?"

The words "we have a bingo" came to mind. "It's possible," I said. With that, I pulled out my cell phone and redialed Kevin Blaylock's number. This time he answered on the third ring.

"Blaylock here," he said.

"My name's Beaumont," I said. "J. P. Beaumont."

"Thanks for calling me back. You wouldn't happen to be Scotty's dad, would you by any chance?"

"You know my son?" I asked.

"I met Scott when he was going through the academy. I was teaching one of the crime scene classes, and we hit it off. He brags about you a lot. When Erin mentioned your name earlier, I wondered if you weren't related, but right then wasn't exactly an opportune time to ask."

"Where are you right now?" I asked him, cutting to the chase. "We need to talk."

"What about?"

"I think I know how your vehicular homicide victim's prints ended up at the scene of Maxwell Cole's fatal fire."

There was a slight pause, but that was all it was—slight. "I live up by Northgate," Blaylock answered. "Where do you want to meet and how soon?"

The bartender had just deposited my to-go bag on the counter in front of me. I wanted to be in on whatever conversation Detective Blaylock had with the bartender, but I didn't want Mel's food to get cold in the meantime. Cold fish and chips are fine for me, but Mel deserved better.

"There's a place on lower Queen Anne called Sneaky Pete's," I told him. "Let's meet up there in half an hour or so."

"How will I recognize you?"

"Just ask the bartender," I said. "He'll be able to point you in the right direction."

CHAPTER 25

I MAY HAVE wanted Mel's food to arrive while it was still hot, but I did not want to explain why I was heading back out to meet up with a Seattle PD homicide detective. To that end, I took the coward's way out. I drove up to the front entrance of Belltown Terrace, called the doorman—a new guy; Bob wasn't on duty—and asked him to deliver the takeout bag to our penthouse unit.

Then I drove back to Sneaky Pete's, where the parking lot was full to the brim. After parking three blocks away I trudged back up the hill in rain that was suddenly more than a "light shower." As a matter of civic pride, people who live in Seattle mostly don't believe in carrying umbrellas. That meant that by the time I got back to the bar, I was soaked. The bar had filled up during my brief absence. I ended up grabbing a table at the far end of the room just in front of the gas log fire. Considering the state of my clothing, that was a good thing.

There were a number of e-mail notifications from Todd Hatcher on my phone. I ordered another tonic and lime and then fired up the iPad to browse through them. They were sorted into separate files by name. Todd Farraday's listings were mostly of the police report and conviction variety. Among them were several DUIs, a drunk and disorderly, and a number of citations for public drunkenness. On three separate occasions he had also been charged with simple assault as well as one instance of assault with intent. Those charges had all been dismissed, something that made me believe that maybe Max hadn't been wrong in thinking that Larry Harden might still have some pull among members of the law enforcement community.

The file on Todd's mother started with her obituary. Natalie Farraday Harden had died five years earlier, at age eighty-seven, of congestive heart failure. Among the links listed for her was a profile piece telling how, after leaving the world of municipal politics and with the help of both her husband, Port Commissioner Lawrence Harden, and her son, Todd Farraday, Natalie had finally fulfilled a lifelong dream by first establishing and then running what had turned into a thriving antique business called Occidental Antiques, based in Pioneer Square.

But the article that really caught my attention was one from the *Seattle Post-Intelligencer*, dated March 2, 2001. It carried a headline that said ANTIQUES EMPORIUM HITS ROCK BOTTOM. The accompanying photo showed Natalie and a man I recognized as a twenty-something version of Todd Farraday standing in a high-ceilinged room and staring down into what appeared to be an abyss. A large decorated chest of some kind dangled precariously on the edge of a black hole that appeared to be eight to ten feet across.

So that's the earthquake in question, I told myself, *the Nisqually Quake.*

Seattle has a long tradition of naming natural disasters for the day on which they happened. Off the top of my head I remember several fierce windstorms, among them the Columbus Day storm, the Inauguration Day storm, and the Hanukkah Eve storm. For a time the 2001 incident was referred to as the Ash Wednesday Quake, but that was early on. Once seismologists established that the quake was traced back to the Nisqually Fault, the event morphed into being referred to as the Nisqually Quake.

According to the article, Natalie Farraday and her son had been alone in her Pioneer Square store late that Wednesday morning when the earthquake occurred. As the shaking continued, what they had thought to be a solid granite floor had abruptly turned the consistency of Jell-O. When it was over, the interior of the shop was littered with fallen bricks and smashed merchandise, including more than one Ming Dynasty vase. The most amazing damage, however, was the gaping hole that had opened up in the middle of the room, revealing a fourteen-foot drop into what turned out to be a previously undiscovered earthen basement space hidden beneath the ground floor.

Anyone who has ever visited Seattle and taken the Seattle Underground tour knows the story of how, on a June day in 1889, an unfortunate local cabinetmaker accidentally knocked over a pot of hot glue and set it ablaze. The resulting fire burned down most of the wooden structures that, at the time, made up the heart of downtown Seattle. The general area known as Pioneer Square had been built on filled-in tidelands that often flooded. When it came time to rebuild, the city fathers decreed that the steeply sloped area would be regraded. As a result, ground floors in the rebuilt buildings would be one to two floors higher than they had been originally. Zoning rules also required that all the rebuilt structures be constructed of brick.

In the mid-1960s, a guy named Bill Speidel started giving tours of those long-disused underground spaces, creating a network of underground passages that went from building to building and paying rent to the existing landlords of the aboveground buildings for the privilege.

Evidently whoever owned the building housing Occidental Antiques on South Jackson hadn't bought into the Seattle Underground program. In the article, Natalie Farraday Harden was quoted as saying she had no idea the empty space underneath her store even existed. My takeaway from the story was that the falling-out between mother and son that had resulted in Natalie disowning Todd must have occurred sometime after the earthquake.

"Striking family resemblance between you and your son," someone said casually, "although it turns out your forehead is quite a bit taller."

There's nothing like having a total stranger remind you of your supposed obsolescence first rattle out of the box. I looked up, fully prepared to take offense, only to see that, when it came to square inches of forehead, the guy doing the talking had no room to talk. What little hair Kevin Blaylock had left made him look like Robin Hood's tonsured friend, Friar Tuck, from that long-ago black-and-white TV series. Not only that, rather than being some sweet young thing of a cop, Blaylock was far closer to my age than he was to Scott's. Even so, he wasn't someone I recognized from my years at Seattle PD.

"Yup," I said agreeably, offering my hand. "Getting old is hell. The name's Beaumont, by the way. Most people call me Beau or J.P., whichever you prefer."

"Beau then," Blaylock concluded, answering my handshake with a firm one of his own. "I'm Kevin."

He set a steaming mug of coffee down on the cocktail table between us and then shrugged his way out of a small leather backpack, little more than an old-fashioned satchel, which he hung on the back of his chair. As he eased himself down into a sitting position, an involuntary grimace told me that Detective Kevin Blaylock's knees most likely hurt like hell. Been there; done that.

"You're new to Seattle PD?" I asked.

"Fairly new," he answered. "I transferred in from Baltimore two years ago. The wife's from here originally. She wanted to come back home so we'd be closer at hand and able to help look after her folks, who still live up in Edmonds. I was a little surprised when the local brass decided to slot me into Homicide, but at my age, beggars can't be choosers. I pick up a few extra bucks now and again by teaching CSI classes at the academy down in Sea-Tac. That's where I met that boy of yours—a very good kid, by the way—who happens to be very proud of his old man."

I couldn't help flushing with pleasure at hearing news of Scott's secondhand praise. With that remark any hard feelings concerning Blaylock's initial comment about my receding hairline dissipated, once and for all.

Settling back in his chair, Detective Blaylock eyed me speculatively. "So what's the deal here?" he asked. "I know you've been involved in looking into the Maxwell Cole case. Erin Howard told me as much. My job is to investigate the hit-and-run death of Duc Nguyen, but what I'd like to know is how you happen to be privy to details of my ongoing investigation."

If Blaylock had been one of those guys who do everything by the book, he would have raised that issue on the telephone to begin with, and he certainly wouldn't have been sitting across the table from me little more than half an hour later. Sometimes you've just got to trust your instincts. Kevin was a newcomer to Homicide, and probably not a particularly welcome addition as far as the old hands were concerned. That helped explain why a dead-end gangbanger hit-and-run case had been tossed in his lap in the first place. That's how bureaucracies function. The last people in are always handed the crap jobs. But Blaylock was also legitimately an "old guy," and sometimes we old guys have to stick together.

"Al Thorne and I go way back," I told him. "No doubt he was speaking out of turn, but we were chewing the fat, and he just happened to mention the fingerprint situation."

Rather than going ballistic about the details of his case being leaked to an outsider, Blaylock simply nodded. "All right then," he said. "That explains how you know where Duc's prints were found, but on the phone earlier you claimed to know how they got there. I've been working this case for days. Other than the fingerprints themselves, I haven't uncovered a single link between Duc Nguyen and Maxwell Cole."

"The link is right here," I said, gesturing in a way that encompassed the whole room. "Sneaky Pete's *is* the connection. According to the bartender, your vic showed up here for the first time ever on the night Maxwell Cole died. The two men struck up a conversation. Cole exited the bar at some point and then came back inside, complaining of a flat tire and expecting Triple A to show up and fix it. Instead, your hit-and-run victim hopped off his chair, left a drink on the bar, and went outside to change the tire."

"Duc offered to change the tire," Blaylock mused thoughtfully. "Were they friends?"

"Strangers as far as I can tell."

"But Maxwell Cole and Duc subsequently left the bar together?"

"That's what I've been told."

"Any security footage to verify that?"

"There might well be," I said, "but considering I'm operating on the sidelines here, I wasn't exactly in a position to ask to see it."

"And your pet theory is that Duc is somehow responsible for the fire that killed Maxwell Cole?"

"Yes, it is. I also believe it's possible that Max's death was a hit of some kind."

"And that whoever called for the hit on Cole took Duc out once the deed was accomplished?"

"That's the idea," I said, "so let me ask you this. What was Duc wearing when he died, and where did it happen?"

"He was run down on South King, down in Pioneer Square. The vehicle hit him hard enough to drop-kick him fifteen yards onto the brick pavers in Occidental Square. The ME put the time of death at between four and five A.M."

"On Sunday morning, the same day as the fire?"

Blaylock nodded, while my head lit up like a Christmas tree. South King just happened to be within a matter of blocks from the location of Natalie Harden's Occidental Antiques. I suspected that wasn't an unimportant coincidence.

"Any damage to the vehicle?"

Blaylock nodded. "Broken headlamp. The crime lab has established that the vehicle in question is most likely a 2015 Cadillac Escalade. As for what the victim was wearing? About what you'd expect of your run-of-the-mill gangbanger—jeans, T-shirt, tennis shoes. And the shoes weren't cheap ones, either. They were the latest hottest-selling, three-hundred-bucks-a-pair Nikes. Everything he was wearing—including the shoes—was filthy and so was he—like he'd been working in a coal mine."

"FYI," I told him, "according to the bartender, when he showed up here a few hours earlier, Nguyen was all decked out in a suit and tie, passing himself off as some kind of engineering type for Google or Amazon."

I could tell that tidbit of information captured Blaylock's attention. "That bartender over there?" he asked, nodding.

"The very one," I told him. As Blaylock excused himself and headed for the bar, my phone rang. "The fish and chips were great," Mel said. "But where are you?"

"Back at Sneaky Pete's," I said. "Meeting with a Seattle homicide cop."

"Far be it from me to interrupt," Mel said. "See you when you get home."

Because Blaylock was still preoccupied with the bartender, I took advantage of his absence to call the ME's office. Since it was Saturday evening, I was relatively sure Dr. Roz would be on duty. When I called on her direct number, she picked up at once.

"Hey, Beau," she said. "What can I do you for?"

"I'm calling about a guy named Todd Farraday. He would have come through the ME's office a little over a week ago."

I heard the clatter of a computer keyboard. "Okay," Roz said a moment later. "Here he is. The body was transported on Thursday, January fifth, but time of death is listed as sometime prior to midnight on January fourth. Autopsy results determined that he died of acute alcohol poisoning combined with severe hypothermia, or, as we like to call it around here, death by Jägermeister. The guy was evidently falling-down drunk, passed out on his stepfather's front porch, and died of exposure. End of story."

"You're sure it was Jägermeister? Since when can autopsy results determine the brand of booze?"

Dr. Roz laughed at that. "That detail came straight from the CSIs," she answered. "There was an empty Jägermeister bottle found near the body, one with Mr. Farraday's prints on it and nobody else's. Why are you asking about this, Beau? Does it have something to do with the Maxwell Cole homicide?"

"With that and with Duc Nguyen's hit-and-run as well."

"Nguyen is the guy whose fingerprints were found at Cole's crime scene?"

"Correct."

"My understanding is that Detective Blaylock of Seattle PD is working that case."

"Yes, he is," I told her. *And so am I.*

Blaylock was returning to the table, so I thanked Roz for her help and hung up.

"Well?" I asked.

"Mike contacted the owner, and he's agreed to come in to give us a look at the security footage. In the meantime, you need to tell me everything you know."

He had used the term "us," but did he really mean it? "Does that mean we're working together on this?" I asked.

"What do you think?"

With that Blaylock reached into his backpack. I expected him to pull out an iPad or a laptop. Instead, he withdrew an old-fashioned stenographer's pad along with a ball-point pen. Back in the day, I hauled around pencils and little notebooks that fit in my pockets. Blaylock noticed that my attention was totally focused on the pad.

"Hope you don't mind," he said, shaking it in my direction. "The guys back at the department call me a troglodyte, and it's true. When I was in high school, boys could take typing but not shorthand. My mom was a secretary, and she took it upon herself to teach me how to do shorthand. Gregg's has served me in good stead ever since."

"However you take notes is fine with me," I told him, "but if you expect me to tell you what I know, it needs to be a two-way street."

Blaylock thought about that for a moment before he nodded. "Fair enough," he agreed. "It will be."

"All right then," I said. "Listen up because, by my count, I may have just uncovered victim number three."

CHAPTER 26

WHILE KEVIN BLAYLOCK made indecipherable chicken scratches onto the pages of his steno pad, I told him the whole story, with zero holdbacks, and that took time. My account included briefing him on Maxwell Cole's reinvestigation of the long-ago school district homicide case, which seemed to be the starting point. When I got as far as the last couple of weeks, I started with Todd Farraday's scheduled meeting with Maxwell Cole and went from there.

I had finished up and was waiting while Blaylock reviewed his notes when a newcomer arrived at our table. "Detective Blaylock?" he inquired.

"That would be me."

"I'm Richard Meece, the owner. I believe you wanted to see me?"

"Yes, and thank you so much for coming in," Blaylock said. "This is my colleague, Mr. Beaumont. We're looking into the death of one of your customers..."

"I know," Meece said. "Maxwell Cole was one of our regulars. If I can do anything to help..."

"You can," Blaylock told him, pausing long enough to consult his notes. "We need to see your security feeds from the last night Maxwell Cole was here. That would be Saturday, January fourteenth."

"And maybe from several nights before that," I added, "including the feeds for Wednesday, the fourth."

"Sure thing," Meece said. "The screens are back in the office. It'll be a little crowded with all three of us in there, but I think we can manage."

Manage was all we did. Meece took the office chair and Blaylock the visitor's chair. I ended up perched on the edge of the desk. I have to hand it to Meece, however. He was a down-home expert at operating his multiscreen security setup. "Max usually showed up around five thirty or so," he explained, as he focused our attention on a screen that showed the interior of the bar from back to front. He put the date stamps at 5:15 and started fast-forwarding from there.

"That looks like Max," I said, pointing to a figure entering the bar at 17:35:46.

"That's him all right," Meece agreed, slowing the feed. "Right on time, too, and that was his usual spot—two stools down from the entrance."

We watched the action, sometimes fast-forwarding and sometimes not. The bartender, the one I recognized as Mike, served him a drink and handed him a menu. He ordered food and another drink. The food came and he ordered drink number three. That was about the time when the two people who had been seated next to Max at the bar got up to leave. Moments later, someone else slipped onto the stool next to Max's.

"Wait," I said. "Can you stop it right there? Isn't that Nguyen?"

With a few clicks on the keyboard, Meece froze the action and then enlarged the frame that was date-stamped 20:46:57. The man now seated to Maxwell Cole's right was indeed Duc Nguyen. The teardrop tattoo was fully visible, but the man bore no resemblance to a gangbanger lowlife. Indeed, he looked for all the world like a sophisticated young millennial out for an evening on the town.

"Is this guy one of your regulars?" Blaylock asked.

Meece shook his head. "Nope," he said. "If he'd been here before, I never saw him."

"Go back a little," I suggested. "Did he just come in or had he come inside earlier and just then moved over to the bar?"

Scrolling back several minutes, we spotted Nguyen enter the room some five minutes earlier and take a seat at an unoccupied table in the middle of the room. He moved from there to the spot next to Max only when the other couple vacated their stools.

"Did Nguyen have a vehicle?" I asked.

"Not one that he owned," Blaylock answered. "Why?"

"So how did he get to Lower Queen Anne from the Rainier Valley?"

"Good question," Blaylock said. "Maybe we should check out the parking lot just before he came inside."

In a matter of seconds, Meece switched over to footage taken by an outside camera, one that afforded us a view of both the building's exterior and most of the parking lot. Meece started reviewing the footage at a time that was ten or so minutes prior to Nguyen's initial appearance inside the bar. When we caught sight of him for the first time outside the building, he was threading his way through the parking lot on foot. He came forward steadily and then disappeared abruptly, dropping completely out of sight behind the sheltering front fender of a parked vehicle.

He remained invisible to the camera for the better part of a minute. When he reappeared, he seemed to be shoving something into the pocket of his jacket before squaring his shoulders and stepping into the bar.

"Do you happen to know whose car that is?" I asked.

"Sure," Meece answered. "That's gotta be Maxwell Cole's Volvo. That was always his favorite place to park—in the gimp spot right out front."

"Unless I miss my guess," Blaylock said, "it looks like our guy there did something to that right front tire—jammed a nail in it maybe?"

"Which goes a long way to explain the flat Max found a little while later when he was ready to leave—the same tire his new best pal here, Duc Nguyen, helpfully offered to change."

We returned to the interior footage where Nguyen and Max sat side by side, apparently exchanging pleasantries while Duc downed one drink and Max had another as well—his fourth by my count—which meant he had probably been legitimately overserved by then, as well. At that point, with the time-date stamp reading 22:10:31, Max paid his bill with a credit card and left. He was outside for a total of three minutes before he came back in, clearly agitated. There were several verbal exchanges before Max and Nguyen left together. Switching over to the outside camera, we watched as Nguyen shed his jacket and then expertly changed the damaged tire, replacing it with Max's spare.

When the job was finished and with a date stamp reading of 22:56:46, Nguyen put his jacket back on and then the two of them left the parking lot together, driving out of sight in Max's Volvo, with Max behind the wheel and Duc Nguyen riding shotgun in the passenger seat. That meant Duc Nguyen had been one of the last people to see Max alive, a little more than three hours before someone made the 911 call reporting the fire.

"What do you think?" Blaylock asked.

"I'm thinking Nguyen's good for it," I replied.

"Anything else?" Meece asked.

After leaning against the desk all that time, my hip was killing me, but I wasn't ready to leave, not just yet. "Yes, please," I said. "Our understanding is that Max was here on Wednesday of the preceding week as well. We'd like to see some of that footage, too."

"Starting about the same time?"

"Yes."

A few minutes later we were once again viewing the feed from the interior of the bar. Max appeared promptly at 17:30:05, took his usual spot, and ordered a drink.

"What was Max's drink of choice?" I asked.

"Vodka tonic," Meece answered at once. Two minutes later, someone joined him at the bar, and the two men shook hands.

"That one has be Todd Farraday," I said aloud.

The two men both ordered food—burgers, from the looks of it. As far as I could see, Todd drank coffee. It was possible the java was spiked with something stronger, but his sticking to coffee tied in with what Patrick had told me earlier—that Todd had been working on staying sober. As for the Jägermeister? There was no sign of it, at least not for as long as he was in the bar.

We were able to fast-forward through most of the footage. Max and Todd ate and talked. Then, when Todd exited Sneaky Pete's an hour and a half later, Max was still seated in the bar, busily typing something into a computer keyboard. A check on the video feed from the parking lot showed Todd, alone and on foot, walking out of camera range northbound—a route that would have taken him up the hill and toward Lawrence Harden's place on Kinnear, only a few blocks away.

"Is that it, then?" Meece asked.

"For now," Blaylock told him. "Hang on to the footage for us, though, because we're probably going to need it."

We made our way out of the office, with Blaylock walking ahead and me limping along behind. Out in the bar, the place was hopping. We managed to find a single table in the far back corner of the room.

"So where are we?" Blaylock asked.

I ticked off what we knew, counting on my fingers. "Maxwell Cole interviews Todd Farraday. The next morning Farraday, who wasn't drinking in the footage, is nonetheless dead of acute alcohol poisoning. A few days later Max meets up with Duc Nguyen right here, and within hours both of them are dead, too."

"And you think Lawrence Harden is the big fish Maxwell Cole was worried about when he talked to you about some kind of pushback?" Blaylock asked.

"I do."

"What exactly did Harden do after he left the department?"

"Got himself elected to the port commission."

"While his wife ran an antique shop of some kind?"

"Far Eastern antiques."

"Imported?" Blaylock asked.

"Presumably."

"Interesting," Blaylock said.

During our long sojourn in the back office, my pair of tonic and limes had run their course. While I excused myself for a trip to the little boys' room, Blaylock reached into his leather backpack and pulled out a standard Seattle PD–issue tablet that could operate either as a stand-alone or as an accessory inside a patrol car. For some reason, I felt relieved to know that Blaylock's investigative skills weren't solely confined to the shorthand contents of his steno pad.

On my way into the restroom, I was busy remembering everything I knew about Natalie Farraday's Occidental Antiques—not only the details Patrick had told me, but also what I had seen and read in that article about the Nisqually Quake. Up to that point, Todd had evidently worked with his mother in the antiques business. Whatever had transpired to wreck their previous working relationship had happened after the earthquake had opened up that gaping hole in the middle of the floor of Natalie Harden's shop.

Suddenly I could see a possible pattern emerging through the fog. Lawrence Harden's work at the port commission would have put him in contact with all kinds of people, both good and bad. But what if some of those folks had been really bad? What if he'd gotten himself mixed up in some kind of smuggling operation? His wife's antiques business—especially in a building that came complete with a cavernous underground storage space—would have provided suitable cover for all kinds of shipments coming and going at odd hours.

This was all speculation, of course, something with

no shred of evidence to support it other than those three recent deaths, all of which, I was convinced, had to be linked. But if Lawrence Harden was the mover and shaker behind all this, what was his connection to Duc Nguyen? How would a former cop and a big-time politico get mixed up with a Rainier Valley gang-banger?

As I returned to the table, Blaylock gave me a furtive glance and then quickly shut down whatever program was operating on his computer. He looked for all the world like a kid caught with his hand in the cookie jar. I was curious about what he was so eager to keep me from seeing, but I didn't ask, not directly. Instead, I posed an entirely different question.

"Tell me about Duc," I said.

"Not much to tell," Blaylock said. "His family immigrated to the States after the Vietnam War. His grandparents ran a hole-in-the-wall restaurant down in the International District. His parents operated several nail salons up until his mother died of cancer about five years ago. That's what the teardrop tattoo is all about—it's for his mother. Duc had been a good student—an honor roll student, before his mother died. When I talked to Duc's father, I learned that the two of them—father and son—never did see eye to eye about much of anything. The mother was the one who maintained the peace between them. Once she was gone, it all fell apart. That's when Duc started hanging out with the wrong kinds of kids. He dropped out of school, got hooked up with the gang, and now he's dead."

"Which gang?" I asked.

"The Local Asian Boys—the LABs," he said. As soon as he said those words, I saw a change of expression flash across his face, as though by simply saying the words something had clicked in his head, but did he tell me what that connection was? He most certainly did not. Instead, he slipped the computer into his satchel and stood up.

A cocktail waitress was finally making her belated way to our table, but he waved her off. "I need to get going," he said. "Thanks for your help."

I have to admit, I was a little puzzled by his abrupt departure. Up to then we had been working together in a fairly congenial manner. I had expected that he'd brief me with a little background on the LABs. Instead, for reasons I didn't understand, our partnership had obviously come to an end.

I followed Blaylock out of the bar and walked down the hill to my car. At least it wasn't raining. Back at Belltown Terrace, I grabbed my now-cold bag of fish and chips from the kitchen counter and went looking for Mel and Lucy. I found them sprawled together on the floor in the family room watching *Dateline*.

You'd think that someone who deals with real cops and robbers day in and day out would find something better to do than watching rehashes of often cold cases on television. The truth is, we do watch them, more often than not picking apart the investigational errors we see along the way and occasionally learning a thing or two. Mel used the clicker to put the program on semipermanent pause when I showed up in the doorway.

"Hey," she said. "Welcome home. Long time no see."

I settled into the surprisingly comfortable easy chair that has permanently replaced that once holy of holies, my recliner, and sampled a bite or two of my Sneaky

Pete's fish and chips. They may have been fine to begin with, but they hadn't exactly improved with age.

"You don't look happy," Mel observed, "so how about bringing me up to speed?"

I did so, starting with my trip to the Evidence Unit and ending with the unexpected parting of the ways with Detective Blaylock.

"My guess is that someone at Seattle PD figured out you were nosing around in some of their cases, and he was ordered to shut you out."

I tossed a soggy french fry in Lucy's direction. She happily caught it in midair and chomped it down. At least someone seemed to like them.

"You're probably right," I said.

"So what are you going to do now?" Mel asked. "Back off?"

"What do you think?"

"Silly me," she said with a grin, "but what's the next step?"

I set the bag of chips aside and pulled out my phone. It needed charging, but not right that minute. Instead I scrolled through my contacts list until I located the number for Big Al Lindstrom.

Years earlier, Big Al and I had been partners at the Seattle PD homicide unit. He had left the department after taking a bullet while protecting the only living witness to a home invasion case—a five-year-old boy named Benjamin Harrison Weston. Ben was a little black kid who had survived the slaughter of the rest of his family only because he'd been playing hide-and-seek at the time and had fallen asleep, hidden away in the safety of a closet.

Not surprisingly, Big Al had taken a personal interest in little Ben's life from then on, and the feeling had been mutual. After leaving the department, Big Al had suffered from any number of health issues and his wife, Molly, had always been his cheerful and undaunted caretaker—up until a few months ago, that is. During the previous summer, Molly had developed a persistent cough. When she had finally agreed to go see a doctor, the diagnosis had been bad news—lung cancer, fourth stage, with very little to be done. She had declined all treatment, focusing her efforts instead on selling their house in Ballard and getting both of them settled into an assisted living facility in the Ballard area, a place where she could be sure Big Al would continue to have the help and care he needed when Molly herself was no longer there to provide it.

And she wasn't. She had died the week after Thanksgiving, less than four months after receiving her diagnosis. The last time I had spoken to Big Al had been at the reception following Molly's funeral, and Benjamin Weston had been there, too, a hulking brute of a young man, who had been helping out at every turn and acting the part of the son Big Al and Molly never had.

I had known all along that he'd gone off to Gonzaga on a full-ride basketball scholarship. What I learned at the funeral was that a knee injury in his sophomore year had taken him out of contention. He had graduated with a degree in criminal justice, however, and had come back to Seattle, where he had joined Seattle PD. Considering that both his father, Benjamin Weston Sr., and Big Al were cops, that was hardly a surprising outcome. What had surprised me when we spoke at the funeral was that Ben was now working undercover in the gang unit.

As I pressed the button to dial Big Al's number, two lumps formed in my body—one in my throat and the other in my gut. What the hell was the matter with me? Why hadn't I called Big Al between the funeral and now? Why hadn't I checked in on him over this first set of holidays without Molly to see how he was doing? Why was I calling now and only because I needed his help? My bout of self-castigation ended when he answered the phone.

"Hey, Beau," he said. "Is it really you?"

"Yes, it's really me," I answered, "your thoughtless, no-good, very bad friend. How are you doing?"

"You're not as bad as all that," he assured me, sounding a lot like his old self. "And I'm doing okay. Molly was so smart to get us settled in here before everything happened. I gave her all kinds of grief about it at the time, at least I tried to, but she wouldn't have it. We were moving and that was that. I can see now she was right."

"So it's an okay place then?"

"It's all right. The food's not nearly as good as what Molly used to make, but it's a hell of a lot better than it would be if I were doing my own cooking. And the people aren't half-bad, either. I enjoy hanging out with some of the other old duffers around here, and I'm turning into a killer when it comes to five-card draw. We've got an afternoon poker group. We only play for toothpicks, of course, but I've developed a bit of a reputation."

He sounded so much like his old self, I breathed a

sigh of relief. Molly had indeed made the right call in getting him established in new digs prior to her passing.

"So why the call?" Big Al asked.

He had me cold there, and my guilt flooded back, big-time. "I was hoping you could put me in touch with Ben Weston. He told me he was working the gang unit for Seattle PD these days, and I have a couple of questions that he may be able to answer."

"No problem," Big Al said. "I'm sure Bennie will be glad to help." He reeled off the phone number to me without having to pause long enough to look it up, and I keyed it into my iPad.

"So with that S.H.I.T. outfit of yours shut down these days, what are you doing to keep yourself busy?"

"A little of this and a little of that," I said.

"And how about that beauteous wife of yours? What's she up to?"

"She's got her hands full running the cop shop up in Bellingham."

"You tell her hello for me." Then, after a little beep sound in my ear, he said, "Oops. I have another call, gotta go. Later."

Wham-bam, thank you, ma'am. Over. As the call ended, I found Mel studying me. "How's he doing?" she asked.

"Fine, I think. He sounded okay—like his old self."

"That's good to hear." She switched off the television and stood up. "I'm going to take Lucy out one more time, and then I'm going to hit the hay. Don't stay up too late. I talked to the kids earlier and told them we'd be by their place early afternoon tomorrow for a late lunch/early dinner before we head back north."

While Mel and Lucy took off, I dialed the number

Big Al had given me. I wasn't the least bit surprised when my call went to voice mail. If Benjamin was working undercover, it wouldn't pay to have calls from cops or ex-cops turning up on his phone at inopportune times.

"J. P. Beaumont here, Ben," I said. "Big Al gave me your number. Call me back when you have a chance."

He called back less than five minutes later, just as Mel and Lucy returned from their sojourn downstairs.

"Hey, Beau," he said. "It's good to hear from you. The last time I saw you was at Molly's funeral. How are things?"

"I'm okay," I said. "I'm working a case, a more or less unofficial one, and I ran up against some questions I thought you might be able to answer."

"About?"

"About the Local Asian Boys."

"Whoa," he said. "The LABs? Talk about a bad bunch!"

"So you know about them, then?"

Ben let out his breath before he answered. "I know something about them, but not nearly as much as I'd like to. They're a tight-knit group, and we haven't been able to get anyone inside. There are rumors out there that the ringleader of the LABs is a woman, but we haven't been able to prove that one way or the other."

"A woman, really?"

"That's the rumor. People sometimes refer to her as the Ghost Girl. What I can tell you for sure is that the LABs are a bunch of bad actors who have suddenly gone from being very small fries to being very big fries."

"How so?" I asked.

"Dealing drugs—fentanyl mostly along with some

meth on the side," he answered. "As far as we're able to tell, they've pretty well cornered the local market on both of those, but they seem to have access to other, more exotic stuff as well, along with a ready supply of weapons."

"Does the name Duc Nguyen mean anything to you?"

"Sure," Ben replied at once. "He was an LAB member in good standing who died last week in what was supposedly a hit-and-run."

"Supposedly?"

"Hit-and-run is Homicide's take on the matter," Ben answered. "Out here in the real world of the gang unit, we're figuring it was more like a straight hit, probably done by a rival gang, one looking to horn in on the LAB's drug-dealing action."

As long as I was at Seattle PD, there had been unresolved rivalries between the gang unit and the homicide squad. Obviously nothing had changed.

"So where are you in all this?" Ben asked. "What's your connection?"

I was reasonably sure that by answering that question, I would be selling Detective Blaylock down the river, but then again, given the fact that the two of us weren't exactly simpatico at the moment, did that even matter?

"Don't quote me on this, but I have it on reasonably good authority that Duc's fingerprints were found at the site of a fatality house fire up on Queen Anne Hill last week. The fire was reported a mere three hours or so before Duc turned up dead down in Pioneer Square."

"Wait, an arson fire?" Ben repeated. "And nobody thought to mention word one about that to us?"

"Most likely they just haven't gotten around to it," I said.

"Sure," Ben responded. "Like hell."

"But what can you tell me about the LABs?"

"A few years ago they were nothing but a bunch of ragtag street thugs. Then, a couple of years ago, they morphed into something else and turned themselves into major players in the drug-dealing world. Word is they're making money hand over fist."

That would go a long way to explain Duc Nguyen's three-hundred-dollar Nikes.

"We've been trying like hell to get an informant inside the LABs to see where their dope is coming from," Ben continued, "but so far it's a no-go. I'd do it myself, but a six-foot-five black man can't exactly pass for a five-foot-nothin' Vietnamese."

"Where do you think the fentanyl is coming from?"

"That would be any number of places in the Far East, China included," Ben said at once. "But we don't know how it's getting here or who's behind it."

I thought about keeping my mouth shut. By speaking up, I ran the risk of putting Ben in harm's way, but then again, if he had signed on to go undercover with the gang unit, wasn't harm's way exactly where he wanted to be?

"I may have a name for you," I said. "Lawrence Harden. Formerly Chief of Police Harden, so if you go looking into this guy, you'll need to be very, very discreet. There are indications that he may still have pull inside the department. These days he runs an antique shop down on South Jackson, a place called Occidental Antiques, that used to belong to his late wife, former Seattle mayor Natalie Farraday Harden."

"Wait," Ben interjected. "South Jackson. Isn't that close to the spot where Duc Nguyen died?"

Yes, I thought gratefully, *someone smart enough to connect the dots.*

"Exactly," I said, "but that's not all. I think Harden may be ultimately responsible for two other deaths as well—the fire that killed Maxwell Cole and the death of Todd Farraday, Harden's stepson, who supposedly died accidentally due to a combination of acute alcohol poisoning and hypothermia. Farraday died some time before midnight on Wednesday, January fourth. Max and Duc died a few days later and within hours of one another early on Sunday morning, January fifteenth. Initially the fire was considered accidental, but the presence of Duc's fingerprints at the scene and the fact that Max's electronics are among the missing moved it over to Homicide."

"Who's been assigned to that one?" Ben asked.

"No idea," I answered, "not so far."

"And the hit-and-run?"

"That would be Detective Kevin Blaylock."

"Mr. Transfer Guy," Ben said. "So the guys at Homicide stuck him with the short stick and gave him the dead-end gangbanger case."

Seattle may be a large city, but in terms of gossip, Seattle PD is still very much your basic small town.

"That would be my take," I agreed. "I met with Blaylock earlier this evening. Between us we came up with some critical video footage that shows Duc meeting up with Maxwell Cole in a bar on Queen Anne Hill on Saturday evening. Later on both men left together with Duc as a passenger in Cole's vehicle. Then, just when I thought we were getting along great and making progress, Blaylock completely shut me out."

"Maybe someone let him know you were bad news?"

"Probably."

"So you're thinking that this Harden guy is somehow behind all of it?"

"That's true, but remember, all of this is pure supposition on my part. So far there's not a shred of evidence to back up any of it."

"JDLR?" Ben asked.

I had to laugh at the ease with which he slipped into cop-speak. "Yes," I agreed, "just doesn't look right."

After that Ben fell quiet for several long moments. "If the stepson's death is considered accidental, nobody's been working that one. What's the deal with the fire?"

"Until Duc's fingerprints showed up at the scene, that one was considered to be an accident as well, and it wasn't being investigated, either."

"Of the three, then, the hit-and-run is the only incident that's been under active investigation. Has Blaylock made any progress on that?"

"Some. When we saw the video footage in the bar, Duc was dressed like some hotshot young businessman out for an evening on the town, except for something odd. On the way into the bar, he paused in the parking lot and appeared to mess with Max's car. Later on, when Max tried to leave, one of his tires was flat. Duc went all Good Samaritan and offered to change it for him."

"The two of them left the bar together?"

"Yes, with Duc still wearing business attire. However, a few hours later, when he turned up dead, he had changed into full gangbanger regalia and looked like he'd been working in a coal mine."

"A coal mine?'

"Yeah, he was covered with all kinds of dirt and muck. According to Blaylock, Duc was run down by a 2015 Cadillac Escalade. I suspect he may have learned more than that, but he didn't bother passing any of it along to me."

"Let me do a little digging," Ben offered. "Word on the street is that Duc was relatively low on the LAB totem pole. He may have agreed to do the hit on Cole as a way of improving his reputation."

Sort of like Todd Farraday's bomb threats. That's what I thought, but I didn't say it aloud. That part of the story would have been ancient history as far as Benjamin Weston was concerned.

"Whatever digging you do," I suggested, "make sure it's discreet digging, and just to be on the safe side, you'd probably be better off if you left my name out of it."

"Do you think I'm stupid or something?" Ben asked with an audible chuckle.

After ending the call, I sat for a few minutes staring into the fire. I was thinking about Todd Farraday and his fatal dose of Jägermeister. Where exactly had the booze come from? Had he downed it willingly, or had it been forcibly administered by someone else? He had consumed several cups of coffee in the course of his visit with Maxwell Cole, but there had been no way to tell whether or not any of those had contained alcohol. He hadn't appeared to be intoxicated when he left the bar on his own, nor had I seen any indication of his buying up takeout booze at Sneaky Pete's. As far as the bar was concerned, that probably would have counted as a violation of any number of liquor department rules and regs.

It was only a few blocks from Sneaky Pete's up the hill to Lawrence Harden's place on Kinnear, with no liquor stores between hither and yon, so either Todd had brought the Jägermeister with him from the Refuge, or it had been supplied to him by someone else. But if, as Patrick had told me, Todd hated his stepfather's guts, why would he go there in the first place?

Just then, Lucy stalked silently into the room on her scraggly, stiltlike legs. She sat down between me and the fire, staring at me with those intense black eyes. It was all slightly unsettling, but then I realized what the deal was. She wasn't really looking at me. She was totally focused on the Sneaky Pete's bag. I might have forgotten about the remainder of my fish and chips, but Lucy had not.

I tossed her a couple of soggy, limp fries. She gulped them down without so much as a single chew.

"Okay, girl," I said finally. "That's enough. Those probably aren't any better for you than they are for me. Let's go to bed."

Then, because my phone was almost dead, I plugged it into a family room charger, and off to bed we went.

CHAPTER 27

I WAS SLEEPING the sleep of the dead the next morning when Mel shook me awake and handed me my phone. "Ben Weston is on the line," she said, disappearing into the hall.

I glanced at my watch before I answered. It was ten past seven. "Hey, Ben," I croaked into the phone. "What's up?"

"It's bad news, Beau."

I sat up straighter in the bed. "What's bad news?"

"Kevin Blaylock is dead."

The hair literally stood up on the back of my neck. "Dead?" I repeated. "What the hell? How? When? Where?"

"Somebody shot the shit out of him down in the Rainier Valley. It happened overnight sometime, but the body wasn't found until early this morning."

I was out of bed and reaching for my clothes. "Where exactly?"

"There's a power line greenbelt that runs north and south through the valley," Ben answered. "Blaylock's unmarked was located in the greenbelt just north of Graham. He was found inside, dead of multiple gunshot wounds. Homicide is all over it, but so is the gang unit. Since he was working the Nguyen hit-and-run, the incident is thought to be gang related."

"Not just gang related," I said grimly. "You can bet your ass it's Lawrence Harden related as well."

"And that's not all," Ben continued.

My heart fell. "There's more?"

"I pulled the vehicle registration information for Lawrence Harden," Ben said. "Guess what? His ride turns out to be a 2015 Cadillac Escalade."

"Bingo!" I said.

"Yes," Ben said, "that's what I'm thinking, too, but what the hell are the two of us going to do about it? If Harden's the big-time political operator you claim he is, my being involved in his takedown in any way is likely to blow my cover."

Ben was right on that score. Bringing down a former police chief who was still a local political mover and shaker would make for headline news. Everybody involved in the operation would end up being put under a media microscope—an eventuality undercover cops try to avoid like the plague.

I was in the closet and grabbing up an assortment of clothing, but with the phone in one hand, there wasn't much I could do about getting dressed. "Don't worry," I assured him. "I'll take care of it."

"How is that going to happen?" Ben objected. "You're not a sworn officer at the moment, remember?"

"That's true," I said, "but I'm the one who discovered the threads connecting all three homicides." I said that and then had to swallow the lump in my throat before

I could force myself to make the appalling correction. "Make that four homicides, since I'm also the guy who pointed Kevin Blaylock in that direction."

"What's your plan?"

"For starters I'm going to talk to Assistant Chief Ron Peters, but don't worry. When I blow the whistle on Harden, I'll be sure to leave your name out of it."

"Good luck with that," Ben said. "We need to nail the bastard. This really sucks!"

I couldn't have agreed more. Once Ben hung up, I immediately dialed Ron's cell phone number, putting the phone on speaker so I could start getting dressed. That call went straight to voice mail, so I dialed Ron's home number next. As the phone started ringing, I glanced at my watch and was dismayed to realize that it was not yet eight o'clock on a Sunday morning. When Amy answered, I immediately launched my "sorry for the early call" apology.

"Don't worry," she said brightly. "We're all up and at 'em. Jared had a sleepover last night. I'm making pancakes."

"I was hoping to talk to Ron."

"Sorry, Beau," she told me. "He's not here right now. He had an early morning call out—some kind of major incident down in the south end. Can I leave him a message?"

Unfortunately I knew far too much about that major incident. "No," I said. "Don't bother. I'll catch up with him later."

I had pulled on a clean shirt and was buttoning it when Mel appeared in the doorway of my walk-in closet. Dressed in a tracksuit and with her hair pulled

back in a ponytail, she held a mug of coffee in one hand
and Lucy's leash in the other.

"What's going on?" she asked. "You look upset."

"I'm a hell of a lot worse off than upset," I told her.
"Kevin Blaylock was murdered overnight, shot dead in
his unmarked down in the Rainier Valley."

"No!" she breathed.

"It's true," I answered bleakly. "I pointed him in Lawrence Harden's direction. I suspect he must have gone
off Lone Rangering it, and now the poor guy's dead."

Mel set the coffee mug down on the counter and
then came over to look me straight in the eyes. "No
matter what happened to Detective Blaylock," she declared, "it is not your fault."

Did I ever mention that she knows me far too well?
But her words barely registered. I was already drowning
in a bottomless pit of self-loathing.

"Who else's fault could it possibly be?"

"How old was he?"

"How old was Kevin Blaylock?"

Mel nodded, and I shrugged. "Late fifties, early sixties maybe."

"And he was a lifetime cop?"

"As far as I know."

"Going after a suspect without proper backup is a
violation of Policing 101. Why would an experienced
cop do something that stupid?"

Mel may be a cop, but she's also a woman. What
Blaylock had done may have been a mystery to Mel, but
it wasn't to me. I understood the poor guy's underlying
issues all too well. If you're someone older who's been
tossed in with a much younger crew, one where you're

trying desperately to maintain your own relevance, it's easy to do stupid things on occasion.

"Blaylock was the new kid on the block," I explained, pulling on a windbreaker. "I'm pretty sure he was being hazed and dissed by all the old hands at Homicide. He maybe saw a chance of hitting a home run. He probably thought that if he could clear all three homicides on his own, the other guys might give him a little slack."

"They'll give him some slack, all right," Mel muttered, "especially now that he's dead."

Grabbing my wallet, keys, and the Ziploc bag of kibble off the dresser, I stuffed all three items into the pocket of the windbreaker.

"Where are you going?" Mel demanded.

"I'm going to walk Lucy and then I'm heading for the crime scene," I said. "Where do you think?"

"Why?"

"I tried calling Ron. I'm pretty sure he's already there, but he isn't picking up. Blaylock was the only one besides me who was privy to the idea all three homicides are connected. Someone needs to put Seattle PD on the right track here, and I'm the only one left to do it."

"We're the ones to do it," Mel corrected, "the two of us together."

I started to object, but she overruled me. "You know as well as I do that you'll need a valid badge to get anywhere near that crime scene, and I just happen to have one of those in my possession. While you fill travel mugs with coffee, I'll take Lucy out. Once we come back and she's been fed, we'll all go visit that crime scene together."

Knowing she was right, I nodded, and then, remembering the kibble, I extracted the bag from my pocket. "You might want to take this along with you when you go," I suggested.

"Why?" Mel asked. "What's that for?"

"It's for a dog named Billy Bob, who belongs to a homeless guy who hangs out down around the dog park."

Mel gave me a look that implied that she thought I'd lost my marbles, but she accepted the kibble and leashed up the dog.

As the two of them departed, my phone rang with Scott's name in the caller ID window. "Hey, Pop," he said when I answered. "Hope I didn't wake you."

"Believe me," I told him, "we were already up. What's going on?"

"I hate to do it, but we're going to have to cancel for today," he said. "I just got called in to work. There's been a homicide—a cop, someone I know from the academy. They're calling for somebody from TEU to fly drone grid surveillance over the crime scene to see if we can maybe turn up the murder weapon."

Of course I could have told Scott that I knew Kevin Blaylock, too, but I didn't. Since when do fathers and sons ever talk about what's really important?

"You go do what you have to do and don't worry about it," I said. "Mel and I will be glad to take a rain check whenever it's convenient."

While Lucy and Mel were gone, I busied myself dishing up the food and fixing the coffee, grateful to have something to do with my hands. Otherwise I might have considered putting a fist-size hole in the drywall.

Only hours after I had watched him doing his chicken-scratch shorthand in that steno pad, how the hell could Kevin Blaylock be dead? How could he?

The possible answer hit me like a ton of bricks. Kevin Blaylock was a cop. Once I'd given him Harden's name, he would have run a routine check on him first rattle out of the box. I was willing to bet that he'd come up with a vehicle registration that seemed to lead straight to Duc Nguyen's hit and run. Thinking back on our dealings at Sneaky Pete's, I remembered the surreptitious way Blaylock had shut down his computer as I approached the table. Was that when he made both the ID and the connection? Was that the reason he'd locked me out shortly thereafter—because he wanted to be the one to get full credit for bringing Lawrence Harden down?

When Mel and Lucy returned, Mel removed Lucy's leash. "Your homeless guy said thank you," she told me. "He thanks you and Billy Bob thanks you. Boy, is that one plug-ugly dog!"

"People who live in glass houses..." I reminded her.

"Yes," she agreed, "but Lucy is starting to grow on me."

We stood in the kitchen, watching and waiting, while Lucy carefully nosed her way through her food. For such a big dog, she's a dainty eater. Mel and I waited, but not in what you could call a companionable silence. It was one of those times when we were having a knock-down, drag-out fight without exchanging a single word. Up to a point, Mel was right about the difficulty of a civilian approaching an active crime scene. Crime scenes are exclusive clubs, with membership limited to sworn officers only. So, yes, having Mel and her badge along would definitely make it easier for me to get where I needed to go.

But having her there would also keep me from doing the one thing I really wanted to do right then, which was to show up on Lawrence Harden's doorstep, look him straight in the eye, tell him what a worthless piece of crap he was, and punch his lights out, an outcome Mel was equally determined to prevent.

It wasn't until we were on our way down in the elevator that the long silence between us was finally broken.

"Are you going to be able to sell any of this to Ron Peters?" she asked. "I can see that the connections you've made all seem to lead back to Harden, but they're tenuous at best and entirely circumstantial. I'm not seeing anything that would give investigators probable cause. And I can't for the life of me understand how a power broker from Queen Anne Hill would get himself mixed up with a bunch of drug-dealing gangbangers."

"According to Ben Weston, the gang in question, the Local Asian Boys, have come up in the world, due in large measure to their having cornered the local market for fentanyl."

"Which mostly comes from China," Mel added.

"And other ports in the Far East, most likely brought in through the Port of Seattle, where Lawrence Harden just happened to be a bigwig for decades."

"Which would have given him a catalog of contacts in the import/export business," Mel said.

"Harden has evidently remarried," I continued, "but his previous wife, Todd Farraday's mother, had an antique shop down in Pioneer Square, which Harden has continued to run since her death."

"Antiques," Mel mused. "An operation like that

would offer plenty of cover for shipments coming and going."

"Wouldn't it though," I muttered. "I remember Max's literary agent telling me Max had stumbled on something interesting in the days just before his death."

"Interesting enough to put this whole chain of events in motion?" Mel asked.

I believed every word, right down to the soles of my shoes, but as we exited the elevator on P-4, I could tell that Mel still wasn't convinced.

"Sorry, Beau," she said. "It's still pretty thin gruel."

Leaving Mel's city-owned Interceptor in the garage, we piled into my aging S 550. Before we even exited the garage, Lucy had already positioned herself in the backseat so her chin could once again rest on my shoulder.

"You let her ride with you like that?" Mel asked.

"If you can figure out a way to get her to wear a seat belt, let me know."

Have I mentioned that, having just been told I was full of it, maybe I was slightly cranky as I pulled out of the garage and turned west on Clay and then south on First Avenue?

CHAPTER 28

LET'S JUST SAY from the get-go that Mel was right. Without her along with her badge in hand, we wouldn't have made it anywhere near the crime scene. We parked outside the perimeter of cop cars and media vans. Then, leaving Lucy in the car, we made our way through the milling mob of reporters and cops until we reached the hive of bustling activity in and around a canopy that had been erected directly under one of the humming power lines.

When we got close enough to make out the details, it was easy to see what had happened. Whoever had been driving the vehicle had probably intended to go a whole lot farther into the greenbelt. Unfortunately, they had somehow missed seeing a hunk of concrete hiding in the tall dead grass. That invisible barrier had brought the speeding car to an abrupt and complete halt.

We arrived on the scene just as people from the ME's office removed Kevin Blaylock's bloodied body from the passenger seat of his car. That told me that he had most likely been shot elsewhere and had already been dead or dying when he was driven here by either his assailant or by an accomplice. It seemed reasonable to assume that someone had driven Kevin Blaylock to the spot where he'd been found and someone else had aided and abetted the driver in leaving the scene.

Mel reached out and took my hand as we watched in silence while the attendants carefully positioned the remains in the body bag already waiting on a nearby gurney. As they zipped the bag closed, try as I might, I could not look away. Fighting back tears I realized that, although I didn't know the name of Kevin Blaylock's widow, life as she knew it was over. Now she would be left to look after her aging parents in Edmonds entirely on her own. And no matter how many times Mel or anyone else tried to tell me Kevin's death wasn't my fault, I would never believe it.

As they rolled the gurney away from the patrol car and over to the waiting van, Ron Peters appeared, speeding along behind the gurney in his electric wheelchair. I understood why he was there. Unfortunately, having brass on the scene of officer-down incidents is something that has become an all-too-common standard operating procedure.

Ron gave Mel and me a half wave when he spotted us standing on the outskirts of the crowd, but rather than coming straight over to us, he stopped off long enough to confer with the ME in charge. Had Dr. Roz been on the scene, I might have tried to horn in on the conversation, but this person was totally unfamiliar to me. Besides, I already knew what the conversation was about—another unfortunate but standard procedure. Ron needed them to delay the van's departure long enough for someone to organize a collection of cops to provide a police escort for that grim trip from the crime scene to the morgue.

When Ron finished with that, he rolled over to where Mel and I were standing. "What are you doing here?" he asked. "Do you know something about this case?"

"Cases," I corrected, "four in all, this one included."

He gave me a quizzical look and then shook his head. "All right then, come on. Let's go sit in my van and get out of the rain."

These days Ron drives a Sprinter conversion that includes a remotely controlled wheelchair ramp. He wheeled himself inside and then motioned for Mel and me to follow. "Talk," he said.

And so I did, giving him an overview of the string of events in as orderly a fashion as I could. He heard me out, making no comments from beginning to end. When I finished, he pulled out his cell phone—the one he hadn't answered earlier—and tapped in a number.

"Captain Kramer needs to be informed," he said.

I had known that was coming. After all, Kramer was calling the shots at Homicide these days, but it would be a lot harder for him to ignore what I had to say if it came by way of Assistant Chief Ron Peters rather than just from me. The cell phone hooked into the Sprinter's sound system, and moments later the voice of my old nemesis came through the speaker.

"Kramer here."

"Are you back from doing the next of kin?" Ron asked.

"I'm back," Kramer said with an audible catch in his throat. "It was tough, damned tough."

Talking to Kevin Blaylock's widow would have been difficult, especially since Kramer himself was most likely the one who had assigned her husband to a supposedly routine hit-and-run investigation that had ended up going horribly wrong.

"Liz's folks came over to stay with her, so at least she's not home by herself."

Now it was my turn. Just hearing him mention the name of Kevin Blaylock's widow hit me like a punch in the gut. Captain Kramer may have assigned the case to Blaylock, but I was the one who had pointed her husband in Lawrence Harden's direction.

"How soon will that escort be ready to roll?" Ron asked.

"In about ten," Kramer answered. "We're waiting for a few more vehicles to show up."

"Maybe you could stop by my Sprinter for a minute," Ron said. "J. P. Beaumont is here. He needs to talk to you."

"Great," Kramer grumbled. "Just when I thought the day couldn't get any worse."

We were certainly on the same page there. I wasn't any happier at the idea of seeing him than he was of seeing me.

"Look," Kramer said impatiently, "I'm out here organizing the cars and parked right behind the ME's van. How about if he comes to me?"

So Mel and I went out into the cold and wet. It was raining harder. Even wearing a slicker covering his dress uniform, Kramer looked like a drowned rat. The windbreaker I wore wasn't much help, either. Since Mel isn't a Seattle native, she doesn't share the locals' natural disdain for umbrellas. Armed with an open bumbershoot, she was dry as can be.

As expected, Kramer greeted us—me especially—

with a snarl. "You're not a cop anymore. What the hell are you doing at my crime scene?" he demanded. "Who let you in?"

I started to respond in kind, but Mel stepped into the fray with the unassailable authority of a grade school principal breaking up a fistfight between two eleven-year-olds.

"The point is we're here," she said, "and Beau has information about Detective Blaylock's case that he needs to share. It's cold and wet out here. Let's get this sorted and be done."

"You have information about this case?" Kramer said. "How do you even know the name of our victim? That hasn't been released."

I had two sources of information—Ben Weston and my son—and I wasn't about to blow the whistle on either one of them, so I simply sidestepped the question.

"I met with Detective Blaylock yesterday afternoon at a joint up on Queen Anne Hill called Sneaky Pete's. I've been asked to look into Maxwell Cole's death, and I uncovered some connections between that case and the hit-and-run Kevin Blaylock was investigating."

Kramer drew himself up, crossed his arms, and glared at me. "The thing about the fingerprints, right? Just how many spies do you have inside Seattle PD? Is your son feeding you information?"

"Scott's got nothing to do with any of this. The point is, while we were in the bar, Blaylock and I located security footage that seems to suggest Duc Nguyen did something to one of the tires on Max's Volvo. Later on, when Max discovered his vehicle wasn't drivable, Duc went out to the parking lot and changed the tire before the two of them left together."

I watched while Kramer processed those two important pieces of information.

"So the connection between Max and Duc is one
part of the equation. Piece number two is Max's connection with Todd Farraday."

"Wait, Todd Farraday? Larry Harden's drunken stepson, the one who just died?"

"Yes."

"What does he have to do with the price of peanuts?"

"Max met with Todd Farraday at the same bar.
Sneaky Pete's was his favorite hangout. They met, had
dinner together, and talked."

"About what?" Kramer wanted to know.

"I'm not sure. Max was working on a book that involved the school district shooting we worked all those
years ago. They may have talked about that; they may
have talked about something else. In any event, when
it came time to leave, rather than taking a cab back to
the Refuge, Todd Farraday left the bar on foot. Early
the next morning he turned up dead at his stepfather's
place a few blocks away up on Queen Anne."

"Todd Farraday must have been drunk as a skunk
when he left the bar. He died of booze and exposure,"
Kramer declared.

"Are you sure?" I asked. "I saw the security footage
from the bar that night. It looked to me like all he drank
was coffee, and he didn't seem impaired when he left."

"Where the hell do you think you're going with all
this?" Kramer wanted to know.

"Tell him," Mel urged.

"I believe Maxwell Cole may have learned something that brought him to the attention of people running a drug-smuggling operation."

"Which people?"

"I'm thinking Lawrence Harden may be behind it."

To my surprise, Paul Kramer burst out laughing. "You've got to be kidding! You think Larry Harden is some kind of evil drug lord?"

"Why wouldn't he be?"

"Because the poor old guy is losing it, for starters," Kramer said. "He was good to me when I first came to the department, and I've never forgotten that. So when I went to the funeral, it broke my heart to see him the way he is now."

"Todd's funeral?" I asked. "I thought that was private."

"It was, but like I told you, we were friends back then, and we never stopped being friends. So yes, I went to the funeral. And there he was in a wheelchair, and so out of it that I doubt he even knows how to wipe his own butt anymore. If it weren't for that sweet little Asian wife of his, he'd have to be in assisted living by now for sure."

I remembered then that Patrick had said something about Todd's having a stepmother, but before anything more was said, a young uniformed cop hurried up to where we were standing. "Hey, Captain," he said, "everyone's here now. We're ready to roll."

"Okay," Kramer told him. "I'll be right with you." Then he wheeled on me. "Just for the record, J.P., Lawrence Harden is not a drug kingpin, and Todd Farraday was a drunk who died a drunk's accidental but totally predictable death. If you want me to think otherwise, you're going to have to come up with something better than this half-baked, unsubstantiated crap of a story aimed at besmirching the reputation of a very good man. Got it?"

With that, he stomped off toward his patrol car.

"Got it, asshole," I answered under my breath as he walked away. "I hear you loud and clear."

"So now we know Maxwell Cole was right," Mel said. "Lawrence Harden was indeed the big fish who used to be inside the department, and Paul Kramer is the guy with the current pull. So what are we going to do about it?"

I looked at her in utter astonishment. "'We'?" I echoed just to verify that I had heard her correctly.

"Yes, we."

"Okay then," I said. "I guess we'd better go home and start digging."

CHAPTER 29

CONSIDERING THAT UNEXPECTED turn of events, it's no surprise that on our way back to Belltown Terrace, we turned off I-5 at Cherry and meandered our way through numerous construction zone detours until we ended up in Pioneer Square. We already knew that this was the neighborhood where Duc Nguyen had been run down. If Occidental Antiques had played a part in any of what was going on, we needed to eyeball the location for ourselves.

Southbound on First Avenue, the first place I could turn left was on Jackson. By then it was a little before nine o'clock on a Sunday morning, which meant there was actually some on-street parking. I pulled into the first available spot. "How about we walk from here?"

"Take Lucy or leave her in the car?"

"We'll only be gone a couple of minutes," I said. "She'll be fine here."

By then the rain had let up. I led us north under the winter-bare trees that lined either side of the urban walkway called Occidental. The shop, Occidental Antiques, was located in the ground floor of a building halfway between South Main and South Jackson. At this hour of the day on a Sunday, I would have expected the place to be relatively deserted. It wasn't.

A utility van with its emergency flashers going had driven into the pedestrian walkway and was parked directly in front of Occidental Antiques. While we watched, two scrawny young men dressed in blue uniforms and with baseball caps pulled low over their heads emerged from the shop, both of them lugging what appeared to be heavy wooden crates. The second one put down his load and paused long enough to lock the door behind them. If they were actually dealing in drugs, would they be hauling them around in broad daylight? On a Sunday morning? Maybe all the assumptions I'd made about what was going on were dead wrong.

"Looks like we came to the right place at the right time," Mel observed.

As the two men loaded the crates into the van's cargo hold, Mel and I took a crack at morphing into hardy, wintertime tourists, posing for a series of selfies, making sure that van's rear license plate was fully visible in the background of some of them. In others we caught the signage on the side of the van—TRAN TRANSPORT, along with a Seattle area phone number. One of the last photos included full profiles of the two guys in their uniforms.

"Follow or not?" I asked, as they climbed into the van and prepared to drive off.

"Follow," Mel said.

We raced back the way we had come. Because of the way the streets are laid out, by the time the van headed south on Fourth Avenue, we were able to pull into traffic three cars behind them. As they went past, I noticed something odd. "Did you see that?"

Mel, whose nose had been buried in her phone, looked up. "See what?"

"The sign's gone," I told her. "It must have been one of those magnetized ones. Now it's a plain white utility van."

"The phone number's bogus, too," Mel told me. "I just tried dialing it." She switched her phone to speaker. "...number you have dialed is no longer in service." Mel switched off without bothering to listen to the remainder of the recording.

At CenturyLink Field, the van negotiated the series of intersections that took us onto southbound I-5. We followed, staying back far enough, I hoped, to avoid notice. Once on the freeway, the van stuck in the right-hand lane and exited at the South Boeing Field Access Road. By then there was only one vehicle between us and them. "They're going to spot us," Mel warned.

"Maybe not," I told her.

While the guys in the van seemed focused on the stoplight, I made a quick right-hand turn and zoomed off in the other direction. At the first opportunity and in a spot where U-turns were clearly forbidden, I made one anyway. We reached the intersection of MLK and Boeing Access just in time to see the van turn into the entrance of what appeared to be a massive public self-storage facility.

"Turn in," Mel said. "I'll go inside and talk about renting a storage unit while you walk around and see if you can tell where they stop. If you're right and those two crates really are loaded with some kind of illicit goods, we need to know where they're going."

We pulled up to the entrance, where we were greeted with a remotely broadcast "May I help you?" delivered through a staticky-sounding speaker box. "We need to rent a unit," I explained, "but while my wife's doing that, would it be all right if I walk around in the parking lot? I've got a cramp in my leg, and I need to walk it off."

"Of course," was the answer.

I stopped in front of the office, and Mel reached for the door handle. "Just get the unit number," she counseled. "No heroics. No Lone Ranger, got it?"

"Yes, Tonto," I replied. "I hear you loud and clear."

The office was in the bottom floor of a low-rise four story structure that, according to the signs, contained climate-controlled storage units. Behind that were four double-sided, single-story buildings lined with rolling metal doors. The van was parked on the far side of the last building. I couldn't see for sure what was happening from where I stood, but it looked as though they were loading cargo from the van into the unit at the far end of the building. When they closed the door and climbed back into the van, I hot-footed it back to my car, where I found Mel already seated inside.

The van rounded the building, drove out through the entrance, and then turned north on MLK. "Not enough traffic to risk following them again," I said.

"Right," Mel agreed. "Let them go, but I'm pretty sure we're onto something."

"Why?"

"I just had one of my guys up in Bellingham run that plate. It came back stolen. If this is some kind of smuggling operation, we've got some idea of where the goods are. Did you get the unit number?"

"No," I said, "but I'm pretty sure I know which one it was, but what do we do now?"

"Gather some more intelligence," she said. "Given Paul Kramer's reaction, we're going to need a hell of a lot more information before we can go back to Seattle PD. I vote that we go home, walk the dog, and go to war. I'm no Todd Hatcher, but these days I have my own access to LexisNexis. This looks like a lucrative operation. If it's been going for years, one way or another, there'll be a cybertrail leading back to it."

I drove, and Mel dove into her iPad. While we'd been screwing around at the storage place, there had been a multivehicle pileup in the northbound lanes that had turned the freeway into a parking lot. I was grateful when the phone rang a few minutes later, because it kept me from stressing about being stuck in nonmoving traffic. The phone number showing on the screen was Rosemary Mellon's private cell.

"Hey, Roz," I answered, putting her on speaker. "What's up?"

"Did anyone ever tell you that you're one smart operator?" she asked.

"Not nearly often enough. Why?"

"Because I just got off the phone with one of my friends down at the crime lab. After I talked to you about our dead Jägermeister guy, you got me thinking. The tox screen results on him aren't back yet and neither are Maxwell Cole's, but I asked one of my pals to check on the contents of the bottle. Turns out what's left in the container is Jägermeister all right, but guess what else they found? There are minute traces of flunitrazepam around the outside rim of the bottle."

"Flunit what?" I asked.

"Flunitrazepam," Roz repeated. "It's sometimes prescribed to treat insomnia. Out on the street, however, it's one of the more popular date-rape drugs, one that leaves its victims incapacitated and confused or, as in Mr. Farraday's case, completely unconscious. I doubt seriously that his dosage was self-administered."

"Would it have been enough to kill him?" I asked.

"Probably not," Roz answered, "but it would have left him disoriented. We already know Todd had a problem with alcohol. Once the date-rape drug kicked in, his sobriety went out the window."

"Could something similar have happened to Maxwell Cole?" I asked. "Could someone have slipped him some of that as well?"

"I suppose so," Roz answered. "We'll know that for sure once the tox screens come back."

"Thanks, Roz," I told her. "Keep me posted."

"Who's Bian Duong?" Mel asked when Roz's call ended.

I was off on a whole other tangent right then and it took me a moment to answer. "Who?"

"Because I just ran a property records search. Didn't you tell me Todd Farraday expected to receive some of the proceeds from the family home on Kinnear once it sold?"

"That's what his friend Patrick told me. Why?"

"Because it sold two weeks ago for two-point-three mill. And the seller is listed as one Bian Duong, with no mention of Lawrence Harden's having had any involvement in the transaction. Looking back, I can see that he quitclaimed the property over to Bian several months ago. And you know that self-storage place we just left? Turns out she's listed as the owner of that, along with several residential properties down in the Rainier Valley."

"That name sounds Vietnamese," I said. "Didn't Kramer just tell us that Harden's current wife is Asian?"

"He did," Mel said.

"So what do you want to bet that this Bian Duong is actually Lawrence Harden's most recent wife?"

"No bet," Mel answered.

A pair of tow trucks had managed to clear the lanes ahead of us. As traffic started to flow again, the circuits in my head jolted clear as well. "Crap!" I exclaimed.

"What is it?" Mel asked.

"All this time I've been thinking Lawrence Harden is our bad guy, but Ben Weston told me last night that the gang unit is under the impression that, when it comes to Local Asian Boys, a woman was running the show—someone the gang unit calls the Ghost Girl. What do you want to bet that Ghost Girl and Bian Duong are one and the same? What if Todd Farraday found out about the sale of the house? Maybe he showed up on Harden's doorstep expecting to have it out with his stepfather and looking for his share of the home sale proceeds."

"And maybe his stepfather turned out to be less of a problem than the new wife," Mel suggested. "Take a look."

The whole time we'd been speaking, Mel's fingers had been flying over her iPad's virtual keyboard. Now she held the device up in a manner that allowed me to see at the screen. What I saw pictured there was a lovely young Asian woman smiling serenely into the camera.

"That's Bian Duong?" I asked. "She's a real looker!"

"Yes, she certainly is," Mel agreed. "When I googled

her name, I found this photo on the Port of Seattle's website, where Bian is listed as a special assistant to the director. It says here that she graduated *cum laude* from the Foster School of Business at the U Dub. She started out as an intern and has held her current position for the last three years."

"They're married, but she still goes by Bian Duong?" I objected.

The words were no sooner out of my mouth than I knew I'd stepped in it.

"That does happen occasionally," Mel Soames observed dryly.

Yes, it does. Point taken.

"What are the chances that Harden met her at work and the two of them hooked up? Next thing you know, the old guy has a lovely piece of arm candy to drag around with him as well as a nurse in his old age. As for that bit of arm candy? Her career is suddenly on a whole new trajectory."

"In this case, the old guy may have bitten off more than he could chew," Mel suggested. "Think about what Kramer told us earlier. He said the last time he saw Harden at Todd's funeral, he was in pretty rough shape. Kramer made it sound as though Harden's mental capacities were severely compromised, but think about this. If his wife and primary caregiver just happened to have ready access to a supply of roofies, she could easily have kept him doped up on those, passing off his periodic bouts of confusion as either Alzheimer's or age-related dementia."

"That would work," I agreed.

"So shouldn't we call Kramer and mention some of this?"

"I doubt he'll listen, but by all means give it a try," I told her.

"Do you have his number?"

I handed her my phone. "I don't, but you can call Ron Peters and ask him to have Kramer call us back."

By then we were exiting at Mercer and had turned onto Denny. Mel was on the phone with Ron when I blew straight through the intersection that would have taken us back home to Belltown Terrace.

She ended the call as we started up Queen Anne.

"I take it we're going to Harden's place anyway?"

I nodded.

"This isn't our jurisdiction," she said, stating the obvious, "and we don't have a warrant."

"No," I agreed, "but we have reason to believe that Lawrence Harden's life may be in danger. Besides, we're stopping by to see an old friend because we've heard he might be a little under the weather. You don't need a warrant to go visit the sick."

"We could be wrong about all this," she cautioned. "What if this goes completely sideways?"

"So be it, then," I said. "I'll claim it was all my fault."

Mel's answering sigh told me that, although she didn't like it, she was all in.

My phone rang then. Even without being on speaker, once Mel answered, I could hear Kramer grousing into phone. "What now?" he demanded.

"Beau and I are on our way to Larry Harden's house," Mel said reasonably. "Since he's a friend of yours, if I were you, I'd get myself there as soon as humanly possible."

"What the hell? Haven't the two of you caused enough trouble for one day?"

Rather than wasting her breath on any further explanation, Mel cut Kramer off in mid-rant by simply ending the call. The phone rang again, almost immediately. This time, instead of picking up, she silenced the ringer, leaving the call unanswered.

For a few seconds we rode on in a silence broken only by the angry buzzings of the unanswered phone. That's when Mel asked the single most important question she had asked all day: "Are you carrying?"

"Yes."

"It's a good thing," she told me. "So am I."

CHAPTER 30

IT HAD BEEN decades since I had last approached Natalie Farraday's art-deco mansion on West Kinnear Place. A black Escalade with a blue handicapped sticker was parked in front of the closed garage doors on one side of the driveway. Next to it was one of those portable on-demand shipping containers generally referred to as PODS. From the looks of it, now that Bian Duong had sold the place, she was in the process of packing up and getting ready to leave.

We drove past the residence and parked several houses away, where we both scrambled out, leaving Lucy alone in the car. Approaching the house, I headed for the front door while Mel ducked behind the PODS and disappeared from view into a small side yard. Stepping onto the porch—the place where Todd Farraday had been left to die—gave me what Johannes, our South African neighbor in Bellingham, likes to call a "skrik"— a fright. One thing I suspected going in was that Bian Duong was most likely a ruthless, cold-hearted bitch.

With me running point, I walked up to the door

and rang the bell. When Bian opened the door, I recognized her at once from the earlier photo. She was dressed in jeans, a pair of those fashionable but idiotically clunky high-heeled shoes, and a University of Washington Husky sweatshirt. She was tiny. Her dark hair was pulled back in a glossy pony tail. She couldn't have been a day over thirty-five. She didn't look like a murderous, drug-dealing crime queen, but I was pretty sure that's exactly what she was.

"Yes," she said, peering up at me with a puzzled expression on her face. "May I help you?"

"Is Larry home?" I asked.

"My husband's here," she said, "but he's not well, and he's not up to having visitors."

"I'm so sorry to hear that. My name's Beaumont, I used to work with him at Seattle PD. I heard from another friend, Paul Kramer, that Larry's been under the weather recently. I live east of the mountains and I'm only in town for the day, but I was hoping to see him. I wanted to say hello, of course, but I also wanted to offer my condolences with regard to the shockingly tragic death of his stepson. I knew Todd, too, years ago. He was always a troubled kid, no matter how much Natalie and Larry tried to help him."

Fortunately I had enough facts about the family at my disposal to make it sound as though Larry and I had once been best buds. The ploy seemed to be working, because Bian was clearly torn. On the one hand, she wanted to tell me to go to hell and leave them alone. On the other hand, her situation was dicey enough right then that she couldn't afford to risk doing anything that might arouse suspicion. Behind her in the room I saw an array of packing boxes. I wondered where she was planning to go.

"I'm so sorry," she said, shaking her head. "Larry's asleep right now, and that's the only time I can get anything done. That's the problem, you see. He hardly ever sleeps at night, and I have to watch him constantly to keep him from wandering off. I'll be glad to tell him you stopped by. I'm sure he'll be sorry he missed you, but under the circumstances..." She left the sentence unfinished.

I put on my most engaging smile. "We were close once. If you don't mind my asking "

"I do mind," she replied, stiffening a little, "but it's hardly a secret. Larry has been diagnosed with Alzheimer's. The truth is, even if he saw you, he most likely wouldn't have any idea who you are. There's really no point in his having visitors."

To my surprise, Mel suddenly materialized over Bian's shoulder, emerging silently from behind the stack of packing boxes lined up in between the foyer and the living room. She had somehow managed to gain entrance to the house, and clearly the situation had changed. With her 9 mm PX4 Storm Beretta in hand, she assumed a shooting stance. It wasn't exactly comforting to realize that if it came down to a shoot-out, I was on the wrong side of Bian Duong, and I most definitely wasn't wearing a Kevlar vest.

"Why would that be, Ms. Duong?" Mel asked. "Would it be because one of those visitors might happen to notice that you keep your husband handcuffed to a hospital bed and trapped in his own filth?"

Bian started at the sound of Mel's voice, and she

spun around. "Who are you?" Bian demanded furiously. "How did you get in here? You've got no right. I'm going to call the cops."

"I'm a cop," Mel assured her. "I let myself in, and it turns out I have every right to be here. Your husband's life is in grave danger. I've already called this in and summoned an ambulance. They'll be here any minute."

Bian Duong may have been a *cum laude* graduate of the University of Washington, but she was also a natural born street fighter. I've spent a lifetime in law enforcement. The moment Bian dropped toward the floor, I knew with absolute certainty that she was going for a knife. I did the only thing that made sense at the time. I grabbed her from behind in a crushing bear hug that lifted her, screaming and kicking, off her feet and into the air.

I gripped her in a way that pinned both of her arms to her sides, but if you've ever tried to bathe a reluctant cat, you know what I was up against. She squirmed and fought in a furious attempt to get away.

"She's got a knife," Mel warned me, pocketing her own weapon. "Down by her ankle. Hold on to her while I get it."

As Mel approached, Bian aimed a powerful kick in her direction. Not only did Mel manage to dodge out of the way, but she grabbed the woman's leg, removing both the knife and a shoe in one fell swoop. The knife skittered harmlessly away on the smooth surface of the marble floor, finally coming to rest under an entryway table on the far side of the room. From my point of view, I didn't know which I welcomed more—having the knife taken out of play or Mel's Beretta.

From outside I heard the distinctive squawk of first one arriving patrol car and then another. "This is going to be tough to explain," Mel said, pulling her badge out of her pocket. "Can you hang on to her long enough for me to clue them in?"

"I'll do my best," I said through gritted teeth.

Once Mel left, Bian continued what I knew to be a life-or-death struggle. There was a good chance that she had another weapon concealed somewhere on her body. I didn't want her slipping out of my grasp long enough to lay hands on that or to grab hold of mine, either, so I hung on for dear life.

The first time I heard the term "KAG," short for "kick-ass-girls," I laughed out loud because it turns out I happen to be married to one. KAGs on TV and in the movies are females who definitely don't fight like females and who aren't afraid to take on all comers.

Bian Duong was one of those. In spades. She kept flinging her head against my chest, trying desperately to connect with my chin. Fortunately, my chin was just out of reach. One of her kicks with her still-shod foot nailed me square in the middle of one of my titanium knees. Pain shot through my body like a lightning bolt, and I came close to passing out.

After what seemed like forever, two uniformed officers burst into the room, one following the other. I was so relieved to see them that I would cheerfully have hugged them had I not been otherwise engaged.

"It's okay, sir," the first cop assured me, grabbing for one of Bian's arms. "You can let her go now. We've got her."

Even then, Bian Duong had no intention of going

quietly. As soon as I loosened my grip, she turned on the officers and fought like a crazed she-devil. It took the combined efforts of both of them to finally subdue her and fasten her wrists with a pair of cuffs. At that point a fire truck and an aid car had pulled up outside. Moments later a phalanx of EMTs rumbled into the house.

"Where is he?" one of them called over his shoulder.

"Down in the basement," Mel answered from somewhere out of sight. "Far back bedroom on the right."

With the fight over, my fake knees—including the bruised one—were knocking like mad. My breath came in short, jagged gasps. Spent with effort, I staggered into the living room, swept a pair of empty cardboard boxes off a nearby couch, and sank down onto it.

Mel showed up an instant later, her face alive with concern. "Are you all right?"

"I'm okay," I said, "but I feel like I just went toe-to-toe with a prize-fighting welterweight."

Mel laughed. "I think you did," she said.

"Thanks for taking that knife out of play."

"We're a team, remember?"

"How did you get inside?"

"There's a backyard patio with a slider that wasn't locked. I let myself in through that."

"How's Harden?"

"Not good. Unless you have a very strong stomach, I wouldn't advise your going down there. My guess is the poor man hasn't been allowed out of bed for several days."

The next person through the front door was, of course, Paul Kramer. "What the hell is going on here?

What's Bian doing in the back of a patrol car? And who the hell do you two think you are?"

Just then, the EMTs trooped back through, pushing a loaded gurney. Even with a sheet spread over the man's body, the stench was appalling. Kramer's florid face went surprisingly pale, and he took a step back. "Larry?" he croaked. "Is that you?"

Larry was in no condition to speak, so Mel answered in his place. "It's him all right," she said. "Bian had him cuffed to a bed frame down in the basement. I believe you'll discover that she's kept him drugged for months on end."

"Holy crap!" Kramer exclaimed. "She's been drugging him? Are you frigging kidding me?"

"No, I'm not," Mel said faintly. "I only wish I were."

Naturally we stayed around to speak to whatever detectives would be dispatched to the scene. While we waited, I noticed a wet bar at the far end of the room. Out of sheer curiosity, I got up and walked over there to take a look. The bottles lined up in a neat row on the black granite countertop were all top-shelf brands.

While Mel and I had been in the process of redoing our new home in Bellingham, Jim Hunt taught me a thing or two about countertops. Black countertops look slick, but they require constant maintenance. If you don't keep after them, they show every speck of dust, grease, and dirt. In this instance, Bian's indifference to good housekeeping definitely showed. A thick layer of gray dust covered the entire countertop, and near the end of the row of bottles, was a dust-free spot where one bottle was obviously missing, leaving behind a distinctive rectangular mark.

"See that?" I said pointing. "That's where Todd's murder weapon was sitting."

"The bottle of Jägermeister?" Mel asked. "How can you tell?"

"Because," I told her, "when it comes to booze bottles, I'm something of an expert."

CHAPTER 31

ON THE WAY down to Seattle PD for our interviews, we stopped by Belltown Terrace long enough to walk Lucy and drop her off upstairs. She had already spent more than enough time stuck in the car, and we knew we were in for a long day of it—a long, grim day of it.

Kevin Blaylock was dead, and every badge in sight was equipped with a black band of mourning. Bian Duong had been booked into jail charged with assault with a deadly weapon, resisting arrest, and elder abuse. But all that was just for starters. An initial inspection of the room where Lawrence Harden had been held prisoner revealed a pharmacy of illegal drugs in large enough quantities that drug possession with intent to distribute was also on the list. My hope was that, once we told investigators what we knew and suspected, plenty more charges would surface.

Naturally, Mel and I were scheduled with two different detectives in separate interview rooms. Mel was led into hers by a baby-faced homicide cop who looked far too young to be a cop, let alone a detective. While

I sat in a small lobby, waiting my turn, the phone rang with Ben Weston's name showing in the window.

"Hot damn, Beau!" Ben exclaimed when I answered. "I just heard you may have taken down the Ghost Girl. And she's Bian Duong? How the hell did you figure it out?"

"I didn't exactly figure anything out," I replied. "It was more or less a case of mistaken identity. All along I thought Lawrence Harden was the bad boy, but it turns out he may have been little more than an innocent bystander right up until he turned into another victim."

"How bad off is he?"

"Pretty bad."

"Anyway," Ben continued, "everybody in the neighborhood is in shock. Bian Duong has always been considered the unofficial queen of the Rainier Valley—top-drawer student at Franklin High, a popular cheerleader, and a college graduate with a high-powered job at the Port of Seattle. She also maintains the reputation of being a dutiful daughter by faithfully looking after her widowed mother."

"And all the while, this supposedly dutiful daughter has been operating a lucrative criminal enterprise right under everyone's noses. How did she do it?"

"It turns out several of the LABs, including Duc Nguyen, were and are blood relatives of hers, and in the gang world, blood is definitely thicker than water."

"Wait, are you saying that hit-and-run victim was related to her?"

"Yup," Ben replied, "Duc was her first cousin—the son of Bian's mother's dead sister. When his father threw him out of the house for hanging out with the

wrong people, that's where he went looking for help—
to his aunty and his auntie's daughter—which got him
caught up with even worse people."

Another connection and another miss. I had been
one hundred percent convinced that Larry Harden had
been the one behind the wheel of that speeding Escalade. Now, of course, I realized that the poor man
would have been in no condition to do such a thing.
The driver had to have been none other than Bian.

"Presumably Bian played a part in getting Duc into
the LABs, but why would she run him down?" I asked.

"Maybe he did something wrong," Ben suggested.
"Everything I ever heard about the Ghost Girl said
that nobody dared cross her and that she didn't tolerate
failure, either."

"Maybe that's why Duc died," I mused. "If he was
supposed to burn down Maxwell Cole's house, he blew
it big-time."

"That could very well have caused her to turn on
him," Ben agreed. "For right now, though, the good
news for us is that the LABs appear to be in a state of
blind panic. They're worried Bian will cut herself some
kind of plea deal and let the cops take down everyone
else. We're trolling the water to see if we can find someone who's willing to beat her to the punch."

And that's when I remembered the two guys in
the van.

"Speaking of LABs, I've got some photos to send
you, some shots Mel and I took of two men removing
packing crates from Harden's antique shop down on
Occidental earlier this morning. With any kind of luck,
maybe you'll be able to ID them for me. Hang on while
I find them and send them."

I scrolled through my photos, located the ones I wanted, and texted the whole batch to Ben.

"Take a look at what I just sent you," I said. "Let me know if either of those two guys looks familiar."

There was a short pause in the conversation. "Okay," Ben said seconds later. "I'm looking at them now. That one shot is especially good. Give me a couple of minutes to run these through the gang unit's facial rec program. We're trying to build up a catalog of all these guys and their various associations. That way, when something bad happens, it makes it easier for us to follow the dots. I'll get back to you on this."

Closing my eyes, I imagined how that would have worked back in the olden days. Searching by hand through reams of paper mug shots would have taken a matter of days or even weeks, but now it's a brand-new ball game. Ben called me back in less than a minute.

"These guys are definitely LABs," he announced. "Bao Tran and An Duong—the latter is another of Bian's cousins on her father's side."

"So she believed in keeping it all in the family," I observed.

"Evidently," Ben said with a chuckle. "By the way, I was just talking to one my fellow GU officers. Do you happen to know what the name Bian means?"

"I have no idea."

"It means Keeper of Secrets."

"Well," I told him, "that certainly suits her to a T."

Ben hung up again, leaving me sitting there with the phone in my hand and thinking about Bian's name. She wasn't merely a keeper of secrets—she was a keeper of deadly secrets. It made me wonder if there's a Vietnamese name for Black Widow. That one would have fit the bill as well.

Detective Greg Stevenson showed up a few minutes later. He had been new to investigations and was still working property crimes at the time I left Seattle PD. He was older now, confident and well seasoned in the job.

"Good to see you again, Beau," he said, offering his hand. "I'm taking the lead on Detective Blaylock's homicide. I understand you and your wife gave us some much-needed assistance today, and that you may have critical information in regard to my case. Mind if I ask you a couple of questions?"

"Not at all."

He led me into an interview room. Although the interview was being recorded, when Detective Stevenson pulled out his iPad and prepared to use that to take notes, it reminded me of Kevin Blaylock's steno pad.

"Before we start, can I ask you some questions?" I said.

"I'm not sure I'll be able to answer them."

"I was with Detective Blaylock yesterday evening at a bar on Queen Anne Hill—Sneaky Pete's—which seems to have played an important part in three recent homicides."

"Three?" Stevenson asked. "Which ones are those?"

"First would be Harden's stepson, Todd Farraday. Next came the fatal house fire where a guy named Maxwell Cole died. The third one is the hit-and-run case Blaylock was investigating."

"Duc Nguyen," Stevenson supplied with a nod. "He's the guy whose prints were found at the site of the fire."

"Correct."

"Okay, so the last two incidents are on the board," Stevenson countered, "but the death of the stepson is news to me. Are you sure the case is being investigated as a homicide?"

"Maybe it isn't now, but it will be soon. Initially it was considered an accidental death—a combination of acute alcohol poisoning and exposure, but it's a homicide all right. Talk to Dr. Rosemary Mellon up at the ME's office. She can tell you everything you need to know."

"So what's the deal with the bar—Sneaky Pete's did you say?"

"Blaylock and I met up there and spoke to the owner—Meece is his name—and he let us take a look at the security footage for the two nights in question. Maxwell Cole had dinner with Todd Farraday the night before Todd was found dead on the front porch of his stepfather's home a few blocks away. Then, the night before Max's fatal fire, we saw footage of him at the bar sharing drinks with Nguyen. The evening ended with Max having car trouble—a flat tire—and with Duc Nguyen offering to help him with it. The two of them left the bar together and both ended up dead in separate locations a few hours later."

Stevenson had been listening with avid interest. "So they're all connected."

"That's what I believe. I think Detective Blaylock arrived at the same conclusion, and that's what got him killed."

"But you don't know that for sure?"

"No, I don't. At some point in the evening, Blaylock cut me off. We were working together and then, all of a sudden, we weren't, so here's my question. Have you located Blaylock's electronics, by any chance, or even his steno pad? He was taking notes in that."

"So far we've found none of his goods," Stevenson told me, "but the last transaction on his computer was a request to the DOL checking for registration information on Lawrence Harden's vehicle."

That was not news to me. I had suspected as much all along. He'd been on the computer doing that just as I returned from the restroom at Sneaky Pete's. That's when Blaylock made the connection between Harden's vehicle and his hit-and-run, and it also had to have been his fatal tipping point. That was when he had decided to shut me out and go off on his own to look into it.

"How did he die?" I asked.

In a typical interview I wouldn't have been asking any questions at all. But this one was different, and Stevenson didn't hedge.

"Multiple gunshot wounds."

"Signs of a struggle?"

"No defensive wounds whatsoever. We suspect that he had been incapacitated in some fashion—either in the vehicle or out of it—and then driven to the location where he was shot."

"We suspect that there was a supply of flunitrazepam in the room where Lawrence Harden was found chained to his bed."

"Flun what?" Stevenson asked.

Thanks to Dr. Roz, I was able to negotiate the pronunciation pitfalls just fine. "Flunitrazepam," I repeated. "Otherwise known as a date-rape drug."

"Like roofies you mean?"

"Exactly. Not only that, but I believe tox screens on

the victims will eventually reveal that the same substance played an essential part in everything that's happened here—in all four homicides and in Lawrence Harden's deteriorating mental state."

"You don't think he has Alzheimer's?"

"No, I think he has a vicious wife who's been poisoning him all along."

At that point we launched off into the real Q-and-A part of the process. Stevenson had promised a "couple of questions." It turned out there were far more than that. The interview continued for the better part of three hours. I started with Erin Howard and worked my way up to the morning's confrontation with Bian. Along the way, I passed along the photos Mel and I had taken down on Occidental.

"Can you think of anything else?" Detective Stevenson asked at long last.

"Nope."

"If you do, you've got my number," he said, handing me a card. "Thanks, Beau," he said. "And now, with any kind of luck, I'm on my way to swear out a whole passel of search warrants—one for the house, one for the antique store, and one for that storage unit. If we can bring down that whole LAB organization, the gang unit is going to love you, and so will I."

CHAPTER 32

TWO TEXTS HAD come in during the course of my long conversation with Detective Stevenson. One had been from Mel, two hours in, saying she was done. The other was a series of outraged questions from Scott:

You're here? In an INTERVIEW ROOM??? WTF?

Okay, so I should have been more up front with Scott when he had called me that morning. When it comes to dealing with kids, I've always come up short. Since it turns out old habits are hard to break, the response I texted back was more of same:

Busy right now. Call Mel.

As a consequence, when Detective Stevenson led me from the interview room back to the lobby, where Mel was waiting, Scott was part of the welcoming committee, too. He was wearing his uniform, his badge, and his black mourning band. He didn't look happy, and he greeted me with a scowl.

"Mel clued me in on everything that's been going on today, but you should have told me yourself. If you already knew Detective Blaylock was dead, you might have at least mentioned it."

Scott was angry, and I couldn't blame him.

"You're right," I said at once. "I should have, and I didn't. I'm sorry." That's something that hanging around with Mel Soames has taught me—if you're going to apologize, do it without making excuses. "Kevin Blaylock told me he knew you. He also said he thought you were a good cop."

I know that was fudging Blaylock's exact words just a little, but right then was not the time to mention that he had actually called Scott "a good kid." That wouldn't have been fair, not when Scott was grieving his colleague's loss right along with every other member of the department.

"He was a good guy," Scott said.

"Yes," I agreed. "I'm sure he was. How did it go with finding the murder weapon? I half-expected Mel and I would run into you when we were at the crime scene."

Scott didn't exactly roll his eyes, but it was close. "Dad," he said, "I fly drones. I don't go to crime scenes looking for weapons—my drones do."

So much for my antiquated ideas about crime scene investigation. In addition, although Scott is a cop, I was glad to know that he hadn't been on hand to see his friend's body zipped into a body bag. Bottom line, Scott may be a cop, but he also happens to be my kid. Kids and crime scenes do not mix. Color me conflicted on that score.

Before the conversation could go completely sideways, Mel stepped in. "Okay, guys," she said. "It's the middle of the afternoon. Your father and I haven't had breakfast or lunch, and I, for one, am starving. What about you, Scott?"

"I haven't eaten, either," he admitted.

"Good," Mel said. "If Cherisse is up to it, why don't we reinstate our canceled lunch date? We'll go out. It can be our treat. That way you won't have to cook. This has been a tough day for everybody, and talking about an upcoming baby will be good for what ails us."

Ironically, Scott suggested Chinook's at Fishermen's Terminal—the same place where I'd met up with Erin Howard to talk back toward the beginning of this whole mess. Since the restaurant is close to Scott and Cherisse's house, we agreed to meet up with them there after stopping off to let Lucy out. I was slowly coming to terms with one of the challenging realities of having dogs in your life—you have to think about their schedules as well as your own.

"Thanks for bailing me out of hot water with Scott," I told Mel as we made our way back to the car.

"You're welcome," she said. "I could see that he was upset about Blaylock and taking it out on you."

Once we were back at Belltown Terrace, I walked Lucy while Mel changed into something a little dressier than a tracksuit. When we left awhile later, Lucy seemed entirely content to stay curled up on her bed in the kitchen.

"Did you know black dogs are the ones least likely to be adopted?" Mel asked as we rode down in the elevator.

That's one of the things I love about Mel. She's a steady source for little-known bits of information.

"Didn't know that," I told her. "I guess Lucy lucked out then."

"I guess she did."

By the time we got to Fishermen's Terminal, the overcast was finally starting to break up. Inside the restaurant, the lunch crowd was mostly gone and the place was relatively quiet. It was late enough in the day that, if Cherisse was still suffering from morning sickness, she had recovered enough to chow down on her very own platter of clam strips. She looked happy. No, make that she looked radiant. My urging her to talk to Scott about the baby had transformed the whole situation, and I couldn't help but be a little proud of myself when Scott started regaling us with his ambitious plans to redo the room that had been intended to be his "man cave" into a nursery. Whew! Bullet dodged!

And Mel was right once again. On a day filled with murder and mayhem, talking about an upcoming baby—a future grandson, as it turns out!—was just what the doctor ordered. We talked about due dates and parental leave and cribs and day care. We said nothing about Kevin Blaylock's murder. It was a needed emotional smoke screen, but once we left the restaurant and headed back to the car, reality intruded.

"I need to talk to Erin," I told Mel. "I gave her information to Stevenson to pass along to whoever is assigned to the Maxwell Cole part of the investigation. We still haven't found his electronics, but once they have permission to access his online accounts, they may be able to find out what it was that put this whole mess in motion."

"Are you going to call her or go see her?" Mel asked.

"I'll call first, but I need to talk to her face-to-face."

"If you go, I'll be glad to ride along."

"I thought you were going to head back north as soon as we finished up with Scott and Cherisse."

"After the day we've had today, I've changed my mind on that," she said. "I'd rather hang in with you tonight and head back to Bellingham early tomorrow morning."

That was more than fine with me. I called Erin before we left the restaurant parking lot. It turned out Sunday was her day off and she was home.

"There are some new developments," I told her. "I'd like to deliver an initial report in person."

"Now?"

"Yes, if you're not too busy. And if you don't mind, my wife might come along. She's a police officer," I added with a wink in Mel's direction. "She's been assisting with the investigation."

Since Mel had probably saved my life, the word "assisting" was understating the case, but Erin didn't need to know that.

"Sure," she said. "Bring her along."

Once I keyed in Erin's address in Renton, the GPS directed us across Lake Washington on 520, on what we like to call "the money-sucking" toll bridge. The clouds had disappeared, and the sky overhead was clear, but the wind had picked up. The water in the lake was grayish-green rather than blue, and occasional whitecaps sent spray splashing across the windshield. And although it was only four o'clock in the afternoon, the sun was close to going down.

"Obviously Bian was on her way out of town. Where do you think she was headed?" Mel asked.

"Out of the country most likely," I said. "I'm sure

she's been working on an exit strategy for a long time, but once Todd Farraday showed up, she needed to accelerate the program."

"I've met some cold-hearted bitches in my time," Mel said, "but Bian Duong takes the cake."

"Yes," I said. "If you ever get that tired of me, don't chain me to a bed and leave me to die. Just shoot me and get it over with."

We both chuckled over that, but it wasn't really funny.

Erin Howard welcomed us into her apartment. It was about as different from Lawrence Harden's Queen Anne mansion as you could imagine. It was a small two-bedroom unit, furnished on the cheap, but spotlessly clean. She directed us to a sagging, butt-sprung sofa while she sat on a beat-up recliner that could have been twins with the one Jim Hunt had forced me to toss into the trash.

"What's happened?" she asked anxiously. "Have you found out something about Uncle Max?"

"Yes," I said. "About him and several others as well."

"Several?" she echoed.

"Have you been watching the news today?"

"I saw that a Seattle PD detective was murdered last night. That doesn't have anything to do with this, does it?"

"Unfortunately, it does."

I told her the whole story then—as much of it as we knew and some of which we could only surmise. In the process of telling, I came to a surprising conclusion. If it hadn't been for Maxwell Cole wanting me to investigate, and if it hadn't been for Erin and I both dutifully carrying out Max's final wishes, Lawrence Harden would no doubt have become victim number five.

"You really think we saved him?"

"Let's hope we saved him," I told her. "It depends on whether or not he pulls through."

"Even if we saved him," Erin said sadly, "we didn't save Uncle Max."

A phone rang then—a landline somewhere in the kitchen—and Erin excused herself to answer it. We heard only her side of the conversation, which was short, and curt to the point of being rude.

"I'm not sure how you got my name or number, but I'm definitely not interested in selling at this point. Don't call me again."

She stalked back to the living room, shaking her head. "That's the third call today from real estate guys claiming to be developers and wanting to buy Uncle Max's house for such an ungodly amount of money that it's probably a scam of some kind. Besides, how can I think about selling it when I haven't even heard from the insurance company about repairing the damage?"

That was interesting. This early on, how would developers have gotten Erin's name? Was that building inspector making a bit of money on the side by alerting potential builders to the availability of possible teardown properties? Or had that information been leaked by someone in Max's attorney's office or even by the attorney herself?

"Have you spoken to the attorney?" I asked. I didn't dare mention Delia Rojas's name, because it wasn't a name I was supposed to know.

"I have an appointment with her tomorrow morning," Erin answered.

If Lawrence Harden's place had sold for $2.3 million, I estimated that Max's wouldn't be worth much less than that. I suspected that the "ungodly numbers," as Erin called them, were far closer to the mark than she realized.

"Talk to her about this," I advised. "In order to evaluate those offers, you'll need to be represented by a reputable Realtor. That flurry of early ones are probably lowball all right, but I doubt they're scams. There are people out there looking for places where they can build megamansions. Max's place certainly..." I started to say, "comes with a killer view." At the last moment, I managed to tone that down into something a little less offensive. "...qualifies on that score. Are you thinking of living there yourself?"

"Are you kidding?" Erin asked. "I'd never fit in with all those fancy people up on Queen Anne Hill, not in a million years. Besides, I need to live closer to work. Commuting back and forth across Lake Washington would kill me."

"Sell the place as is, then," I told her, "without going through all the agony and effort of fixing it. Let the insurance company write you a check for whatever they owe. I wouldn't be surprised if the insurance settlement combined with proceeds from the sale of the property didn't leave you in a position where you'll be able to pay cash for whatever you want."

"You think I'd have enough to be able to pay cash for a house? Really?"

Erin shook her head as though the whole idea were completely preposterous. She had yet to grasp exactly how much Maxwell Cole's generosity had changed her circumstances. And that reminded me of something else I had so far neglected to tell her about a few additional items about Max's life, the secrets he hadn't entrusted even to her.

"Did you know Max was gay?"

Erin shrugged. "I always supposed he was, but I never asked him. It wasn't any of my business. Why?"

"Did he ever mention someone named Amelia Rourke?"

"No, who's she?"

"That's a complex question," I replied. "Amelia was one of Max's friends. She's also a transvestite who runs a place called the DQC."

"You mean Drag Queen Central over in Wallingford?" Erin asked. "I've heard it's some kind of stand-up comedy place."

"Yes," I said, "one that caters to other drag queens. Max was a minority partner in that establishment—and now you are, too. Max's attorney should have the details on that as well. I wouldn't be surprised if, once you contact Amelia, you'll find that she's willing to buy out your share."

That added another sizable ka-ching to what would probably turn out to be an amazing total, but when Mel and I left the apartment half an hour or so later, Erin, still in a state of disbelief, had yet to come to terms with any of it.

As we drove away from that dodgy apartment complex, I couldn't help but remember that old black-and-white TV show from the late fifties, *The Millionaire*, the one where a wealthy recluse named John Beresford Tipton delegates an assistant to show up unexpectedly on someone's doorstep and hands over a check for a million bucks.

I was old enough to remember the show, but I didn't bother mentioning it to Mel. That's one of the life experience hazards of being married to a younger woman. I doubt she ever saw it.

CHAPTER 33

IT WAS FULL dark now. We were on our way up 405 when my phone buzzed. I had turned it off during our visit with Erin. I pulled it out and handed it over to Mel. She turned it on speaker before she answered.

"J. P. Beaumont's phone," she said.

"Greg Stevenson here. Can I talk to him, please?"

"He's driving. You're on speaker."

"Hey, Beau, give yourself a gold star." There was a hollow echo to his voice that made me think he was using a speaker for his end of the conversation.

"Why? What's happened?"

"We executed the search warrant on that storage unit and came up with two crates of high-powered weapons. We've called ATF in on the case. Bian Duong is now looking at federal charges in addition to the others."

"You found illegal weapons but no drugs?"

"Nary a one."

I had been wrong about so much on this case that it hurt to think maybe I was wrong about the drugs, too.

Then again, maybe I wasn't. "Since she owns the storage facility," I suggested, "maybe the drugs are stored in one of the other units."

"That thought occurred to me, too," Stevenson agreed, "but we have a warrant for only this one. We can't go rifling through other people's units and stuff. We're in the process of bringing in some drug-sniffing dogs to walk past and check out the exteriors of those storage units. If they alert, we'll have probable cause to obtain warrants."

"Any sign of drugs at the house?"

"We found some substances that tested positive for roofies in Mr. Harden's bedroom. In the meantime, I've got someone going through everything in the PODS. So far they've come up empty."

"What about the store?"

"No dice here, either. That's where I am right now. The place is cleaned out slick as can be—no merchandise, no shelving, no nothing. It's completely empty."

"Did you check the basement?"

"What basement? I've been over every inch of this space. There's no basement."

But I remembered that newspaper photo, the one with the gaping hole in the floor of Natalie Farraday's earthquake-damaged shop.

We were just past Coal Creek, northbound on 405. Rather than sticking to the left lanes and going back home by way of 520, I swung onto the entrance to westbound I-90. "Mel and I are on our way," I said into the speaker. "We'll be there in a couple of minutes."

"Beau," Stevenson argued, "I'm telling you, there's nothing here, and it's been a very long day."

"Please," I begged. "Humor me just this once."

"All right," he said with an exasperated sigh. "We'll wait."

Ten minutes later we pulled into a parking place on Jackson, two spots up from where we'd parked earlier that morning. As we walked back toward Occidental, Mel noticed I was limping. "What's wrong with your leg?"

"Bian kicked me in the knee," I confessed. "It hurts some."

Actually it hurt a lot. I was looking forward to going home, taking an Aleve, and putting my foot up.

"Look, Stevenson already executed the warrant and didn't find anything," Mel said reasonably. "If your leg is bothering you that much, let's just leave it at that."

"I know there is a basement under that shop," I insisted, "and I'm going to find it."

Mel's sigh of resignation mimicked Detective Stevenson's. "Did anyone ever tell you that you are one stubborn man?"

"It may have been mentioned once or twice."

When we arrived at the shop, the place was ablaze with lights. We were greeted by Detective Stevenson and three very grouchy crime scene techs. It didn't take long to see that Stevenson was right. The place was bare-bones empty. There were lines on the floor that showed where display tables had once been located, but the tables themselves were gone. The only structure remaining in the room was the built-in cash-wrap counter toward the front of the shop, complete with a collection of electrical outlets.

"See there?" Stevenson said. "What did I tell you?"

I stood in the center of the room and turned in a circle. That's when I spotted a door in the far back corner of the room.

"What's that to?" I asked pointing.

"Utility closet," one of the techs said. "I already checked. It's completely empty."

Determined to see for myself, I limped over to take a look. It was a small closet, about four-by-four. Other than an electrical service box on the wall just inside the door, the closet was, as reported, completely empty. It smelled of disinfectant and janitorial supplies, but still, there was something odd about it ... If there was a circuit breaker on the wall inside the closet, I couldn't help wondering why there wasn't even so much as a dangling lightbulb to provide illumination.

"Hey, Mel," I said. "Do you have your Maglite?"

Dumb question. Mel may be a cop, but she's also a woman who, in uniform or out, wouldn't be caught dead in public without a large purse and her own personal Maglite. If a bag isn't big enough to hold that, it isn't the bag for her.

She handed me her flashlight and I switched it on. With the extra light I could see that there was some difference in shading between the flooring in the rest of the room and the flooring in the closet. I remembered that the earthquake article had mentioned something about a granite floor. When the floor was repaired, granite tiles had been replaced with now grimy hardwood. I noticed, however, that wood flooring in the utility room was slightly different from that in the rest of the room, and so was the stain.

I knew just from looking that I was onto something.

There was a basement here, and the closet had to be the entrance. "Anybody here have a saw?" I asked.

"A saw?" Stevenson repeated. "You're thinking about cutting a hole in the floor? Are you nuts?"

"I've got a Sawzall out in the van," one of the techs said wearily. "I'll go get it. With any kind of luck we'll all make it home sometime tonight."

While he was gone, I swung open the door on the electrical box. There were several breaker switches inside, and I began flipping them one by one. The first one operated the lights out in the main room. The next one handled the lights in the front window. The one after that took care of the lights in the outside overhang, but the next one surprised the hell out of me. As soon as I hit it, the floor inside the closet dropped two inches and began to slide silently under the outside flooring. Grabbing on to the door frame, I somehow managed to lurch backward and pull myself to safety as a gaping black hole appeared just underneath where I had been standing.

"What the hell?"

Reaching back inside, I flipped the bottom switch in the breaker box. Fluorescent lights suddenly illuminated the hole. Then, with a low rumble and the distinctive smell of hot hydraulics, a rough, wooden-planked platform seemed to rise from the floor. It stopped six or so inches below the surface of the floor where we were standing.

I turned to Detective Stevenson, who was standing just behind me. "What comes up must go down. Care to join me?"

"How does it work?"

"There's got to be a control switch here somewhere," I said. "All we need to do is find it."

It turned out to be two switches rather than one. I found them built into one corner of the platform, both of them mounted in the cover of a metal junction box. One of them was marked UP and the other DOWN. I hit the DOWN one with the toe of my shoe, and away we went.

"Do you believe this!" Stevenson exclaimed once we dropped below floor level and could see the extent of Bian Duong's secret warehouse. I was excited, too, until I saw what was missing. The room was full of state-of-the-art big-box store metal shelving but, as in the floorspace above, every bit of it was completely, bare-bones empty.

Whatever goods had been stored in that damp, musty cellar would have required plenty of moisture-proofing. I stepped off the platform and onto wooden decking that had apparently been installed over damp earth. I pushed the button marked with the up arrow and sent the platform back to the ground level so the others could come down and join us. The device was simple enough—basically a mechanic's garage lift with the wooden platform added so it could be used to raise and lower heavy boxes rather than cars.

Looking around and realizing we were out of luck, I shook my head in frustration. Whatever illegal goods Bian Duong had stored here were long gone. We had discovered her hiding place a day late and a dollar short!

As the lift returned, bringing Mel and two of the techs, I stalked off on my own, wandering through the empty shelving in the faint hope that something had been overlooked and left behind. The far end of the room wasn't as well lit as the rest, but when I spotted a bump of some kind, I walked over to investigate.

In the far corner I found an eight-by-ten area where the decking had been pried up and stacked off to one side. Next to the planking was the mound I'd seen, which consisted of a pile of damp earth that had been dug out of the ground. I stepped around the dirt and stared into the resulting hole. What I saw there sent a chill down my spine. The distinctly shaped cavity—six feet long and three feet wide—was clearly intended for one purpose only: to bury a body.

Since the lights in the room behind me didn't quite penetrate this gloomy corner, I switched on Mel's flashlight and shone that into the hole. It wasn't all that deep—only four feet or so—but what I saw lying at the bottom of it made me catch my breath. A heap of what appeared to be men's attire—suit jacket, shoes, dress shirt, and tie—lay scattered on the ground.

"Hey guys!" I called over my shoulder. "You'd better come take a look at this. I think we've just found Duc Nguyen's missing clothing."

Moments later, with the whole crew gathered round, Mel was the first to speak. "Why do I get the feeling that this is where Lawrence Harden was supposed to end up?"

I nodded. "I'm guessing Bian got Duc to dig the hole, willingly or not. At some point in the process, though, he may have started worrying that the grave would end up being his."

"And that's when he took off," Mel said.

"That's when he tried to take off," I corrected. "The kid was running for his life, only he didn't quite make it."

One of the CSIs stepped forward then and bodily shoved me out of the way. "Off you go now, folks," he said, sounding far more chipper than he had earlier. "We have to go to work."

CHAPTER 34

WE WENT HOME. Finally. It had been a long, complex, tiring day, one Mel and I had been lucky to survive. Even though I knew she'd have to be up at the crack of dawn in time to make it to work, I was glad Mel had decided to stay at the condo that night rather than driving back north. I wanted her nearby—needed her nearby.

"You're still limping," Mel observed as we walked through the P-4 garage level toward the elevator. "Do you think the knee is permanently damaged?"

"Just bruised, I think."

"When we get upstairs, take an Aleve and put some ice on it," she said. "I'll walk Lucy. Since she's been locked up all day, I may take her around the block a couple of times just to get the kinks out."

On the surface, all of that seemed perfectly reasonable. Upstairs, while Mel changed back into her tracksuit and running shoes, I made a necessary pit stop—aging prostates are no joke. Once Mel finished leashing up the dog and the two of them left, I did as I'd been told—took my Aleve, two of them for good measure, and got an ice pack out of the freezer.

I hit the easy chair in the family room. Then, with my foot resting on the hassock and with the ice pack on my swollen knee, I leaned back and closed my eyes. It wasn't that late, only ten or so, but it really had been one hell of a day.

I must have dozed off for a moment, because when our landline phone rang, it startled me awake. Yes, we still have landline phones—two of them—primarily because we still use them to let visitors in and out of the building on those occasions when the doorman is temporarily unavailable. One phone is located on my bedside table and the other is on the side table next to my chair in the family room.

These are phones only—the old-fashioned kind. They ring and you answer them. There are no built-in cameras or Internet access. They do have caller ID, however, and I immediately recognized the number in the display as belonging to our doorman.

"Mr. Beaumont?"

The voice on the phone was that of our weekend relief doorman, Charles Little. Charlie is young, relatively new, and a bit unsure of himself. His stature pretty much mirrors his last name. He's a little bit of a guy, five five or so and 130 pounds soaking wet.

"Hope I didn't wake you," he said.

"No," I lied. "I'm up. What can I do for you?"

"Something weird happened this evening. Some big old guy—a homeless guy—came by asking for you. You may have seen him hanging around the neighborhood—the black guy with the big dog. Anyway, he was looking for you and wanted to talk to you.

When I saw that dog of yours dragging Ms. Soames past the door just now, it reminded me, and I thought I should mention it."

"I know them," I said. "I don't know the guy's name, but the dog is named Billy Bob."

"The man didn't know your name, either," Charles continued, "and that's kind of what worried me. He wanted to know if the guy with the big black dog was home. I tried calling on the phone. When no one answered, I asked if I could take a message. He said no, he'd stop by later."

"Okay," I said. "We're home now, but what did you just say about Mel?"

"She came tearing past the front of the building a minute ago with that dog pulling so hard it looked like Ms. Soames was about to be turned into a human dog-sled. That is one big dog!"

Lucy was pulling on the leash? Lucy, who was an absolutely 100 percent graduate of the Academy of Canine Behavior, was pulling on the leash? Talk about JDLR or rather JDSR—sound right rather than look right.

"Thanks for the heads-up, Charlie," I said. "I'll check it out."

I ended the landline call, reached for my cell, and dialed Mel's phone. Because she uses the health app to keep track of her steps and her runs, the phone goes with her everywhere, zipped into the pocket of her tracksuit.

When she answered, Mel sounded out of breath and out of sorts. "What?"

"Are you okay?" I asked.

"Of course I'm okay, but I don't know what's gotten into this damned dog," she complained. "We were doing fine, then all of a sudden she turned around and wanted to go racing off in the exact opposite direction."

"Did you try telling her 'right here'?" I asked.

"Yes, I told her that," Mel snapped. "Don't forget, we've been down in Myrtle Edwards Park a couple of times, and she's never been like this. She even growled at me just now."

"She growled? Hold on. I'll come down and give you a hand."

"Don't bother. I'm completely over the idea of taking her for a walk around the block. We'll go pee and crap and call it a job."

I got the message. Mel had just given me the human equivalent of "sit and stay." The problem is, I've never been especially good at taking orders. By then I was already limping toward the entryway closet to collect my jacket. "I'll meet you there," I said into the phone, but she had already hung up.

The elevator was evidently on a nearby floor, because the doors opened mere seconds after I pressed the button. I had exited into the garage on P-1 and was starting toward the outside gate when I heard a muffled cry of alarm followed immediately by a bark—a ferocious bark.

Worried that Lucy had somehow turned on Mel, I sprinted toward the gate, pressed the button, and then stood there waiting impatiently, dancing on first one foot and then the other, while the gate took its own sweet time in rising far enough for me to duck underneath.

When I burst out onto the sidewalk, I saw some kind of melee happening over in the dog-walking area on the far side of Clay. Several people seemed to be caught up in a scuffle. Fearing Mel was somehow involved, I sprinted toward the fight with my heart in my throat. Since I was entering the fray alone and unarmed, at the very least I needed to sound threatening.

"Break it up!" I shouted. "Knock it off!"

My cop-speak voice had the desired effect. There was the slightest pause in the action, then one of the struggling figures staggered away from the fight and collapsed soundlessly on the ground. A moment later I heard a roar of human outrage—a man's roar of outrage—which was immediately followed by both a whine and a whimper. At that point another figure—a dog this time—dropped away from the fight.

That left only one figure standing—a man, who swung around to face me. As he did so, the glimmer of a nearby streetlight caught on the blade of a knife. He was still grasping the knife in his right hand, but I could tell from the way he was cradling his wrist that the guy was hurt—maybe even badly hurt. That fact, however, was of little comfort. I know the statistics and the grim realities because even badly wounded assailants can prove to be downright deadly, especially if they're packing knives and their opponents aren't.

I had been running pell-mell toward the fight. Now, with the armed man's eyes fully on me, I skidded to a stop. Lucy was on the ground, and so was Mel. That meant I was totally on my own. To my surprise I was close enough to recognize the guy from his mug shot. It was none other than Ken Purcell, the domestic violence creep someone had thoughtfully bailed out of jail. What the hell was he doing here? How had he found us?

"Drop it!" I shouted at him. "Drop the damned knife!"

"Make me," he said.

Lucy whimpered and tried to struggle to her feet. And then, because Ken Purcell was, is, and always will be an asshole and a bully, he aimed a vicious kick in the dog's direction. It never landed.

From somewhere behind me, someone shouted the welcome words "Get him, Billy Bob! Go get him!"

And Billy Bob did just that. I barely glimpsed the brown and white streak as it shot past me. Because Purcell had one foot in the air, he was already off balance when the dog slammed into him. Both of them tumbled and rolled, and the knife went flying. I went after the knife while Billy Bob went after Purcell, tearing into him, biting and snarling. By the time I had the knife in hand, Purcell had had enough and was howling like a banshee. "Get him off me! Call him off! Please!"

Billy Bob's owner strode forward and stood looming over the fight, but he didn't immediately leap to Purcell's rescue. In fact, he let the thrashing continue for several beats before putting a stop to it.

"Enough, Billy Bob," he ordered finally. The dog immediately backed away and went to stand at his master's feet. "As for you, asshole," Billy Bob's owner continued through clenched teeth, "if you move so much as a muscle, I'll set him on you again."

Obviously Billy Bob had turned Purcell into a believer. With the assailant under control, I turned my attention and my dread in Mel's direction. Sure she'd been stabbed, I was surprised to find her on her hands and knees, crawling toward Lucy.

"I'm okay," she gasped. "He sucker-punched me in

the gut with his elbow. He was after the dog. Oh my God! Lucy's bleeding. We've got to get her to a vet."

She was right, of course. Lucy was bleeding from a deep cut on her right shoulder, but the only vet I knew personally was eighty miles away in Bellingham. While Mel leaned down to apply pressure to the wound, I looked around for help, and there was plenty to choose from. In a matter of moments, the street had filled up with curious onlookers, most of them equipped with cell phones. One of them used his flashlight app to focus light on Purcell. The man was bleeding profusely. There were bites on his hands, arms, face, and neck. One guy made a move to help him.

"Don't you dare," Billy Bob's owner warned. "Let the cops take care of him when they get here."

As for Billy Bob? Having done his job, he lay down on the grass, closed his eyes, and went to sleep, looking as harmless as the day is long.

"I called the cops," someone else said. "They're on their way and so is an ambulance."

By then Mel was sitting on the ground with Lucy's head cradled in her lap. "We need an ambulance for this dog!" she exclaimed. "Otherwise she's going to bleed to death."

"No, she won't," another helpful stranger chimed in. "There's a good emergency vet on the far side of Lake Union. If someone can help get the dog into my car, I'll take her there. And you, too, lady," he added belatedly, looking in Mel's direction. "I'll take you both."

The car in question was an older-model Dodge Caravan. The Good Samaritan put the center seats into the floorboard. Then with two men helping to carry Lucy, they eased her into the van. A bloodstained Mel crawled in behind her. My last glimpse of them as the side panel door slid shut was of Mel kneeling on the floor next to the dog, still applying pressure and probably praying, too.

I know I sure as hell was.

CHAPTER 35

FOR MY SECOND knife fight of the day, things didn't go quite as well as the first time around. For one thing, with Mel off at the animal ER, we didn't have her valid cop-shop chops or her badge to help smooth things over. It took some serious convincing on my part to persuade the two young uniforms who turned up on the scene that things weren't as they seemed, as in a) the bloody guy on the ground was the aggressor; b) the guy holding the knife—namely me—was not the problem; and c) the "vicious animal" who had torn the hell out of the guy doing all the bleeding shouldn't be summarily handed over to animal control.

Fortunately, Sam Shelton (that was the homeless guy's name, by the way) was a seasoned street person—a Vietnam War vet with PTSD and a terminal case of fear when it came to being shut up in enclosed spaces. I was impressed by the quiet dignity with which he dealt with the young cops. Their natural arrogance ran off Sam's weathered hide like water off a duck. He shuffled off across the street and retrieved his heavily laden grocery cart, which had been squirreled away some-where near the KIRO building. After sorting through numerous plastic bags, he was able to produce not only Billy Bob's valid license and tags but also a current shot record, courtesy of a vet who volunteers his services by holding periodic pet clinics for homeless pet owners at the Union Gospel Mission, which, it turned out, just happened to be the address listed on the paperwork as Billy Bob's place of residence.

The cops were not happy that Mel and Lucy, the purported victims of what they called an "alleged" at-tack, were not available to be interviewed, but Sam was able to fill them in on the details. Earlier in the day, word on the street had spread about someone going around offering to pay various homeless people for in-formation about a new dog somewhere in the neighbor-hood, a big black dog. That evening, after Sam and Billy Bob had settled into their little fire escape hidey-hole, that same guy had turned up and offered Sam a hun-dred bucks for them to clear out.

Sam had been happy to take the money. He had packed up and moved his camp to another location, one directly across the street that just happened to af-ford him a view of the dog-walking area. He had also stopped by Belltown Terrace, trying to warn me. Un-able to reach me, and worried that something wasn't right, he had kept watch. As soon as Purcell went after Mel and Lucy, Sam and Billy Bob went after him.

"Thank you for being their guardian angels," I said gratefully, when he finished telling his story.

"Turnabout's fair play," he said. "Thank you for the kibble."

"Billy Bob is one hell of a dog!"

"He is that," Sam agreed. "Out here on the streets, he's got my back, and I've got his."

About then, the sergeant—a guy I happened to know—showed up and took his young hotshots in hand. By the time he finished with them, they had a) apologized to Sam and b) allowed as how it would be fine for Mel to come down to the department at her convenience to give her statement. In the meantime, Purcell had been hauled off to Harborview. The sergeant assured me that the information I had provided about his being out on bail on the domestic would be enough to ensure his being placed under arrest on that until other charges could be brought against him.

"Sir?" I turned around to find the minivan driver standing behind me. "Do you want me to show you where I took your wife and dog?"

"Yes, please," I said. "I'll need to go get my license and car, then I can follow you there."

I hurried into the building to gather my goods. Knowing Mel, while I was at it, I stuffed a clean tracksuit for her in a grocery bag and brought it along.

Urgent Pet Care was a little over a mile away on Eastlake. It turns out an emergency room for pets is... well...an emergency room, one filled with sick and worried dogs and cats along with their sick and worried owners. I found Mel off in a corner by herself.

"How are things?" I asked.

She looked up at me with unexpected tears in her eyes. "She's still in surgery," Mel said.

I sat down beside Mel and took her hand in mine. "Lucy must have known Purcell was there," Mel continued. "That's why she was acting up. She must have smelled him. And when he came after us, I don't know if he was after her or after me, but Lucy was right there, fighting him off. I'm pretty sure she nailed him a couple of times before he...you know..." Unable to complete the sentence, Mel fell silent.

"Which means that, however much this emergency surgery costs, her bill is paid in full." I handed Mel the grocery bag. "You might want to change out of those bloody clothes," I added. "You're scaring people who already look scared enough."

With the bag in hand, Mel stood up and disappeared into a nearby restroom. While she was gone I sat there worrying about Lucy and remembering that other Irish wolfhound, the one in that heartbreaking poem. Gelert had died after saving that child. With a clutch in my gut, I feared Lucy might be lost as well.

Mel returned from the restroom looking a little less wan, but not by much. Had I really been on my toes, I would have grabbed her purse and hence her pouch of touch-up makeup as well. Let's face it. Nobody's perfect.

"Thanks," she said, sinking back down on the chair next to mine.

"Purcell is at Harborview being treated and stitched up. After that he's on his way to jail. I blew the whistle about his being out on bail. You're expected to go down to Seattle PD tomorrow to give your statement."

"I figured as much," she said. "I already called in and told my people that I won't be in. Depending on how Lucy's doing, I may not be in on Tuesday, either."

"Lucy will be fine," I said, offering reassurance with no real basis in fact, other than the fact that Mel needed to hear it, and I needed to say it.

"How do you think Purcell found us?" she asked.

"The only thing I can think of is that he got Lucy's location by way of her chip provider. They gave me all kinds of hell when I called in looking for information, but maybe Purcell was able to talk to someone a bit more accommodating."

"If Lucy had been with Nancy and her kids, he would have been able to find them the same way he found us, only they would have been far more vulnerable. Speaking of which, while I was in the bathroom, I used my phone to take a selfie. I've got a hell of a bruise on my belly from that elbow."

"Bastard," I muttered.

She gave me a small smile. "Thanks," she said.

A young woman in scrubs entered the waiting room. After pausing for a moment to look around, she came straight toward us, smiling as she approached. Mel sprang to her feet, and we both went to meet her. "Is Lucy going to be okay?" Mel asked.

Although the new arrival looked like she should still be in high school, she turned out to be Dr. Jillian Lawes, Lucy's vet. "Your dog is out of surgery," she said. "We had to give her a transfusion, but she should pull through. Your keeping pressure on that wound is what saved her."

Mel sat back down. "Thank you," she murmured. "That's such good news."

"We'll want to keep her overnight," Dr. Lawes continued. "That deep puncture wound in her shoulder will take time to heal. Be aware, though, that due to the extent of her injuries, she may end up with a permanent limp."

"Not to worry," I said. "These days there's a lot of limping going around."

"In the meantime, she'll need to be kept quiet, and she'll probably need some assistance when it comes to walking. You'll have to try to keep her from putting too much weight on that shoulder."

"How do we do that?"

"I suggest you get one of those canvas or leather slings people use to carry firewood. That way you can give her some support."

"I'll find one of those first thing tomorrow," I promised.

Dr. Lawes looked up at me. "Are you Mr. Soames?"

Sometimes you just have to go with the flow. "Yes, I am," I answered.

"Glad to meet you," she said.

Before we left the building, I forked over my credit card and made a thousand-dollar payment toward the bill. The clerk handling the finances for us mentioned that Lucy's remaining charges would be totaled and due at the time of pickup. The truth is, I would willingly have paid twice that.

Meanwhile, on the counter next to us sat a birdcage containing a droopy, almost featherless parrot. The parrot's tearful owner was talking to another clerk. "I can't possibly afford that much for treatment," she said. "I've had Louie for years, but I guess I'll have to put him down."

I caught the clerk's eye. "How much?" I asked.

"Somewhere between two hundred and five hundred dollars."

"Whatever it turns out to be, I'll leave a credit card to cover it," I said.

"Really?" The clerk looked dismayed while the woman was utterly dumbfounded.

"Why would you do that?" she asked.

"I owe big," I told her. "You and Louie are helping me pay it forward."

Fifteen minutes later we pulled off Second onto Clay. As we waited for the garage gate to open, Mel looked toward the building across the street.

"Do you think Sam and Billy Bob are out there right now?"

"I'm pretty sure they are."

She shivered. "It's so cold. Can't we help them find a warmer place to live?"

"I'll ask," I said, "but I get the feeling that Sam Shelton is on the streets because that's where he wants to be."

I had thought I was beat hours earlier. Now it was after 2 A.M. and I was done. Up in our unit, we stripped off our clothing and tumbled into bed. Mel cuddled up next to me and was asleep in an instant. She snores a little, but it doesn't bother me. I lay there listening to her for a long time and thought about how differently this night might have turned out for all concerned if it hadn't been for that single bag of kibble.

CHAPTER 36

MONDAY BEGAN WITH our spending two hours at Seattle PD, where both Mel and I were interviewed about what was referred to as "the Clay Street incident" as opposed to "the Kinnear Place incident." Believe me, I'll be happy to go a very long time without having two incidents of any kind on the books in a single day.

Because I finished up earlier than Mel, I went upstairs to talk to Scott and bring him up to speed. While I was there, he gave me an insider's tour of the Tactical Electronics Unit. These days I'm fairly conversant as far as electronic gizmos are concerned, but some of the stuff he was talking about was, as they say, Greek to me.

I was back in the waiting room when Greg Stevenson stuck his head inside. "Somebody told me you were here. You'll never guess what we found in that hole in the ground under Duc Nguyen's clothing."

"What?"

"A whole pile of electronics—a laptop, an iPad, a phone, and an old-fashioned desktop PC, all of them apparently belonging to your Mr. Cole. We have people analyzing the contents of his files and his correspondence to see if it will give us any clues about how all this came together."

"Wait, you're able to access his files? How?"

"Mr. Cole wasn't exactly big on cybersecurity. His birth month and year were enough to let us open his phone, and in his message file there was one called Passwords that listed them all."

"In the manuscript for his book there, too. It's called *Tangled Web*."

"Could be," Stevenson said.

"When you find out, be sure to let Erin Howard know. It'll be up to her to see if there's any way to finish the project and get it published."

"Will do."

"What's the deal with Bian?"

"Her arraignment is set for tomorrow afternoon," he said. "I'm not sure on what charges exactly, but they're adding up fast. There's no way in hell the woman is going to make bail. We found a whole cache of false IDs. Combine that with the funds she has available? In my book that makes her a serious flight risk."

"What about Lawrence Harden?"

"As far as we can tell, he had nothing to do with any of the criminal activity. I think she's bamboozled him from the very beginning."

"How's he doing physically?" I asked.

Stevenson shook his head. "Not good. They're still not sure if he's going to pull through. Even if he does, months of being fed mind-altering drugs may have done permanent damage. If that's the case, he'll probably have to go into some kind of assisted living facility."

Stevenson's phone rang. He answered and then

waved to me as he walked away, leaving me thinking about Lawrence Harden. I hadn't liked the man, not at all, but I certainly hadn't expected or wished for this kind of an outcome. And then there was Kramer. He had thought his friend Harden was fortunate to have a sweet young thing of a wife to keep him out of assisted living when, in fact, she was the one who would most likely end up putting him there.

Shaking off that disturbing thought, I opened my iPad and searched until I located a barbecue supply place in Ballard that had two different versions of canvas firewood slings for me to choose from—medium and large. "Put a reserve on the large one for me," I told the clerk. "I'm pretty sure that's the one we'll need. We should be there within the hour."

By one o'clock in the afternoon we were parked outside Urgent Pet Care. When a male attendant brought Lucy out to the waiting room, he was using a sling as well. His was a lot more official-looking and probably cost a lot more than the one I'd just purchased, but they both did the job.

Lucy seemed overjoyed to see us. It took the joint effort of both the attendant and me to lift her into the car. I was afraid she'd try to pull her usual stunt and stand with her chin on my shoulder. Seeming to grasp that she was in no condition to do so, she immediately stretched out across the length of the backseat, closed her eyes, and went to sleep.

Mel and I had already come to the conclusion that Lucy's recovery meant we needed to be at home in Bellingham rather than in the condo. Using the doggy door was out of the question for the time being, but being able to go out to the yard from inside a single-story house would make for far shorter trips than riding up and down in the elevator, trudging through the garage, and crossing the street.

Lucy rode with me and slept all the way from Seattle to Fairhaven. Once we made it home and got unloaded, I launched off on my new career as caregiver in chief. Lucy adjusted to her changed circumstances and the necessity of using the sling in short order, while I, on the other hand, had to learn to read her distress signals. Whenever she started struggling to get up, I figured out that probably meant she needed to go outside. She's tall enough that I could use the sling without wrenching my back. Even so, between her injured shoulder and my bruised knee, we were a matching pair of gimps, and going in and out of the house that way took a toll on both of us.

Mel went back to work on Tuesday. For the first several days we were home, Lucy mostly slept. Dr. Lawes had sent us home with a full set of meds, some of which were designed to alleviate pain and others to stave off possible infections. I started out mixing the meds with Lucy's food. That was a definite no-go. Her kibble would disappear, but whatever pills had been mixed in with the food would be left in the bottom of her dish. Peanut butter sandwiches were the answer to that. We had already figured out that Lucy adores peanut butter sandwiches. Once we slapped her medications inside one of those, her gigantic tongue couldn't separate the pills from the sticky spread.

Tuesday afternoon, I went out to the street and brought in the snail mail. Front and center among the collection of bills and unwanted catalogs was the wedding invitation from Harry I. Ball and Marge Herndon.

Looking down at Lucy snoozing comfortably on her bed, I knew at once that Mel's and my circumstances had changed and a weekend trip to Vegas wasn't in the cards. I had no intention of leaving a recuperating Lucy in the care of some anonymous dog sitter.

The wedding invitation, smelling faintly of cigarette smoke, included an RSVP card along with a self-addressed stamped envelope. I filled out the card saying Mel and I would not be in attendance. Next I wrote out a check, one that was probably big enough to handle both their hotel and airfare. I slipped that into the envelope along with the card. So what if their wedding present didn't come complete with beautiful gift wrapping and a flowery verse? Harry has never struck me as the flowery sort. That goes double for Marge, but seeing her name reminded me of Bob, Belltown Terrace's head doorman. Knowing he would be on duty at that time of day, I gave him a call.

"Heard you had some excitement out in the dog park the other evening," he said.

"We certainly did."

"How's your dog?"

"Lucy's recovering, but that's actually why I'm calling—about a dog, the other guy's dog."

"You mean the homeless guy's dog?"

"That's the one," I said. "The two of them really saved our bacon, and I'd like to ask you for a favor."

"Sure thing," Bob said. "Whatever you need."

"Go upstairs and let yourself into our unit. There's a bag of kibble stored under the kitchen sink and a box of Ziploc bags in the drawer next to the dishwasher. I want you to fill a bunch of those bags with kibble and keep them in your desk downstairs. Then, in the evenings, when whoever is on duty is about to leave work, he can go out and drop two of the bags off in the fire escape alcove on the back of the church on the far side of Clay."

"Two a day?" Bob asked.

"Yes, one for morning and one for evening."

"Wouldn't it be easier to just give the guy a whole bag of dog food?"

"No," I answered, "it wouldn't. A full bag of kibble would be too much for someone whose only means of transportation is a grocery cart. If it starts to look like you're about to run out of either kibble or Ziploc bags, let me know."

"Sure thing, Beau," Bob said. "We'll see to it."

I had every confidence that he and his fellow doormen would follow through. Each year during the holidays, the condo association gives its employees bonuses in lieu of tips, but since Mel and I routinely give the door staff generous gifts of our own, I knew my request wouldn't be regarded as a problem. In addition, the next time we were back in town, I fully intended to have a talk with Sam Shelton to see if there was anything we could do to otherwise improve his and Billy Bob's living arrangements.

A jubilant Ben Weston called me late Tuesday afternoon. "I just came from the arraignment," he said. "The Keeper of Secrets's ass is grass!"

"Why? What happened?"

"An Duong, Bian's other cousin and the guy considered to be her first lieutenant in the LABs, has agreed to turn state's evidence. In exchange for taking the death sentence off the table, he's admitted to being the shooter in the death of Detective Blaylock, but his written confession lays out the whole shebang, and she's been formally charged with all of it—drug and weapons violations along with two counts of conspiracy to commit, one count of vehicular homicide—"

"You even got her for Duc Nguyen's death?"

"You bet. Bian had that same cousin of hers take the Escalade to a local chop shop to have the broken headlight fixed. She wanted that done off the books rather than taking it to a dealership. Guess what? The chop shop guys didn't do a very good job of detailing it because CSI was still able to find Duc's DNA profile in the seams around some of the chrome."

"Good-o!"

Ben continued his recitation. "After vehicular homicide comes two counts of assault with a deadly weapon, two counts of resisting arrest, and…wait for it…one count of elder abuse and one of fraud. There's a good chance that the quitclaim deed turning Harden's Kinnear property over to her is a forgery. Not surprisingly, when An's judge locked him up, he issued an order that An Duong be held in isolation from the general population."

"In case Bian might put out a hit on him?"

"Exactly. As for the lady herself? Since she wasn't granted bail, Bian Duong is locked up, too. With any kind of luck, she'll stay that way for a very long time."

"Amen to that."

Down on the floor, I saw Lucy attempting to scramble to her feet. "Sorry to cut you off, Ben," I said into the phone. "Duty calls."

A week went by—a quiet week. Time slowed to a crawl, because that's how it is when you're caring for an invalid. Your life adjusts to their needs and schedules rather than the other way around. Lucy and I spent a lot of time in the living room, looking out at the water, primarily because that room was closest to the front door and required the fewest steps to negotiate.

The news as far as Ken Purcell was concerned was almost as good as that on Bian Duong. Ken's father was the one who had posted his $500,000 bail. That had been revoked. As the old song says, "Now ain't that too damned bad!" Not! After being released from Harborview, Purcell had been transported back to the jail in Bellingham, where he remained under arrest on both the assault and the domestic violence charges. Charges for his attack on Mel and Lucy were still pending, ones far more serious than that worthless assault in the third degree.

Erin called to say she had met with Max's attorney. She was still in shock, but the extent of her good fortune seemed to be sinking in. "I just can't believe it," she said. "I always knew Uncle Max had some money, but I had no idea how much. And it turns out, you're right. I really will be able to pay cash for a house. I'm about to make an offer on a town home here in Bellevue, and I'm driving his Volvo. I've never had a car this new."

I gave myself a mental note to put Jim Hunt in touch with Erin. After Karen threw me out of the house in Lake Tapps with nothing but my recliner, Jim was the guy who had taken me in hand and outfitted my first condo in the Regrade. With Erin's new digs, her household goods and furnishings would need the same kind of upgrade. My housewarming present for her would consist of a decorating consultation with Jim accompanied by a generous allowance for furniture.

On Thursday, when I took Lucy down for a checkup, I drove on down to Renton to see Erin. We talked about the complications of bailing Max's electronics out of the evidence locker, something that was proving to be very difficult.

"What about the book?" I asked.

Erin sighed. Obviously I had just touched on a painful subject. "I've talked to Mr. Raines about that. He thinks that once he lays hands on the files, the publisher may want to find a ghostwriter to finish the project so it can still be published."

I had a feeling that a book written by a murdered author might be a sure bet as far as bestseller lists were concerned. Erin might not have thought about that, but I'm pretty sure both Maxwell Cole's literary agent and editor would have taken that possibility into consideration. As far as I could see, having *Tangled Web* make it big was the best possible outcome. Max had been worried about getting pushback from writing the book. Whatever pushback resulting from the book would now come from Max himself.

"I'm pretty sure that if Maxwell Cole had a vote," I told Erin, "he'd rather see it published than lost. After all, not only is it part of his legacy, but also yours."

That remark reminded me of the man I'd once known as Pete Kelsey. I took a steadying breath before broaching the next topic. "Have you thought about being in touch with John Madsen?" I asked.

Erin drew back in her chair as though I'd just reached out and slapped her. "Why on earth would I do that?" she demanded. "Besides, I have no idea where he is."

"I happen to know he lives in Chehalis," I told her. "Did you know he came to Max's funeral?"

"He did? I never saw him there."

"You didn't see him because he didn't want you to,

but he came hoping to catch a glimpse of you. He and Max evidently stayed in touch over the years. Did you know that?"

Erin shook her head.

"Max kept him updated on what was going on with you and Chris. He still cares about you, Erin. He took care of you when you were an abandoned orphan in Mexico, and you were his little girl for a very long time after that. Although his and Marcia's relationship wasn't one that most people would regard as standard, they lived the way they did in order to protect you. And it turns out you needed protecting. Jennifer came after all of you, Pete Kelsey lost everything, including the two women he loved more than anything in the world. The poor guy has spent years wandering in the wilderness with two holes in his heart. Your reaching out to him would go a long way toward filling one of them."

A silence settled between us then, and I let it sit there for a time, giving my words a chance to sink in.

"I'm not promising," Erin said at last, "but I'll think about it."

"Fair enough," I said.

It was the best I could do.

When I stood up to leave, Erin walked me to the door.

"Thank you," she said. "Thank you for everything you did for me—and for Chris."

"You're welcome," I told her. "Any time."

On the drive home, all I could do was hope that what I'd said had been enough.

Considering Lucy's condition, Mel and I were no longer meeting up for lunch. When she came home that evening with that day's selection of takeout, I told her about my visit with Erin. While we were cleaning up after dinner, Mel stopped in the middle of scraping a plate into the trash and gave me an appraising look.

"Aside from the actual knife fights, this whole thing was good for you, wasn't it?" she said. "You really enjoyed helping Erin."

Why accept a compliment when it's so easy to deflect one? "Max is the one who helped her," I said.

"You're still helping her," Mel pointed out.

She had me there. "I suppose you're right."

"So I'm signing you up for your own subscription to LexisNexis," she said.

"Why on earth would you do that?"

"Because you need it. I also brought home the paperwork for you to apply to become a PI. It's in my purse. All you have to do is fill it out. Think about it. You have a whole lifetime's worth of people that you know in Seattle. If some of them show up on your doorstep in the future, asking for help, as a PI you'll have the benefit of some official standing, and you'll also have some up-to-date tools to work with. Being able to work when you want to and call your own shots will be a hell of a lot better for you than waiting around until TLC decides to call you in on one of their cases."

When Mel handed me the application, I said the same thing to her that Erin had said to me about Pete Kelsey. "I'll think about it," I said, but later on that evening, I stuffed the form into my in-basket on the kitchen counter and left it there.

On Friday morning both Mel and I declined to drive down to Seattle for Kevin Blaylock's funeral. Lucy and I had gone down and back the day before. Mel's excuse

was based on the fact that she had already missed one
day of work that week. Rather than going herself, she
dispatched her second in command along with a group
of officers to participate in her place.

Let's just say I've attended far too many fallen-officer
memorials in my time. Even though I'm sure there was
wall-to-wall coverage of all the pomp and circumstance
on TV, I didn't watch any of it, for the very real reason
that I was still struggling with having pointed Kevin
Blaylock in Bian Duong's direction.

Friday evening, Mel came home from work and gave
me the latest. "Nancy Purcell called today."

"How are she and the kids doing? What are their
names again?"

"Chrissy and Lonny," Mel answered. "And it sounds
like they're doing fine. Great, even."

It turned out that's exactly the news I'd been
dreading—that they really were doing well. Any minute, they'd be out of the shelter and into either tran-
sitional or permanent housing. Once that happened,
they'd probably also be ready to take their dog back.

I looked down at Lucy, who was lying peacefully on
her bed in the kitchen. She caught the glance and obligingly thumped her tail.

"I told Nancy all about what happened with Lucy,"
Mel continued. "By the way, they still call her Rambo."

I didn't say anything at all. I was too busy waiting for
the other shoe to drop.

"Then, just before I came home, Nancy called me
back and told me that she and the kids talked it over
as a family and decided that, if we don't mind keeping
Rambo, once they get into a place where they can have

a pet, she's promised the kids they'll get a new dog—
only a small one this time."

I cannot tell you how happy that news made me feel.
I didn't let on, or at least I tried not to let on, but Mel
probably figured it out all the same.

CHAPTER 37

OVER THE WEEKEND, with Mel home to help with Lucy, I decided it was time to contact Patrick Donahue. Bian Duong's story had been getting blanket coverage in the media, and Todd's death was now considered a homicide, but I felt as though I owed Patrick more information than what was public fodder. We still didn't know exactly what had prompted Todd Farraday's visit to his stepfather's home, but I still suspect it had something to do with Bian's illicit property transfer.

When I called the Refuge and asked to speak to Patrick Donahue, the response was curt. "I'm sorry, but Mr. Donahue is no longer with us."

I thought I recognized the voice as belonging to the very unhelpful Mr. Bannerman. Under the circumstances, those words, "no longer with us," could mean two very different things—that Patrick might have pulled up stakes and gone to live elsewhere, or else he was dead. I knew for sure that if I asked for details, I'd get zilch, so I gave up and was able to spend the rest of the day castigating myself for not trying to reach him sooner.

On Monday morning I woke up gasping for breath and thinking I was having a heart attack. I couldn't breathe. At all. When I turned on the light, I found Lucy standing next to the bed, with her lips almost touching mine and with her intense black eyes boring into me. She was up to her old tricks again, and robbing me of air at every breath.

When Scotty and Kelly were little, I remember Karen complaining about my being able to sleep right through the sound of crying babies. Later, when the kids were older and needed something during the night, they always went to Karen's side of the bed rather than mine. Now, with Mel sleeping soundly on her side of the bed, Karen Moffitt Beaumont was getting a little of her own back.

"How did you get here?" I whispered to Lucy as I scrambled out of bed, although the answer to that was pretty obvious. She had gotten up from her bed all on her own and had come to waken me.

I grabbed the sling and put it around her, but as we headed out it was clear that Lucy needed less support from the sling than she had before. I hadn't taken the time to put on slippers. Out in the yard, the wet grass was cold as hell on my bare feet. Thankfully Lucy didn't linger. She did what needed to be done, and we went back inside.

By then it was five o'clock in the morning. I suppose I could have gone back to bed, but there wasn't much point. I made a cup of coffee, and then Lucy and I decamped into the living room, where I lit the gas log fireplace and sat down to think. Lucy lay down next to my chair, close enough that periodically I could reach down and stroke her head. Whenever I did so, she thumped her tail at me. A man and his dog, what could be better?

I sat there thinking about everything that had gone on in the previous couple of weeks, starting with taking Scott to the dentist that Friday morning and then, later on that evening, running into Max at the restaurant. Those events seemed forever ago now, but they weren't, not really. The time between then and now had been scary and exhausting and exhilarating. Bringing down Bian Harden and Kenneth Purcell had given my life a sense of purpose that had been missing for a very long time.

When I went back to the kitchen for my second cup of coffee, I retrieved the PI application from the in-basket and sat down at the kitchen island to fill it out. When Mel came into the kitchen awhile later, the completed application was sitting on top of the coffee machine.

"What's this?" she asked, picking it up.

"Remember Scott and Cherisse's sonogram?" I asked.

"Sure," Mel said, "but what does that have to do with this?"

"It's the same thing," I told her. "Let's just call it proof of life. It turns out this old guy's still got it."

Since the disbanding of the Special Homicide Investigation Team, J. P. Beaumont's biggest concern is pondering whether he and his wife, Mel, should finally get a dog. But one voicemail from his old friend Ralph Ames is about to change that. Through Ralph, Beau has become involved in an organization called The Last Chance, which enlists a number of retired homicide investigators to tackle long unsolved cold cases. And one has just dropped into Beau's lap.

The facts are muddy at best; thirty years ago, Janice Marie Harrison's car was found abandoned near a bridge, and scratched in the dirt nearby was the word "sorry." It's possible her death was a suicide, but her body was never found. And as Beau begins to investigate, he discovers that no one connected to Janice—not her once all-star football player widower, Anders; not her long-grieving sister, Estelle; not sheriff Gavin Loper, who was deputy sheriff at the time of Janice's disappearance; and not Anders's second wife, Betsy—is exactly what they seem. The question is, which of them knows the truth?

And why have they kept it buried?

Turn the page to join Beaumont as he faces one of his most harrowing trials yet in the novella

STILL DEAD

STILL DEAD

"SO," MY WIFE, Mel Soames, said to me offhandedly over coffee one stormy Saturday morning in November, "have you given any more thought to maybe getting a dog?"

We were at home in Fairhaven, a part of Bellingham, Washington, sitting in the living room of our recently remodeled and even more recently occupied home. The house is situated on a bluff overlooking Bellingham Bay. That blustery morning, our floor-to-ceiling triple-paned windows offered a relatively unobstructed view of wicked waves hurling themselves toward the perpendicular cliffs at the base of our bluff. When I say relatively unobstructed view, I was referring to the sturdy wooden fence we'd installed at the base of the lawn in order to keep overly adventurous grandchildren from venturing beyond the yard and out onto the cliffs themselves.

Mel is my third wife—as in third time's the charm—and I like to think that I'm a little older—well, much older—and a little wiser than I was with numbers one and two. Unlike my younger self, I was able to sense the possible presence of a trap long before the iron jaws themselves clamped shut around my ankle. The fact that I regarded the question as a trap has nothing to do with my hating dogs in general, but there's some unfortunate history here—with me, dogs, and ankles.

I met Karen Moffitt, my first wife, back when we were both students at the University of Washington— the U-Dub as it's affectionately referred to by residents of Washington State. Karen showed up at one of my fraternity's formals on the arm of one of my frat brothers, a guy by the name of Maxwell Cole. By the end of the evening, Karen and I were an item, and Max was in a permanent state of snit, a situation which has lasted for decades. The fact that Karen and I divorced eventually and she subsequently died of cancer has had no effect on Max. His nose is still out of joint.

All of this was back in the old days—the sixties. Although dinosaurs no longer roamed the earth, it was still a time when boys taking girls out on first dates were expected to show up on the front porches of family homes, dressed to the nines, and prepared to meet the parents before escorting their daughters out of the house. I was worried about making a good impression on Karen's father, Amos Moffitt—Pop, as he later insisted I call him—and on her mother, Doris. I should have been more worried about the dog, whose name was Snooks.

Snooks was an ill-tempered, full-sized, wide-load dachshund who took one look at me and promptly bit a big chunk out of my ankle. One of his canines went straight through my sock and into my Achilles tendon, deep enough to draw blood. Karen's dad dragged the dog off me and locked him in the kitchen. Karen's mother treated the wound with mercurochrome and a Band-Aid, all the while assuring me that Snooks had indeed had all his shots. With the bleeding stopped and me noticeably limping, I escorted Karen out of the house to go to a movie—*Around the World in Eighty Days*, as I recall. As for Snooks? For the next five years, as long as the dog remained on the planet, he viewed me as evil incarnate—a reality that made going to the in-laws' home for Sunday dinners and holiday get-togethers somewhat problematic.

So, yes, I admit straight out that I have dog issues. Maybe if I'd had a dog when I was younger and had known something about them, Snooks wouldn't have regarded me as a mortal enemy, but that wasn't the case. I grew up as the son of a single mother—an unmarried World War II not-quite widow. My parents hadn't managed to tie the knot when my father, a sailor based in Bremerton, was killed in a motorcycle accident on his way back home. My mother gave birth to me eight months later, leaving her with all the responsibilities of wartime widowhood and none of the benefits. She raised me totally on her own, with no help either from her family or from my father's, by working as a seamstress. We lived in an apartment over a bakery in Seattle's Ballard neighborhood. The fact that we had no yard automatically precluded the idea of having a dog, nor could we have afforded one. What I do remember is that all my friends who did have dogs were forever complaining about having to take care of them.

All this is to say that, as far as dogs are concerned, Mel and I might just as well have been raised in separate universes. Mel grew up as an army brat, but her family was always attached to at least one dog as well as the occasional cat. Whenever her father was posted overseas, whatever pets were then in residence were carted off to Mel's maternal grandparents' farm near Odessa, Missouri, where they remained for the duration.

I find it amusing that Mel is always more effusive when it comes to talking about her lifetime's worth of dogs than she is about Greg, her ex-husband. For example, she'd been far more dispassionate in telling me about coming home and finding Greg and her best friend in bed together than she had been when it came to relating the story of having to take her beloved sixteen-year-old springer spaniel, Marty—named after Marty Robbins—to the vet to be put down because his back had given out and he could no longer walk.

Her loss of Marty had occurred shortly after her divorce and just prior to her move to Seattle, where, I like to think, she had exchanged one old dog for another—yours truly.

Mel is something of a physical fitness buff. Before I got my relatively new fake knees, I liked to say that my favorite form of exercise was jumping to conclusions. I've upped my game in the walking department some since then—a lot, actually—but Mel was of the opinion that having a dog would kill two birds with one stone—get me out walking more and provide me with some companionship while she was off at work. In other words, this conversation had been ongoing for some time.

"Well," Mel prompted, "have you?"

I had wandered so far off into the woolgathering woods that I had lost track of her original question. It took a moment for me to get back in the right groove.

One thing I knew about any venture into dog ownership was that, with Mel working long hours and with
me performing househusband duties, I would be the
one looking after said dog.

"No," I admitted, "not really."

Which was probably not a good answer, either, since
Mel immediately got up, took her cup to the sink, rinsed
it, and placed it in the dishwasher.

"Where are you going?" I asked.

"To work," she said.

"But today's Saturday," I objected. "Do you have to?"

I probably sounded like a petulant four-year-old objecting to his working mommy's very necessary work-
day departure.

"If we're going to be going to Ashland over next
weekend, I need to clear some of the paperwork off my
desk," Mel said. "That mountain of paperwork is going
to be the death of me yet."

When I was a street cop and a homicide investigator,
I always considered paperwork the bane of my existence. To my way of thinking, it was something forced
on the rest of us from the top down. But now that I was
married to a police chief, I realized that the gods of
paperwork rain the stuff down on everyone's head in a
totally indiscriminate manner—top brass included. In
addition, our upcoming Thanksgiving weekend jaunt to
Ashland to see the kids and grandkids would amount to
a four-day road trip, including two full days—ten hours
apiece—in the car. However, since this was the first
official long weekend Mel had scheduled off since assuming the role of chief, I didn't want anything—most
especially an accumulation of unfinished paperwork—
to screw it up.

"You'd better hop to it then," I told her, "and I'll quit whining."

Mel went off to work. I may have stopped whining, but that didn't mean I stopped thinking. I did the tasks that pass for doing housework these days. I started a load of laundry. I ran the dishwasher, and then, with the gas log fireplace burning and with the iPad on my lap, I set out to do my crossword puzzles, but it didn't work. The printed clues didn't add up in my head because I was too busy thinking about my mother. Thinking about my not having a dog as a kid had reminded me of my mother—Carol Ann Piedmont.

Remember that old Frank Sinatra song, the one that that goes "regrets, I've had a few"? As far as my mother is concerned, regrets are all I have. I wish she could see me as I am now: sober, for one thing. She was the first one who ever told me I had a booze problem back when I was still in high school. I seem to remember telling her she was dead wrong about that, but of course she wasn't. I wish she could see my kids—her grandkids, to say nothing of her great-grandkids. I was only twenty years old when I spent all those hours sitting by her side in a hospital room, one long night after another, while she lost her brief but fierce battle with breast cancer. Karen came to the hospital with me, too, on occasion, but we weren't yet married at the time, and our kids, Scott and Kelly weren't even a blip on the radar.

A sudden rain squall blew in off the bay, leaving the westward-facing windows covered with a scenery-blurring sheet of flowing water. I looked around our spacious great room—at the clean surfaces; the stylish furnishings; the massive island; the gleaming stainless steel appliances in the kitchen—and remembered the dingy, cluttered apartment filled with other people's cast-off furniture where my mother raised me entirely on her own by dint of the one thing she most assuredly inherited from her father—stubbornness in its purest and most unadulterated form.

My mother was only seventeen and still in high school when she discovered she was pregnant. Upon learning the news, her parents, Jonas and Beverly Piedmont, had immediately packed their daughter off to Portland to a home for unwed mothers, where she stayed for the better part of a week before running away. When my mother told her father that she was keeping the baby rather than giving me up, Jonas had banished her from his house and his life.

That was one of my profound regrets, of course, that although my mother always hoped there would be some kind of reconciliation with her family—that was one of the reasons she named me after her father—she never lived to see it. My grandparents didn't become part of my life until much later when I was in my forties—at a time when I'd already been divorced and remarried. Jonas and Beverly Piedmont got to meet their great-grandkids, Scott and Kelly, and even their great-great-granddaughter, Kelly and Jeremy's baby girl, Kayla. My mother missed all of it.

So there she was—a high school dropout, seventeen years old, unmarried, and pregnant. Only in recent years have I learned that initially she turned to my father's parents for help. They declined to do so, leaving her to make her way entirely on her own. She got a job as a dishwasher in a neighborhood bakery—the one under the apartment where we lived the whole time I was growing up. It wasn't until those long nights in the hospital that she told me that Olga Johansson, the woman who owned the bakery, had despised my grandfather for the way he treated us. Olga's way of getting back at him had been to give my mother a job and a place to live along with providing a way for her to make a living—by gifting her with a treadle Singer sewing machine Olga had rescued from a local pawnshop.

The first things my mother made—under Olga's guidance and tutelage—were aprons for the people who worked downstairs. Soon she had a thriving business making aprons for some of the other neighborhood businesses—cafés and coffee shops. Eventually she became a skilled seamstress—with an excellent eye for fashion. Over time her business model changed. She could look at a designer dress in a photograph and create a respectable knockoff for far less than the original. By the time I was in high school, she was making what amounted to inexpensive haute couture dresses for the money-conscious Scandinavian ladies of Ballard who would never consider parting with enough hard-earned cash to pay for an original design.

That's one of my major regrets—the one that, even now, can keep me awake at night—that I didn't appreciate what my mother did; that I didn't understand the terrible price she paid for not giving me up for adoption; that I was ashamed of having to wear "homemade" shirts to school when all the other boys had store-bought shirts. One day when I was in the fourth grade, I told her that I wouldn't go to school if I couldn't wear a "real" shirt.

"Fine," she said. "Take it off then, but you're still going to school. By the way," she added, "it's February. Running around without a shirt may not be such a good idea."

She was right, of course; it wasn't a good idea at all. She won that round fair and square.

On the subject of shirts, however, homemade or not, I never said another word about them to my mother, and the reverse was also true. When I got an after-school job in high school and was able to buy my own shirts, I did so, but it wasn't something she and I ever discussed. Is it possible some of old man Piedmont's stubbornness came down through her DNA to me? You be the judge.

But during those long, empty nights in the hospital, did I ever mention anything about that to my mother? Are you kidding me? I was a twenty-year-old kid who thought I knew everything, even though I didn't know squat. I was arrogant enough to feel sorry for myself and to think that it wasn't fair for her to up and die on me— ON ME—when I wasn't even out of college yet. What an unmitigated twerp I was!

By then it was only ten o'clock in the morning, and I was deep in the emotional weeds. Finally, since there wasn't a damned thing I could do to make things right with my mother, I pried my butt off my self-pity pot and did the only thing that made sense at the time— found an eleven o'clock meeting and went to it. I've spent a long time in AA. One of the hallmarks of Alcoholics Anonymous is knowing the difference between what you can change and what you can't. Having had that pointed out to me, I emerged from the meeting at noon in time to meet up with Mel afterward for lunch, where she had a chef's salad and I had a chili burger.

"What have you done with yourself all morning?" she asked.

"I've been thinking about getting a dog," I told her.

Surprisingly enough, my nose didn't start growing like Pinocchio's, but it should have.

"Have you come to any conclusions?" Mel asked.

"Not so far," I answered. I believe that's what's called a sin of omission.

I went home after lunch, determined to fill the hours between then and the time Mel came home with something worthwhile besides thinking about whether or not to get a dog. I left my phone and keys on the kitchen counter while I went to change into my current favorite at-home wear—a pair of sweats. Picking up the phone a few minutes later, I was surprised to see that I had a voice message. When I played it back, I was even more surprised.

"Gus Loper, here, of the Island County Sheriff's Department. We've got a hit on that print! Call me."

A hit on a print in a cold case? And just like that, even though the Special Homicide Investigation Team is no more, worrying about getting a dog was off my list, and I was back in the harness.

The case had started out a couple of weeks earlier with a call from Ralph Ames. Ralph has been my attorney and my friend for decades now, but we met back when he was my second wife's attorney. Anne Corley is a whole other story and one I won't go into right now, but after her death, I discovered that not only had I inherited her fortune, she also had bequeathed me Ralph. His abiding friendship and wise counsel are things I've come to treasure more with each passing year. And it's due to him that I became involved with an organization called TLC—short for The Last Chance—that uses the volunteered skills of retired homicide investigators and forensic folks to tackle long-unsolved cold cases.

TLC was started by one of Ralph's longtime clients, Hedda Brinker. After taking home a fortune in a Mega Millions lottery, she had used her winnings as seed money to establish the cold case unit. In the aftermath of the shuttering of the Special Homicide Investigation Team, Ralph had realized I was at loose ends, and he had brought me onboard, putting me in touch with a number of TLC operatives located in far-flung corners of the country. And that is how I became involved in the Janice Harrison case—a more than thirty-year-old missing persons case in Washington State, one that had been closed without ever being solved. As far as TLC is concerned, if there's a case based in Washington, I'm their go-to guy—their boots on the ground.

At Ralph's suggestion, I had contacted Estelle Manring—the woman who had connected with TLC, asking for help. Speaking with me over the phone, she supplied me with part of the story—her side of the story anyway—about her long-lost sister.

On Saturday morning, June 22, 1985, a 1983 Ford T-Bird belonging to one Janice Marie Harrison was found parked near one of the viewpoints on the Whidbey Island side of Deception Pass on Washington State Route 20. People from Washington often refer to it as "the bridge at Deception Pass," but that's actually . . . well . . . deceptive. The crossing between Whidbey Island and the mainland is composed of two two-lane bridges—one over Canoe Pass and the other over Deception Pass.

A Washington State trooper discovered Janice's abandoned vehicle at 1:45 A.M., not far from the two bridges. The keys were still in the ignition, and her purse was on the front seat. There was no sign of a struggle or of foul play. Scratched into the dirt next to the car was a single printed word, "SORRY." The implement used to write out what was assumed to be a one-word suicide note was never recovered, and neither was Janice's body. If she had leapt to her death from the bridge deck, the assumption was that her remains must have been washed out to sea, since they were never seen again.

Janice's grieving husband, Anders, was a local guy— a Whidbey Island native—who had been an all-star football player at Oak Harbor High and who was expected to go on to a stellar football career at the University of Washington. Unfortunately, once he arrived at the U-Dub, it hadn't all been smooth sailing. He had partied too much and washed out of college halfway through his freshman year. Had he been born in other circumstances, not completing his education might have been the beginning of a permanent downward spiral, but that wasn't the case. Anders's forebears had been early settlers on Whidbey Island, and coming from pioneer stock meant that, with a degree or without, his future was padded with a certain amount of a: money and b: pull.

Once Anders was back home, his somewhat disappointed but very well-heeled father helped set Anders up in a family-owned auto dealership. A short time later he had married Janice in a quirky wedding that should have amounted to a happy ending but didn't—at least not for Janice. According to the way her sister, Estelle, told the story, Janice had gotten pregnant out of wedlock while Anders was still on the rebound after the breakup of a long-term relationship with his high school sweetheart.

As the story unfolded, it seemed to me that, at the time of their shotgun wedding, both Janice and Anders had had plenty of growing up to do. Anders still liked to party. He drank too much and played poker too much. As for Anders's parents? They tolerated their new daughter-in-law, but they felt their son had married beneath his station in life, and they made it clear that they were none too happy with the match. When that first unplanned pregnancy ended in a miscarriage, the elder Harrisons probably thought the marriage would end as well. Much to their surprise, however, it didn't, and soon Janice turned up pregnant yet again, this time with Tiffany Anne.

After losing the first baby, Janice had been overjoyed to welcome Tiffany into the world. Although she had adored her new role as mother, there had been some dark clouds on the marital horizon. In private Janice had complained about her in-laws' constant harping and disapproval and about Anders, who continued to drink and party and generally behave like an arrogant jerk.

"I told her that if worse came to worst, she could always bring the baby and come home," Estelle said. "The folks and I had moved to Mukilteo by then, and I was still in high school. It would have been crowded living in a little two-bedroom apartment, but if we'd had to, we would have made it work. But then Tiffany died."

"What happened?" I asked.

"She died of SIDS," Estelle answered. "Sudden Infant Death Syndrome."

"At the time of the baby's death, do you believe Janice was actively thinking about leaving her husband?" I asked.

"I'm not sure how serious she was, but I do know that she had mentioned it to me more than once, after Tiffany was born and before she died."

"And afterward?"

"I can't tell you about that," Estelle answered sadly, "at least not for sure. Janice sort of shut everyone else out after that, me included. I've always felt I wasn't there for her when I should have been."

So that was the other part of Estelle Manring's deal. She blamed Anders for her sister's death, but she also blamed herself.

"She was depressed then?" I asked.

"I suppose."

"Were there any other reasons for Janice to want out of the marriage in addition to concerns about her husband's drinking and partying?" I asked.

"You mean, did he hit her?" Estelle asked. We had been speaking by phone, and there was a long pause before she resumed speaking. "Janice never came out and said as much, but I always wondered about that. He was a control freak and expected her to do as he said. Sort of one of those 'my way or the highway' kind of guys."

"Tell me about the baby," I said.

"Tiffany was three months old when she died," Estelle answered. "Janice put her down for a nap one afternoon. When she came back an hour or so later, Tiffany was cold to the touch. Janice called 911 immediately, but it was already too late. She was beside herself with grief—blamed herself for being a terrible mom, for not going in to check on the baby sooner, for everything. And then, two months after that, Janice was gone, too, with everybody claiming that she took her own life by jumping off that bridge."

"But you hold Anders responsible, don't you?"

"Yes, I do," Estelle declared. "He was Janice's husband. Isn't it always the husband?"

Not always, of course, but I could see Estelle's point. She had also spent the last thirty or so years mired in the unshakable belief that her former brother-in-law had somehow played a part in her sister's death.

"So where was Anders on the night in question?" I asked.

"It turns out he had an air-tight alibi," Estelle answered. "He had a regularly scheduled Friday night poker game that night with two of his best buds from high school, one of whom turned out to be an Island County deputy sheriff. There were usually four of them, but the other guy couldn't make it. According to Anders, after the game broke up, he went back to the house a little after midnight and discovered Janice wasn't there. According to him, she had been moody lately and threatening to go visit us. Assuming that's what she'd done, he went to bed and was sound asleep when the cops showed up a while later to say they'd found her car on the bridge."

That was the gist of my hour-long phone call with Estelle Manring that Thursday morning. Her sister, Janice, was dead; the world thought she had committed suicide; and Estelle thought her former brother-in-law responsible. But here's the deal, I'm an old-fashioned kind of guy. In talking to witnesses, I prefer working eyeball-to-eyeball, so I made an appointment to meet up with Estelle at her real estate office in Poulsbo the following afternoon in order to continue our conversation.

Bellingham is a small city with a population of right

around 85,000. Running a cop shop anywhere means living in a pressure cooker on a daily basis. Since Mel—the girl of my dreams—is currently the one inhabiting said pressure cooker, I try to get her out of Dodge for a day or so on the weekends by making sure we spend at least one night a week at our condo in Seattle's Denny Regrade area. Yes, there's an eighty-mile drive coming and going, but there are times when even fighting your way through gnarly traffic can be a useful form of decompression.

I figured I'd hop over to the Kitsap Peninsula in the early afternoon on Friday, spend some time interviewing Estelle, and then take the Bainbridge ferry to Seattle in time to have dinner with Mel. And because I could tell from the weather report that the seas might be rough that day, I took the added precaution of bringing along the seasickness prevention bracelets that had been a gift from my grandmother, thank you very much. I didn't end up having to use them, but knowing they were right there in my pocket and readily available should the need arise gave me a lot of reassurance.

Bainbridge Realty and Trust has its offices just off the highway in Poulsbo, but from the waterfront photos prominently displayed on their walls, most of their business dealings were on Bainbridge Island rather than on the mainland. When I arrived, I was told that Estelle Manring was involved in an unscheduled but complex meeting of some kind, so I spent some time cooling my heels in the reception area, reading through the company's obligatory and laudatory literature, which let me know that as far as sales were concerned, Estelle Manring was one of their top brokers.

The brochure not only contained a listing of the

company's current hot real estate offerings, it also included Glamour Shots–style photos of their several brokers. The one above Estelle Manring's name showed a reasonably good-looking and well-dressed business-woman somewhere in her forties. However, no amount of deft photoshopping had been able to correct two very visible flaws in Estelle's appearance. The fixed smile she showed to the camera didn't reach all the way to her eyes, and there was no concealing the permanently downturned cast of her lips at both edges of that forced smile. I've seen features like that all too often, etched into the faces of the grieving after some sudden and impossibly tragic event has stolen away someone near and dear. Janice Harrison may have been gone for more than thirty years, but the pain of that loss was still writ large on her sister's somber face.

When Estelle finally emerged from the meeting, she greeted me with an apologetic shake of her head. "Sorry," she muttered. "The more someone pays for a house, the more unreasonable they become."

"Your basic well-heeled toddlers?" I asked.

This time Estelle's smile was genuine. "Yes," she said. "I need to remember that line the next time I get cornered by someone who decides that the Sub-Zero in her otherwise 'perfect' house isn't the 'right' Sub-Zero."

She led me into a conference room where the only item visible on the otherwise empty surface of the table was a high school yearbook—the 1981 issue of Oak Harbor High's *Acorn*. Once we were seated and she passed the book in my direction, I noticed it was already open to the page depicting that year's big-hair version of homecoming royalty—none other than Anders Harrison and Betsy Davis.

"That's my former brother-in-law with his first love and second wife," Estelle told me. "Janice was just a brief side trip—a detour as it were—along the way. Betsy Davis Parmenter was someone who believed in playing the field. She broke up with Anders right after their senior prom, and the split left him in a world of hurt. Betsy immediately married guy number two, Ron Parmenter, only circling back to Anders once she tired of husband number one. Or once he tired of her. I was never sure which was which."

"Were Anders and Betsy still an item while he was married to Janice?" I asked.

"Not as far as I could tell," Estelle answered. "Betsy claimed that after their senior year, she didn't see Anders again until long after Janice's death."

"Does that mean you asked her about that directly?"

Janice bit her lip. "Nobody else was asking any questions," she said. "Someone had to do it."

Estelle might not have uncovered evidence to the effect that Anders and Betsy had been fooling around behind Janice's back, but it clearly wasn't for lack of trying.

I changed the subject by once more focusing on the yearbook. "Is Janice in here, too?" I asked.

Nodding, Estelle took the book, thumbed through a few pages, and handed it back. "She was a junior when Betsy and Anders were seniors," Estelle explained, turning the book back in my direction with a different page showing—one containing pictures of members of that year's junior class. The photo featuring Janice Marshall showed her to be a serious-looking young woman who had resisted the big-hair look—her long, dark locks pulled back in a simple ponytail. The thick-rimmed glasses she wore gave her a studious look. The contrast between the two young women couldn't have been greater. Betsy, dolled up in her homecoming finery, looked like a beauty pageant contestant while Janice was your basic plain Jane.

There were paperclips attached to some of the yearbook's pages. Sorting through those, I found a photo that featured the co-captains of the football team—Gus Loper and Anders Harrison. "Wait," I said, "wasn't that the name of the deputy sheriff who was playing poker with Anders the night Janice disappeared?"

Estelle nodded. "You've got it. Gus was a deputy back then. Now he's the local sheriff."

"Are the sheriff and Anders still tight?" I asked.

Estelle nodded. "As far as I know, they are," she said bitterly. "Anders and Gus are in Rotary together. Gus runs the sheriff's department, Anders is on the school board, and Betts is the mover and shaker behind the garden club. You could say they're all just one big happy family."

It wasn't hard to see how Estelle had arrived at the conclusion that the close friendship between the two men might have impacted that original investigation, and I found myself asking some of those same questions. Had the poker game been nothing more than a manufactured story aimed at providing a bulletproof alibi for a friend badly in need of one? Or was it possible that the deputy's involvement in the case had helped contribute to the ready acceptance of the premise that Janice's disappearance could be attributed to suicide rather than something more sinister? If that were the case, I wondered, wouldn't there have had to be some signs of a cover-up? As President Nixon learned to his everlasting regret, doing the crime is one thing. It's the cover-up that gets you every time.

I spent the better part of an hour with Estelle that afternoon. Like so many cold case family members, she was grateful that, at long last, someone was willing to hear her out. Estelle maintained that Janice was someone who, no matter how upset she might have been over the loss of her child, would never have taken her own life. And she also hinted that at that juncture in Anders's career, losing his wife in what was commonly regarded as a horrible tragedy had been far more socially acceptable around town than a rancorous divorce would have been.

When it came time for me to leave and head for the ferry, I asked if it would be possible for me to borrow the yearbook.

"Sure," Estelle said. "Keep it as long as you like."

Even though it was Friday afternoon, it was a winter Friday afternoon, and I made it onto the Bainbridge ferry on the first try. Then, rather than go upstairs, I stayed on the car deck, turned on the reading light, and paged through the book. I was struck by how young all those kids looked—young, hopeful, and incredibly innocent. I found a few more photos of Janice Marshall scattered throughout the book. She was on the yearbook staff. She was also a member of the National Honor Society and the Future Teachers of America.

Becoming a teacher had never happened because Janice never actually graduated. Ed Marshall, Estelle and Janice's father, was injured and permanently disabled in a logging truck accident the summer before Janice's senior year. She and Anders had started dating late in the summer, just before he went off to the U-Dub. When she turned up pregnant later that fall, the couple had married over Christmas vacation. Janice had dropped out of Oak Harbor High School about the same time Anders had dropped out of the University of Washington. She had suffered a miscarriage only a month or two later. By 1985, at barely twenty-one years of age, Janice Harrison had already lost two children and was stuck in what was reportedly a challenging marriage. Those circumstances made the idea of her committing suicide seem a lot more plausible.

As for the yearbook photos of Betsy Davis? Her pictures were everywhere. She seemed to be Oak Harbor High's version of the "It" girl. Like Janice, Betsy, too, was in the National Honor Society. In addition, she was a member of the varsity tennis team and a cheerleader, along with serving as student body treasurer. Sometime before their springtime breakup, she and Anders had been photographed together after being voted most likely to succeed.

As the ferry slowed at the Coleman ferry dock, I closed the book thinking sadly about those very young kids. I thought about how, in the four short years between 1981 and 1985, so many of those hopeful innocents would find their lives indelibly touched by tragedy. And I thought, too, about Janice Marie Marshall Harrison— long gone now but thankfully not forgotten.

Mel and I went to dinner that night at our favorite walking-distance hangout—El Gaucho on First Avenue. Over our split steak, I told her about everything I had learned about Janice Marshall Harrison's long-ago disappearance and presumed death. Mel heard me out without comment.

"It sounds like a familiar story," she said when I finished. "The popular in-girl drops the guy, your local big man on campus, who immediately seeks out a second-choice girl and knocks her up. A year or two later, Janice is dead while everybody else apparently lives happily ever after. No wonder Estelle's upset. So what's the next step?"

Obviously Mel had come down solidly in Janice's and Estelle's corner and fully expected that a next step on my part would soon be forthcoming.

"First thing next week, I guess I'll make a pilgrimage over to Whidbey and pay a call on the Island County sheriff."

And that's exactly what I did bright and early the following Monday morning. On my way back to Bellingham after our weekend in the city, I swung off I-5, drove across Camano Island, and motored over to Whidbey via Deception Pass. On my way to Coupeville, I stopped off at the overlook where Janice's car had been found abandoned. These days there are plenty of WDOT surveillance cameras in the area. Back in the eighties, however, that wasn't the case. I turned up at the sheriff's office in Coupeville at around eleven that morning and handed Sheriff Loper's receptionist one of my TLC business cards.

"May I tell him what this is about?" she asked.

"Janice Harrison," I answered, "Janice Marshall Harrison."

When the woman ushered me into the sheriff's private office a few minutes later, two things were immediately clear. For one, Sheriff Gus Loper's big-hair days from back in the mid-eighties were long gone.

He wasn't exactly bald as a billiard ball, because he did have a close-cropped fringe running earlobe to earlobe around the back of his head. As for number two? He wasn't the least bit happy to see me.

"Don't tell me," he said, sending the business card his receptionist had just handed him spinning back across his desk with enough force that it spiraled off onto the floor. "Estelle Manring's back at it again, right? So who the hell are you and what the hell is a TLC?"

I stooped down, retrieved the card, and put it back on his desk. "My name's J. P. Beaumont," I told him, "formerly with the attorney general's Special Homicide Investigation Team. I'm currently associated with The Last Chance, aka TLC. It's a consortium of retired homicide and forensic folks who volunteer our services to resolve long-unsolved homicides."

"You're out of luck then," Sheriff Loper declared. "Janice Marshall's death is not unresolved; she committed suicide."

No matter how many decades pass and no matter how many feminists would like it to be otherwise, women who hail from small-town America are forever stuck in a time warp and referred to by their birth names—their "maiden names" as it were. Thirty plus years later, this was still the case with Janice.

"Look," Sheriff Loper continued, "Estelle Manring lost her sister. I get that. But Anders lost big, too—his wife and both of his babies. Everybody acts like it was all so much water off a duck's back as far as he was concerned, but it wasn't like that. He was devastated. Went off the deep end for a while—drinking, drugging, you name it. It was the better part of two years before he started getting his act back together. If it hadn't been for Betts turning up and taking him in hand, he probably would have ended up dead, too."

"Betts?" I asked.

"Betsy Davis Parmenter—Anders's second wife. They had been close in high school. They lost track of each other for a while, married other people, and got back together much later. She was the thing after Janice's death that made Anders decide that maybe his life could still be worth living. They married and raised three kids together—Betts's son from a previous marriage and two daughters of their own. All good kids, by the way. They're all through college and doing well."

"So a good second act then?" I said.

There may have been the smallest hint of sarcasm in my question. Loper caught it and called me on it. "Losing Janice wasn't an act, Mr. Beaumont, and marrying Betts wasn't an act, either."

"You never considered that Anders Harrison might have played some role in his wife's disappearance."

"Not once," Loper declared, "and neither did anyone else, except for Estelle Manring, that is. Why can't she just let it go?"

"Because her sister is still dead," I replied.

The answer was an understated rebuke calculated to sort out real cops from the pompous assholes of the world. It worked like a charm, and Sheriff Loper landed squarely on the correct side of that equation.

"What do you need?" he asked with a sigh.

"I'd like to go through the case files," I said. "That's what we used to do at Special Homicide, and it's what we do at TLC as well. We go through the records with new eyes. Occasionally we spot something important that everyone else may have missed."

Loper picked up my card again and stared at it in silence for a long moment. "You know that Anders Harrison and I have been best friends since grade school?" he asked at last.

"I do."

"Well, go ahead and knock yourself out then," Loper told me.

With that he turned back to the receptionist who had lingered in the doorway, watching and listening goggle-eyed as words volleyed back and forth between us. "Daisy," he said, "would you please be so kind as to take this gentleman down to the evidence facility and tell Stanley to give him whatever assistance he may require."

"Yes, sir," Daisy said. To me, she added, "Right this way."

The so-called evidence facility was in one of those modular buildings that school districts usually refer to as "portables," although once installed, they are anything but. Deputy Stanley House, the evidence clerk, was a wheelchair-bound former Island County officer who mentioned to me in passing that he had been run down ten years earlier by a drunk driver. I had to give Sheriff Loper credit on that score, too. He was the kind of guy who looked after his own.

Deputy House took me in hand. He gave me his undivided attention and complete access to everything I needed.

As I sorted my way through the materials he provided, I was forced to conclude that Gavin Miller, the

Island County sheriff back in 1985, had done a pretty thorough job of investigating the case. I'm in favor of making video recordings of all witness and suspect interviews. Most people aren't trained actors. When you're looking at videos, it's relatively easy to spot when somebody is hamming it up and faking a level of grief that's as phony as a three-dollar bill.

But the Janice Harrison investigation predated the now routine practice of doing video recordings of everything. Back then the department had relied solely on audio recordings. Among the case artifacts I found a whole cache of labeled audio cassettes that indicated the interviews had been conducted in a timely and orderly fashion.

Deputy House wasn't able to produce a working cassette player, and even had he done so, I think there's a good chance that the tapes themselves would have deteriorated to the point that listening to them would have been impossible. Fortunately, someone had gone to the considerable trouble of transcribing each of the interviews. Reading through the transcripts didn't allow me a window into any of the visible or audible emotions behind the words of each individual, but in reading the words themselves, I was unable to find anything amiss.

The interviews with the three poker players—Anders Harrison himself, Deputy Gus Loper, and Clyde Lewis—all seemed to substantiate each other's story. They reported that they'd started playing about eight, paused for pizza around ten or so, and then shut the game down for good a little after midnight, whereupon everyone went their separate ways. In answer to questions about the topics discussed that night, all three mentioned Anders's concern about his wife's current state of mind, but there was no indication that he feared she might do herself harm. The fourth transcribed interview had been conducted with a guy named Buzz Buford who was the other regularly scheduled poker player, the one who had missed that night's game due to the late arrival of a load of cement at a home construction site where he was project foreman.

I paid especially close attention to every word of Anders's interview. He claimed that he'd arrived home at his and Janice's place outside Coupeville around 12:30 A.M. and had discovered that Janice wasn't there. Relatively unconcerned by her absence, he'd gone to bed, only to be awakened some two hours later when an Island County deputy, alerted by the state patrol, stopped by to report that Janice's abandoned vehicle had been found near Deception Pass.

Reading through what Anders said at the time, the words sounded right to me—like the bewildered maunderings of a grieving man trying to come to terms with the inexplicable losses of first his two children and now his wife. Nothing he said in the transcript raised my hackles or my suspicions. In addition, he was entirely cooperative with every aspect of the investigation. He had invited the cops to search both the house and the grounds even though Sheriff Miller had insisted on having a valid search warrant in hand before allowing his officers to set foot inside the property.

But the resulting exhaustive search had yielded nothing. The house held no sign of any kind of altercation or any trace of homicidal violence. Nothing was missing from the residence. A single unidentified fingerprint was lifted from the front door, suggesting that Janice might have had a visitor on the night she disappeared, but no one came forward to admit to having called on her.

Several days later some tourists from British Columbia had called in to report that they'd been driving back to Vancouver in the early morning hours that Saturday morning and had seen what appeared to be a lone woman walking along the shoulder of the road, coming west from the bridge and walking in the direction of Oak Harbor. Assuming she was a stranded motorist, the husband had wanted to turn around and offer assistance. His wife initially rejected the idea but eventually relented. When they made a U-turn and returned to where they had spotted her, the woman had disappeared.

The presence of a mysterious woman on that stretch of roadway on the night Janice disappeared had given rise to the idea that perhaps Janice had faked her suicide as a way of escaping a life that had turned out to be anything but what she'd expected, but that theory had never gained any traction.

A forensic examination of the abandoned T-Bird had come up empty. Janice had been a little bit of a thing—only five-foot-two. The seat and mirror adjustments had both been in what appeared to be their normal positions for someone of that size and stature. The only fingerprints found on the steering wheel or anywhere else in the vehicle had belonged to either Janice or Anders.

After spending three hours browsing through the Janice Harrison files, I thanked Deputy House for his assistance and made my way back to Sheriff Loper's office.

"Well," he asked, looking up from his desk when

Daisy once again ushered me into the room. "Did you find anything of interest?"

"Not much," I admitted. "But I'm curious about one thing. Did you ever run that one unidentified print through AFIS?"

If you want to be picky about it, the proper term should be IAFIS—for Integrated Automated Fingerprint Identification System—but most old-time cops, yours truly included—drop that initial I in favor of sticking with the original acronym. Regardless of what I called it, Sheriff Loper wasn't amused.

"This was 1985, remember?" he said. "I don't think AFIS was even a glimmer in the FBI's eye back then, and my department didn't have either the necessary equipment or the capability of getting on line with AFIS until sometime in the mid-nineties, years after Janice Harrison was declared legally dead and the case deemed closed."

"So that would be a no then?"

Sheriff Loper answered my question with a baleful shake of his head.

"Did you read through the interviews?" he asked.

"I read them," I answered. "All of them were surprisingly consistent."

"Did you see any indication that Anders Harrison was anything other than a grieving husband?"

"No," I admitted, "I did not."

"And did you notice we all mentioned the same thing—that Janice's state of mind was one of the topics we discussed that night. Anders told us he was worried about her, too, but I don't think any of us even remotely considered the possibility that she'd drive out there in the middle of the night and throw herself off a bridge."

"What about that woman who was spotted out walking along the highway?"

"That was looked into but never corroborated," Loper told me. "In fact, a search was conducted along that stretch of roadway to see if perhaps there had been some kind of hit-and-run with a dead body lying hidden in a ditch somewhere. Nothing was found. We also had people out searching the coastline for miles on either side of the bridge. Nothing ever turned up, and nothing is going to turn up."

I didn't like having to agree with him, but there wasn't much choice. "All right, then," I said. "Thanks for the help. I'll get back to Estelle Manring and let her know that I've come up empty."

I had made that difficult phone call the same afternoon as I drove from Coupeville back to Bellingham. It had not gone well. "So you're giving up," Estelle demanded, "just like that?"

"I went through all the files," I said. "And came up with nothing."

"I should have known," she said.

"So what should I do about the yearbook. Do you want me to mail it back to you?"

"As far as I'm concerned, you can burn the damned thing," she stormed. "Or put it where the sun don't shine." Whereupon she hung up.

Right, I told myself, *yet another dissatisfied customer.*

Now, however, just days after my giving up on the Janice Harrison case, here was a message from Sheriff Loper saying they had a hit. Really? My finger shook as I dialed him back.

"A hit?" I repeated.

"Yes," he said. "I'm about to send out an invitation for her to come in for an interview."

"Her?"

"Betts," he said. "Betsy Harrison. Five years ago she signed up to be a substitute teacher."

"And these days teachers are required to give prints," I concluded.

"Exactly," Loper replied. "So after you left my office the other day, I called down to Seattle PD and did some checking on you. Everyone there gives you pretty high marks. That's when I decided to take your advice and run that print after all."

Obviously in his conversations with Seattle PD, Loper hadn't turned over the rock labeled Captain Paul Kramer. If he had, Loper and I probably wouldn't have been having a cordial conversation. And although our discussion was most likely leading somewhere at that point, I had no idea where that might be.

"Are you saying it came back as hers?" I asked.

"Yes, it did."

The simplest answer to any given question is usually the right one. "Maybe this Betsy person stopped by for a visit—maybe a condolence call of some kind."

"No, she didn't," Loper said.

"You're sure about that?"

"I was best man at Anders's wedding," Sheriff Loper told me. "At both of his weddings, as a matter of fact. I remember talking to Betts at their reception. She was talking about how, after she left Whidbey, it was years before she came back. She said that Anders had always been her one true love, and that she felt as though she had behaved so badly toward him that she couldn't bear facing him. Then, a year or so after Janice's death, they accidentally crossed paths at a mutual friend's house in Seattle, that was it. She claimed it was only after they reconnected and started dating that she was finally able to come home to Whidbey."

"The presence of that print tells us she lied about that."

"Yes," Loper agreed somberly, "and that got me wondering about what other lies she might have told."

"And?" I prompted.

"I'm looking at a copy of her first husband's death certificate," he said. "It says here that Ron Parmenter died of an accidental drug overdose on August 8, 1985."

I was starting to connect the same dots that Sheriff Loper had already connected. "That's only a couple of months after Janice died. Are you thinking maybe it wasn't accidental?" I asked.

"Do you?" Sheriff Loper's voice was bleak. "I'm thinking Betts came up here determined to take Janice off the board so she could have a clear shot at getting Anders back. That would only be possible, of course, if Betts got rid of her own husband, too."

"This Ron person, her husband," I said. "What about him? Was he a known drug user?"

"Not exactly. Ron Parmenter was a hotshot, name-brand snowboarder, back when snowboards were the new thing on the block. That was a big part of his appeal. At the time, he was way more showy than Anders was. The problem is, Ron had an accident of some kind, screwed up his back real bad, and was ruled permanently off the slopes."

"Was he an invalid then?"

"Pretty much. He was bedridden. Betts had to look after him."

"So rather than having to take care of him for the rest of her life, you're thinking Betts got rid of him?"

"What do you think?"

"How can I help?"

"I want to get Betts Harrison inside one of my interview rooms, but if I tell her straight out that we're reopening Janice's case, she either won't show up or else she'll lawyer up."

"So?"

"I'd like to lure her into stopping by. I want to tell her that you've come around asking questions about the case, and that I suggested you talk with her rather than bringing all this bad old stuff up with poor Anders. I'll assure her that the conversation is for informational purposes only, and that just chatting about what went on will most likely be enough to set Estelle's mind at ease. Once your interview with her is over, that will probably be the end of it."

I was listening to what Loper was saying, but I was pretty sure there was something he was leaving out. I needed to know about that missing piece of the puzzle.

"What else?" I asked.

"What do you mean?"

"There's more to this story," I told him. "Something you haven't quite gotten around to telling me."

Sheriff Loper took a deep breath. "It goes back to what Betts said at the wedding reception," Loper answered reluctantly. "The part about Anders being her one true love."

"You're saying that wasn't true?"

"Not exactly. It turns out Betts Davis had a lot of true loves. I happen to know there was at least one other guy who both predated and postdated Anders."

It has taken me years to learn the art of keeping my trap shut long enough for the other shoe to drop. This was one of those times.

"Buzz Buford," Loper said at last in a strangled whisper.

"The construction foreman?" I asked. "The one who missed the poker game that night?"

"He's the one," Loper answered. "Buzz and Betts were a hot item our sophomore year, before Betts hooked up with Anders." He paused for a moment. "I happen to know that they were involved for a while after Anders as well. I always thought it was a harmless little affair that had ended long before Janice died, but . . ."

"But the ID on that fingerprint sheds a whole new light on things."

"Yes, it does."

"Did anyone ever look at Buzz's alibi for the night in question?"

"There didn't seem to be a need to. Now there is. I just stopped by the evidence room and read through the transcript. He said he was pouring footings at the Creagers' new house. That's located just a half mile or so up the bluff from the place where Anders and Janice were living at the time. I'm thinking that could be where Janice's body ended up—buried in a load of wet cement. Maybe that's why we never found her."

I could see Sheriff Loper's dilemma. This was all circumstantial evidence at best, and in order for this to work, he would have to have a confession. The suspects involved were longtime friends of his—lifelong friends—and he was about to throw them under the bus. No, that's not true—he needed a fall guy there to do the actual throwing.

"Obviously you can't be part of the interview."

"Obviously."

"So who will be?"

"Detective Gonzales," Loper answered. "He's ex-navy who was stationed here on Whidbey while he was in the service and decided to come back once he got out. He's a good guy who spent some time working NCIS. Smart, too. My department is lucky to have him."

I could see Loper's strategy here. By sending in two relative outsiders—Detective Gonzales and me—Loper was unofficially recusing himself from the investigation. He suspected where at least one body was buried, and now so did I. My next job was to bring Gonzales up to speed.

"When do you want to do this?" I asked.

"Tomorrow afternoon, maybe?" Loper suggested. "A Sunday afternoon sit-down will look a little less official than inviting Betts in on a weekday."

"How about if I bring my wife along?" I asked. "That'll make it look even less official."

"By wife I take it you mean Mel Soames, the new chief of police in Bellingham?"

Clearly Sheriff Loper had checked me out. "That would be the one," I said.

"Why the hell not?" Loper replied. "That way there would be two sworn police officers in that interview room rather than just one."

"Are you going to brief Detective Gonzales before-hand?" I asked.

"How long were you a homicide cop—thirty years or so?"

"Give or take."

"Here's what I'm going to do. I'm going to tell him who you are, that you're investigating a long-closed case, and that Betts Harrison may be a person of interest in said case. I want you to put him in the know. At this point, I don't want to do or say anything that could be prejudicial to the case."

After getting off the phone with Gus Loper, I did not immediately pick up the phone and call Estelle back to let her know the playing field had suddenly shifted under our feet. I had a feeling Sheriff Loper and I were on to something, but I wanted to deliver results rather than promises of results. The person I did call was Mel. I was determined that she would be briefed well in advance of the interview even if Detective Gonzales wasn't.

Late in the afternoon, sitting in front of the gas log fireplace and watching the sunset, I told her everything I knew or thought I did. "So you and Sheriff Loper think the bad actors here are Betts Harrison and this Buzz guy, and that Anders Harrison is just some kind of innocent bystander?"

"That's how it looks to us."

"I don't think so," Mel said.

"Why not?"

"Because he's the husband. It's always the husband."

I might have pointed out that this was sexual stereotyping of the first water, but I didn't. Sometimes maintaining marital harmony is more important than making a point.

On Sunday afternoon, Mel and I showed up at the Island County Sheriff's Office in Coupeville at 1:45, fifteen minutes ahead of our scheduled 2:00 P.M. meeting with Betts Harrison. Mel, with her hair pulled back in a ponytail and dressed in a pair of slim jeans topped by a bright blue cashmere sweater, didn't look the least bit police-chiefy. When I introduced her to Detective Emilio Gonzales as my wife, I couldn't help but notice the appreciative way in which he looked her up and down.

"I'm not with TLC," she told him with a disarming smile during their initial handshake. "I just came along for the ride."

Sure she did, and I'm a monkey's uncle.

Betts Harrison drove up a few minutes later in a slick little Mercedes SLK Roadster that was several years newer than my aging S550. As she exited her tiny car, I noticed that she was tiny, too—five-two at the very most. And that's when I remembered the forensic report about Janice Harrison's T-Bird. Because the seat and mirror adjustments hadn't been changed, everyone had assumed Janice was the last person to drive the car. What it really meant was that Anders Harrison liked his womenfolk to come in small packages.

Entering the lobby with all the gracious assurance of a homecoming queen, Betsy Davis Parmenter Harrison greeted Sheriff Loper with an effusive hug. "Why, Gussy," she said, "I didn't think you were going to be here."

I caught a glimpse of the shocked expression that momentarily shot across Detective Gonzales's face. I doubt any members of the department had ever heard that schoolboy nickname applied to the man who was their tough-guy boss.

Sheriff Loper fended off Betts Harrison's enthusiastic greeting and pointed her in my direction. "I have to run," he said, "but before I do, I wanted to make the introductions. This is J. P. Beaumont. He and Mel here are with an organization called TLC. And Detective Emilio Gonzales who's with my department is here to provide whatever assistance might be required."

"Of course," Betts said. "That makes perfect sense."

She turned a dazzling, white-toothed smile on me. Taking in that perfectly sculpted face, it occurred to me that she'd most likely had some work done. The short jacket she wore looked like a David Green mink for sure, and the rings on her fingers collectively boasted several carats' worth of diamonds. Clearly she had cashed in by marrying Anders Harrison, and she was making the most of it.

"So you're the ones who are looking into Janice's case?" Betts asked. "I thought that whole mess was cleared up ages ago."

"It was," I said, "but Janice's sister, Estelle, still has a few questions, and Sheriff Loper thought it would be better to discuss them with you rather than bringing them up with your husband."

"Absolutely," Betts said. "It was a terribly difficult time for poor Anders, and I'm happy to spare him the emotional pain. Be advised, however, since I wasn't on Whidbey at the time everything happened, what I have to say is bound to be secondhand rather than first."

Bingo! As the saying goes, the first liar doesn't stand a chance. Betts had no idea we were there for her—none at all. She had gotten away with lying about all this for so long that it never occurred to her to think otherwise.

Mel stepped into the discussion just then. "We've made arrangements to use an interview room," she said. "TLC likes to maintain a video record of all proceedings—if that's all right with you."

"No problem," Betts said. "I'm glad to do whatever I can to help out."

Detective Gonzales ushered us into an interview room crammed with a table and four chairs. It was very tight, but in terms of putting the squeeze on Betts Harrison, tight and uncomfortable was exactly what was needed. We waited while Detective Gonzales activated the recording equipment. Mel and I had strategized about this in advance. Following our game plan, she asked the first question.

"You weren't actually in town during all the unpleasantness?"

"No, not at all," Betts said. "I was living in Seattle at the time with a toddler of my own and a gravely injured husband—my first husband."

"It sounds like things weren't smooth as glass for you back then, either," Mel observed.

Betts took Mel's proffered hook of sympathy and swallowed it whole. "You can say that again," she agreed.

I made a show of turning on my iPad and consulting the screen. "My understanding is that you and Anders dated in high school prior to his marrying Janice Marshall. Is that correct?"

Betts nodded. "It was one of those young love things that ended badly. I married for the first time on the rebound after that breakup, and so did Anders. Both of those first marriages ended in tragedy. Afterward, Anders and I somehow found our way back to each other. Nobody expects to be widowed while you're still in your twenties."

"Your first husband died, too?" Mel asked.

Betts nodded. "Ron was a championship snow-boarder who had messed up his back. He overdosed on his pain meds."

"So an accidental death then?"

"Totally," Betts replied. "Anyway, when Anders and I got together again, we were both trying to pick up the broken pieces of our lives. I had my son, Anthony, to look after, while poor Anders had lost everything. At first we were like our own little private grief-support group. Before long, though, we realized that the feelings we'd once shared were still there, and in between we'd both had a chance to grow up. What is it they say about love being lovelier the second time around? That's what it's been like for Anders and me. It's been great. Anders helped me raise Anthony, and then we had two girls together—Amber and Jasmine."

"Sounds like you were both incredibly unlucky and incredibly lucky at the same time," Mel observed. Betts nodded in happy agreement. Believe me, when it comes to playing good cop, nobody tops Mel Soames, and by then she had Betsy Harrison eating out of her hand.

"Where exactly were Janice and Anders living at the time she disappeared?" I asked.

"On a bluff south of town," Betts told us. "When Anders and I were dating in high school, his grandmother was still alive, and that's where she lived. By the time Anders and Janice got married, Grandma Harrison had passed on, and his folks let the newlyweds move in and live there rent-free. If they'd had kids, that little cabin probably would have been tight quarters. I doubt they would have stayed on there permanently."

"So by the time you and Anders got together, he was no longer living there?"

"No, he was back in town with his folks."

"And you never visited their house, the one on the bluff?"

"Never," Betts said. "Why would I?"

Why indeed!

The interview didn't end there. We kept Betsy Davis Parmenter Harrison jabbering away for another hour and a half, but we had the one thing we needed from her on tape—the woman's bogus claim that she had never been anywhere near the house where Janice and Anders lived. We had nothing but circumstantial evidence at the moment, and I figured this was only the tip of the iceberg as far as building a case was concerned. What I hadn't anticipated, however, was that Gussy Loper was about to throw a Hail Mary.

When the interview concluded, we left the room and escorted Betts back down the hall. We entered the lobby to find a middle-aged man seated in front of the windows on the far side of the reception desk. I was following Betts and saw her shoulders stiffen with recognition when the new arrival looked up at her as we came through the doorway.

"Hey, Buzz," she said, catching herself and trying to paper over what had clearly been a shock to her system. "Long time no see. How's it going?"

"Fine, fine," Buzz Buford said quickly. "Just stopped by to see Gus for a moment."

"Okay then," Betts said. "See you."

The pallor on Betsy Harrison's face as she hurried out to her car was a joy to see. Just then, Sheriff Loper emerged from his office. "Oh, there you are, Buzz," he said to the newcomer. "Sorry to keep you waiting. I've just been out to the Creager place, looking at the footings. I've got a guy with a specially trained cadaver dog coming out tomorrow. The remains may be old, but he's pretty sure if there's anything to be found, his dog will be on it."

All color drained from Buzz Buford's face. Watching a six-foot-something fold into himself and almost disappear is an amazing sight to see, but that's exactly what happened. Buzz seemed to shrink before our very eyes. As for cadaver dogs? I've never heard tell of one that could sniff out remains more than three decades old, but that's the interesting thing about cops and suspects. In situations like that, cops are allowed to lie their heads off, and we do.

"What was she doing here?" Buford asked, nodding in the direction of the parking place Betts Harrison's SLK had just vacated.

"It's about Janice's case," Sheriff Loper said quietly. "It's just been reopened. Betts stopped by to discuss the possibility of taking a plea deal. No agreement was reached, at least not yet. In instances like this, the first one to sign a confession and turn state's evidence usually gets the best deal."

Clearly Buzz Buford was panicked. "What did she say?" he demanded. "What did she tell you?"

"That getting rid of Janice Harrison was all your idea," Loper told him. "That you're the one who knocked her off and then came up with the idea of dumping her body in freshly poured cement over at the Creagers' place."

"Why that lying bitch!" Buzz blazed. "It wasn't my idea; it was hers. She's the one who did it. I just helped get rid of the body."

Sheriff Loper smiled. "Here you go, Detective Gonzales. Maybe you should take Mr. Buford here back to an interview room and read him his rights. As I said before, the first one to sign a confession usually gets the best deal."

This time Detective Gonzales had the suspect and the interview room all to himself, but Sheriff Loper, Mel, and I used the video hookup to follow the action from the sidelines. The story came out gradually at first and then in a rush. Betts had come to Coupeville that day for the express purpose of having it out with Janice. Betts's own marriage was over, and she wanted Anders back. The two women had argued. Rather than agreeing to Betts's terms, Janice had ordered her out of the house. On their way outside, Betts had plunged a syringe loaded with some of her husband's powerful painkillers into Janice's bare neck. Then Betsy had called her old beau and asked for help.

"Betts told me Janice had fallen and hit her head. She said it was an accident but no one would believe her. She asked me to help her get rid of the body. You don't know what Betts was like back then," Buzz murmured. "It was like she was bewitching me or something, so I did what she asked. But then . . ." He stopped cold. For the better part of a minute, he said nothing at all. He just sat there staring at his hands.

"What?" Detective Gonzales urged.

"That's the worst part of it," Buzz groaned as tears suddenly coursed down his cheeks.

"What's the worst part?"

"Janice wasn't dead. We were carrying her from the car to the footings when I realized she was still alive."

"And you dumped her into the cement anyway?" Detective Gonzales asked.

"God forgive me but I did!" After that, with an anguished groan, Buzz Buford buried his face in his hands and sobbed.

For a long time, that was all we heard—the sound of Buzz's broken sobs. Finally Detective Gonzales reached across the table and shoved pen and paper in front of him.

"If you want God to forgive you," Gonzales suggested gently. "Maybe you'd better write this all down."

Four hours later and decades too late, Mel and I sat in the conference room at Bainbridge Realty and Trust and told Estelle Manring about her sister's horrifying last moments.

"They buried her alive?" Estelle gasped.

The prospect was too awful to consider, but it was the truth. I nodded, and for the next very long minute, no one in the room said a word.

I had taken the yearbook along with us to the interview in Coupeville, so now it was here with us, lying on the conference table in front of us. Finally, Estelle reached over, picked it up, and opened it to the homecoming page.

"You're saying you don't think Anders had anything to do with what happened to Janice?"

"We don't believe so, no," Mel said.

"And that Betts killed her first husband, too?"

"That has yet to be proven," I told her. "And we may not be able to so, but with Buzz's signed confession in hand, she's for sure going down for Janice's murder. When Mel and I left Whidbey to come here, Detective Gonzales and a pair of deputies were on their way out to the house to take Betts Harrison into custody."

"It's over then," Estelle murmured at last. "It's finally over."

We spent the better part of an hour with Estelle after that, talking to her, grieving with her. It was dark and raining sheets when we finally headed out to drive back to Bellingham.

"You did a good job," Mel told me. "You found a way to give her the answers she needed."

"Awful answers," I said. "I never should have told her the truth."

"Necessary answers," Mel corrected. "Estelle wanted the truth, and she's right. It finally is over."

"That's the whole problem," I said.

"What's that?"

"Answers or not, this will never be over."

"Why not?"

"Because," I said, "no matter what, Janice Marshall Harrison is still dead, and she always will be."